Totally Bound Publishing books by Makayla Roberts

The Royal Gordanos
A Royal's Touch
A Royal's Pursuit

The Royal Gordanos

A ROYAL'S TOUCH

MAKAYLA ROBERTS

A ROYAL'S
TOUCH

Chapter One

Humans are such mundane creatures. They carry on with their lives, unaware of just how vast the world truly is.

They're unconscious of the immense number of demons roaming through their cities, living secret lives among them. Demons hide behind magical glamour spells to make themselves invisible to mortal eyes, but many of them just blend in with only the subtlest indications of their natures. Vampires have stunning, heart-wrenching beauty – shifters, the sweltering heat of their skin that is far hotter than a human's and trolls have impenetrably thick skin and a brief flash of red in their eyes when they grow angry.

That was one of the things Ava loved most about humans. They were simple-minded. Where her world was filled with danger, darkness and children of the underworld, humans were oblivious to the mystical existence around them.

She envied that about them. To be able to live their lives with no clue that they were always surrounded by creatures that go bump in the night. It was miraculous how blind they were.

Yes, envious indeed. Yet, at the same time, she couldn't help but admire them.

To have a demon strolling past them every day, even serving the food at a restaurant they frequented — *cough, cough* — yet never even knowing... She only wished to trade places with them. Maybe then she'd be able to get a full night of sleep.

"Don't tell me you're daydreaming again, Ava," a friendly, yet gruff voice called out.

Ava turned a smile on her boss, who was raising a bushy gray eyebrow at her through the small square window separating them. Though he was a rough-looking old man with a perpetual scowl, he had a heart of gold. He'd give the clothes on his back to someone in need.

A trait lacking in the majority of demons.

"Sorry about that, Mr. Tommy," she said. She picked up a thin white rag and tasked herself with wiping down the countertop. The diner she worked in was fairly empty at this time of the morning. The early morning rush had ended, but there were a few customers seated at the tables, finishing off their meals.

Tom's Place wasn't anything special, but there was a certain charm about the diner that made Ava feel comfortable working there. A gray-and-white checkered tile floor complemented baby-blue booths and metal tables. The walls were the same blue, with aged pictures from the diner's first opening in the twenties hanging on the walls. The windows had a faint tint on them to keep the inside cool and shaded, which was perfect for Ava.

She had a mild allergy to the sun's rays.

In all honesty, she didn't need this job. She'd managed to save up a considerable amount of wealth over the years to keep herself comfortable for a while.

However, as a waitress, it was a great way to interact with humans. She enjoyed studying them, learning more about their ways. She'd been sheltered from them until she reached adulthood. When she'd gone off into the world to discover for herself what was out there, she'd developed a substantial fascination with the fragile beings.

It had quickly become her small bit of joy in life — *which is rather...bizarre, isn't it?*

They were a puzzling race. The smallest of incidents could be fatal for them, and they were foolishly driven by their emotions rather than their minds. She didn't understand it in the slightest, but she wanted to. It was intriguing.

But no matter how much she enjoyed watching humans, she couldn't get involved with them any more than that. She'd never forgive herself if anyone was hurt because of her carelessness.

Especially not *that* human. There was one in particular her body craved like no other, which was a very, very dangerous thing in her predicament.

The bell above the diner door rang and the delicious scent of sandalwood filled her nose. *Speak of the devil...* She frowned to herself and looked up at the two men who took a seat at the diner bar, right in front of her. As always.

They were both dressed in uniform and both as handsome as could be. However, it was the one to the right who made her heart skip a beat. The human cop was so good-looking it was almost painful. In all her hundred-plus years of living, she'd seen her share of handsome men. But this one? He took the cake.

He had a crew-cut hairstyle, his hair cut close to his head on the sides, while the remaining dark hair on top was longer and neatly brushed backward. His eyes were a bright golden color, framed by thick, dark lashes that were long enough to make any woman seethe with jealousy. He had a thin, straight nose and a chiseled jawline so sharp that only a master craftsman could have sculpted it with such perfection. And his lips? Full, flawless and made to please a woman.

And when he smiled...

Good gods, when he smiles. His teeth were even and white, his cheeks bearing the deepest set of dimples she'd ever seen. Add to that his six-foot-three muscular build and he was a walking sexual invitation affecting women within a five-mile radius. And Ava was no exception.

Which was what frustrated her more than anything. She couldn't get involved with anyone right now — least of all a human — no matter how much her body ached for his touch.

"Good morning, Aaavaaaa," Marc drawled, those dimples flashing when he grinned.

Ava kept her face blank at the lazy way he drew her name out, but inside her heart was pounding. Even his smooth voice had her shifting her feet as heat began to pool in the pit of her stomach.

She gave him and Duncan a simple nod, ignoring her body's reaction to the sexy male. "Good morning," she responded, avoiding Marc's simmering gaze. "Edith will be over to take your orders shortly."

His dimpled smile never wavered. "Ahh, still too shy to talk to me, are you? It's been how many months now?"

Ava didn't respond as she turned to walk through the door to the kitchen area of the diner.

Too shy to talk to him? Gods. If he knew how bad she wanted him, he'd be running in terror until he reached the Atlantic Ocean.

Shaking the thought from her head, she headed toward the stock room where the other waitress, Edith, was gathering a few items.

She looked over at her. "I was *not* expecting that morning rush today," the aged woman said. "I know it's Friday, but golly."

Ava nodded in agreement. "Right? I have no idea where that crowd even came from. Is there some sort of special event going on in the city?"

Edith's gaze turned thoughtful. "If there is, I haven't heard about it. Chicago is pretty big, so there's no telling."

"Hmm. Well, your favorite customers are here. I'll finish stocking while you take their orders."

Edith blinked in surprise, her wrinkled gaze turning dreamy. "Marc and Duncan?" She let out a little happy squeal, dropping her handful of straws and condiment packets. "Oh, cripes," she muttered, crouching down to pick them up.

Ava got down to help her. "Don't worry about it. I'll get these. You go on."

Edith gave her a small frown. "Ya'know, Ava, I've been wondering for a while now… You're so nice to everyone that comes in but you always avoid those two. Why is that?"

Ava felt her cheeks heat just a bit. *Damn those old eyes of hers.*

She kept her head down, focusing on picking up the dropped items. "No reason," she mumbled. And damn herself for not being a good liar. What was the purpose of being a demon, known for their manipulation and cunning mental prowess, if she couldn't even master the art of telling a lie?

She knew that pathetic excuse wouldn't stop the other woman from prying. She was like a fluttering

11

grandmother, always attempting to piece things together.

"Child, they're both drop-dead gorgeous," the woman continued. "They're cops, and neither of them has a ring on his finger." She paused for a second. "Wait! Could it be *because* they're cops? I know some people who tend to avoid the law at all costs. Is that the reason?" She looked around suspiciously before lowering her voice to a whisper. "Are you on the run from the authorities? Are you worried about getting deported? Don't. I won't rat on you."

Ava let out a small chuckle. In the few months since she'd been working there, she'd learned how much of a chatterbox Edith was. She voiced all her thoughts and opinions without a care in the world. Half the time Ava was sure the woman didn't even realize it. "Deported?" she asked, smiling.

Edith nodded, tapping a bony finger to her wrinkled cheeks in thought. "Yes, deported back to Mexico where you came from."

Ava shook her head. "I'm Italian, Edith, not Mexican. Two completely different countries on two completely different continents."

Edith waved that away. "Whatever. I'm not so good with all these different accents. Too many of them sound alike."

Ava only continued to smile. Despite Edith's claims, Ava's Italian accent was very faint. She'd spent a great number of years all over America, so she often picked up on their ever-changing lingo. The only time it became noticeable was if her emotions surged, which had yet to happen since working here.

"There are plenty of other police officers who come in here, and I have no trouble talking with them," Ava responded. "Honestly, I don't have an issue with either

Duncan or Marc. Let's just say I'm fairly shy around men who look that good." It was a lie, but she couldn't very well tell the woman she didn't talk to Marc because his very presence was enough to make her body tingle with desire. *Talk about embarrassing.*

"Oh well, I suppose that makes sense. Ever since you started working here, you would clam up and act all shy with only those two. Especially Marc. *That's* the one you need to shag."

Ava shook her head again. "Shag? What does that even mean?"

The woman stood up, raised a brow and put a bony hand on her hip. "You know what I mean. He's young and virile. You're young and gorgeous. You're both single. And I see the way you look at each other when no one's looking." She winked at that. "If I was just a few years younger, I'd mount that stallion in a heartbeat."

Ava bit the inside of her cheek to keep from laughing out loud. *A few years younger? Yeah, right.* They both knew full well that Edith was in her seventies — wrinkles, gray hairs and all. "Polite pass, Edith. I'm just not interested in seeing anyone right now."

That much was true, at least. Dating or even purely sexual relationships were impossible for her. *Hell, with my bad luck, it'll probably always be that way.*

"Oh well, your loss then, honey," Edith said, shrugging. She smoothed the front of her apron and straightened her thin shoulders. "How do I look?"

Ava rose as well, smiling warmly. "Fabulous."

Edith grinned and made her way back to the front, putting a little sway in her steps. Ava shook her head, still smiling. *That woman is really something else.* She was living proof that anyone is only as old as they feel. Well, to humans anyway. Time had no meaning to most demons.

She'd grown quite attached to the woman and her husband, Mr. Tommy. Though they had incredibly different personalities, they were both so sweet and generous. There'd been a few times when she'd seen them take people off the streets, offer them a hot meal and warm bed, clean them up and give them a job at the diner before helping them find something better. There weren't very many demons, if any, who would do such a thing without expecting something in return. It was the kind of pure, human love that made them want to help each other.

She placed the fallen items into the trash and washed her hands. She then pulled on a fresh pair of latex gloves, grabbed more condiments and went back to the front, where Edith's flirtatious giggling could be heard.

Ava hid a smile and began stocking the bins underneath the counter a few feet away from them. The woman was married and old enough to have great-grandchildren, yet she still flirted away with the younger men. It was fairly amusing, and the guys all went along with it.

As always, she was aware of Marc's presence. Over the smell of grease, butter and the other employees and customers, his scent stood out the most. It was a mix of his aftershave and his own personal aroma that filled her senses, making her head spin. That alone was enough to drive her mad with want.

And it was such a nuisance. She loved humans, but he stood out like a sore thumb—a very sexy, enticing sore thumb. And it was bloody frustrating because she didn't even know why. Why was it just him she felt so enamored with? Why did she feel such an intense reaction? Why did her heart jump every time her eyes met his? Yes, he was extremely attractive. Then again, so was his partner and several other men she'd come across. *So why only him?*

Speaking of his partner, she looked over at the Scot out of the corner of her eye.

Duncan looked normal enough, but he wasn't human. Oh, he very much smelled like one and did well to hide it, but she knew better. Demons could always sense another demon's presence.

Unlike Marc, Duncan's reddish-brown hair was longer and brushed back, the tips curling around his ears. His face was clean-shaven with a faint scar running from his chin up to his ear. However, it did nothing at all to take away from his handsome features. If anything, it gave him more of a gruff, sexy look, like those proud Highland warriors she'd seen on the covers of romance novels. But there was just something in the air around him that was demonic — a deadly, powerful aura that never failed to make her wary.

Oh, she wasn't afraid of him. She could hold her own against most demons. She did, after all, possess the blood of Royal vampires, some of the strongest demons to ever walk the earth.

However, Duncan was... Hell, she didn't know. His eyes were dark green with flecks of yellow around the pupil, but they held a predatory gleam that hinted at his demon side. It was like he was always searching for his next meal. That made her think he was some sort of shifter. Whether it was canine, feline or something else, she had no idea, but either way, he'd be a dangerous adversary.

Duncan was talking to Edith, making her laugh. When the woman turned away to place their orders, he looked over at Ava out of the corner of his eye, catching her watching him at bay. He winked and gave her a knowing smile. He knew she was a demon as well. It had been evident when they'd first met each other months ago, though neither of them had ever once mentioned it.

And why should they? Most demons were naturally private creatures. It wasn't like they often sat around a campfire holding hands and singing songs about peace and love. The thought made her give a soft snort.

Still... More than once she'd wondered what kind of demon he was and why he was parading around as a human cop. The intelligent look in his eyes told her he was far older than he appeared. He was a demon who'd lived a long life and had many stories to tell.

She gave another small shake of her head. *Oh well.* No need for dwelling on such trivial thoughts. Even if she had the answer to that question, it wouldn't change anything. As much as it would be nice to have demon friends she could feel comfortable around and let her fangs down with once in a while, so to speak, she would just have to keep dreaming. She wasn't the safest person to be around. And Marc...

He was a human. Getting involved with one was something she'd sworn to never do. She'd interact with them, even take their blood when she needed it. But with Marc, she wanted him in a way she hadn't ever felt before.

That in itself was dangerous. She would have to keep her distance from him. She feared that once she gave in to her carnal desires, it would be hard to stop.

And she would never forgive herself if something were to happen to him, all because she'd brought him into her world.

"Hey, Ava, come listen to this story," Edith suddenly called out. "It's intense."

Jarred from her thoughts, Ava bit back a sigh. *Damn you, Edith,* she thought. She was a character, but she was nosey as could be—nosey, and always trying to play matchmaker between her and Marc.

Ava picked up a clean blue towel and slowly walked over to them. The closer she got, the more Marc's scent clouded her mind. He was smirking as if he knew the effect he had on her. *Damn him too.*

Even as she silently cursed him, she was powerless to fight the way her body clenched in response to his look. *I'm worse than a harpy in heat, for crying out loud.*

"Thanks for joining us," he said playfully. Ava shrugged, annoyed that her tongue was dry. The more she looked at him, the more drawn she became. He was undoubtedly human, but he had a certain pull about him that could rival that of a full-grown incubus.

She began to dry the already-dried coffee mugs under the counter, setting them in their proper places as she listened.

Duncan was the one continuing the story. From what she'd learned from Edith, he had been born and raised in Scotland up until he'd been a teenager, then he'd moved to the US where he'd become a full citizen. He still had a thick accent when he spoke.

Although, with him being a demon who probably aged much more slowly than humans, it was no doubt just a cover. Not that he wasn't Scottish... The thick brogue and powerful aura gave him a warrior's presence that couldn't be faked. However, he could have spent several centuries in his homeland before coming here. *Who knows?*

"Anyway, one day we got a call about this drunk guy running down the street in this old neighborhood. It's broad daylight and he's just running, screaming at the top of his lungs. So we answer the call and roll up on this guy, expecting him to be high as shit. When we found him, he was rolling around in a field of grass screaming *'They're inside of me!'* This wasn't the first nut case we'd come across, so the procedure was pretty standard."

While Duncan continued with his story, a prickling sensation slid down Ava's neck, causing her to look up. She glanced around the room, but none of the patrons were out of the ordinary. The feeling became stronger and it was one she was all too familiar with. She narrowed her eyes, peering out of the large, shaded windows. She trusted her senses more than anything, and right now they were telling her something sinister was nearby.

She was never wrong.

Sure enough, across the street in the narrow alley stood a lone, cloaked figure. Even with the daylight outside, it was still dark between the two buildings. The humans on the other side of the street continued walking, completely oblivious to the danger standing within feet of them. To anyone who could see it, it would look like an ordinary person dressed for the changing weather.

To Ava, the figure stood out. It wasn't a human. It was hidden deep in the shadows, but she could make out two glowing-red eyes from under the hood it wore. Even with the distance, her enhanced eyesight allowed her to see the creature open its mouth in a wide grin.

Found you, it mouthed.

Her heart raced in her chest as she broke out in a cold sweat.

Damn, damn, damn. She'd known it might only be a matter of time before she was discovered, but she'd been too reckless. She'd hoped she had finally shaken the ghouls off her tail and had allowed herself to get too comfortable. *Curse it all.*

There was the sound of glass breaking, followed by a sharp pain in her hand, but she didn't even flinch. She glanced down at the shattered cup she'd grasped too tightly, watching as her blood flowed onto the sink and countertop.

She hissed, quickly running the water and holding her hand under the faucet.

By the gods. Now, with the scent of her blood in the air, it'd be even harder to make an escape. She'd just dug her own damn grave.

Edith appeared at her side, trying to help Ava with her wound, even as she was beginning to panic. Even Marc and Duncan look alarmed, and she could see Duncan's nostrils flaring, his eyes widening as he caught her scent.

Shit and double shit.

She had to make a quick escape.

Though most ghouls preferred night over day, there were a few who were strong enough to withstand the burning sunlight for a certain amount of time — like the one across the street, for example. And they were definitely not afraid to kill any humans who came between them and their target. If she stayed much longer, no doubt everyone in the diner would be injured...or worse. They would be collateral damage.

Wrapping her hand in the blue cloth towel, she turned to the small square window separating her from Mr. Tommy. She clutched her bleeding hand to her chest. "Sorry, Mr. Tommy, but I've got to go." She didn't even wait for a response. She took off her apron and sped out of the back, ignoring calls from her coworkers. She burst through the door and raced down the street. She knew the ghoul was following. She could feel it moving swiftly through the streets and alleys, following her scent. Her superior speed was near blinding compared to the ghoul's, but even then she didn't have much time. Once one of those creatures caught a scent, it was damn hard to get rid of them.

She only prayed her sudden departure would cause the creature to avoid harming anyone near the diner.

* * * *

Marc stood outside the diner's front door, looking around. Patrons were walking back and forth along the sidewalks and a few cars drove past, but other than that, nothing seemed out of the ordinary.

So what was it that got Ava so spooked all of a sudden?

He replayed the image in his mind. Duncan had been telling the story of them responding to one of their calls. Halfway through, she'd suddenly tensed up. Marc had been watching her—as he usually did—and had noticed the change in her posture. She'd looked around the diner, frowning. But then, glancing just out of the window, she'd frozen, zoning in on something. He'd followed her gaze to try to see what she was looking at, but there had been nothing. Well, the dark alley across the street had seemed like there were shadows moving around, but he'd thought maybe those were from the cars passing.

Then she'd turned a shade whiter. After being a cop for years, he'd studied all types of body language. Even the slightest of moves could reveal what someone was feeling.

And Ava had definitely been showing signs of fear.

Which only further proved his point when she'd squeezed the glass mug hard enough to break it. A surprising display of strength, given her slender build, but he'd been more concerned with the amount of blood that had started flowing from her hand.

However, before he could say anything, she'd turned away, dashed toward the back and fled. The other workers had tried to follow her to see what was wrong, but she was long gone. It was as if she'd disappeared into thin air.

"That was strange," Duncan commented. He rubbed his nose for the hundredth time, it seemed, since Ava had left.

Marc nodded. He couldn't explain it, but something definitely wasn't right. He felt a nagging sense of worry. "I have a sinking feeling she saw something we didn't."

Duncan raised a brow. "What? You mean like a ghost or something?"

Marc gave his partner a lazy glare. "Don't be ridiculous. That shit isn't real."

Duncan just flashed an amused smile before stuffing his six-foot-six frame into the passenger seat of the patrol car. "Hey, man, you never know. We've seen some pretty screwed up shit before. I wouldn't be surprised if those types of things really did exist."

Marc just shook his head, getting into the driver's side. That was true enough, but he didn't comment. Whatever it was, he hoped Ava would be okay. Edith had given him Ava's apartment location so he could check on her when his shift was over. The ever easy-going woman had been tense with worry ever since Ava had gone, and she'd requested he make sure her coworker was all right.

Well, in truth he'd already planned on doing so, but now he had a genuine excuse so she wouldn't think he was some lunatic stalking her.

He hoped she had the sense to go to the hospital to get her hand looked at. Judging by the amount of blood pouring into the sink, she'd need some stitches.

He continued the rest of his day as normal, but he just couldn't shake the feeling of dread in his gut.

And when he had that feeling, nine times out of ten it meant things were going to end badly.

* * * *

As promised, Marc made his way up the flight of stairs to Ava's apartment on the third floor. Though he was off duty for the day, he hadn't yet been home to change into his regular clothes, so he still wore his dark-colored uniform. He'd been in a hurry to get there and make sure Ava was all right—if she'd even made it back from the hospital. It had been the only thing he could think of.

He exited the stairwell and stepped onto the third-floor landing. Her door was at the far end of the hall. He made sure to remain alert, because with each step he took, the feeling of dread in his stomach tightened more and more.

Even as a kid, he'd always had a strong intuition. He trusted his gut more than anything. It had saved his life more times than he could count.

When he finally made it to her door, his heart sank. There were obvious signs of forced entry. The wooden panel of the door was broken in, splinters dusting the floor. He pulled out his gun, holding it straight with a firm grip. He pushed the door open and entered the apartment with light footfalls. The living room light was still on, but even so, he had his flashlight on above his gun. As he looked around, he saw the telltale signs of a struggle.

And from the looks of it, whoever was here had put up a *big* fight.

The beige couch was overturned and the glass coffee table was shattered to pieces and coated with blood. The insides from the torn couch and other bits of glass lay scattered around the floor. The living room connected to the open kitchen. On the opposite side was a narrow hall with three doors. He cleared the first two doors—a spare closet and a bathroom— before going to the bedroom.

From there he had to pause, covering his nose. It took a large amount of willpower to prevent himself from gagging at the putrid smell of sulfur.

Ava's bedroom was even more destroyed than her living room. It was clear that this was where the main fight had occurred. Her floor was cluttered with broken and torn bits of furniture, and her TV had a large, gaping hole in the screen. Even her bed frame had been busted, the single mattress slumping at an awkward angle. There was more glass on the floor, but what caught his attention was the pitch-black dust on the ground in the shape of a body.

What the hell is that? Whatever it was, he was willing to bet all the money he had that it was where the horrific smell was coming from. It was so strong that he was close to throwing up every bit of food he'd consumed that day.

Which was saying something, because he had a damn strong stomach.

There was a large splatter of black and red gunk on the cream-colored walls, causing him to frown even more. He didn't know what the hell the goop was, but he was almost positive the red stains were blood. Something terrible had gone down in this apartment— and recently.

Making sure to keep a grip on his gun, he used one hand to pick up the radio on his belt. He pressed a button to contact dispatch, but before he could get any words out, something struck him on his head with enough force to cause him to drop to his knees. There was another blow, then the world around him faded to black.

Chapter Two

"I can't do this on my own," a woman cried out. "How am I supposed to raise this…this…thing by myself?" Her sobs filled the night air, echoing throughout the the house. There was a rumbling response in a deep baritone that was drowned out by the woman's sobs.

The front door leading outside slammed shut, leaving the woman to cry harder. A child peeked around the corner, seeing his mother curled on the floor sobbing. The child took a tentative step inside the living room.

"Mommy, why are you crying?"

The woman jerked her head up. Her eyes were red and swollen and makeup streaked down her face from her tears. When she glanced at the child, her eyes grew wide with horror. She pointed a shaking finger at him. "Stay away from me, demon!" she yelled. "I hate you! I hate you!"

She threw her head back and screamed at the top of her lungs. She reached for a knife lying beside her on the floor and began frantically slicing at her wrists and forearms. The child covered his ears, his own tears forming. He ran back into his own room, locking his door and hiding his small body *under the bed. He squeezed his eyes shut, but nothing he could do would block out the sounds of his mother wailing.*

"Marc... Marc, can you hear me? Wake up."

The soft, whispery voice floated over Marc, chasing the nightmare from his mind. He cracked his eyes open, wincing at the pounding in his head. *Jesus Christ.* If this was a hangover, he'd never had one this bad. He felt like his skull had shrunk and his brain was pressing against the bones to be free.

He blinked a few times to get his vision to focus, but it took several minutes for his eyes to adjust to the blinding light. When they did, he realized there actually wasn't a bright light at all. There was a faint orange glow from a torch hanging from the wall several feet away, sending shadows flickering across the walls. He blinked again. Confusion swamped him, causing him to frown.

He felt weak, and it took a great amount of effort to push himself up into a sitting position. He had to close his eyes until the wave of nausea began to subside. He reached up his hands to rub his temples but paused. With each movement, he could hear metal rattling.

He looked down at his wrists, frowning even more when he saw they were bound in chains. "What the—?"

"Thank goodness you're okay," that voice whispered again, a light Italian accent present in the soft tone—a familiar one.

He jerked his head up and squinted his eyes through the pain to focus even more. He was pressed against a wall in some kind of cell and, in the far corner across from him, he could see bright green eyes glowing in the shadows. The torch allowed just enough light for him to make out the slender body of a female in a sullied blue-and-white-striped uniform. She was watching him intently.

"Ava?" he asked, his voice a mere croak. *Damn, cottonmouth is a bitch.* He felt as if he'd eaten a pound of saltine crackers without even a sip of water. *What the hell is going on here?*

"Yes, it's me," she whispered. In the faint shadows, her eyes had an odd shimmer to them, almost like a cat's when a light shone on them in the dark. *How...odd.* He guessed he must've drunk even more than he'd assumed if he was still seeing things.

"Where are we? Why am I in chains?" he questioned. He appreciated kinky sex as much as the next man, but this wasn't anything he was used to. And he damn sure didn't like it.

"I don't know where we are," she answered quietly. "Do you remember anything?"

He squeezed his eyes shut. The pain in his head was so great that he felt like throwing up. "Ah... I went to your apartment to check up on you — at Edith's request, mind you. There were signs of a struggle, and I was about to call for backup but... That's it. I woke up and here I am now." Alarmed, he recalled being hit in the head before even uttering a word to dispatch. *So much for this being a hangover*, he thought with annoyance. Someone had snuck up on him and knocked him out cold.

"I'm so sorry," she said, her voice cracking. "You should have just let me be."

He opened his eyes, doing his best to fix her with a hard look. Those were some guilty words. "Tell me what's going on."

She paused for a moment. "I...can't. You wouldn't understand."

He kept his expression serious. "Tell me," he demanded, gritting his teeth. "I deserve to know after this shit."

When she didn't answer, his frustration bubbled inside. He was just so confused that it was annoying. He'd always thought Ava was a secretive person, but he'd never seen this coming. He didn't even know what kind of background she had or what kind of person she truly was. Hell, this could be a gang-related kidnapping or some shit. Whatever it was, she knew something about their predicament but didn't want to share that information. It pissed him off, especially since he'd been worried about her all day — *is it still Friday night?* — and had gone out of his way to check up on her.

He heard footsteps approaching and whipped his head around to the closed door of the cell. He smoothed his expression to be impassive and void of any emotion. During his days at the academy, he'd learned what to do and what not to do if he was ever held captive. Rule number one? Always stay calm.

As the heavy footfalls drew closer, two men wearing ski masks suddenly appeared outside the cell. One unlocked the door and they both stepped inside. Their body language displayed malice, but there was something…off about them. It was as if the very air around them was…unearthly. *Which is ridiculous, isn't it?* They were just men — no different from the other criminals he'd come across in his career.

The taller of the two, who seemed to be the dominant one, let his gaze roam to Marc. In the darkness, they were a burning red color. *Contacts?* No doubt another means to conceal his identity. "So, you're both awake," the man said, his tone bored. He had a Russian accent, though it was faint like Ava's Italian one.

"What do you want to do with him?" the other asked, using his head to indicate Marc. His accent was stronger.

"He's a human," the first man stated with disgust. "Just kill him and dump his body somewhere."

When the shorter man took a step toward him, as if to carry out the order, a loud growl sounded, causing Marc to blink in surprise. He looked around, half expecting some kind of animal in the room with them, but all he could see was Ava. Her eyes were narrowed to slits as she glared at the two men. He realized belatedly that the feral noise had come from her. She had actually growled. *What. The. Hell.*

"Lay one finger on him and I'll rip your throat out," she said darkly.

Marc swallowed. It was hard trying to imagine this angry woman being the quiet, meek Ava he'd thought her to be these last few months. It was almost terrifying. *Almost.* He wasn't a man who was easily frightened.

The two men laughed at that. "You're hardly in a position to make such empty threats, princess," the leader said.

Ava bared her teeth. Marc squinted his eyes. Her canines were looking fairly long, almost like...*fangs?* Red eyes, fangs and animalistic growls... Someone had definitely hit his head a little too hard.

"Consider it a friendly promise," she retorted.

In two quick strides, the leading man was standing before her. He swung his hand back and a loud smack rang out, echoing off the walls. Marc tensed, feeling his rage scratching to be released. One thing he could not stand was to see a man put his hands on a woman, especially not a woman he'd spent the last few months pining for like a dog in heat.

Every instinct in his body was urging him to beat the shit out of the man, but he had to hold back. Another rule of thumb was to never try to antagonize your captors.

"Watch your tone, bitch," the man spat. "Our customer may want you alive, but I have no problem sending you over to him with your tongue missing."

Ava raised her head, her glare firmly in place. Marc's body clenched. Her look was filled with a deep, personal hatred. There was no doubt in his mind that she knew these men.

Their customer *wants her alive?* Did that mean they were traffickers? Or were they bounty hunters?

As the man began to walk away, she muttered something so low that even Marc couldn't hear it. But the man did. He whirled around, his red eyes narrowing on her. "What did you say?"

She just gave them a feral smile, those sharp canines glinting in the firelight. "Ethan Warren and Ivan Sokolav, two bounty hunters from the Yashin house. Nice try with the ski masks, but it was a failed attempt to hide your human identities. You'd better pray I do not make it out of here alive."

Marc watched in suspicion as one stiffened and the other's skin went pale around his neck. He didn't know what the hell was going on, but whatever it was, it seemed Ava had them on their toes. The second male grabbed the other guy by his arm, pulling him out of the cell. "Come on, man. Let's go. We gotta get this set up."

The first male shrugged him off. He sent Ava one last glare before they stormed off. A door slammed shut in the distance. After that, Ava slumped against the wall, letting out a small sigh.

Marc peered at her. Ava was five-foot-eight, slender and couldn't be any older than twenty-one. She was a bit taller than the average woman, but she in no way looked imposing or dangerous, most of all not while chained to the wall. Even her looks had always been serene.

And yet with just a simple threat, she'd had two stocky men scrambling away in fear.

Yeah, she couldn't be an ordinary waitress. He had a brief image of her being the daughter of some high-class Italian mobster. That would explain why her knowing their names would cause them alarm. It would also explain why she had been so reserved in his and Duncan's presence every time they'd entered the diner. No doubt having policemen snooping around and digging into her personal life would raise some suspicions.

Marc cleared his head of the animated thoughts and tugged on his chains. They were long but secure. Judging by the length of them, he wouldn't be able to reach the cell door.

He looked down at his waist. The men had removed his utility belt, along with his attached gear. He dug in his pockets and frowned when he realized that they were empty. He'd left his cell phone in his car outside Ava's apartment.

Yeah, some cop he was. *That's me, always prepared for anything.*

Idiot.

He looked over at Ava, who was stroking the cheek the man had slapped. Already it was swollen, a small cut having formed across the gentle curve of her cheekbone. A huge part of him wanted to draw her into his arms and comfort her then beat the shit out of the bastards who'd harmed her, but he had to refrain. Ava was involved in something much bigger than anything he could have imagined. He didn't know what was happening here, but she definitely wasn't the person he'd thought she was.

"Ava," he called out, his voice steady, "I need to know what's going on here, so I can know what I'm up against. If this is some kind of gang issue or drug matter, I need you to cooperate with me. And it'll help you in the long run."

She didn't move. Her breathing was growing raspy in the silence, making him frown.

"Marc...you wouldn't believe me, even if I told you. Hell, I wouldn't even know where to begin."

"That's okay," he said with reassurance. He had to get her to open up to him, so he could better assess the situation. "Just give me a rundown. Who are those guys and what do they want from us?"

She shifted her head, her bright eyes opening to peer at him. There was that odd flash again, making him wonder if she was wearing contacts as well, though he had to admit he'd never heard of any that were able to flash like a cat's.

"They're bounty hunters," she murmured. "Apparently, I have a large price on my head, and they managed to catch me off guard in my apartment."

"Is that why you took off this morning?" he asked. "You recognized one of them?"

She tilted her head to the side. "Yes. One of them was standing across the street watching the diner. They want me alive so they can receive payment, but you? These guys aren't your ordinary criminals. They will not hesitate to kill you if you do not benefit them in any way."

He frowned at her words. Her voice sounded...sad, as if she were worried for his safety over her own — something that had him a bit touched before he squashed the feeling.

This was her doing to begin with.

Focus.

A sudden thought occurred to him. "Is that why you diverted their attention away from me? You wanted them to center on you, so they'd be distracted and forget about me being here?"

Her eyes widened a fraction. Yeah, he was damn good at reading people.

"Yes," she stated. "I would not be able to bear it if something were to happen to you because of me."

Marc watched her. The nearby torch outside the cell flickered about, sending shadows dancing around the small room and the hall beyond. Ava was huddled in the darkest corner of the cell, but now his eyes had adjusted more to the dim light. As a kid, he'd always been able to see in the dark after a few moments. He could see how her cheek was swollen and the other side of her face was bruised. Every time she spoke, he could see those flashes of fangs, the two tips looking sharp as razors.

"What's up with your teeth?" he questioned bluntly. "They weren't like that this morning. And what's with the whole *'he's just a human'* thing? Is this some kind of…lunatic cult or something? If you can't tell me everything, just give me something to go by, Ava. That's all I ask."

She closed her eyes and was quiet for several long minutes. As the time passed, her breathing became worse, almost as if the simple act of inhaling and exhaling was painful. He recalled the state of her apartment and worried she had endured quite a beating since she had been taken. *Two big burly men against one female?* She couldn't have stood a chance. The way she was clutching her side, she might have a broken rib.

Yet he earnestly hoped that was not the case. Though it was her fault they were in this mess, he didn't want her harmed, not even a little. He'd spent months growing more and more attracted to her, though they'd never held a full conversation before. Even him being knocked unconscious and chained up like some wild animal didn't change the fact that he still cared about her.

Ludicrous as that may be.

When she spoke at last, it was clear it took great effort for her to do so. "Those two men you just saw are not human. They're demons. Ghouls, to be exact." Her eyes met his and she gave a dry snort. "Clearly you don't believe that, but it's true. Demons are decidedly real, and I don't mean in the metaphorical sense."

Marc only fixed her with a blank look.

I knew it. I knew it was too good to be true. A woman as pretty as Ava couldn't possibly be normal. He shifted, turning away from her with a frustrated huff. "This is not a joking matter, Ava — or is that even your real name?"

She sighed again. "Yes, it's my real name. You wanted to know the truth."

"So I did," he snapped. *What is it with me, always being attracted to the crazy ones? Good Lord.* He had to be cursed. That was the only explanation.

Whatever, then. He'd get out of here himself. It wasn't the first time he'd been in a hostage situation, and if he kept it up with this blind heroism, it wouldn't be the last.

He lifted his arms, inspecting the chains. He looked around, searching for anything he could use to pick the locks. Aside from a few pebbles, there was only the cold stone floor beneath them.

He stood. He tugged at the chains, but they were thick as hell and bolted to the stone wall. It would take a blowtorch and the strength of a thousand men to break through them.

He looked over at Ava. Her eyes were closed again, her breathing labored. He tilted his head. Though he was pissed at her for many reasons, he couldn't help the gentle tone he used to talk to her. "You sound awful. We need to get you to a hospital."

She opened her eyes. If he wasn't mistaken, she looked pale. "Human hospitals will not be able to help me."

He frowned. There went that 'human' crap again. "What is it?"

She lifted her hands. "These chains are mixed with silver. The longer they're touching me, the more they sap my strength, not to mention that it's been a while since I last fed, and I took quite a beating before they brought me here. I'm pretty sure one of my ribs is broken, too."

He walked as far as the chains would let him go, stopping a few feet away from her. He crouched down to be eye-to-eye. His frown deepened. She really had gone pale. Her exotic bronze skin was now almost gray in color. She was sweating and her features were tight with pain. Her mouth was parted a fraction, the tips of her canines peeking from under her lips. At this proximity he examined them closer.

"Let's pretend what you said was true," he stated. Worry for her was gnawing away at him. Whether it was some kind of drug or poison the two men had given her, she looked sick. Delusional or not, she still needed to be treated. "Those two men were...ghouls or whatever. And I'm just a human. What does that make you? Are you a ghoul too?"

She looked taken aback, almost offended. "Don't compare me to those...*things*," she muttered.

Okay, she was upset. "So what are you? Going by the fangs, I'm guessing you're, like, a vampire or something?"

Her eyes widened before closing again. But she gave a faint smile. "Or something."

Yep, totally bonkers. "Okay, so is whatever you are the reason you have bounty hunters after you?"

She gave a single nod, a sweat-dampened strand of midnight hair falling over her shoulder.

"Is this something dealing with trafficking? Some kind of...demonic slave trade?"

Her lips twitched again. "Demonic slave trade is a good way of putting it."

He rolled his eyes at her vague answers. But if he played into her imagination, no doubt she'd reveal some useful information. Some *real* information — none of this demon hokey-pokey bullshit. "Okay, so this is some kind of demon transaction, and because I was in your apartment, I was just caught in the middle of everything."

This time when she smiled, her perfect white teeth were showing, including those elongated fangs. It was odd how the more he looked at them, the more real they appeared.

"I know what you're doing," she said, humor lacing her tone, despite the pain she was clearly in. "You think I'm crazy, but if you go along with my fantasy, I'll talk, right? However, everything I'm telling you is the truth. Humans just have a hard time believing things they don't understand. It's only natural for you to fear the unknown."

He rocked back and forth on his heels. *Loony, but smart.* "You're right. I don't believe you. But, hypothetically, if all of this *was* real, isn't it against the underworld law or something to tell humans about your existence?"

She opened her eyes, giving him a half-lidded gaze. Despite the circumstances, he felt his lower body clench at the unintentionally sexy look. "You've been watching too many Hollywood movies. The underworld is an entirely different place, Marc. For the demons in the human world, it's a bit more complex than that. Different species follow different rules, depending on who their leaders are, similar to how America has a president, but other countries may have kings, dictators or emperors..." At his dumbfounded look, she waved that away. "Look, I don't have the energy to completely explain it to you. But it's best that you find a way out of here before they come back."

He shook his head, putting their conversation on the back burner. Crazy or not, it seemed she thoroughly believed what she was saying. Oftentimes that made people all the more dangerous. "You want me to leave you here?"

She leaned her head back against the stone wall, looking up at the dark ceiling. "I will be fine. It's not the first time something like this has happened to me."

Again, her voice sounded dejected. He furrowed his forehead. "What does *that* mean?"

She remained quiet. He sighed impatiently and rose to his feet again. "Ava, I'm not going to leave you here. We'll both escape, and as soon as I get to a phone, I can call for a unit—"

He cut himself off at the sound of a door being opened and closed again, followed by rapid footsteps. The two Russian men came back, still wearing the ski masks, even though Ava obviously knew their identities. One of them unlocked the cell door so they could step inside. They both turned to Marc.

"Get him," the leader commanded.

The shorter, yet burlier male came at him, and Marc backed all the way against the wall to slacken the chains then got into a defensive position, though there wasn't much he could do, being shackled. To his surprise, in the blink of an eye Ava was on her feet as well, her chains stretched taut as she pulled against them. It was as if she'd forgotten the pain she had been in a moment before.

Her fangs were bared, her eyes narrowed to dangerous slits. "Don't you *dare* touch him!"

The two men ignored her. Marc put up a fight as they came close, but they were both strong as hell—so strong that it was unnerving. He managed a double punch to one man, catching him in the nose and throat. The attack caused the man to let out a sharp yelp. Soon after, the other one delivered a powerful blow to Marc's stomach. He doubled over, gasping for air. *Holy shit.* He was sure the thug had just ruptured his spleen.

One man quickly unlocked Marc's chains, while the other had him in a tight hold, pinning his arms at his sides. He struggled against them, but he might as well have been trying to push at an elephant.

There was a loud, furious roar and Marc looked up in time to see Ava's chains pop free from the stone wall. His eyes grew wide. *No way in hell…*

Someone let out a cry of terror. In the blink of an eye, Ava threw an arm forward, and with perfect aim, she wrapped her chain around one man's neck, as if she'd wielded a whip. He was snatched away from Marc and thrown against the wall, crumpling to the ground with a deep gash in his head. The other man cursed, preparing to bolt.

Too late. Ava caught him and picked him up by the neck. Marc scrambled backward, watching in wide-eyed panic. The man was bigger than Ava, yet she was holding him in one hand with his feet dangling from the ground like he was a sack of potatoes. The man was clutching at her wrist, clawing to be free. He was the one who had slapped her earlier.

"I make good on my promises," she growled. Then, in a swift movement, she sank her teeth in the man's throat and yanked her head back, tearing the flesh wide open. She dropped him to the ground, while he tried futilely to stop his neck from bleeding.

This time, Marc wasn't able to hold back. He leaned over and released the contents of his stomach. Even when it was empty, he continued to dry heave, using one arm to remain stable against the stone wall. When he was done, he looked up to see Ava frisking the man. She reached into his pocket and found a set of keys. She tried every one of them before finding the correct one to unlock the bindings around her wrists. Once free, she kicked the offensive metal away from her and used a clean portion of her sleeve to wipe at her mouth.

"Disgusting piece of trash," she grumbled. She paused, looking over at Marc with glittering eyes.

He pressed more firmly into the wall, unable to comprehend what he was seeing. "Y-you killed them."

"Yes, as I said I would."

He pointed a shaking finger at the man who had literally choked on his own blood. "You... How... Why... What the *hell?*"

She looked down at the man then back up at Marc. "I don't understand your shock. Have you never seen a dead body before?"

He swallowed thickly, not understanding how she was so calm about it. "You didn't have to... I mean, they could have been subdued and brought in for questioning! Now we can't — "

"You just don't get it, Marc," she said on a sigh, as if *he* were the frustrating one. "These are not ordinary men. They are *ghouls*. They are not humans, so you can't expect to treat them as such. See for yourself."

She pointed at the man against the far wall. Marc's gaze tentatively followed her finger and he did a double-take.

The first man she'd killed was no longer there. All that was left was a puddle of blood and black dust in the shape of his body. That same sulfuric smell from her bedroom filled the cell, and Marc covered his nose before he puked again.

He looked over at the bigger man. If it were possible, Marc's eyes grew even wider. The man whose throat had been torn open was now dissolving into a mass of black dust, leaving behind the only evidence that he had even been there. That...and the puddle of black blood.

"What the fuck is going on?" he demanded. This living nightmare had taken a sudden, dramatic turn into Wonderland. A very dark, very creepy Wonderland. He had to be dreaming...or hallucinating. Or...anything else that could explain why he was delusional. Because this shit could *not* be real.

Ava turned to face him, her lips twisting with disdain. "I told you that they are not what you think they are. This world is bigger than anything you can imagine. These men are the type of demons who will kill without a shred of remorse. It was either you or them." She shifted, toying with a button on her uniform. "Although I do apologize that you had to see that side of me. I understand how disturbed you must feel."

'Disturbed' was a polite way of describing what he was feeling.

Marc's heart was pounding in his chest. He watched as she approached him as if he were a skittish animal. After witnessing what he had, of course he'd appear that way. Those two men — demons, or whatever — had been killed by Ava and their bodies had dissolved, leaving black ash behind. As he looked at the bloody pools that remained, he noticed how there wasn't any red color. The two men had bled out, but their blood was pitch black.

Just like the goop he'd seen in her apartment earlier.

He looked back up at her and she was within arm's reach. The front of her shirt was soaked with the black blood, and though she still looked sickly, a bit of color had returned to her pallor.

"What are you — ?"

He cut himself off when her cold fingers touched his cheek. A healthy mix of desire and fear flooded through him, waging war until he couldn't decide whether he wanted to press her into the wall and kiss those full lips silly or curl into fetal position in the corner of the cell and pray that he'd wake up in his own bed and find he'd suffered a terrible hangover. It was the lusty side that had him cringing with disgust. This was *so* not an appropriate time to feel such a thing.

Her forehead furrowed.

"What is it?" he asked, his voice tight.

Her lips tightened to a thin line and she took a step back. "Nothing," she murmured, though her expression was pinched with worry. "We need to leave before more of them come after us."

She turned away and walked out of the cell. Mark rubbed his cheek where he could still feel her lingering touch, annoyed at his body's heated response. Though his mind had just witnessed the horror of her ripping a man's throat out, apparently his cock wasn't prejudiced at all.

This is madness. This is impossible. No way in hell is any of this real.

All his life he'd prided himself on his bravery. He'd been in some pretty scary situations out in the field. He'd even come close to death a time or two.

But nothing had been half as weird as what he'd experienced in the past few hours.

He shouldn't follow her. He should find his own way of escaping and go home, shower and take his ass to sleep. He just wanted to forget this day had ever happened. Even if he did report it, there was nothing he could do to prove, especially with no bodies. If what Ava had said were true, then this was something far bigger than anything the police force could handle.

It was out of his hands. All he could do was go home, sleep it off and pretend that instead of checking on Ava, he'd gone home with a six-pack of beer to drink the night away. Maybe he'd even attend a few therapy sessions.

Yeah, and have the good doctor determine I'm unfit to wear my badge.

With a deep sigh, he exited the cell and followed Ava. Hell, though he didn't like her method of doing it, she *had* saved his life, after all. He owed her for that, at least. He was honorable, if nothing else.

He shook his head. Years of police training and experience had all gone down the shitter in a matter of minutes.

All thanks to the slender, deceptively innocent-looking woman walking a few feet ahead of him.

Just freaking great.

Chapter Three

Lucian Gordano walked through the winding halls of his father's mansion in St. Charles, Illinois, his signature scowl in place. Dressed in denim jeans, black biker boots, a black leather jacket and with a half-dozen weapons hidden on his body, he was always prepared for a fight and constantly alert.

As the eldest son of the king of the vampires and the leader of one of the most powerful clans in the world, he was always vigilant. While most of their people admired and respected Cyrus, his father, there were a great number of them out there who opposed his rulings. There were even a few non-vampires who had tried to start a war with him. A man didn't live well over three thousand years without making a few enemies.

And, of course, though rare, there were a few who were foolish enough to actually try attacking one of the king's six sons. That was always fun and usually ended in an army of vampires ripping the opposers to shreds.

As Lucian approached the large wooden doors leading to his father's private library, he could hear loud guffawing through the thick paneling. He sighed in exasperation. He only wished his brothers could take their positions as seriously as he did.

Much to Lucian's annoyance, his father had called a meeting at a very inconvenient time. As Chicago's sole clan chief, he was tied up with a lot of shit as it was. A few Rogues had banded together and were wreaking havoc in his territory, killing humans and leaving their corpses in the open, drained of every last drop of blood.

He had been in the middle of an investigation when his father had called the mandatory meeting with his sons. It was a royal command of their king, not a polite request from their father, meaning he couldn't refuse.

Damn him.

The two hooded vampires standing guard bowed their heads in respect at Lucian's approach. He nodded in return before entering.

The library was massive, easily the size of a small house, with a second floor above them. There were thousands upon thousands of books and scrolls on the shelves, some as old as Cyrus himself. Some of them were even older. In the center of the room was an elegant living room set placed around a wide fireplace, allowing the guests to face each other when sitting. The gold-and-white décor of the furniture gave it an even more lush appeal. The high ceiling was painted in a way that rivaled Michelangelo's work on the Sistine Chapel.

As ancient as his father was, it was no surprise he'd accumulated a tremendous amount of wealth over the last few millennia. His estate here, just an hour away from Chicago, was only one of many he kept around the world.

All five of Lucian's brothers sat on the couches, laughing and talking while his father sat in a lush wingchair, watching them with a guarded expression. When Lucian entered, they all paused and looked up at him.

"Finally!" Andreas, the youngest, exclaimed. In a room full of men with matching pale blue eyes, he and Lucian stood out. Lucian's eyes were more silver than blue, but Andreas' were a bright amber, the only true sign that he wasn't blood-related to the rest of them.

Lucian only nodded in greeting, keeping his expression impassive. He went to lean on the fireplace, crossing his arms. As much as he cared about his family, he had things to do. The faster they got this tedious meeting over with, the better.

While he trusted his hunters to continue the investigations without him, he still wanted to be there himself. Some Rogues out there possessed the actual balls to hunt in his territory, taunting him with the trail of dead bodies they'd left in their wake. And when he caught the bastards, he'd make sure they knew not to step on his toes.

Rogues were mindless, bloodthirsty heathens, but they at least knew to stay out of clan areas. It was an internal instinct that was lacking in those mongrels.

"Ah, always the loner," his other brother Cassander said with a dramatic shake of his blond head. The others began to murmur their agreement but Lucian ignored them. Of all the people in the universe, Cass had some nerve calling *him* a loner. The man spent more time locked away in his gloomy lair than stepping foot outside.

"Enough," Cyrus said. His voice was loud and booming, holding the expected commanding tone of a king. There was a slight edge to it, letting Lucian know his father was bothered by something. Everyone quieted and looked to him. Even as old as Cyrus was, like all vampires, he looked to be in the prime of his life. With his pale blue eyes the color of a glacier and his hardened frame draped in a fancy toga-style robe, he looked every bit the Etruscan warrior he'd once been.

"My sons, I'm just going to cut straight to the point. I called you all here tonight because we have an immense problem on our hands." Like his three eldest sons, he spoke in a thick accent that was no longer used, the four of them having been brought up with Latin as their primary language.

"Let me guess," Salvator, the third-oldest, drawled, a chalice filled with blood held in one manicured hand. He was the more extravagant of the bunch, with his long silver hair flowing neatly over his shoulders. He was wearing a red silk shirt tucked into smooth black dress pants. Though he often spent his time keeping his appearance immaculate and flashy, he was just as skilled and dangerous as Lucian himself. All his brothers were. They weren't necessarily intimidating in appearance, but the rare, noble blood of the Ancients flowed through their veins. They were the strongest of the strong. "The twins got into a brawl with the shifters again?"

"Hey!" Julius, the younger twin, snapped with annoyance. "That was a one-time thing, and those mangy wolves started it."

Darius, who was an almost-mirror-image of him, crossed his arms much like a petulant child. "Yeah, those fleabags were asking for a fight, so we gave it to them."

Lucian sighed deeply. 'Dumb and dumber' was far too polite to describe those two imbeciles. They were more troublesome than a tribe of mischievous imps. It was rare that a story gets told about them that didn't end with them making another enemy.

Cyrus waved that away. "No, this is far more serious." He pointed a small remote at the large flat-screen TV hanging above the fireplace. The screen came on. Lucian looked up at the monitor. His arms fell and he straightened, widening his eyes.

The image on the screen was of a gorgeous woman dressed in a blue-and-white pin-striped uniform standing inside a diner.

In the close-up, she was smiling at an elderly couple at the counter as she poured them a cup of coffee from latex-covered hands. The image was so clear that it was easy to make out her sharp angular features, wide emerald eyes, thick black hair and exotic skin tone. It was perfectly bronzed, revealing her mother's Egyptian descent.

Like all vampires, she possessed the sort of unearthly beauty that could have an entire room full of patrons stopping and gazing in awe.

However, that wasn't the reason Lucian's heart hitched.

"No way," someone breathed.

"Is that—?"

"Yes," Cyrus cut in. "An informant sent this to me. From what they gathered, someone's been hunting her for a long time and, a few days ago, they found her. We don't yet know who it is or why they want her, but one thing is certain. Ava is in a lot of danger. We have to find her before they do."

Lucian swallowed hard. It had been damn near a century since any of them had seen their estranged younger sister. She'd only lived with them for a short decade after losing her mother when she was thirteen, but one day she'd disappeared and no one had seen or heard from her since. Lucian had traveled far and wide looking for her, and just when he'd picked up on her trail, it had vanished, leaving him with no clues to her whereabouts.

Her disappearance had hit him hard. As the eldest sibling, it was his duty to protect his brothers and sister at all costs, and he'd failed to do so. Given that she was the baby of the family, he'd created a strong brotherly bond with her. He'd gone above and beyond to make sure that she in no way felt like an outcast among their family. He'd even trained her in several forms of martial arts and taught her how to defend herself wielding the most common weapons.

After she'd left, a cavernous hole had formed in his heart. It was almost as great as the pain he'd felt when his own mother had died.

The room was silent for several moments.

Lucian narrowed his eyes on the picture, taking in the surroundings of the diner. It looked pretty damn familiar. He turned to his father, whose pale blue eyes were filled with sadness and worry. "Where was this photo taken?"

He hesitated a moment, no doubt worrying the next thing out of his mouth would alarm his sons. And it did. "Downtown Chicago."

"Fuck," Darius breathed, scrubbing his hands across his face.

Lucian felt his very breath leave his body. She'd been living practically in their backyard and not once had they ever known. He clenched his fists at his sides. As much as he told himself it wasn't his fault that she'd gone missing, he couldn't help feeling otherwise. If only he'd been better at protecting her...

"*Merda,*" he growled. He took one last look at the picture, confirming the location of the diner. He pushed himself away from the wall and stalked toward the exit.

Chicago. That was *his* territory, where he and his clan resided. She'd been right under his nose for gods knew how long, and yet he hadn't even thought...

His nails were biting into his palms. He was so pissed with himself.

"Luc, where are you going?" Cass called out, running after him. Lucian paused with his hand on the doorknob.

"I'm going to bring our sister home."

Each of his brothers stood. Cass gave him a solemn look and strode over to place his hand on Lucian's shoulder. "We share your pain, *fratello.* We're coming with you."

In the background, Cyrus rose as well, smoothing down the elegant fabric of his toga. Lucian gave a curt nod and continued out of the door, all five of his brothers following behind him. Though they all bumped heads and fought more often than not, one thing was certain. When it came to family, they would march through hell and back to protect their own.

"*Be safe, Ava,*" he called out in his mind. "*We're coming for you.*"

* * * *

An old superstition claimed that if your nose was itching, it meant someone was talking about you. Ava frowned as she used her fingertips to pinch her nostrils closed in an attempt to relieve the mild itch.

She shrugged it off. *Oh well.* If that were true, then no doubt whoever had discovered those two ghouls' remains were the ones doing the talking.

Either them or the bastard who has been hunting me down for the last few decades.

She stood by the window, peering out of a small slit in the curtains of the motel room in Madison, Wisconsin. Somehow, in the time since she'd been kidnapped, the ghouls had managed to drag her across state lines nearly three hours away from Chicago. The sun had just begun to set when she and Marc had escaped. Though she was able to walk in daylight without combusting into flames like Turnblood vampires, she was still naturally a creature of the night, so being in the sun drained her of her already-sapped energy. Even pureblood Royal and Aristocratic vampires avoided venturing outside during the day if they had the choice. Doing so meant they'd need to consume more blood to keep up their waning strength.

She peered down at her wrists. The silver shackles had blistered her skin pretty badly. If they had been left on much longer, the metal would have burned straight down to the bone. It hurt like a bitch, but she had to suck it up until she could feed. That would speed up the healing process, not to mention ease the painful cramps in her stomach.

She looked over her shoulder at the closed bathroom door. Though neither she nor Marc had had their wallets on them, Ava had been able to use her vampiric charm to get the office clerk to give them a room key, making him think she was just a normal guest traveling the countryside from town and not a gaunt, beat-up creep covered in demon blood. She'd then had him go out on his break and buy them a change of clothes and some food.

When she saw the clerk approaching their door, she opened it. She made sure to stay out of the doorway as she took the bags of food and clothing from him. She looked at his name tag and smiled warmly. "Thank you, Dillon," she said, touching his hand. "If anyone asks, tell them this room is paid off for the next two days. Other than that, forget you ever saw me."

She watched his blank expression. She peered inside his mind, nodding with satisfaction as his memory was wiped clean, save for her orders. *Good.*

The young boy bobbed his head and walked off, unaware of what was going on. On the plus side, this motel was in the countryside where very little action happened, and only one person was working the office. She doubted anyone would question him about the occupied room, but she had prepared for it just in case.

Ava turned back and set the bags on the single full-sized bed. Her cheeks flushed. Her heart was throbbing at the thought of Marc and her sharing a bed, heat pooling low in her stomach as the mere image of his body pressed up against hers flashed in her mind.

Though she really needed to feed and rest, she would just have to stay up and keep watch — or sleep in the armchair in the corner near the small dining table. Even after the danger they'd just escaped, she craved him in a way that both excited and terrified her. She'd already gotten him involved enough. She didn't want him to become a part of her world. He had nearly been killed, for the gods' sake.

Besides, with the horrified way he'd looked at her in the cell, no doubt he now wanted nothing to do with her but to get as far away as fast as he could. She certainly didn't blame him for that.

She looked at her fingertips, thinking back over what had happened in the cell. She'd tried to wipe his memory earlier and replace it with something else to explain what was going on, but she hadn't been able to get inside his mind. Normally, she could just peer into a human's eyes and get them to do her bidding by charming them, and when that didn't work, she could touch them with her fingertips and see their memories, even alter them. But she hadn't been able to do that with Marc. She'd thought maybe it was because of her weakened state. However, that couldn't have been it, since she'd been able to use her powers on Dillon.

Then again, he was a young lad, barely out of his teen years. No doubt being several years older and a cop with strong mental stability, Marc had much stronger willpower. With proper feeding and rest, she'd be strong enough to make him forget these last two nights had ever happened. It was for his own good, after all. Being knocked unconscious and kidnapped by demons then witnessing her — another demon — kill them right in front of him? *Yeah, what mortal wants to remember seeing that?*

The shower had cut off several minutes before, and now the door opened and she looked up at Marc as he stepped out, the steam from his shower leaving the bathroom and swirling around him as if begging him to step back in.

Ava's breath caught in her throat and her mouth went dry.

By the gods, she thought Marc was fine in uniform, but looking at him now with only a towel hanging low on his waist made him downright sexy. He ran a hand through his wet hair, every movement causing his muscles to flex. His hard chest was free of hair and his stomach was tight with the faintest indication of abs. A thin line of dark hair made a trail from his navel, disappearing under the thick white towel that was unable to conceal the bulge tantalizingly hidden underneath the fabric.

Despite the pain in her body, Ava reacted to him in a way only he could make her feel. It took sheer strength to tear her eyes away from him and focus on going through the bag of clothes. She took out a pair of women's sweatpants and a sweatshirt.

Marc stayed put, watching her warily. She didn't look up at him for fear he would see her flaming cheeks. "The clerk brought us a change of clothes and something to eat. I'll shower while you change." She walked past him, pausing just before closing the door. "If you're gone by the time I get out, be safe." With that, she closed the door and leaned against it. She blew out a long breath.

The steam from Marc's shower caused her skin to dampen, making the collar of her uniform stick to her neck. Gods, he'd been so close — so close that the smell of clean skin and pure male had teased her nose, causing wetness to grow between her legs. Her fangs throbbed as she wondered if his blood tasted as good as the rest of him looked.

She shook her head furiously. *No.* She wouldn't do that to him. If she did, she'd definitely crave him even more — more of his blood, more of his touch...everything.

With a frustrated sigh, she pushed away from the door and began to undress. She definitely needed to feed or she feared she would pounce on Marc.

And wouldn't that be awful? The poor thing had already been through enough because of her. She didn't need to scare him any more than he already was. The horrified look in his eyes in the cell and even the wary gazes he'd kept sending her as they had made their way to the motel told her he couldn't possibly be okay with all this. It was only a matter of time before the reality of the past few hours set in and panic took over. It was the norm when humans were suddenly thrown into the demon world.

Turning the water on high, Ava stepped under the steamy spray of the shower. Nearly an hour later she was feeling refreshed. With her skin scrubbed pink and pruney, she wrapped her body in a thick towel and used another one to dry her hair. She wiped the tall, foggy mirror clean, wincing when she saw her reflection.

The left side of her face was still red and purple from bruising when the ghouls had knocked her out. She had a few scratches and cuts along her arms, plus the red blistered skin around her wrists. Where her skin was normally bronze in color, she looked pale. Her eyes had dark circles under them, her cheeks almost hollow. *Holy freaking hell, I look like shit!* No wonder Marc was so scared. She probably really did look like a demon to him.

She grunted and donned her new clothes. Then she stepped out of the bathroom, enjoying the cooler air hitting her skin.

She peeked around the room, her heart squeezing in pain when she saw it was empty. She gave a small sigh and perched on the edge of the bed. *Well, I expected it, didn't I?* Marc was only human, after all. Only a small number of humans knew about the demon world and were able to accept it. As she'd told him earlier, humans were afraid of what they didn't understand. She felt foolish for having just a shred of hope that he'd still be here when she got out the shower.

Her musings were cut short when she heard a card key slide into the lock. She jumped to her feet, reached for the nearby TV remote and held it above her head, ready to fight. She was certain she looked downright stupid, but if one were cunning enough, anything could be used as a formidable weapon — even a cheap piece of plastic that was the size of her hand.

However, only Marc stepped in, blinking at her in surprise. He held his hands up in mock surrender. "Calm down, Selene. It's only me."

Ava found herself relaxing, an unexplainable sense of relief filling her. She hadn't realized just how tense she had been at the thought of him leaving. "Selene?" she demanded, confused.

He stepped into the room, closing the door behind him. "As in the movie *Underworld*? The main character who's a total badass female vampire?" At her dull look, he waved that away. "Forget it." He eyed the remote control suspiciously, a dark eyebrow raising. "What the hell kind of damage is that thing going to do?"

Ava tossed the plastic on the dresser next to the TV, folding her arms with indignance. She refused to be embarrassed. "Never mind that. What were you doing?"

He shook his head, sliding his hands into his pockets. "I just went to check the perimeter. Not exactly sure who or what I was looking for, but everything seemed fine."

He was dressed in a black-and-white jogging suit, his large frame filling the outfit. He raked his hand through his hair as he eyed her with caution. Then he waved it to indicate the opened bag of food sitting on the bed. "I saved you some."

Ava removed the towel from her head, allowing her long hair to fall down her back. She tugged at a damp lock that fell over her shoulder. "That's not necessary. I-I'm going to have to leave for a little while."

He frowned. "Why? Where to?"

She repositioned herself. He watched her with an intensity that made her feel guilty, even though she hadn't done anything wrong. "As I told you before, I need to feed."

His look was filled with confusion. "There's a burger in there. Are you — " He broke off as realization hit him. "Don't tell me you don't eat regular food."

She pressed her lips together to keep from smiling. "Yes, I eat regular food. However...as the story of vampires goes, I need blood to survive. If I go too long without it..." She used her hands to suggest her current condition.

He was quiet for several moments, just watching her with those sharp golden eyes. She couldn't read his expression, which frustrated the hell out of her. *Damn cop.*

He was always good at hiding his expressions. Ava envied him for it. She was the vampire, after all. 'Darkness and mystery' were in her nature.

When he spoke, his voice was strangely harsh. "And where are you planning to get blood?"

She frowned, tilting her head to the side. "I'm not understanding your question. How else am I supposed to get blood? I'll find a donor willing to spare a vein." She paused, a sudden thought occurring. "If you're concerned I'm going to kill or hurt someone, rest assured. I never take more than a pint from anyone, and from what I hear, a vampire's bite is actually quite pleasurable for the donor."

He grimaced. "From what you *hear*? You've never had a bite from your own kind?"

Ava shook her head. For vampires, the act of giving their own blood took an immense amount of trust. It wasn't something they did just for the hell of it, no matter how pleasurable it might be. "Once I finish, I erase their memory of ever encountering me and send them on their way."

Anger and confusion warred on his face. "Wait just one damn minute. I have so many questions. So you really *are* a fucking vampire?"

She raised her brows, shifting her weight to one leg. "Yes, more or less."

"Again with these vague-ass answers," he grumbled. "Explain this to me clearly."

She tugged on her hair again. "My father is a vampire, and my mother was a fey."

He huffed in annoyance, like a child. "Ava," he said through gritted teeth, "I don't abuse women, but I'm about half a step away from launching across this room and tossing you out of the window. I already watched you rip out a man's throat then watched that same man dissolve into ashes. I was even knocked unconscious by some demons for something that has absolutely nothing to do with me. My patience is beginning to wear thin, so you would be doing us both a favor if you cooperate and stop bullshitting me."

She paused, weighing her options. She could refuse to answer, and they both knew who the winner would be if they battled it out — not that she would wish such a thing. However, he was right. He'd already been dragged into this mess. The least she could do was be honest. With a heavy sigh, she responded, "Fine. Let me start from the beginning."

So as to not collapse, she walked over to sit in the armchair she'd thought about sleeping in. She turned the chair to face him then waited until he sat on the edge of the bed, as if half-prepared to dash out the room. She could catch him in the blink of an eye if she really wanted to.

Well, in her weak state she was sure he could outrun her. She'd used up most of her remaining energy breaking free of the chains back in the cell. It had only been her desire to protect Marc that had given her that bit of strength. That and the fact that those two idiot-ghouls had used shackles that weren't full silver. The metal had been mixed with other elements, making them weaker than they could have been.

In the end, though, it had cost her. She was already shaking from trying to stay upright.

"As you learned tonight, there are creatures other than humans walking this plane. However, we all generally prefer being called 'demons'. There are literally hundreds, if not thousands, of different types of demons, but most of them live in the underworld, also known as Hell—not necessarily the fiery pits of eternal torment exaggerated in religions, but still a place humans don't want to go. But again, that's another world entirely. Where we are now is what we call 'the human plane'. The gateways to Hell are heavily guarded and closed off, so it's almost impossible for anything, human or otherwise, to cross planes, not without being summoned for a short period of time. Every so often it does happen, but as long as demons keep to themselves and don't cause harm to humans, it's okay. And that's a simple introduction to the demon world." She paused, giving him a moment to soak that bit of information in. *Gods, is this Demon Studies 101 or what?*

It was clear he was having a hard time believing everything, but after seeing with his own eyes, he had to know what she was saying was true.

"Okay, I think I understand that," he said. "Kind of. Demons are real. But those two guys looked normal to me. I mean, they had some kind of weird vibes and red eyes, but visually they looked like regular men. I thought demons would look more...demonic. You know, misshapen bodies, multiple eyes, razor-sharp teeth…that sort of thing."

Her lips twitched again. *He is so cute.* "Yes, demons come in all shapes and sizes, some of them horribly grotesque like you just mentioned. Some are able to take on a humanoid form, and some are simply born like that. For example, those two bounty hunters who captured us were demons called 'ghouls'. They're stronger and faster than humans and they're pretty good hunters, but that's about it. They mostly love causing destruction wherever they go. They're the disposable creatures you call on when you want someone else to do your dirty work for a small fee. They have the ability to take on a human form, though in reality they look more like…well, imagine a man-sized, two-legged body with a praying mantis head and oily black skin."

He gave her a horrified look and she nodded in rueful agreement. She'd only seen a few ghouls in their natural form from afar, and it had definitely not been pretty.

He shook his head in disgust. "I'm glad I didn't see that shit." He peered at her with narrowed eyes. "So what about you? What is your real form?"

She raised her brows at the accusing tone. "You're looking at it. I look the same as I do now, minus the bruising. I'm one of the demons who were born with a humanoid body, thank the gods."

"Mm-hmm. Okay," he said, still cautious. "You said you were a vampire, right?"

"Half vampire, half fey."

He waved that aside. "So, if that's true, then how come you can walk in daylight and eat regular food and wait— Aren't vampires dead? Or *undead*? So how were you *born* a half-vampire? Aren't vampires created by a bite or something?"

She drummed her fingers on the small table next to her, leaning back. Well, as far as Hollywood movies went, she supposed they weren't *too* far off the mark. Still, they could never completely capture the truth of her race. "Vampires are a bit more complex than the way we're depicted in movies. There are four types — Royals, Aristocrats, Turnbloods and Rogues. Royals are the highest ranking. They are purebloods, descended from the Ancients — the very first vampires to walk this earth. They are the most powerful. The Aristocrats are born vampires as well, though they do not have a drop of Ancient blood in them.

"Also like the Royals, they can walk in sunlight and eat regular food. The main differences are that Royals are much stronger and faster, and they each have a special power that no other vampire has. The next level is Turnbloods. They are the more common vampires in folklore. They're the ones who were once human but were turned into vampires. They cannot walk in daylight and can only drink blood. And though their body is technically undead, they are able to sire children so long as their mate is fully alive. For instance, a Turnblood siring a child with a human will result in an Aristocratic child. A half-breed, but still…

"Lastly, there are Rogues. Rogues can be either Royal, Aristocrat or Turnblood, but they are all very dangerous, and highly unpredictable. They're vampires who have given in to their most primal needs. They do not belong to a clan, nor do they follow the laws we live by. They will kill without mercy and drink every last drop of blood from their victims. Once a vampire succumbs to their bloodlust, there is no bringing them back. The only thing to do is put them down, which is a job given to our hunters.

"So, all in all, though we're all different, every vampire has one thing in common. We all need blood to survive. Some can go days without it, while some can only go hours."

She could see the wheels turning in Marc's head as he soaked in all this information. Though she hadn't wanted to involve him any more than she had, he had deserved an explanation. After all, it didn't really matter in the end, because once she had her strength and made sure he got back home safely, she was going to erase his memory of everything anyway. She owed him that. He didn't need to have those scary memories in his life.

"Let me get this straight," he murmured, obviously trying to understand the complex information. "Royals, Aristocrats, Turnbloods and Rogues. All are vampires, and yet they are all different from one another."

"That's correct."

"And so vampires are able to have children? Like...give birth?"

Her lips twitched in suppressed amusement. "Yes. We do not lay eggs, if that's what you're thinking."

His own amusement flashed in his eyes. "Smartass. How is that possible, though? Even for the...Turnbloods. They're killed as humans and brought back to life. How is it that their reproductive organs are even working?"

Ava thought it over a moment before shrugging. "I'll admit it's a mystery to me. I've never studied them much. There are many different theories, though. If I had to choose one, I'd say the blood they take from a live host is able to awaken their bodies, making it possible for them to do mundane activities such as…giving birth. However, it's only effective if one of them is alive. For example, Turnbloods wouldn't be able to produce a child with each other, but a Turnblood and an Aristocrat, or a Turnblood and a human, are able to. It's strange, but again, I've never fully researched any of it."

"That's as good an explanation as any, I suppose. So these Royals are like the head honchos, huh? Since their blood is rare, I guess that means not too many of them are around."

She tilted her head to the side, her wavy hair sliding down her shoulder. "So rare that, from what I know, there are only eight left."

He widened his beautiful eyes considerably, letting out a low whistle.

"Damn, almost extinct."

Ava's heart gave a painful lurch at that, but she just gave a small shrug. She knew he didn't mean any harm by his simple words, but she couldn't help the sadness that her people would eventually die out.

Marc continued his questioning. "Back in the cell, you said those two ghouls weren't able to be tried as regular people," he stated.

She nodded. "That is correct."

"So you all just kill each other? Is there no order?"

Ava grimaced. "At one point in time, there was none, but things have changed. As I said, different demons follow different rules, depending on who their leaders are. For vampires, we form clans all around the world. To not belong to a clan is equivalent to saying you do not need help or protection from other demons who may wish you harm, to enslave you or gods know what else. Every clan has a leader that clan members answer to. Above them, we all answer to one king. His very word is law among vampires. It is because of him that clans were formed, and most demons choose to not cause any trouble with vampires." She rubbed a hand against her jaw, flinching at the pain it brought. With her lack of feeding, all of her bruises, cuts and burns were going to take forever to heal.

"One thing all demons in this world have in common, however, is that we are forbidden from harming or killing humans without just cause. Demon-on-demon crime isn't nearly so strict, though. Demons fight each other at their own risk. For example, if a werewolf decides to attack a vampire who belongs to a clan, then that wolf has essentially challenged the entire clan. If a vampire doesn't belong to a clan, then they are an easy target for other demons to attack. They are, what the kids call, SOL."

Marc soaked in the information, leaning back on his elbows as he watched her. Ava eyed the length of his body beneath his track suit. Even under the clothes, she could see the powerful muscles.

Nice. Very nice.

Marc finally said, "Let's say, hypothetically speaking, all the demons want to fight each other in a mass, flat-out war or that an entire species decides to take over the humans and kill them all — or harvest their souls, or enslave them or...something. Or what if some evil demon lord decides to destroy the world? Wait! Is there even a such thing as a demon lord?"

Ava smiled, even as she shook her head. "Seriously, Marc. Ease up on the movies. None of those scenarios would ever happen, because all demons answer to the Imperials."

Marc shook his head. "Imperials?"

"Basically the Supreme Court of the demon world. They usually mind their own business and let demons hash out their own problems, but every so often they interfere and prevent...an apocalypse."

"Very well." He rolled his head from side to side, cracking the bones.

Ava had to bite her tongue to keep from offering a massage—a long, full-body massage...without any clothes. *Yum.*

"I'm assuming you don't belong to a clan?" he asked.

An old pain scratched the surface of her heart. "No." The flat answer came out a bit harsher than she'd meant it to.

"Why not?"

She frowned, unwilling to share that particular piece of information. "It's complicated."

He frowned in return but didn't press, thank the gods. He probably sensed she wouldn't tell him, no matter how persistent he was. To say it was a touchy subject was an understatement. Instead, he asked, "So which one are you?"

"Which one what?"

"You said you're a half-vampire and half-fey, whatever the hell that is, so what kind of vampire are you?" He paused, thinking it over. "You're clearly able to be in the sun. Also, you can eat regular food, but you still need blood. So that means you're either an Aristocrat or a Royal. Which is it?"

Another pain tugged in her chest as a memory flashed in her mind. "My father is a Royal." She didn't dare tell him the full truth, that her father was the king. "It's the reason I have a bounty on my head." That also wasn't a lie, but it wasn't completely true either.

"Only eight Royals, huh? Including or not including you?"

Another painful tug. "Including."

He widened his eyes again. "Jesus. Don't tell me it's one of those situations where you have to marry one of them and reproduce just to keep the bloodline pure."

Ava gave him a horrified look. *Keep the bloodline pure? Considering the other seven Royals alive are my brothers and father, no freaking thanks. Gross.* "That's..." She shook her head. "No. It isn't one of those situations."

A look of relief crossed his features. "Okay. You also said back in the cell that it's been a while since you last fed. How long is 'a while'?"

She was still shaking the disgusting thoughts from her mind when she registered his words. Heat rose in her cheeks.

"Well?" he pressed.

She bit her lip then muttered, "A week."

His eyes almost bugged out of his head. "A week? You just said vampires need to feed every few hours or days."

She gave a single nod. "That's correct."

His mouth parted in shock. "Is that why you look so..." He snapped his mouth shut, appearing to not want to offend her.

Unconcerned, Ava only smiled. "I look terrible, right?"

His cheeks turned an endearing shade of pink. "I set myself up for that one, didn't I?"

Ava chuckled. "I know I look bad. To answer your question, yes. Going this long without feeding, plus the fight with those ghouls, plus being chained in silver, plus being in the sun every day? I'm really drained."

He frowned. "But you're able to walk in the sun. How is that draining?"

"Royals and Aristocrats are able to walk in sunlight, but it takes a toll on our bodies. We don't turn into ash, like Turnbloods do, but we experience great amounts of fatigue, especially when we don't feed during that time."

"Huh," he commented. He was observing her, though all traces of fear were gone. All that was left seemed to be curiosity. Not for the first time, Ava wished she could see what he was thinking.

"So, whenever you feed from someone, you're able to erase their memories?" He asked. She nodded. "How?"

"It's a skill that comes with being a vampire. We use our powers to charm humans. It's what's kept our identities hidden for so long. Along with that, we have the usual superior senses, speed, strength, eternal youth and the ability to heal even the gravest of injuries. And every Royal has a special skill that is unique to only them. For example, one can have the ability to manipulate ice or fire, to command animals... It varies."

"What's yours?" he demanded.

Ava bit the inside of her cheek. For a Royal to give disclose their special ability was to reveal a way for their enemies to discover a weakness. Even if Marc wasn't a true threat to her, she still found herself reluctant to unveil such a secret to him. "That's...personal."

He was quiet for several moments, thinking everything over. When Ava's stomach began to tighten, she stood, using the table for balance. "We can continue with this conversation later. Right now, I really need to feed while I still can." If not, she would attack the nearest blood source she could find.

Which was Marc, a thought that tempted her far more than it should have.

Marc stood as well, moving to block the door.

She frowned. "What are you — ?"

"I've been thinking about it," he said, his tone serious. "It's too dangerous for you to go outside right now, right? If one of those things were to see you, you wouldn't have the energy to fight back."

"Marc, I'll be fine. As you saw, I can handle myself. Move."

His eyes turned hard, those golden orbs burning. "Drink my blood."

Chapter Four

Ava reared back, appalled at the mere thought of drinking his blood.

Appalled, but tempted. Very, very tempted.

"What? No."

"Look... I'm perfectly healthy," he stated. "That's important, isn't it? I have no history of family illnesses, I have regular physicals and checkups due to my job and I have plenty of blood to spare."

"Marc, I don't have time for this."

He wasn't budging. "Ava, stop being so stubborn. Instead of going off into the darkness searching for someone to...do whatever, you have a capable donor right here. Besides, one of those ghouls could be lurking outside." He turned his head to the side and tapped his jugular, as if to entice her. It was working. "Come on."

Ava gulped. Even from across the room she could hear the pulsing of his veins, could practically smell the blood rushing underneath the skin. "I...can't," she said weakly. Her stomach only clenched again, the cramps becoming worse in retaliation of her refusal. Gods, she wanted him. She wanted him bad. But she couldn't. She had to find someone else...anyone else.

Marc was far too precious. She feared that if she took even one small taste, she'd be addicted for the rest of her life.

And considering I'm constantly on the run, wouldn't that just suck – no pun intended.

"Why not?" he demanded, narrowing his eyes. "Even at the diner, no matter how much I tried to get you to open up, you acted cold toward only me. Right now I'm standing before you willing to give you some blood to heal yourself, and you're still pushing me away. It's clear you want me as much as I want you, so what the hell is keeping you from giving in to something as simple as this?"

Something as simple as this? There was nothing simple about her taking his blood. Even now her fangs were throbbing painfully with the need to sink into his flesh – *his and only his.*

Ava's heart gave an odd thump at his words. He actually wanted her to like him still? Even now, knowing she was a demon? *How confusing.*

But his words had struck a chord deep within her. In the blink of an eye, she was standing before him, leaning into him. Her heart was pounding, the pain in her stomach nothing compared to the one in her chest. She wanted him more than anything else – his blood, his touch, everything. And for his own good, she'd kept him at a distance. It was her fault he was in this mess to begin with. She'd already told him more than he needed to know about her world, and he'd seen things no human should have to see.

And even so, he wanted to help her. He should be afraid, not wanting her anywhere near him. She didn't understand it one bit.

But as she looked deep into his darkening eyes, her resolve slipped away. *Damn him and damn those ghouls for putting me in this position.*

She would do it. She'd take a little bit of blood from him. And afterward, when they made it back to Chicago, she'd erase the whole thing from his mind. At least that way he'd be safe...and sane.

"Fine," she whispered. She took his wrist in her hand and led him over to the bed. They both sat down on the edge, facing each other. "Are you sure you want this?" she asked cautiously.

He swallowed. "Yes."

It was all she needed to hear.

Ava tilted his head to the side, exposing the smooth skin of his neck. She leaned forward, inhaling deeply. *Oh, he smells so good. So deliciously good.* She placed one hand on one side of his head and the other on his broad shoulder, admiring the hard muscles flexing beneath his jacket. She placed her lips to the pounding vein in his neck, scraping her fangs ever so softly across the warm skin. He shuddered and she could smell his sudden arousal.

He snaked his arm around her waist and pulled her closer, urging her on. She licked the tender spot above his vein before allowing her elongated fangs to sink into his flesh. He gasped aloud, and she let out a small moan as his hot blood flooded her tongue. It was sweet and tangy, a perfect combination that had her longing for more of him.

His arousal was strong, and her body reacted immediately. She pushed more fully against him. He used both of his hands to pull her in, and without realizing it, she was soon straddling him. With each pull of his blood, she ground against the erection straining in his jogging pants. He was letting out tiny, soft sounds of encouragement, gripping her ass and sliding her across him.

She didn't understand what was going on. She'd taken blood from hundreds of males and females, and though they had always become aroused, not once had she ever responded like this. She had just taken their blood and left them in a state of pleasure as she went her separate way — no sex, no extra touching, nothing.

But Marc...

This was unlike anything she'd ever experienced. Whatever pull he had on her, she didn't know if it was good or bad, but in this moment, she was loving every second of it. She'd desired him when she'd first laid eyes on him. His looks, his charisma, his dimpled smile, his scent... Everything called to her in a way she'd never felt before.

She should be terrified of these strange feelings. And she had no doubt that if her mind wasn't clouded with lust, she would be.

For the moment, however, she reveled in the sweet bliss. After months of fantasizing and dreaming, she was finally taking his blood and feeling his hard body against hers.

With a sudden movement, with her still drinking deeply of him, Marc stood up with her in his arms. He turned and gently laid her on the bed, settling between her legs. Ava closed her eyes as pleasure overcame her. He untied the string holding up her pants. Soon they were sliding down her legs then being tossed across the room. With one hand grasping the back of his head, she used her free hand to unzip his jacket. She allowed it to slide down his smooth torso, stroking her fingers over the hard planes of his chest.

Warm velvet over steel. That was what he felt like, and she loved it. She wanted to lick and kiss and suck every delectable inch of him just as she had in her dreams. Unfortunately, she couldn't drag this out tonight. She wanted him far too much and she was about to explode in his arms. Drinking blood allowed vampires to experience their donor's every feeling, and right now, Marc's pleasure was skyrocketing. There was no confusion, no fear, no wariness, just a deep-seated longing to be drenched in her heat.

She allowed her hand to sweep down the taut muscles of his stomach and dip underneath the stretchy waistband of his jogging pants. When she found his hardened shaft, she wrapped her hand around the hot skin, giving it a gentle squeeze. He gasped again and gripped her waist.

He spread her legs wide and found the center of her pleasure. She moaned against his skin, using the pad of one of her fingers to swipe at the drop of moisture at his tip and swirl it around his cockhead.

"Ava," he breathed. With his thumb still massaging her clit, he allowed a finger to dip into her damp core. Another followed, slowly stroking back and forth.

Ava tightened her hand around his shaft and she pulled it free from his pants, stroking its length. She withdrew her fangs from his neck, licking the twin puncture wounds to seal them closed. He pulled back a bit, peering down at her with a sexy half-lidded gaze. His once-bright golden eyes were now nearly pitch back with his lust, only the thinnest ring of gold circling his pupils.

He moved his hand away from her dripping sex, much to her annoyance. But, before she could utter a complaint, he grabbed his erection and guided it to her entrance. He stuck the tip inside, teasing her opening and making her hiss in pleasure. Then, in one smooth motion, he sank completely inside her.

Ava arched her back at the penetration and they both moaned aloud.

She wrapped her legs around him, bringing him close as he moved with steady strokes. Never once skipping a beat, he leaned down and placed his lips to hers. She made sure not to nick him with her fangs as she kissed him back. He slid his hand under her sweatshirt and cupped one breast, toying with her hardened nipple. She moaned again, running her nails lightly down his back. *Damn, damn, damn.* Nothing had ever felt so right.

He broke away from her mouth and kissed a trail down her cheek to her neck. He licked over the sweet spot where her neck and shoulder met, kissing and sucking her with fevered passion.

With each deep thrust of his hips, she met him with her own, her desire gaining momentum. He suddenly tightened his hand on her waist, and his strokes grew faster and shorter. They were both breathing hard, a moan escaping from her lips with every pound. *Just a little...more...*

He brought Ava to the very edge, and with one final stroke, she cried out her release as wave after wave of pleasure rippled through her core, clenching his erect member. He threw his head back and gritted his teeth as his own orgasm exploded. After what seemed like an eternity, both their bodies went weak. He collapsed on top of her, pinning her to the bed.

If not for her demonic strength, she would've been crushed under his weight. But she was pleased. His warm skin mixed with his delicious scent caused her to smile softly.

He stroked her hair and she nearly purred with delight. She'd never felt this kind of peace before, such tenderness from a man she'd longed for like a stray dog peering through the glass display at a bakery. For the first time in several decades, she was...happy.

A dangerous notion, no doubt, but she couldn't find it in herself to care at the moment. She just tucked her arms under his and stroked the muscles of his back soothingly, her eyelids growing heavy.

She let out a wide yawn and, in a matter of seconds, sleep overcame her.

* * * *

When Ava awoke the next day, it was already afternoon. Feeling well-rested and magnificently sated, she sat up, peering around. She blinked a few times in confusion.

Instead of her small bed with the black-and-white comforter, this one was full-sized with red-and-white etchings. The walls were bare, save for one bland painting of a flower. The TV was an older model bubble back with two large antennae on top. She frowned. This definitely wasn't the bedroom in the apartment she'd been living in for the last year.

Then it hit her—the ghouls, being chained in that damp cell, Marc, this motel room, her feeding from him.

Her face heated to scorching temperatures. *Oh, nononono*, she thought in a panic. She jumped out of bed and dashed to the bathroom, peering into the mirror. The circles under her eyes were gone and her skin had returned to its normal lightly bronzed tone. Her face was still bruised on one side, but it was far less noticeable than it had been the night before. She bit her nail as a nervous energy filled her.

She and Marc... It wasn't just a dream. *Oh, gods.* She felt so ashamed. She had only meant to drink a bit of his blood, but instead, she'd turned into some kind of lust-crazed maniac. Her body reacted in remembrance, but she shook her head, glaring at herself in the mirror.

What did you do?

She'd had sex with Marc...while drinking his blood.

Granted, it had been great sex. Amazing sex. Earth shattering, best-sex-she'd-ever-had-in-her-life sex. But she'd sworn to not do anything with him. Sure, she'd dreamed about it plenty of times in the last few months, but she had chastised herself to not let it be anything more than that.

She scrubbed her hands over her face. *Damn it all.* She had to get away from him — the sooner, the better. She'd erase his memory of the last few days, make sure to formally quit her job at the diner, say her goodbyes to Edith and Mr. Tommy and get the hell out of Dodge. She'd still remember her night with him and still think about him, but as much as it would sadden her, she would get over it...sooner or later. She was a vampire, so she'd have an eternity to do so, granted the gods allowed her to live that long. She had no idea what Marc thought about her now, and to be truthful, she didn't want to know.

Gods, she was too embarrassed to even stand before him.

She splashed some water on her face and put the spare toothbrush and toothpaste to use, a bit rougher than she meant. She then left the bathroom, found her discarded pants and put them on. She was in the middle of pulling her thick hair into a braid when the room door opened. Marc stepped inside, and their eyes met and held for several awkward moments before she turned away.

"We lucked out," he said, his tone cautious. "I found an older couple heading toward Chicago. They're willing to give us a ride, though it'll be in the back of their truck."

Ava only nodded, doing her best to hide her flushed face. Marc was quiet for several more moments, but she could feel him staring at her.

Just kill me now, she thought in distress. She was a vampire, for the gods' sake. Taking blood and satiating their lusts were the norm. She should in no way feel so embarrassed.

Yet, here she was, acting all shy and skittish like a virgin after having sex for the first time.

And she *so* wasn't a virgin anymore. But it had been so long since she'd last done anything other than take blood from someone. And Marc... Goodness, she'd gone the whole nine yards with him.

Finally, Marc let out a soft sigh. "Ava, listen. About last night... If you're — "

"It's okay!" She said. She looked up at him and saw his worried eyes. She forced a smile. She didn't need to hear his rejection or have him apologize. That would just be...embarrassing. "Thank you for helping me out, and I'm sorry for getting carried away. It won't happen again."

A hurt expression crossed his face, but just as quickly as it had appeared, it was gone. He was now looking at her in such a way she'd never seen before. It was cold and impassive. It almost reminded her of her brother Lucian.

"Right. Glad to have been of service," he drawled. "It's the black pickup truck with the trailer attached. Don't take too long." With that, he turned on his heel and left the room, slamming the door shut behind him.

Ava watched him leave, an odd ache forming in her chest.

Somehow, she got the feeling that he was...angry.

She frowned then shrugged it off. Whatever the case was, it was for the best. If being mad at her would help to keep the distance between them, she would suffer through it.

No matter how much it made her heart hurt.

* * * *

When they reached her apartment complex in Chicago, the sun had already set. They thanked the polite couple warmly, who in turn wished them good luck in life. When they drove off, Ava glanced around, spreading her senses out to check for anything that might be lurking in the shadows.

She couldn't be too cautious. Though she'd killed all three ghouls that had followed her from the diner to her apartment, there was no telling how many more of them were left or who or what was watching her right now.

Her location was now exposed, so she was no longer safe.

Once satisfied no demons were nearby, she turned to Marc. They hadn't spoken a single word to each other during the three-hour drive. Even when the couple had stopped for gas, they'd kept to themselves. It had been awkward, even more so now that they were here alone.

He was watching her with that same unreadable mask. She hated not being able to know what he was thinking.

Where exactly do we even go from here?

Did they shake hands and say goodbye? Should she just wave and turn away? Was there supposed to be some kind of hug or embrace and *I'll-miss-you*? Well, she knew that last one was out of the equation. With the way Marc was looking at her, no doubt touching her was the last thing on his mind.

Then again, she'd pretty much dismissed him in the motel room, right? Perhaps she'd wounded his pride in a way she hadn't realized at the time, and though she felt bad for it, she couldn't take it back, not now that he could be in danger just from being with her.

She tugged on the sleeve of her sweatshirt. "Um…well, do you need money for a ride home? My wallet is in my apartment somewhere. I doubt the ghouls found it."

He tucked his hands in the pockets of his pants. "No, but I think they may have taken my duty belt off when they knocked me out. If so, it should still be in there."

Ava nodded. She turned on her heel and led the way up to her apartment.

It was an older building, but it was well-maintained for its low cost. It was nothing fancy or high-class, but not as run-down as one would expect from the surrounding neighborhood. It was the type of place where tenants could lease month-to-month and pay in cold cash, so if they decided to move out of the blue, nothing would be complicated.

And since the entire neighborhood was a risky area, everyone kept to themselves. That was one thing she liked about living here. Even if they saw her door broken in, her neighbors would pretend not to notice.

The exact kind of privacy a vampire on the run would need.

Standing out in the hall, she listened to see if anyone was inside. All that was left was the faint sulfuric smell of the one ghoul she'd killed before they'd caught her, though even that odor was fading. She was about to enter when Marc wrapped his warm hand around her wrist, stopping her.

"What—"

He just went around her, stepping inside first. He pushed the door open and made his way in, checking to make sure the room was secure before relaxing. It was obvious those police instincts of his were still as sharp as ever.

And though they both knew very well she was better equipped to fight off a demon attack, she still felt a small, girly thrill zing through her at his actions.

Then she told herself he wasn't trying to protect her because he cared. It was just the nature of his job. He was a natural-born guardian.

When he motioned that everything was clear, Ava glanced around her apartment, frowning at the mess. She hadn't needed the furnishings. They were cheap anyway. They were just to keep her landlady from getting suspicious, should the woman ever pop in one day. Even so, there was a huge mess to clean. The couch was ripped open, its stuffing scattered about. Her blood was splattered on the ground, her lamp and side table broken to pieces.

She went inside her bedroom and saw it looked no better. The rotten scent of dead ghoul was still in the air, but it was far fainter than after a fresh kill. Within days, it would disappear completely, along with the black dust and blood left behind.

Her gaze landed on Marc's belt, which had been thrown across the room, and he went to pick it up, inspecting it to make sure everything was in place. Ava turned her back to him and kneeled before her nightstand. The drawers were wide open, but in the very back, she'd hidden a black box.

She took it out and opened it, thanking the gods that the ghouls had been too impatient to check everywhere thoroughly.

Inside was a large wad of hundreds, along with multiple fake IDs and a knife. The wicked blade was silver with a gold-and-white hilt. She stroked it lovingly before tucking the weapon and its strap around her ankle under her pant leg. It was her most prized possession. It was the one thing she'd had to keep her sane these past years. The blade had been a gift from her father on her fourteenth birthday, the first birthday she'd spent with him and her brothers.

She went over to her closet, making sure to avoid stepping in the dust left behind by the dead ghoul. She reached up to the top shelf for her traveling bag, which was already filled with clothes for her to just grab and go if need be. She took out a few of the hundreds and stuffed them deep into her pants pocket before shoving the rest inside the bag and slinging it over her back.

She looked up at Marc, who was tucking his gun into its holster at his hip. Their eyes met, and again there was that awkward silence.

He eyed her, frowning. "What are you going to do now?"

She shrugged. "Now that my whereabouts have been discovered, I have to move on. I can never stay in one place for long."

"You're just going to up and leave Chicago?"

"Yes," she said simply. *Obviously.* "It's best for me to leave Illinois altogether. Although, I must see Edith and Mr. Tommy. They've been good to me." She turned to face him fully. *This is it.* She extended her hand. She lowered her voice to be more compelling, lacing it with her charm. "I'm really sorry about everything you had to go through. I understand how…difficult everything must've been."

He eyed her warily, as if knowing her hidden intentions. But, he slowly reached out. His big hand engulfed hers, the appendage warm and strong — just like the rest of him.

Ava tightened her grip and took a step closer, looking him deep in the eyes. His sandalwood scent wrapped around her, sending a thrill of excitement straight to her core.

She ignored her sudden arousal, focusing instead on her powers. She unlocked her mind, letting her Royal powers flow into where their hands connected. This was her Royal gift — her ability to see into another's memories and alter them at her will.

Just like when they had been in the cell, her mind met a blank wall. She put more force into trying to get into his head, but it wouldn't budge. She held his gaze, and with a smooth, lowered voice, she said, "Forget the last two nights. You went to check on me, I was fine, then you went home and had a normal weekend."

He crinkled his forehead and snatched his hand away as if she'd burned him. "You— Are you trying to erase my memory?"

Ava reared back, frowning. Neither her charm nor her Royal powers were working on him. "How is this possible?" she muttered to herself.

Marc took a step back, glaring at her.

Gods. If looks could kill, she'd be as dead as the ghoul whose ashes lay a few feet away from them. "You tell me. You're the vampire, after all. Don't go trying using that demon mumbo jumbo on me—or whatever the hell you do. I don't want my memories altered. I'll pretend this weekend never happened, but I definitely don't want to go back to not knowing demons are fucking real, especially when they live all around us." With that, he stormed away.

Ava just watched him, her mouth parted. *What the hell?* Twice now she'd been unable to use her powers on him. Even with most of her strength returned, there was no way it should have been possible. After all, he was just a human. They were the most vulnerable to enthrallments.

She began to walk stiffly out of the bedroom behind him, shaking her head in confusion. *Of all people, it just had to be him.* The gods were surely against her.

When she made it to the living room, she saw Marc standing by the door with his arms crossed, facing away from her. She frowned. "Are you waiting for me?"

He glared at her over his shoulder. "Of course I am. What kind of man would I be if I just let you wander off alone?"

"Marc, we both know I can take care of myself. Trust me when I say I'm not defenseless."

"That's beside the point. I'll drive you wherever you need to go. It's the least I can do after you saved my life."

She began walking toward him, crossing her arms. "You gave me your blood in return. We're even."

"Christ, woman, why do you have to be so damn difficult?"

Despite her worrying over her failed powers, Ava pressed her lips together to keep from laughing. After several months of him getting under her skin, she was more than happy to return the favor. "*Merda*, you're one to talk. Seriously, you don't have to do anything. I'm better off on my own."

"Well, I want to. How about that. You don't have anywhere to go, and it isn't safe here. At least at my house you can rest until you figure out your next move. I have to work in the morning, so you can have some peace and quiet. You can even use my computer to plan everything. I'd feel better if you actually had a decent strategy instead of just wandering the streets."

Ava blinked in surprise, a denial on her lips, but she paused, thinking it over. On one hand, hadn't she decided that she didn't want to get any closer to him than she already was? But it hurt just thinking about never seeing him again. Plus, she'd have to move across the country just to shake off her tail.

On the other hand, he was right. It could help her in the long run to plan things out first before hopping on the next bus out of town. After a few days, she would have all of her affairs in order. It would definitely make things easier.

That way she could give herself more time to figure out why her powers weren't working on him. She'd feed again — from someone else, of course — and regain the rest of her strength. Though she had no idea what human in their right mind would like to keep the memory of nearly dying by demons, it was at least comforting to know he wouldn't forget her entirely.

She frowned, thinking about the forces hunting her down.

Then again, perhaps if he had no memory of her, he wouldn't be a target for anyone who came looking for her.

With a deep sigh, she looked up at him. "Okay. I'll do it your way."

His expression didn't change, but something in his eyes told her he was very pleased with her answer.

Gods, she thought as she followed him out of her apartment. She made sure to leave an envelope containing the month's rent on the counter top before walking out.

What am I getting myself into?

* * * *

Tuscany, Italy

Mikhail Nilsen was a very pissed-off vampire. He knew it and his Rogues knew it, by the agitated shuffling and fang-snapping they continued doing while watching him. The worthless imp curled into a ball in the corner of the room also knew it.

The coward was terrified, as well he should be. He'd allowed Mikhail's most prized possession to escape. It had taken years to find the bloody siren — and now she was gone. Granted, he'd already taken what he needed from her, but there could never be enough of her precious blood to satisfy him and his cause.

And given that he'd learned she'd been the top assassin at her guild, it would only be a matter of time before the bitch came after him, seeking revenge. Worse yet, he wouldn't even have anything to keep her in check, as he'd had the first time he'd captured her. While he was so powerful a vampire that very few were foolish enough to challenge him, he had a plan that he needed to execute perfectly. He didn't have the time or patience to be constantly looking over his shoulder on the off chance that the siren bitch would ruin everything.

It was time to act *now*. He'd finally caught up to Ava, and though it was a fucking pain in the ass that she was exactly where he *didn't* need her to be, he could still turn a shoddy situation to his benefit.

That was the only reason the damn imp was even still alive. Stripped naked of everything except for a tattered piece of loincloth covering his mangled junk, the fey was shivering under the freezing drop in temperature that came with Mikhail's rage. He was also covered in a myriad of bruises and fresh lashings from a recent flogging.

"Gather your bearings, you pathetic worm," he barked, his voice ringing off the walls of the cavern he'd taken residence in. "I still have use of you. Open a portal to Chicago and send the hounds. I want Ava alive. Cyrus' daughter has eluded me for far too long. It's time I get my revenge."

He called forth a couple of Rogues and gave them precise instructions to follow before he left the cavern.

He bared his fangs on a snarl as he stormed through the tunnels toward his own room. He'd worry about the missing siren in due time. Cyrus Gordano had been in power for far too long. That bastard would soon get what was coming to him. Revenge was so close that Mikhail could taste it on his tongue. But, first things first. He needed Ava, the precious and only daughter to the king of vampires. Anticipation sent a delicious shiver down his spine.

Soon.

Chapter Five

It was only around three p.m. when Lucian exited the diner where Ava had been seen working in the picture. As a Royal, though he was able to eat human food, he'd stopped caring for it centuries ago. Even the smell of fresh waffles and coffee only made his stomach turn in disgust.

It was just another sign of how aged he'd become. Though he looked to be in the prime of his life and held the same alluring beauty all vampires possessed, he certainly felt as old as dirt. Very little excited him these days, and he was in a foul mood more often than not. His brothers often taunted him about his sour personality.

Oh well. Even as a youngling he'd never been the open, friendly type. He'd always borne the heavy responsibilities that came with being a prince and had worked hard alongside his father to ensure their people would see a day where they could all live in peace. Not to mention that after living for damn near two thousand years, he was a realist and he'd seen more than enough of the world's grim ways.

While his mind wandered, he rubbed at his chest as he made his way to his sleek black Jag that was parked down the road.

Ava had indeed been working there for the last few months. The waitress named Edith was awfully fond of her, he could tell. At first, when he'd asked, the woman had been suspicious and reluctant to reveal any information to him. He admired her loyalty to his sister. Fealty wasn't nearly as common to others as it was among clan members. So often humans and demons turned on one another if it would benefit them. To see the woman had a genuinely pure heart and devotion to his sister was...refreshing.

Admirable as it was, he hadn't wasted a second before using his charm to get the information he needed from the woman before erasing her memory of him being there. It had been necessary. Someone outside of their family was looking to capture Ava. No doubt, if they got the woman to reveal he was there looking for her as well, they'd become alarmed and hasty. More often than not, that could result in someone getting killed.

And he preferred to deal with things with as little bloodshed as possible when it came to his family.

He was far from a pacifist, but after endless centuries of fighting and killing, he preferred a more diplomatic approach to things.

Most times.

On Friday morning, Ava had suddenly left the diner after cutting her hand on some glass, and they hadn't seen or heard from her since. She had been scheduled to work two shifts over the weekend but hadn't showed up to either one — or even made a call. The waitress had been over-the-moon worried, but he'd used his charm and told her Ava was safe and unharmed. She was just resting after being hurt.

He only wished that was the case. Truth was, no doubt Ava had seen the ghouls that were looking for her and had taken off. Luck was on his side for he'd gotten an address from the waitress before he'd left. He doubted she'd be at her residence by the time he got there, if it was even a legit address. But at least it could give him some clues to her current whereabouts.

After starting up his vehicle, he sent a text to his brothers to meet him where her apartment was located. He knew they were just as eager to find their lost sister as he was. Though they'd only known her for a little over a decade — so short a time for their kind — she'd become a vital member of their small family. Even after a hundred years of her being absent, it still wasn't the same without her.

He made his way through the winding streets of the city until some thirty minutes later, when he slowed to a stop across the street from the small apartment complex the waitress had told him about. He got out of his car and made his way to the entrance, where Cass, Sal and Andreas were waiting for him. The twins were in the city seeking information about the person or people looking for Ava, hopefully staying out of trouble in the process.

Those two were perfect recipes for disaster. They were formidable opponents during battle, but more often than not, the two idiots didn't know when to keep their mouths shut. There had been far too many occasions where they had pissed off the wrong person at the wrong time.

He nodded to his three brothers and, as one, they entered the building. It was nowhere near close to the luxurious lifestyle they'd lived all their lives, making Lucian frown. *Is my sister so impoverished?*

They cleared the third-floor landing. The worn carpet was clean, though there were old stains visible behind. The same went for the beige walls. There were only four apartments on each floor — two on each side of the hall. Ava's was at the very end on the left.

He procured a hidden dagger when he saw the door had been broken in, and he caught the unmistakable scent of dead ghoul. Worry settled in his gut, fear gripping his heart that the ghouls had caught her before he could.

He looked to his brothers. They nodded, and on the count of three, entered the apartment.

They ignored the mess and checked every inch of the small enclosure.

He made it to her room and, after deciding it was clear, he sheathed his weapon. He grimaced as he looked around, his worry turning to dismay.

"We're too late," he murmured to his brothers. One ghoul was dead, but it was clear Ava was long gone, most likely against her will. He looked at the fading blood on the walls. The thought that she'd gone down fighting lifted his sunken spirits just a tad.

At least his sister was able to defend herself.

Andreas stood in the middle of the room and everyone began to explore.

"It's been so long since we've last seen her that her scent isn't even the same," Andreas said, his dark brows furrowed. He squeezed his eyes shut. "There were three ghouls here a few days ago." With his eyes still closed, he pointed at the fading black spot on the floor. "She killed that one and the other two took her away."

Lucian slammed his fist into the nightstand, almost breaking it in half. "*Cazzo*," he growled. If they had known she was here just a bit sooner, they could have saved her.

"Let him finish, Luc," Sal said, his tone somber.

He huffed and turned away, looking for something to rip apart. What was the point? They could look at the room and tell exactly what had happened.

As Royals, they each had one special power that no other vampire had. Andreas' was the most useful in this situation, his hunting skills greater by far than even the most elite of demons. By scent alone, he could see the past of an area he was standing in. But even so, hadn't he just told them what had happened?

"A human came here after that," Andreas continued. His nostrils flared as he inhaled the stale scents in the air. "A police officer."

Lucian paused, recalling the waitress telling him about the two cops who frequented the diner. She'd asked them to check in on Ava after her sudden departure.

"He was here looking for Ava, but he was rendered unconscious by a ghoul who was hiding." He walked over to the bedroom door, following an invisible trail to the closet door. "I'm guessing they managed to escape, because Ava and the cop returned here last night."

Lucian spun around, his eyes widening a fraction. A sliver of hope made his heart give a sudden jump. He took a step closer to his brother, holding his breath for his next words.

"She walked over here for a bag of clothes. Then, she and the male stood in the living room for a while. They were discussing something." He opened his amber eyes, a small smile curving his lips. "She ended up leaving with him. It'll take a while, since their trail is faint, but I can track his scent to their location. If we don't find her, at least we can find him and get more information about what happened to her."

Lucian found himself grinning as he clapped his youngest brother on the back. "*Bene, fratello.* Well done." He turned to the rest of them, who also looked more hopeful with this bit of news. "Lead the way, Andreas."

* * * *

Ava scratched at her nose, sniffling. As far as she knew, vampires didn't get allergies, so someone must be talking about her again.

Sitting on the plush leather couch in Marc's spacious living room, which was decorated in various brown and beige tones, she placed his laptop on the glass coffee table in front of her and sighed deeply.

It had been two nights since they'd left her apartment. As expected, Marc had gone to work the next day as if all had been well. He'd given her a small tour of his house, which was located in a quiet suburban neighborhood near the edge of the city, before showing her to one of his spare rooms where she could stay. He'd then gone to his own bedroom and that had been the end of it. Through the wall, she had heard him showering and moving to lie down in bed, though it had taken several hours before his heartrate slowed, telling her he was asleep.

No conversation whatsoever.

In all honesty, she'd been hurt by his coldness, though she had no choice but to accept it. As long as she kept telling herself it was for the best, she could deal with it. It was a lie, but she was sticking with it.

He'd stopped by later that day, only to tell her he wouldn't be coming home that night because of the large amount of paperwork that he needed to do. She was free to make herself at home and fix whatever she wanted to eat from his fridge. In the meantime, she'd busied herself with his computer, looking for her next location to hole up in before she was found again.

Still, she couldn't shake the feeling that he was avoiding her.

The next day had come and gone, and now it was late in the evening. The sun had fallen hours ago, the streetlights the only sources of light outside.

Though she was glad for the distance between them, she felt a terrible amount of loneliness that had settled in her heart, and it wasn't showing signs of disappearing anytime soon. She'd spent the last hundred years running all across Europe and North America, never staying in the same place for more than a few months. And each time, she'd had to refrain from getting close to anyone.

Chicago was by far the longest she'd been settled in one spot, and she'd thought for once she could make it her home. She'd liked the city, so had taken a job where she could interact with humans every day.

Also, she'd known Chicago was the heart of a particularly strong vampire clan. She'd hoped that by hiding in the midst of the city, she'd go unnoticed. Even though vampires and demons weren't allowed to enter clan territories without permission from the clan chief—especially if they planned on staying for more than a few days—she'd managed to mingle with the humans long enough to keep her presence under wraps.

For a while it had worked. She'd hidden from both the clan members and the man searching for her. She'd felt she could finally relax.

Until those damned ghouls had found her. She had to come to terms with the fact that no matter how far she ran or how long she remained hiding, there was no avoiding the darkness following her every move. It would be so simple if she could just kill everyone who stood in her way, but that was impossible. She'd need a whole army to fight off Mikhail. She was only half Royal, after all, and he was an older vampire with a lot of power and authority. She was no match for him.

She thought about her father and brothers but dismissed them right away. She didn't know how to contact them, even if she wanted to. It had been almost a hundred years since she'd last seen any of them, and that had been halfway around the world in Italy. Even when she'd lived with them, it had only been for about twelve years—long enough for her to create memories, but only a mere blink in time to immortals. She doubted they even remembered her or cared about her being alive.

After all, she had just been a burden to them.

She scoffed as the hole in her chest opened even more. She missed them so much, but she couldn't go back. As she always said, it was for the best.

It was better for everyone if she kept to herself—disappeared from the world and hid very, very far away, somewhere deep underground. Hell, maybe it was time to just throw in the towel completely.

She wasn't meant for this world. All it had ever done was crap on her and take away the people she cared about most.

It was those kinds of feeble thoughts that would make Lucian scold her if he were here.

'Ava, giving up is only for the weak-minded. If ever you feel you cannot take another step, just remember how many steps you've taken so far. What's a few more going to hurt?'

She snorted. Yes, he'd say some wise froufrou crap like that. Though he'd been several centuries older than her, he had been her best friend. On her lowest days, he always had just the right words to say to keep her going.

With a deep sigh, she nodded to herself. *Okay, Luc. I'll take a few more steps. Just a few.*

Her stomach clenched painfully, reminding her that she needed to feed again. She couldn't keep going days and weeks without blood. It was only making her weaker. Even when she'd fed from Marc a few days before, it hadn't made up for her starving herself for a week prior. It was a bad habit she would have to break if she wanted to continue surviving.

She rose from the couch and stretched her arms high above her head. She'd made sure to delete the browsing history from Marc's computer. If he knew where she was going, it would take just a moment for a vampire to use their charm to get him to tell them where she was.

Then again, even as a Royal, her powers wouldn't work on him. It was entirely possible that other vampires with lower ranks would have the same issue—a thought that gave her comfort as much as it worried her.

She shook her head and made her way to the bedroom she'd slept in. It was October in Illinois, which meant the weather was growing cooler day by day. While she didn't get cold as much as humans did, she was still affected by the weather if she was exposed to the elements for long. She changed into some black leggings, a simple black zip-up jacket and dark tennis shoes.

Not the most fashionable attire, but it would help her blend into the shadows as she sought out her meal.

Ava was just about to place her hand on the brass doorknob of the front door when it swung open.

She blinked in surprise to see Marc standing there. His golden eyes were shining bright as they roamed her with hunger.

He stepped inside, and she stepped back. He raised an eyebrow at her. "Going somewhere?"

She gave a nod. It felt as though she was seeing him for the first time in years, though it had only been hours. And with the way he was looking at her, she couldn't help the heat that was pooling in the pit of her stomach.

Her fingers twitched. It took all the strength she had to keep from reaching to rip his uniform off.

"I need to feed," she said, doing her best to keep her tone even. *Gods, why do I always get like this around him?* Just one look at Marc and she turned into a puddle of fumbling clumsiness, much like a teenage girl with her first crush.

It was downright embarrassing.

His face immediately turned into one of irritation. "Oh, really," he drawled. "Do what you have to do then." He stepped around her and made his way to his own bedroom, where he slammed the door behind him.

Ava frowned, not understanding his sudden change of mood. Granted, he'd been cold to her since she'd tried to erase his memory in her apartment — hell, since they'd left the motel room — but this somehow seemed...different. He was pissed at her.

Her heart gave a painful thump. Was her reminding him of her vampire needs the issue? Could it be that he couldn't accept that she wasn't a human?

She took a step back as a familiar sadness engulfed her. Of course he didn't accept her. He was a human, and she was a demon. There wasn't a single drop of human blood in her veins. While some were able to accept her kind, not all could. And it seemed that Marc was one of the latter.

It was evident she'd been reading him wrong. By offering her a place to stay for a few days, he'd only been trying to help her, not because he cared. Just to repay a debt.

With a deep sigh, she chided herself for being so stupid.

Falling for a human was something she'd sworn she'd never do, under any circumstance. She could study them, interact with them and occasionally take their blood and satisfy her urges. But nothing more than that.

However, she'd just discovered that not falling for him was something far easier said than done.

Absently rubbing the ache in her chest, she closed the door behind her, breathing in the crisp night air. Whenever she returned tonight, she'd gather her things and leave when Marc fell asleep. No need to say goodbye. She'd just leave a small 'thank you' note and be on her way.

It was for the best.

This time, it was for her own good.

Chapter Six

By the time Marc had finished showering and eating, he'd still been in a foul mood. He'd sat around dressed in just a thick robe and briefs, waiting, watching TV, reading, browsing the web on his laptop. Anything to pass the time. Hell, he had to go to work at the crack of dawn. His ass needed to get some rest before it was time for him to get ready, but much to his dismay, he was far too distracted.

All because Ava had yet to make it back from feeding.

Sitting in the middle of his couch with his legs sprawled apart, he leaned his head back, looking up at the motionless ceiling fan. *It's been nearly four hours. Too damn long to drink blood.* Not that he really knew how long it took, but he could only imagine it didn't take four freaking hours.

His mind traveled back to when they were in the motel room — her fangs sliding into his neck...pressing his lips to hers...sinking deep into her dampness...

Good God Almighty. He'd never felt such pleasure.

With his allure and looks, he was used to women fawning over him. He'd dated women hot enough to be on the cover of *Playboy* magazine. With just a cock of his lips, they had been putty in his hands

And yet Ava was in an entirely different league.

When he'd first seen her, all he could imagine was how much she looked like Esmeralda from *The Hunchback of Notre-Dame*. She was beyond beautiful. With her exotic golden skin tone that spoke of Egyptian descent, thick midnight hair falling in waves halfway down her back and wide emerald eyes framed by the longest and thickest lashes he'd ever seen, she had been a mighty attraction from the very first day. Her features were sharp and carved to absolute perfection. There wasn't a single flaw, not even the faintest of childhood scars as everyone had. She'd had such an unearthly beauty that he had thought it was impossible to look that good without surgery and layers of makeup.

But it wasn't even just her looks that had drawn him.

Though she had always been aloof toward him, he'd admired the gentle, almost loving, way she treated her customers. She'd fix them with a warm smile as if they were family to her.

It was as if she were genuinely happy just to be talking with them.

Underneath her sunny disposition, however, he'd sensed a deep sadness that had called out to his own. She did really well hiding it, but something about her had revealed that she wasn't just a naïve, pretty face. He'd catch her scanning the crowd with sharp eyes. Her posture was always straight and poised, as if to be ready to bolt or fight at any moment.

He had been intrigued, even if he'd known there was something she was hiding. Actually, it was the fact that she was hiding something that made him itch to uncover all her secrets.

He just never in a million fucking years would have guessed it was because she was a damn demon on the run from other damn demons.

He blew out a breath of air. That still freaked the hell out of him. Knowing demons were real, seeing them for himself, even having sex with one? It was a lot to take in.

He knew he should have been terrified, but somehow, he wasn't. In fact, it was pretty damn fascinating—beyond his comprehension, but interesting. Maybe it was because he'd never been quite normal himself, so it was easier to accept her strange life. Then again, knowing there was an entire world of magic and supernatural creatures all around them, hiding in plain sight, sent a shiver of excitement down his spine. It was bizarre in the greatest way.

He then wondered if he was losing his sanity. No doubt he was, due to all that had happened in the past few days, but he couldn't find it in himself to care. Ava had opened his eyes to an entirely new world, and while he should want to flee far, far away from her, he only felt more drawn to her.

He wanted to know more—about her, about her life, about her world...everything. He wanted to know about it all.

He perked up like a puppy at the sound of the door opening, and he watched as Ava stepped silently inside. She was wearing skin-tight leggings that were molded to her long, shapely legs. He licked his lips, remembering those smooth limbs wrapped around his waist as he'd made love to her. His body was already hardening at the thought.

She fit him wonderfully. She was tall and slender, curved in all the right places, sweet and funny — and just...perfect. *God, she is absolutely perfect.*

And he wanted more.

He'd craved her the day they'd first met, and he still wanted her, fangs and all.

He looked at her flushed cheeks and remembered why she had even been gone for so long. Disappointment slid through him and he felt his foul mood returning. Just the thought of her sucking blood from anyone else was enough to drive him mad with jealousy. He didn't like picturing it, and he sure as hell didn't want her getting all hot and bothered with someone else as she had with him.

"Enjoy your meal?" he asked, his tone petulant.

Christ, am I a child or what? It wasn't any of his business who she took blood from — or fucked, whichever the case may be. She was a grown woman — over a hundred years old at that — and could do whatever the hell she wanted. He didn't give a rat's ass.

He didn't.

As he looked at her standing there with her eyes lowered sadly, he felt the bitterness quickly fading. *Okay, maybe I do care a little.*

Hell, he cared a lot, a damn lot. More than he should have.

Biting back a sigh, he rose to his feet, rubbing the back of his head. "Ava, I'm sorry for being a dick. I'm just... Honestly, just the thought of you and another man... It's frustrating, is all. I don't mean to take it out on you."

Her beautiful eyes widened and her full lips parted. His gaze was drawn to those lips and he imagined them kissing all over his body. He wondered how her tongue would feel on his —

"You're jealous?" she asked, bewildered.

He met her eyes again, blinking several times to clear his head of his perverted thoughts. When he recalled what he'd just said, his cheeks heated. *What the hell?* Men were not supposed to blush. "I, er... What I mean is... Um..."

Dammit! Men did not stumble over their words, either. *What the hell is wrong with me tonight?* He inhaled a deep breath before letting it out. *Get it together, man.*

"Yes," he replied. "When you said you needed to feed, I imagined you did — you know — to another male. And it makes me jealous."

Fucking loser, he yelled to himself. He felt like a damn teen all over again, just awkward and ridiculous.

He expected her to laugh at him. Or scoff. Or tell him how he was a big wimp. What he wasn't expecting, however, was to see those expressive green eyes widen and her sensual lips curling into a smile.

Alarmed, he shuffled his feet. "Damn, don't laugh at me. It was an honest confession."

She shook her head and wiped the moisture that had formed in her eyes.

Smiling and crying?

Jesus, what in the hell? Could he screw this up any more than he already had?

Ava sniffled. "I was planning on leaving tonight," she said at last.

Marc's blood ran cold at her words. He swallowed several times. "What?"

She looked up at him. "While you were asleep, I was going to leave a note and take off."

His body tensed and his annoyance rose. "Why would you sneak away like that?"

She sniffed again then sighed. "I thought maybe you hated me because of my being a demon — and that I tried to erase your memories. You were acting so…cold that I thought it would be better that way."

He reared back, looking at her as if she'd grown two heads. *Hate her?* Just the mere thought of her not being at his side was enough to make his knees buckle and his chest get tighter. It was as frightening as it was painful.

"Ava, I was angry at you for trying to get into my head, but I don't hate you one bit." *Quite the opposite.* He cupped her chin, making her eyes meet his. Her skin was smooth to the touch, like warm silk he wanted draped over his body. "And you being a demon doesn't bother me. I mean, it's still strange to accept that demons are actually real, but it doesn't make me see you any differently. You're still as beautiful as ever, and honestly…I've never wanted someone so bad in my life."

She gasped at that, and he nodded. It was the truth. Everything about her called to him in the most primal of ways.

Which was pretty damn ludicrous, given that they came from two different worlds.

Almost literally.

"It's not safe for me to be around you, Marc," she whispered. She reached up and placed a shaking, leather-gloved hand on his cheek. "If anything happens to you, I'll — " She bit off her words.

Marc just gave her a small, reassuring smile.

He leaned forward and wrapped his arms gently around her slender frame, pleased when she didn't back away. "Though I'm just a human, I'm not nearly as weak as you think, Ava. I've always been a bit on the strong side."

When she looked like she wanted to protest, he pressed his lips to hers. "Don't leave tonight," he whispered against her mouth, reveling in her sweetness. He kissed her again, and again, pausing between words. "Let me make love to you one more time before you go, so you'll always remember me."

She hesitated, but only for a moment, before she opened up to him, molding her body against his. "I'll never forget you."

There was a low grumbling noise between them, breaking the mood. He furrowed his forehead in confusion, taking note of the way her cheeks turned bright pink. "What the devil was that?" he inquired, bewildered.

She darted her eyes to the side, as if embarrassed. "I... I still need to feed."

He leaned back a bit, lifting his eyebrows. "You didn't get enough the four hours you were gone?"

Her blush only deepened. "Well, about that... I wasn't able to." She looked up at him shyly. "I couldn't think about drinking from anyone else but you."

He widened his eyes, but then he smiled, an inexplicable sense of gratification sliding through him. If that was one of those corny vampire pickup lines, it certainly worked. He'd been worried about her sucking on someone else's neck all night, when in actuality she'd been unable to do so.

Which could only mean he wasn't drowning alone in the unyielding feelings he had for her.

Good.

In one swift movement, he scooped her off her feet and cradled her in his arms. She let out a squeak of shock, wrapping her arms around his neck as he carried her to his bedroom.

He hadn't been lying when he'd said he'd always been strong. Growing up, he had been far faster and stronger than his peers. Throughout high school, he'd received many sports medals because of it. Lifting her slim, athletic body in his arms and carrying her across his house was nothing.

He kicked his bedroom door closed behind him and laid her on the soft sheets on his bed, as if she were a fragile artifact that could break with the slightest bit of force.

Which was utterly false, given that she'd held a man twice her size above the ground by his throat.

Marc shook the image out of his head and went to work undressing her, all the while planting gentle kisses across her face. He was already hard for her, but he wanted to take his time. The first time they'd made love had been fast, rough and over far too soon for his liking.

Tonight he wanted to savor having her sprawled out on his bed. He wanted to explore every inch of her, to burn her very image and scent into his brain. He wanted to be able to relive this moment over and over again, long after she left him behind.

Tonight was all about Ava.

With her fully naked, he paused and stared down at her in appreciation.

He let his gaze roam her. Her skin was polished to perfection, as if she spent a lot of time in the sun, and it looked smooth to the touch. She was tall and slim with soft curves that women would kill to have. He surveyed the swell of her breasts, two full mounds with lovely pink-tinted tips that were begging for his touch.

Just a minute, he silently promised them in his mind. He'd give them both all the attention they deserved the moment he finished drinking in the lush sight of her.

He admired her toned, flat belly, the bare skin between her legs displaying her wetness, her sleek, shapely legs, and even her small feet. He didn't even care for feet, yet hers looked enticing.

And with her stretched out on his black sheets with her thick black mane loose around her and her half-lidded gaze watching him with stark hunger, he was tempted to the fullest.

She was so damn beautiful. She was perfect.

Mine.

The thought was sudden and held a savage possessiveness behind it. It startled the hell out of him. But, at the same time, he couldn't ignore the fact that he indeed felt a powerful need to claim her as his own, whatever the hell that meant. Just being around her made him want to drop to his knees and worship her, tell her with his touch just how much he desired her.

His need for her was terrifying, but welcome. He'd never, ever felt so smitten by a woman.

With Ava...it was more than just sex. He hadn't been interested in other females since meeting her, which had landed him a few mocking taunts from his closest friend Duncan and some of the other coworkers he frequently hung out with. The deep-seated longing he had for her had taken a front-row seat in the center of his chest the first day he'd met her, and it refused to go away. And after finally having a small taste of the fiery desire inside her, he wasn't even sure he wanted it to.

When his eyes met hers again, the ravenous look was enough to rival his own. She clearly wanted him just as much as he wanted her.

That alone gave him a kick to fill the small space between them.

He covered her body with his, kissing her with stark yearning. Her lips parted, and his tongue met hers, swirling together in a wet dance, tasting and pleading. Her fangs were extended, and he subconsciously made sure not to pierce his tongue on the sharp tips in his desperation.

Hell, not that he minded a little pain. He wasn't into any of that hardcore shit that required whips and torture to get off, but he knew precisely what those razor-like fangs were capable of. They could either bring a man to his knees in pleasure or rip his throat out with excruciating pain.

He pulled away and trailed a path of hot kisses down her cheek to her throat, where he went to work nibbling and sucking her delicate skin.

He smiled against her, at the way she let out a soft moan whenever he found a particular sensitive spot. *So damn sexy.*

He traced a wet path with his tongue, down her collarbone and over the swell of one breast until he made it to its hardened peak. Making good on his secret promise, he gave the tight bud a gentle kiss before pulling it into his mouth. Ava arched her back on a groan.

Marc used one hand to massage the other breast before turning his attention to the neglected nipple. After several minutes of sucking until both tips were stiff and she was making soft keening sounds of need, he continued his path along her body, pausing here and there to lick and nibble and kiss.

He scooted down the bed and parted her thighs. He continued kissing all the way to her dainty little feet then back up the other leg until he got to the place where she was dripping wet for him.

He licked his lips in anticipation. She smelled so sweet.

He gave her pussy a loving lick, smiling when her body jerked in response.

Tastes sweet as well.

Settling more firmly between her legs, he began licking at her dampness, loving the way she gripped his hair, holding his head in place.

He lapped at every bit of her, sliding his tongue along her folds. Her loud moans only encouraged him as he flicked his tongue inside her. She clamped her thighs around his head and breathing became a struggle, but if he died like this, then damn it all, he'd die a very happy man.

He broke away for just a moment to suck gently on the bud of nerves hidden within her soft flesh. Her body gave a sudden jerk and he knew she was about to come. Still, he continued to lick and suck, slowly inserting one, then two fingers.

She cried out her release, all the while pulling at his hair. The small pain only fueled his own lust and he ground his hips into the mattress in a failed attempt to soothe his aching erection.

He licked every drop of her sweet juice before crawling back up the bed. He threw his robe onto the floor and yanked his briefs down, preparing to enter her. However, the wind was knocked from his lungs as Ava pushed him onto his back.

He looked up in astonishment to see her straddling him. Her green eyes were dark and filled with so much desire that his body twitched in response. "Your turn," she growled, her fangs flashing in the soft glow of the lamp on his nightstand.

He allowed his body to relax. Call him demented, but he was far from afraid. She was a demon, but she was still the sexiest, most beautiful woman he'd ever seen. And the way she was looking at him only further stirred the carnal need he had for her.

She began kissing a hot path down his chest. She flicked her tongue over his nipples, eliciting a low groan from him. She continued, pausing every so often to pierce him with her fangs and lap up the blood that welled, before licking the wounds closed.

Lord almighty. It was amazing, better than anything he'd ever felt in his life. Her fangs sliding through his skin and pulling his very essence from his body was the most erotic sensation he'd ever experienced. He wanted so much more that he felt he'd explode. But he refrained, letting her continue her trail of torment down his body.

How many nights had he stayed up fantasizing about this very moment? Now that it was happening, he wasn't about to screw it up by coming so fast.

His cock was standing at attention, drops of precum sliding from its tip. *Good grief.* It was embarrassing how much effort it took to control himself.

He'd always been a patient man, able to take his time and drag out foreplay for hours.

However, he was still learning that Ava was unlike any woman he'd ever encountered. She was a sensual, libidinous goddess who could set his body on fire with just a mere glance. The lightest of touches were enough to send him flying over the edge. Control was just a myth when it came to her.

She gripped the base of his shaft and stroked him. She brought her head down and when she wrapped those lush lips around him, licking the tip, he let out a strangled gasp. Her mouth was hot and wet, her tongue pressing flat against his length as she moved her head up and down his member. He threaded his fingers through the silky strands of her hair, holding her head in place as he pumped his hips with gentle movements.

Fuck, this is amazing. She *is amazing.*

A feeling that was all too familiar was coming over him, and with a gasp, he pulled her away. He refused to embarrass himself further by blowing his load before even entering her.

She looked confused for just a moment, but he rushed to say, "I need to be inside of you."

She grinned, showing off those pretty white teeth. She climbed on top of him, hovering her heat just an inch above his cock.

"Marc," she breathed, her eyes filled with passion.

A strange emotion overcame him, causing his heart to clench. Something primitive shifted inside him, and he again felt that possessive need to claim her.

Shaking it off, he gripped her hips, and in one swift motion arched into her wet core. She stiffened, crying out in pleasure. She pushed forward and Marc let out a loud groan.

Once she'd adjusted to his entrance, she began moving her hips in the most tantalizing way. *Fuuuuuck.* It was incredible. He'd spend the rest of his life buried inside her if he could. She was so tight and wet, fitting him like a glove. Nothing had ever felt so wonderful. The entire universe was in perfect alignment, it seemed.

Her pace quickened, and soon she was riding him as if her very life depended on it.

He was right there with her, pumping his hips into her. Her breasts jiggled with every bounce, and, still buried inside her, he sat up and pulled one puckered nipple into his mouth. She continued her movements, moaning as her pleasure obviously mounted higher and higher.

"Marc," she panted, her tone pleading. "I'm so close."

He groaned in response. He was too. It was miraculous he'd even restrained himself this long. Ava was a delicious temptation, and he feared he wouldn't be able to hold out much longer.

She let out a low noise, and when he looked up at her, her eyes were glittering, just like they had been back in the cell. Only this time, there was a raw, animalistic craving in them.

At this moment she looked the demon he knew her to be.

And though he should have been horrified, all he could feel was the near overwhelming desire to claim her somehow, to leave his mark for her to carry wherever she went.

He tilted his head to the side, baring his neck to her. With another low growl, she leaned forward and sank her fangs into him.

Like the last time he'd offered his vein, there was just a tiny prick of needles that was soon followed by a monumental wave of pleasure, shooting straight toward his dick. She let out a soft sigh as she drank his blood. He gripped her hips like a vise as he slammed into her over and over again, the sounds of their lovemaking the only thing to be heard throughout the room.

She yanked her mouth free, a drop of blood sliding down the corner of her lip, leaving a crimson trail.

He arched himself as deep into her as he could go and roared his release. She cried out as well, her tight center clenching him, milking him of every last drop.

After what seemed like an eternity, her body relaxed. She slid off him and landed on her side, breathing hard. He was in much the same condition as he fell back on the mound of pillows, his chest heaving.

Good...God.

That...

That was unlike anything he'd experienced. It was so passionate — and hot, and heavy. It had been magnificent.

Still breathing hard, he turned his head to look at her. She looked sated and pleased, making him grin. *Good.*

Because he damn sure was.

As he studied her features, he felt that odd tightening in his chest again. It was as if a hidden part of him had unlocked, bringing forth new feelings that both frightened and warmed him.

He didn't know what to make of it, but as he gazed down at Ava, he couldn't help but know the change was happening because of her.

And, in all honesty, he didn't dislike it at all.

Chapter Seven

Feeling an intense amount of satisfaction, Ava snuggled closer to Marc as he curled his muscled arm around her.

That. Was. Incredible. Absolutely the best sex she'd ever had in her life.

Well, not that she had much experience to go by, but he was definitely someone she'd never, ever forget.

The mere thought of leaving him behind stung her heart in the most painful way, but she pushed it aside. No matter how bad it hurt, leaving him was inevitable. But she was more than thankful to carry these memories with her. She was going to enjoy her time with him while she could.

Speaking of memories, she didn't know what to make of her not being able to see his. As a Royal, her power allowed her to see into someone's past if she touched their skin. It was how she'd known the names of those two bounty hunter ghouls. The man's open palm had struck her cheek, and brief as it had been, she'd already been expecting it. She'd unlocked her powers and seen just enough to get their names.

Her powers were another reason why she didn't take lovers. Even though she hadn't had the time while being on the run, it was also very unnerving to be able to see someone's every thought and memory while having sex.

Talk about disturbing, being in the throes of passion and all of a sudden seeing a lover thinking about his cousin Frieda touching him. Yuck.

Yet nothing had happened with Marc. They'd been connected in the most intimate of ways, yet his mind had still been blocked off from her.

It made her able to relax with him and enjoy the experience. And she had. Goodness, the man truly knew how to please a woman.

At the same time, it worried her. She knew her powers weren't failing, but how was it that Marc, a human, was able to block access into his mind? No human she'd ever come across had been able to do so. Even most demons were vulnerable to Royal powers, most of all telepathic ones like herself.

What was even more frustrating was the fact that he didn't even know he was able to do it. *So why...*

"Tell me about your childhood," she blurted.

Her sudden demand caused him to stiffen, and she could sense his reluctance. She could feel the muscles bunching as she stroked her hand over his chest. She hadn't meant to sound so intrusive, but she had to get to the bottom of this mystery or else she would stress over it long after she left.

She also had to admit she was interested in learning more about him. He'd intrigued her from the start, and as easygoing as he'd been, he'd never talked about himself. He was better at getting others to reveal their own pasts.

Instead of refusing, as she assumed he would, he relaxed with a deep sigh, and she felt his mood lighten. "I grew up in foster care," he stated at last.

She raised up onto her elbow and frowned at him. "Really?"

His warm gaze landed on her and he flashed his sexy dimples. "Yes. Since I was about four or five."

Ava's heart lurched. Though he was smiling, she sensed a deep sadness within him. "So you never knew your real parents?" she asked.

He shook his head, looking back up at the ceiling. "Not at first, no. Well, I was really young when I was taken from my mother, so I don't really remember much of her."

He paused, grimacing with a bad memory before he shook his head. No doubt what little he did remember wasn't pleasant.

"I grew up in many different foster homes. I wasn't the most well-behaved child, I admit. I was always so angry. Not a single one of my foster parents had an ounce of parental instinct. They were only interested in the money. So I always thought, if no one cared about me, why should I give a damn about them?" He gave a humorless laugh and shook his head. "I've been beaten, gotten into fights and run away more times than I can count. I hated life and I hated my parents for abandoning their own flesh and blood. I ended up doing some pretty stupid shit. Got hooked on some hard drugs, overdosed twice, broke a lot of laws — stupid shit."

"I can imagine a lot of kids would be troubled under the circumstances," she murmured.

His mood had darkened again, and Ava ran her fingers across his smooth chest in what she hoped was a comforting way.

"When I turned fifteen, I was placed in the care of this older couple who were really good people. I was so horrible to them, but they didn't give up on me. They encouraged me to look at the world in a different way. It took a while, but their gentle patience and loving arms eventually got through to me. I got clean, started going to the local high school, even joined several clubs and sports. I wanted to become a someone they could be proud of."

He gave her a genuine smile this time. "On weekends we would all go to volunteer around the community, helping other troubled kids like me. It gave me a sense of purpose, and I knew it was something I wanted to do with my life. So, when I graduated, I busted my ass to join the police academy. Fourteen years later, here I am. It's difficult, and more often than not I come home bone-weary and exhausted. But every now and then I get to save someone's life or help them get off the streets. It's rewarding."

Ava continued stroking his chest. "You are a natural protector. That's what I've always thought of you. It's amazing how you've dedicated your life to helping others."

He beamed down at her, placing a kiss to her forehead. "Thanks, love. Still, I want to do more. One day I want to open my home to kids who are lost on the streets — give them a safe place to grow up, teach them values. Not everyone is fortunate enough to have loving parents like my two foster parents, but I hope to one day help as many kids as I possibly can."

If it hadn't already happened, Ava's heart melted for him. For someone so big and powerful, he had such a pure soul. She loved that about him. "I'd love to do that too," she whispered. At his shocked look, she rushed on to say, "And what of your foster parents? Are they still...?"

His gave a small shake of his head. "Unfortunately, no. As I mentioned, they were an older couple. They died one after the other shortly after I left the academy. I was sad, of course, but they went happily. It was their goal to make a difference in someone's life, and I can assure you they did. I wouldn't even be here today if not for them. One day, I want someone to be able to say that about me."

Ava laid her head on his chest, his heartbeat drumming in her ear. It was a soothing rhythm. "You said you didn't really know your birth parents at first. I'm assuming you learned of your heritage?"

He paused for several moments, and Ava worried he wouldn't answer. After all, it was a deeply personal question. It didn't take an empath to know that.

Then he sighed again. When he spoke, he tried to keep his tone steady, but she could hear a small amount of bitterness in it. "After I joined the force, I spent years tracking them down. My mother turned out to be living on the streets, strung out on drugs. It took her several minutes to recall she'd ever had a child, but when she did remember, she went on a rant about me being a monster. She gave me away when I was little because she didn't want to raise me. When I asked about my father, even she didn't know who he was. She was... Well, let's just say she'd had many, many partners in her day. And the number of drugs she'd consumed over the years had damaged her brain, so she wouldn't have been able to remember, even if she'd wanted to. Still, I did my best to help her get sober and off the streets, but it ended up being futile. She OD'd just a few years ago."

Ava swallowed the lump in her throat. He was like her in a way, all alone in the world.

At least she'd had loving parents.

"I'm sorry," she whispered.

He turned to look at her, his hardened face relaxing. "Don't be," he said with a smile. Those deep dimples flashed, never failing to make her heart lurch. "It's life. In the end, I'm happy with mine. I got to experience what it meant to be loved by parents, and I get to help people every day. Even though sometimes I don't succeed in assisting someone, I was told that as long as I gave it my all, in the end only those who want help can change."

It's a nice notion, Ava thought with remorse. In truth, she wanted help in her situation. She wanted it so bad, but she didn't know how to go about receiving it. Mikhail Nilsen wasn't just any ordinary demon. He was a powerful man and slandering his good name would only bring war and shame to her family.

Though she killed when she needed to, she didn't want anyone dying over her. If there must be bloodshed, she didn't want it on her hands if it could be avoided.

Marc tightened his arms around her and placed a lingering kiss to her forehead. "You have that look again," he murmured.

She frowned. "What look?"

"The one where you're thinking really hard about something but don't want to share."

"How do you know that's what that look means?"

"I just told you I've been a cop for fourteen years, love. I know body language. Besides,"

—he grinned sheepishly—"despite the fact that we've never held a one-on-one conversation, I've come to recognize your various expressions." He paused, shaking his head. "Sorry. That must make me sound like a creep."

Ava forced an easy smile. If that made him creepy, then the same could be said about her. She'd spent a lot of time watching him, too. "Not at all. I'm only thinking you and I aren't that much different."

His eyes flared with interest. "Tell me about *your* childhood."

Her heart froze for several seconds. Her life was very, very private. Even with the few friends she'd made over the years, she'd never told them secrets. It was a sensitive subject for her.

"It's okay," Marc said with a small smile. The man was always smiling. She was beginning to think he'd forced it so many times in his life that it had become a natural part of his face. Either that or he just loved showing off those deep dimples. No doubt sensing her distress, he said, "You don't have to tell me if you don't want to. I know how hard it can be to open up to someone after bottling everything inside for so long." He paused long enough to place another kiss at her temple, sending a jolt of heat through her. "But I want you to know you can trust me with anything."

Trust.

A dangerous word that should have no place in her heart, but somehow it managed to wriggle its way past her defenses. Everything about Marc was a strong, solid force—a sturdy wall for her to lean on when it'd been so long since she'd last rested.

That's right. Marc would understand if no one else would.

Well, not completely, but he'd try to. That was the type of man he was—arrogant and stubborn, yet a constant beacon of comfort. She could trust him.

After all, he'd opened up to her, and she'd known full well it had taken a great deal of effort.

"I was born in Europe in 1897—" She paused when he started to choke, clearly startled over her revelation.

"Sorry, sorry," he said hastily, at her glare. "It caught me off guard. I felt like I was watching *Interview with a Vampire* or something." He waved that away when her eyes narrowed even more. "Sorry, love. Continue."

She huffed. "As I was saying, I was born in 1897 in Europe. My mother was fey."

"Fey, as in fairies?" he asked softly, kissing the curve of her ear.

Ava shuddered in delight. "Fairies, imps, sprites, nymphs, elves...the types of magical creatures you hear about in fantasy tales."

"Hmm," he murmured. "So all this time I had a right to be scared of those creepy gnomes in my foster mother's garden?"

Ava's lips twitched. "Actually, gnomes aren't real. Your fear was rather trivial."

He let out a small curse, continuing his nuzzling. "Disregard that question then. So your mother was one of these fey? Does that mean you can grant me any wish I want?"

Ava chuckled. "No. I'm half fey, but my father's vampire blood is dominant. I can't wield any kind of magic but I can sense it. Sounds boring, I know, but magic is essentially invisible to all but a handful of vampires."

"Hmm," he murmured into the curve of her jaw. "Were your parents married?"

She unconsciously flinched at the question, but he tightened his arms around her, comforting her. "No. They didn't even know each other." When he froze and fixed her with a lift of his eyebrows, she explained, "From what my mother told me, she had just recently lost her best friend, so she was sad and lonely. One night she met my father, and she could sense his own pain and sadness. It called out to her, so she sought him out. They spent a long night...erm, *comforting* each other, then went their separate ways."

Basically, they'd had a one-night stand. She didn't have to say the words, because they both knew the hidden meaning. Marc only hummed an "I see," and continued nuzzling and kissing her.

Ava tilted her head to the side, giving him better access to her neck. His lips felt so good on her skin. Already she could feel her desire rising once again — a common occurrence when it came to him. "She was a wood sprite. Her particular tribe was fairly old-fashioned, and they were very strict on keeping their bloodline pure. It's because of that that their blood and powers are considered a treat among the demon world. So when my mother became pregnant by my vampire father, she was exiled, as you can imagine."

Marc let out a low whistle. "Sounds a bit harsh. Her people seem really uptight." He paused. "No offense to you."

She shook her head. "None taken. I agree that they are conservative. They keep to themselves and refuse outsiders, so I've never met them." The was a trace of bitterness in her tone, but she bit back the harsh words she really wanted to say.

"My mother was very loving and protective of me, and because of my mixed blood, we were always on the run. Given that my mother's pure blood was desired by many demons and I was the daughter of a Royal, it did not take long for word to get out that we had no protection. The main ones seeking my mother out were members of a rival sprite tribe." Ava's mood darkened in remembrance. Marc tightened his arms. "When I was thirteen, we were hiding in a human inn somewhere in Italy. We awoke in the middle of the night because a fire had broken out. We were on the third floor, and there was only a small window."

She swallowed several times, closing her eyes tightly. *Gods, it still seems just like yesterday.* She could practically feel the smoke burning her nose. She slowly inhaled, held it then let it go.

That had been a long time ago. She was far away now, safely tucked under Marc's strong arms.

"Long story short," she continued sadly, "my mother used her powers to help us escape. However, we realized too late that it was a trap. There were tribe hunters waiting on us, and they were the ones who had set the fire to lure us out. My mother was already weak from using her powers, but she fought them off. She told me to run away and she would follow. I hesitated, but I was so scared that I took off. I believed her when she said she would be behind me. So when I made it far away, I took shelter in an old barn and waited for her to join me. I waited for three d-days."

Ava's voice cracked on the last word, and hot tears leaked from her eyes. She hadn't thought about that night in decades. It was always easier to push it to the very back of her mind and pretend it hadn't happened.

But right here, right now, she felt as if she'd opened an old wound, one that had never healed properly. She covered her face with her hands and curled into herself, sobbing. She was faintly aware of Marc sitting up, pulling her onto his lap and holding her as if she were a small child.

Yeesh, how embarrassing. She had prided herself on her years of being strong and not allowing her emotions to get the best of her.

Right now, however, the tears kept coming, with no likelihood of slowing anytime soon.

She cried for her mother's loss. She cried for Marc's loss. She cried at having to leave her brothers and father behind.

She cried for the people who'd been unfortunate enough to cross her path and had been caught in the fray.

She cried for everyone whose memories she'd come across who were hurting over the loss of someone precious to them.

She cried for her ninety-six years of pure loneliness, always having to look over her shoulder, and gods knew what else. Like all vampires, she had superior physical strength. However, there was a vulnerable gray area in her soul that was ever-present. No amount of forcing it away could change the fact that deep inside she was as sensitive as they come — oftentimes more so than others.

It was all just a part of her 'gift', she supposed. Her empathic powers not only allowed her to see memories, but she could feel others' pain. Even if someone was standing at the opposite end of a football field, she could always sense if they were feeling a strong emotion.

After what felt like hours but had only been minutes, her crying slowed to a stop. Marc handed her the box of tissues that had been sitting on his nightstand, and she put them to use. All the while he held her, rocking back and forth and rubbing a comforting hand across her back.

She felt a small flare of envy. He would make a great husband to someone one day. He was sexy as hell, a good listener, an amazing comforter, a magnificent lover and a police officer who loved kids. What better package could a woman ask for?

After a few more minutes of getting herself together, she peeked up at him. He was watching her with tender eyes. Her sorrow was still palpable, but somehow, being in Marc's arms provided her with a consolation she hadn't known she'd needed. It was as if his gentle caresses were enough to soothe the decades worth of pain.

"I'm sorry about that," she murmured.

He flashed those dimples in a soft smile. "Don't be, love. It's good to let those feelings out every now and then. Don't you feel a bit lighter?"

To her surprise, she did. It was as if a tremendous weight had been lifted from her shoulders. Though she still had a lot more of it to get rid of, she did feel as though she could breathe again.

Just a little.

"Yes, I do. Thank you," she said, snuggling into him. "I really needed it."

He kissed the top of her head, stroking her arms and back. "My pleasure. I feel you still have more to say, though. What happened after those three days?"

Ava nodded, marveling at how easy he was to talk to. He was so attentive.

"After three days, it hit me that she wasn't coming. I felt so guilty for leaving her behind — like, I should have helped her."

He planted soft kisses along her cheeks. To her relief, each touch of his soft lips sent heat flooding to her most intimate of places. She wanted that distraction.

"You were only a child, Ava. There was nothing you could have done. You would have suffered the same fate she did, and it's clear she didn't want that."

Yeah, she knew that. *How many years have I spent telling myself that?*

A damn lot.

She continued. "At that point, it had been a while since I'd last fed. Up until then, my mother had helped me find blood donors. But without her, I didn't know what to do. I starved myself until I couldn't take it anymore. When a vampire goes so long without feeding, their instincts take over and they lose control of their mind. It's what creates most Rogues. I was on the brink of becoming one and I nearly killed a human in the process. It was only thanks to a hunter that I was stopped. Normally hunters are to kill all Rogues without a second thought, but seeing that I was only a child and hadn't yet gone fully over the edge, he allowed me to feed from him to gain control of my sanity. When I did, I realized I was able to trust him. I told him all that had happened. Something about my story must have sounded familiar to him, because I later found out that the hunter knew my mother and who my father was. I was brought to his home and it was there that I learned I had another family on my father's side."

"You didn't know anything of your father prior to that?" he asked, bewildered.

She shook her head. "Just that he'd been a hook-up she had fond memories of."

Ava's nose crinkled at the thought, remembering that terribly awkward moment she'd accidentally brushed against her mother's bare skin and had seen her memories of her and Cyrus' night of passionate lovemaking. Ava hadn't really known what sex was at that point, but she remembered wanting to throw up after that scene. She gave a small smile, even as she shook her head. "When I met them, I learned I had six brothers. They were all much older than me, but they accepted me and treated me as though I really belonged. For the first time in my life I felt...safe. I had a family who cared about me. It was a nice few years."

Marc had a frown in his voice. "A few years? You didn't stay?"

She shook her head, lowering her eyes. "I left when I was twenty-five. Some things...happened, and I realized I couldn't stay any longer. So I ran away."

Behind her, Marc stiffened. "What happened? Did someone...?"

She didn't know exactly where his train of thought was leading, but she had a guess. Being a young girl in a house full of men, no doubt it would cause concern. She rushed to shake her head in denial. "No. Gods, no. I..." she sighed deeply. *How can I tell him the full truth? He'll only push me away.* "My father was a very powerful vampire. He had many servants under him, and there were a few who...well, they didn't approve of my being there. One of them said I was just a burden to my father and brothers. My being a half-breed was tarnishing their name, since they were all purebloods. So as to not cause them any more disturbance, I left. Of course, it led to me living a life on the run from bounty hunters, but I've become used to it."

He pulled back and she turned to look at him. His face was filled with disbelief.

"What?" she asked uneasily.

"Ava, you've got to be kidding me," he said, his tone matching his look. "You ran away and left the protection of your father and brothers, who seemed to adore you, all because of something someone else said? You deliberately put yourself in danger and exposed yourself to the world over some lowlife bastard's petty words?"

Ava swallowed. She didn't dare tell him her father was the king of *all* vampires, and so having a half-blood daughter was a mockery to him.

Or that the lowlife bastard in question was a man whom her father trusted with his very life.

Or that the man was the one behind her being hunted in the first place.

Marc gave a slight shake of his head. "Okay, so you've been on the run for...roughly ninety-six years. Why haven't you joined one of these vampire clans for protection?"

"It's...complicated."

"Complicated," he repeated with a scoff. Then he demanded, "Ava, where is your family now? I don't want you running away anymore. You need their help to—"

She was already shaking her head. "No, Marc. Even if I wanted to reach out to them, I don't know how. Besides, that was nearly a century ago, and they're most likely still in Italy."

He let out another scoff, his expression both angry and bewildered. Then, he paused, pulling away from her. "Wait a minute. Six brothers?"

Ava nodded. "Yep."

"All...vampires?"

She lifted a brow. "Yes, all vampires."

He pulled away another few inches, his eyes widening. Her lips twisted at his look, unable to determine what he was thinking. "What?" she demanded.

"You told me there are only eight Royals left in the world, including you," he said suspiciously. "So, that makes you like a princess or something?"

Ding, ding, ding! We have a winner, she thought wryly.

Well, so much for keeping it a secret. She hadn't thought he'd piece that tidbit of information together. *He's far too perceptive for his own good, damn it all.*

A sudden prickling slid down Ava's spine. She tilted her head back and inhaled the air, opening her senses to detect the source of her unease. She stiffened. The distant howling in the night could very well be from the neighborhood dogs or even distant werewolves on the hunt during the full moon. However, her hairs suddenly standing on end told her otherwise.

Dogs didn't sound that feral, and werewolves were forbidden from hunting near the city.

Which only left one thing.

Gods, why now? "Shit," she growled.

Marc became alarmed, reaching into his nightstand drawer for his gun. "What is it?"

She rushed to her feet and quickly began pulling on her clothes, urging him to do the same.

"Hellhounds. We need to leave. *Now.*"

Chapter Eight

With a pair of faded jeans and a hoodie thrown on in his haste, Marc hopped into the driver side of his car and turned the engine on, peeling out of the driveway the moment Ava closed the passenger door.

He didn't know what the hell was going on, but she sensed something he didn't.

Hellhounds. What the hell are those?

Hounds from hell, obviously, he thought with a wry snort. He hoped they weren't disgusting and grotesque like Ava had described ghouls to be. He didn't even like regular dogs, let alone demonic canines. Sure, some dogs were cute, but he was allergic to them.

He shook his head. Whatever they were, they had Ava scrambling from his arms and rushing to leave the house. That had been his first clue something wasn't right.

Well, that wasn't true. He'd felt the hairs on the back of his neck stand up a moment before she'd hopped out of bed. It was a stark warning that something dangerous was close. It was a sense he'd had from a young age and that had saved him countless times in the field.

Never easing his foot off the gas, he sped through the city, praying none of his fellow policemen would pull him over. He wouldn't stop, even if he wanted to. Whatever Ava had sensed had to be something big. He feared if he slowed down or paused, they would be caught, and he was damn sure not in a rush to be chained in a damp cell again.

Over an hour later, he was speeding through the outskirts of town. The houses stretched farther and farther apart until the streetlights disappeared and Chicago was growing smaller and smaller in the background.

He glanced over at Ava, who was turned around looking out the back window.

"Is it still following us?" he demanded.

Her face was so intense that she seemed t have changed from the soft, innocent woman with a delicate heart to a hardened warrior. Her vampire mode was pretty scary, but he couldn't deny it was also still damn sexy.

Yep, I'm definitely losing my mind.

"They," she corrected, "and yes. Can't you go any faster?"

Go faster? Hell, his foot was damn near touching the floor beneath the gas pedal. He was already going well over a hundred. There were no vehicles behind them that he could see, so just what the hell kind of speed did demons have?

He looked in his rearview mirror again, but all he could see was the reflection of his own red taillights on the pavement behind him. "I don't see —"

Before he could utter a statement, the car slammed into something with enough force to send them swerving across the ground and tumbling down the side of a small hill. Only the restraint of their seatbelts held them back from bursting through the windshield as the car spun over and over. In a blink, both airbags deployed, one smashing into Marc with a stunning impact that forced his head into the driver's-side window. The car was still spinning, hurtling downhill until the passenger side crashed into a tree, bringing them to a halt.

Minutes later, Marc's ears were still ringing, and it took several moments for his vision to clear. He shook his head, feeling a warm liquid slide down his temple. He touched the spot, pulling his fingers back to see blood.

"Damn it," he grumbled, undoing his seatbelt. It hurt like hell to move, but he had to get out of the car. "Ava, are you okay?"

When she didn't answer him, he opened his eyes and looked over at her. Crippling fear sliced through him at the sight of her, unconscious and bleeding over her face and neck. The car had impacted the tree on her side, one of its low-hanging branches having broken through her window. Even in the dark, he could see her blood dripping from the wood.

He reached out a shaking hand to her, checking her pulse. It remained strong, but she was still as a statue. "Ava, love, wake up," he said, a hint of urgency in his voice. "Come on, baby. We've got to get out of here."

She still didn't budge—not even a twitch of muscle. *Fuck, that isn't a good sign.*

He unbuckled her seatbelt and had just pulled her out of the car through the driver's side and laid her on the ground when every last one of his hairs rose. He whirled around, standing over her protectively, and he drew his personal gun. There were no lights nearby, but his eyes had adjusted to the night.

A man and a woman were approaching them, along with five large dogs.

Well, at first glance he'd thought they were dogs. As they neared, Marc realized they weren't—not conventional ones, anyway.

These mutts were far larger, far uglier and if his gut was correct, far deadlier than the average poodle.

They were larger than an adult Great Dane with glowing red eyes, pitch black skin instead of fur and very, very long teeth, dripping saliva.

The two people weren't any less dangerous. They had the same mysterious air around them that Ava had, though theirs was far more sinister. Even their eyes were glowing, flickering in the dark like hers did.

But what unnerved him the most was the sheer rabid madness haunting their stares.

These two... They were vampires.

And Rogues at that. They had to be. He didn't know how he knew, but he was certain.

"A human," one growled, his voice hardly comprehensible, like a zombie trying to talk.

"Food," the other rasped.

"Master wants the girl but not the human," the man husked. His gaze landed on Marc and he grinned, flashing two sharp fangs. "What a feast we have."

He swallowed. He wasn't afraid of them, not anymore. He'd accepted that demons existed. He'd even fought two of them.

However, with Ava unconscious, he feared he wouldn't be enough. Oh, he would protect her with his very last breath. Somehow, though, he felt with one human against two Rogue vampires and five demon dogs — or whatever — the odds weren't in his favor.

Ava uttered a soft noise, and he stiffened when one of the dogs gave an ear-splitting growl before charging forward. He let out a line of bullets into the ugly mutt. It whimpered and faltered, but only for a moment.

"Shit," he growled, tossing his emptied gun to the side. Even if he had time to grab more clips, he had a sinking suspicion regular bullets wouldn't work on these demons. From what Ava had said, silver was the main thing that could be effective against vampires. He wondered if the same could be said for all demons.

If that were true, he didn't know who the hell made silver bullets, but he damn sure didn't have any on him.

He took a wider stance over her, more protective as the mutt drew closer. Ava made another soft noise as she battled consciousness, and he felt a fierce power flow through him.

Mine.

That possessive thought rolled through his mind again, bringing forth a searing heat throughout his body. A low noise rumbled from deep within his chest. His need to protect her was the only thing he focused on.

White-hot fury welled within him. The thought of anyone trying to harm one precious strand on her pretty little head pissed him off to uncharted levels.

He wouldn't let these demons lay one damn finger, claw or paw on her.

The mutt made a large leap at him, and he struck out with his fist, slugging the thing right in the snout. There was a sickening crush of bone followed by loud whining, but he ignored it. He wrapped his huge arm around the creature's neck, and with a strong jerk, crushed the demon's windpipe.

It dropped to the ground with a thud, and Marc kicked the immobile creature away from him. He hadn't known if it would actually kill the thing, but he was glad it was at least down. There was no time to feel remorse when he knew good and well the demon mutt would have killed him first.

His actions only seemed to infuriate the remaining hounds and, as one, they charged. He experienced another powerful surge of strength and kicked out at the closest demon, sending it sliding across the ground. The remaining three pounced. He caught one by the throat and slammed it to the ground. One of them bit into his shoulder, causing him to shout aloud, while he used both hands on the mutt below him to snap its neck.

Another one bit into his leg, and the one that he'd kicked came running back.

It seemed like a downhill battle—*literally*—but he wasn't about to give in to these freaks, not when he had something so precious to protect.

There was another dark growl, only this one was far more familiar. A smirk slowly curled his lips. One of the mutts was pulled off him. The other, Ava then pinned to the ground. It kicked out at her, but all she did was use her glinting silver blade to slice its throat open. It would have been a sickening sight to Marc a few days ago, but now, all he could think about was his fierce need to protect her.

No matter how gruesome the kill, he'd stick to it.

The last two hellhounds got to their feet and began to charge. At the same time, he saw the two Rogue vampires dash forward with near-blinding speed, their fangs bared.

Before they could reach him, however, Ava jumped in front of him, fending them off while he dealt with the last two hellhounds.

Now that she was awake and fighting alongside him, it seemed a much easier task.

The scent of blood filled his nostrils, belonging to more than one person. However, it was Ava's whose stood out the most. He instinctually knew it was hers, because it was burned into his senses. The sweet scent fed his rage at the demons attacking them.

One dog leaped at him, and he ducked low, dodging the creature. The other rammed into him, knocking him to the ground.

The beast's massive paws were on his chest, pinning him in place. Breathing became a pain, and he feared that with any more pressure, his entire chest cavity would cave in.

He felt the ground around him for something, anything, to use. *Give me something,* he growled to himself.

As if a silent force was answering his prayer, he found a long, jagged piece of glass that had broken from his car. He gripped it in his hand, not at all caring about the way the sharp edges bit into his palm and fingers.

In a swift movement, he stabbed the glass into the leg of the beast on top of him.

It yipped and scrambled away, giving Marc just enough time to rise to his feet. The other mutt came at him. He clasped his hands together and swung his arms up at the creature, as if he were swinging a baseball bat.

The blow hit the animal dead in its jaw, hard enough to crack bone. It fell to the ground and Marc brought his foot down on its throat, killing it.

One left to go. The creature snarled at him, limping on its injured paw. Marc bared his teeth and spread his arms wide, daring the creature to make a move. "Bring it on, Cujo," he said darkly.

To his astonishment, it didn't. It lifted its snout to the sky as if scenting it. With a frightened yip, it turned around and dashed away.

Huh. That was...odd.

But no odder than the fact that demons were real, and twice now he'd been attacked by them in less than a week.

He turned to Ava to see her several yards away fighting with the two vampires.

He'd taken all of three steps toward her but stopped dead in his tracks. Two loud shots rang out in the cool night air, making him freeze. The Rogues suddenly dropped like flies to the ground, their bodies swiftly fading to ashes. Ava held her blade up defensively, her fangs bared. He scanned the darkness, stiffening when an icy blast of air prickled over his skin.

Somehow, he knew for a fact that it had nothing to do with the weather.

There was another vampire nearby.

Ava was prepared for another attack.

After awakening to find herself on the ground and Marc fighting off a pack of hellhounds, she'd felt all the blood in her body go cold.

He was defending her, which both excited and terrified her. He was only a human. He couldn't possibly take on five hellhounds and two vampires alone with no weapons.

Certainly not Rogues.

All vampires were dangerous creatures. In the demon world, it was widely known that they sat at the top of the food chain. Though vampires were separated by levels of hierarchy, only a fool would underestimate a single one.

Rogues, however, were in a slightly different league. They possessed all the strength and speed their brethren shared, but they were crazed. In their eyes, everything was either an enemy or food, and only death could stop them from attacking. So there was no way Marc could stand a chance against two. He was strong, cunning and a skilled officer, but compared to demons, he was far too weak.

That was what she'd thought, anyway. While she'd killed one hellhound and defended him against the two Rogues, she'd been astonished to see him holding his own. He'd moved with incredible speed and strength.

It was almost as if he wasn't even a human.

Which was...impossible.

Isn't it?

Just when she was about to finish off the Rogues, two gunshots broke through the silent night, torturing her sensitive ears.

The two Rogues dropped to the ground, their heads bleeding from the gunshot wounds. In a matter of seconds, they were reduced to a pile of ashes. "What the—?"

The air around her suddenly dropped to freezing temperatures, and the scent of more vampires filled her nose. *Damn the gods, can I get a freaking break?*

She brought her dagger up, prepared to fight off the newcomers.

She only hoped Marc'd had the sense to run for safety. Somehow, though, she just knew he wouldn't. He was awfully stubborn. He'd demand to stay by her side, perhaps even try to push her behind him, as if it would do any good.

From the shadows, a tall vampire made his presence known. He was taller than Marc and just as built, with tan skin covered in faded jeans, heavy biker boots and a black leather jacket. His narrowed eyes were a pale silver with the same glittering all vampires had in the dark. His hair was pitch black, like her own, and pulled into a short tail at his nape. His face was as cold as the air around him, his lips pressed into a flat line, as if he was bored.

However, she sensed a great power beneath that impassive stature—a power that took centuries to accumulate.

When her narrowed eyes met his, his scowl disappeared and a small smile formed, easing his cold expression into one of relief. Had she been anyone else, she would have felt uneasy with the towering physique and the cold power swirling in his eyes.

But she wasn't anyone else. She was someone who instantly recognized the man others would be wise to fear.

With a small laugh, she dashed forward, wrapping her arms around his neck. He hugged her back, lifting her off the ground and spinning her as if she were still a child.

When he set her on her feet, he pulled back but didn't let her go, as if he were afraid she'd take off the moment he did.

"Lucian," she breathed, "I can't believe it's really you."

He pulled her in for another long hug, squeezing the air from her lungs. "Neither could I believe it's you, *piccolina.*" He pulled back again, smoothing her wild hair back. There were years of pain in his eyes. "I'm so...relieved."

A primal growl filled the air, and in the blink of an eye her brother was pushed away from her, stumbling backward. Marc was standing in front of her, a strange heat radiating from his body. He was standing tall and rigid, clenching his hands. She only then realized that the animalistic sound had come from him.

It was pretty...odd.

Odd, but sexy, she thought, hiding her smile. She couldn't explain it, but something about having this man defending her sent a tingling desire that was all feminine through her body.

Just as fast as he'd been pushed aside, Lucian was in Marc's face, his icy glare set. Marc didn't back down, just bared his teeth.

Ava didn't understand what was going on, or if what she was seeing was real. Tiny black dots were beginning to dance before her eyes. Whatever it was, it appeared to be some show of testosterone, and she wasn't sure what to do.

"Back off," Marc growled, his fists clenching at his sides. "She's *mine.*"

Ava and Lucian's eyes widened at his words. *Mine?* Such a small simple word, but the way he said it was...predatory. Even his eyes looked to be glowing a bit. *Or am I just seeing things?* The world around her was starting to spin.

Just what the hell is going on with Marc?

Lucian scowled darkly, and he had Marc by the front of his hoodie. "Listen here, bastard. My sister isn't some property for you to claim — "

"Ava!"

At the delighted shout of her name, Ava turned to see three more men approaching. The three couldn't look any more different, and yet she knew them all too well. Her heart gave a painful thump when more of her brothers emerged from the shadows.

It took a great amount of resolve to keep her tears at bay. Lucian, Cassander, Salvator and Andreas... Four of her six brothers, whom she hadn't seen in almost a hundred years, were suddenly standing before her.

This had to be a dream — or a nightmare, depending on who was asked.

"Wait... Sister?" Marc asked with surprise, turning to peer at her.

Ava nodded at him. "Marc, these are my brothers. Most of them, anyway."

He turned back to Lucian, sizing him up before taking a step back. "Oh." Lucian still looked disgusted and was glaring daggers at Marc.

Ava shook her head, worry filling her. When the black dots grew larger, she squeezed her eyes shut. She had to be losing her mind. No doubt the head injury had something to do with it.

For the last several months she'd been so sure Marc was only human. He'd smelled completely ordinary — sexy and tantalizing as hell, but ordinary. Even when she'd taken his blood it had tasted human. A bit tangier than most, but still human.

However, in that moment, he smelled different — not to mention the voracious way he'd fought for her, the strength he had to kill those hellhounds, the territorial way he was now acting…

None of that was human-like. Even now as she watched him, he seemed…different. The only problem was she couldn't figure out how.

Too much was happening all at once. The spinning world was gaining momentum with each second.

"Ava, your wounds!"

My wounds? Warm liquid was dripping down her face. Blood slid into her mouth. *Oh yeah, I was injured in the car accident.* And fighting those two Rogues hadn't been easy. They'd managed to get a few bites in and those had hurt like a bitch, too.

The voices around her were beginning to sound far away. She reached out, looking for something to hold on to. She felt as if the entire world was falling beneath her feet and she was powerless to stop it. She grabbed at the night air as she fell backward.

Marc, her brothers, the night sky… Everything faded to darkness.

Chapter Nine

"Ava? Quickly, sweetie, wake up."

Ava opened her eyes wide at her mother's frantic voice. She sat up on the feather bed, covering her nose as the unmistakable scent of smoke filled the room. She coughed and got up.

Her mother took her gloved hand and led her to the small window, where she used her foot to kick the glass out. "Here, Ava. Breathe through this."

The window was far too small for either of them to crawl through to escape, but Ava pressed her face into it, inhaling deep gulps of the fresh night air. Her heart was racing, and in the distance, she could hear the sounds of humans crying and screaming.

How had a fire started? The inn was made of wood, so had one of the servants accidentally left a fire burning in the furnace, and it had gotten out of hand? Where was the fire brigade?

Ava turned to her mother, who had torn a piece of fabric and pressed it to her own nose. Her emerald eyes were wide with fear as she seemingly contemplated what to do.

She was shaking, her bronzed skin awfully pale. It was a sign of her failing health. Alarmed, Ava rushed to her side. "Mother, are you unwell? Come... Breathe out of this window."

Her mother shook her head. "Ava," she said, holding out her hand, "hold on to me, sweetie."

Without a moment's hesitation, Ava ran to her mother, gripping her mother's hand like a vise. Her mother began a low chant in a foreign language. A pale blue light slowly surrounded them, growing into a sphere big enough to engulf them both. Ava hardly ever got to witness her mother using her powers, so despite the danger of the fire and smoke in the air, she was awestruck.

With a soft 'pop', Ava felt a tingling in her body and in a flash of light, they were outside in the open air, the inn blazing in the distance.

The blue light vanished, and Ava's mother dropped to her knees, panting.

Ava kneeled in front of her, worry gnawing at her. She might still be young, but she knew sickness when she saw it. "Mother, what ails you? Is it because you used too much power?"

Her mother gave her a sad smile, placing a brief kiss to the top of Ava's head. "Ava, darling, you're so bright. I don't — "

Her mother bit off her words and she rose to her feet, pushing Ava behind her. The hair on the back of Ava's neck stood on end. There was a loud hiss then three large, scary men were looming before them, slowly closing in. Going by the swirling tribal patterns on their bald heads, Ava knew they were some kind of fey, but she wasn't sure what breed. What she did know was that from the menacing air around them they weren't nice.

She gripped the back of her mother's skirts, a familiar fear washing over her. Tears welled in her eyes. "Mother — "

"Ava, listen to me," her mother said sternly. Her voice was tight, and the scent of her mother's own fear filled her nose. "Run away. Run far away from here, as fast as you possibly can. Do you understand me?"

Ava shook her head visciously. "No, Mother! I won't leave you here alone. They'll — "

"Now, Ava!" her mother demanded. Then her tone softened, as if she were trying to ease Ava's fear. "I'm right behind you, darling. I promise. Just run and don't look back."

Hesitating briefly, Ava let out a small sob before turning around and using her vampire speed to take off. She heard one of the men protest, followed by her mother's battle cry.

Her mother had promised to join her. She would kill those demons and come find her.

Her mother never broke her promises. Never.

Despite her mother's wishes, Ava looked over her shoulder as she continued running.

Her mother was fighting off the three men, but with her sickness and being weak from teleporting them out of the inn, it was clear that she was losing the battle. One man knocked her feet from under her and she fell to the ground. He then raised a large blade above his head and brought it down.

"No, Mother!"

With a deep gasp, Ava sat up, clutching her chest in a futile attempt to still her pounding heart. Tears were in her eyes and she was soaked with sweat. Her body was trembling like a leaf in the wind.

She blinked several times, telling herself over and over that it had just been an old dream — a terrible one she hadn't had in ages. She heaved a deep sigh and wiped her tears. *Damn it all… Just when I thought I was done reliving that hellish night…*

Inhaling deeply, she glanced around, frowning at the unfamiliarity of everything.

The room alone was big enough to contain her entire apartment and still have extra space to spare. There was a wide fireplace with an impossibly big flat-screen TV mounted to the wall, a connecting bathroom, a furniture set over to one side and varying ivory and crimson colors decorating the walls.

The bed she was lying on was large enough for at least ten people, with the softest silk sheets she'd ever felt. She splayed her hands across the fabric, marveling at the sensation. These alone must have cost a fortune.

Thick, heavy curtains shielded the windows, but she knew by instinct that it was late in the evening, the sun having already set. All vampires had amazing internal clocks.

The sound of soft breathing next to her caught her attention, and she turned to peer at Marc sleeping beside her. He had a small square of white gauze bandaged to his temple and a larger one taped to his bare shoulder. He was frowning, as if even in his sleep he was worrying over something.

With a faint smile, she leaned over him, giving him a gentle kiss. Just as she began to pull away, he snaked his arms around her, holding her in place.

She let out a small noise of surprise as he met her eyes. He curled those delicious lips of his into a sensual smile, twin craters forming in his cheeks. *Gods, will I ever get tired of seeing those dimples?*

"Hello, love," he purred, his tone husky.

Ava felt an immediate rush of heat slide through her. *Hot damn, he is so sexy.*

He pulled her closer, burying his face in her neck. "I'm so glad you're okay," he murmured.

A shiver ran down her spine. Oh, how good his lips felt on her. She wanted nothing more than to have him kissing all over her again, trailing his lips down the curve of her throat, over her tender breasts and down to the damp heat that was begging for his touch...

As if sensing her sudden arousal, Marc rolled her over onto her back, settling his big body on top of her. He kissed a searing hot path down her collarbone to the plunging neckline of the silky nightgown she wore. The gown was foreign to her as well. It was a luxury she hadn't ever bought herself, since she had always been prepared to bolt in the middle of the night if need be. *So, where did this one come from?*

She moaned when he toyed with her erect nipple that was covered by the white silk. He watched her as he tugged the peak between his teeth, giving it a soft nip.

By the gods, he was a deviant. He knew all the right spots that made her arch and moan and gasp. She was soaking wet, ready for his entrance. She wanted him to take her right here, in this beautiful, elegant room where only the two of them resided.

Wait a minute.

She pushed Marc off her and sat up as the memories of the previous night slammed into her with full force.

She and Marc had left his home when she'd sensed the presence of hellhounds. She'd known for a fact they were heading straight for her. They'd gotten into his car and driven away from the city, though the demons were still after them. They'd crashed into one of the hellhounds, and...well, she had been in a world of pain when she'd woken up, but she'd seen Marc fighting the hellhounds alone and she'd had to help.

Then...

She gasped, placing her hand over her mouth. *Was it all a dream?* It had to be. Her brothers had appeared so suddenly, and even after all the decades away from them, they'd remembered her.

"Ava, what's wrong?" Marc asked worriedly, sitting up beside her.

She gnawed on her fingernail. *What the hell is going on? Did I hit my head so hard that I imagined everything?*

Marc cupped her cheek, making her look him in the eye. "Talk to me, love. I can't help if you don't tell me what's on your mind."

"Wh-where are we?" she demanded.

He frowned, his concern evident. "Do you remember anything about last night?"

She bit her lip and pulled her eyebrows together. "I'm not sure. It feels like a dream. We were in a car accident, we fought those hellhounds and Rogues, and...my brothers showed up. But that's not what happened, right?"

"Ava, love...it wasn't a dream. All that really happened. You lost a lot of blood in the accident and ended up passing out. Your brothers brought us here to St. Charles. We're safe, but you've been asleep ever since."

A lump of dread formed in her stomach and she clutched at it, feeling a panic attack coming on.

She hopped out of the bed — well, tried to anyway, since it was like trying to crawl across a sea of silk — and began to pace the length of the room. This... This couldn't be real, not one bit. She'd left her brothers behind in Italy, thousands of miles across the ocean, ninety-six years ago.

What the hell are they doing here, in the same city as me, no less?

It was too much. It couldn't be a mere coincidence.

Somewhere in her brooding she became aware of Marc's gaze. He was no doubt trying to understand her reaction. Hell, she didn't blame him. She didn't understand it herself.

She was happy to see her family after so long. Ecstatic, even.

Yet, at the same time, how could she tell them the reason she'd run away? Or why someone was hunting her down like a wild animal? She didn't know how they would respond to any of it.

Would they even care? Would they hear her out? Believe her?

Or would they call her a liar and lock her away for making up accusations about someone in a high position

Hell, it was too much — and far too soon.

Tears stung her eyes as she clutched at her head, wincing at the pain from her still-open wound. Marc had said she'd lost a lot of blood. It explained why none of the cuts or bruises had healed. She needed to drink to replace what she'd lost.

She glanced over at Marc, who was still studying her. Somehow, he made her think of an animal watching its prey.

Those intense eyes of his never missed a thing. The room was dark, but she could see him clear as day. He watched her as if he, too, could see her just as well, and his eyes even had a faint glow to them. No doubt because she was so upset, she was just imagining things.

"You need to feed," he stated.

It wasn't a question. Him being a cop for so long helped him adapt to his surroundings. It was no surprise he'd caught on to her lifestyle so fast. Well, it was still shocking how calm he was about everything, but at least he wasn't crying and freaking out as most other humans would do. While those reactions were expected, they were insufferable.

She gave a simple nod, dropping her eyes to his bare neck. The last two times she'd fed from him, they'd ended up having sex.

Hot, delicious, glorious sex.

But now was not the time or place to do so. There were things to be discussed. She was sure her brothers were all waiting on her to awaken before seeking her out.

As if reading her mind, there was a sharp knock on the door.

She stiffened, not yet prepared to face them.

So she was thankful that Marc could read her body language. In several long strides, he made his way over to the door. He cracked it open just enough to peer out. Though he and the other person spoke in low tones, her vampire hearing picked up on it.

"Is she awake yet?" a deep baritone demanded in an accent that was a perfect mix of Old English and Italian. She recognized the voice as Lucian's, sounding impatient. He'd been born in the days when the Roman Empire had still been at its peak, so he spoke with a Latin brogue. Even if she couldn't hear his voice, the cold prickling of his power was always a dead giveaway. He had the Royal ability to command ice, and his powers tended to cloak around him like a dangerous cologne.

Marc's own voice was one of authority, not a shred of fear to be detected. "Yes, she is."

"Then step aside, human. We are here to see her."

We? As in more than just Lucian? Panic bubbled inside Ava, but Marc didn't budge, not even a twitch. "She's awake, but she needs a few moments before facing any of you."

"Excuse me?" Lucian demanded with outrage. "We are her family, not her enemy."

"What I mean is, she needs to feed and clean herself up before then. Give her some time." He dropped his voice to a low volume, though Ava still heard his words. "She'll come out when she's ready."

There was a moment of silence, as if Lucian were contemplating bursting past Marc or throwing him out into the hall. Hell, Lucian was a Royal and a rather old one, at that. With a small flick of his fingers, he could send Marc flying across the room.

Granted, Ava would beat him to a bloody pulp if he did, but it could happen.

Much to her relief, however, Lucian heaved an exasperated sigh. "For a human you certainly have a lot of balls. I'd advise you to tread wisely in the future. There are bags of blood in a miniature refrigerator in there, along with a microwave for her to heat them up. Whenever she's ready, we'll be in our father's private study. There will be a servant waiting to lead you there."

With that, Ava could sense he was walking away, though his steps made no sound.

Marc closed the door and turned back to her, a look of smug satisfaction gracing his handsome features. "I'm quite sure your brother would like nothing more than to eat my heart for breakfast, quite literally."

Despite her inner turmoil, Ava found herself smiling. "He wouldn't dare, so long as I can help it. He's always been...protective. I guess after a hundred years that hasn't changed about him, at least."

Marc shook his head. "And to think there are five more of them."

Ava's smile turned wry, and she went searching for the mini fridge Luc had mentioned. Yes, she had six brothers. Lucian, Cassander, Salvator, Darius, Julius and Andreas. Despite their closeness, they'd all had vastly different personalities. She wondered if they were the same way or if maybe they'd changed over time.

To vampires and most other demons, time had no meaning due to their immortality. A century to humans was merely a year to demons.

For Ava, perhaps because she was still so young, it had been a long century. So much had happened in that time that it felt longer.

She walked over to the large chestnut armoire and opened the doors, feeling pleased at seeing the three-foot-tall black mini fridge, along with a microwave and several glass goblets. She opened it and, as Lucian had stated, there were multiple bags of blood inside.

"What are you doing?" Marc asked, coming to stand next to her.

His scent washed over her, making her mouth go dry. She didn't think she'd ever get tired of his smell. "I'm about to feed," she stated, her voice thankfully even. His effect on her was embarrassing as it was. If he knew just how much his presence alone was enough to drive her mad, he'd never let her live it down.

Well, until I have to move away and leave him behind for good.

"Don't you want it straight from tap?" he teased, turning his head to the side to bare his neck.

She gulped but continued to busy herself. Of course she preferred her meal straight from the source. Well, when it came to Marc she did. She knew a lot of vampires these days preferred bagged blood because it was more convenient than hunting down real donors. However, she didn't have access to blood banks like most clans did.

She placed a handful of bags in the microwave. "You and I both know what'll happen if I take blood from you again."

He chuckled at that. A few moments later, she could sense the humor dissipating. "Ava..."

She kept her back turned as she emptied the heated blood into one of the cups. She knew that tone. He was about to ask her something personal.

In an effort to prepare herself, or maybe just create a distraction, she downed the glass of blood, resisting the urge to gag. Bagged blood was just a good as fresh blood, but after feeding from live hosts most of her life, she supposed it was an acquired taste.

Ick.

"What is it about your brothers that makes you so uneasy?" he asked, concern lacing his tone. "You were clearly happy to see them last night, but now it's... What are you afraid of?"

She felt her wounds begin to heal and the pain of hunger faded away, but even so, she heated another glass.

She knew he wouldn't drop his questioning until she answered, so she turned to face him. "You wouldn't understand, Marc. It's best that you don't know any more than you already do." Even as the words left her mouth, she felt foolish.

A low growl erupted from deep in his throat, making her raise her eyebrows in surprise. He leaned down to glare directly into her eyes, emphasizing their difference in height.

"In less than a week I've come to accept that demons are real, you're a vampire and hellhounds are giant, hairless mutts with a nasty bite. And yes, I may have done a bit of complaining a time or two, but I've accepted all of it, all of *you*. So don't you dare try to use that bullshit excuse on me. You're right. Maybe I won't completely understand your reasoning, but I can damn sure try—because I *want* to. Something is eating you alive and holding you back from being around your own family, whom you haven't seen in decades, and I want to know why."

He reached out a hand, and despite his angry words, tucked a strand of hair gently behind her ear. "I care about you, love. I want you to be safe and happy, not constantly running away from whatever or whoever is desperate to get their hands on you."

Ava swallowed. He was right. She wasn't being fair to him. He'd done so much for her, and in spite of suddenly being thrown into her world, he really had been rather accepting of everything. He'd even nearly gotten himself killed trying to protect her.

He more than deserved her honesty.

She sighed deeply, downed the second glass of blood then nodded. "I mentioned how one of the servants told me I didn't belong here, right? He said I was just a burden to my father, that it was best if I wasn't around and that a Royal having a half-breed for a child was sure to ruffle the feathers of other vampires." She rubbed away the chills that formed on her arms. "Well, he was a bit more than a servant. He was my father's second-in-command. He knew my father better than anyone else. So for him to say something like that to me, I thought it had to be my father's own feelings."

She gave a wry laugh, moving across the room to sit on the edge of the bed. Marc followed slowly, standing before her. She forced herself to look down at the ivory carpeting.

It was either that or gawk at his chiseled torso, or worse, reach up to rub across the hard planes of his body.

"Tell me about these people hunting you," he said, shifting to fold his arms. "I know you said those ghouls were bounty hunters, but they're not necessarily the only ones after you, are they?"

Ava's spine stiffened, her breath lodging somewhere in her throat. Shocked, she looked up at him. "H-How did you know?"

He gave her a disbelieving look and tapped his temple. "Remember, love. I've been a cop for years. There isn't much I don't catch on to. When we were both held in the cell, those two guys said they had a customer wanting to pay for you. Yet those two Rogues we fought last night said their *master* wanted you alive. That tells me that while some people want you alive so they can earn a profit, there's someone out there trying to capture you for some other reason."

Ava's mouth parted, shut, then parted again. *Well…damn. He knows.*

She shouldn't have been surprised. Marc was far more intelligent than the average human. It seemed he always knew when something was bothering her. *Reading body language must be a rather tenacious skill of his.*
"That's correct."

"Why? Who is it?"

When she didn't answer right away, he crouched down, looking up at her. His lashes were dark and long, making his eyes seem even brighter. They still looked to be faintly glowing, a thought that made her curious. His jaw had a shadow from him not shaving in a few days. With his hair bedraggled, he looked even more rugged and sexy than when he was clean-shaven and groomed.

"Every Royal vampire, even mixed breeds like myself, has a special power. For me, I'm a telepath. If I touch someone's skin, I am able to see all of their thoughts and memories, even alter them to whatever I want."

He frowned. "I thought all vampires were able to manipulate their victim's memories?"

She shook her head slightly. "All vampires have the ability to *charm* humans, meaning we can make them do whatever we want then erase their memories of encountering us. However, my power goes beyond that. It can affect both humans and demons. From the time they're born up until the very moment I touch them, I practically relive their entire lives."

He widened his eyes with interest, and he glanced at her bare hands folded in her lap. "Is that why you wear gloves a lot? I just thought you were a germaphobe or something."

She gave a wry smile. "Yes, they're necessary. I can mostly control it now, but if I or the other person is feeling some strong emotions and we so happen to brush each other's skin, it just...happens. That's why I try my best to wear long sleeves or gloves." She shrugged. "One day I came across someone and I bumped into him, and... Well, I saw something I shouldn't have seen. It is because of that he wants to capture me, for fear I will expose him. No doubt he wants to kill me himself or see if I've snitched on him or something."

Marc's frown only deepened, his features tightening. "Who is he? Someone you know?"

She looked to the side then back again. "My father's second."

His eyes widened again, and he rose to his feet. "What? Ava, you have to tell your father."

She hopped to her feet as well, pacing. "I can't, Marc. This man… He's very powerful and my father trusted him more than anything. Do you understand how people would react if I, a mere half-breed, were to accuse the king's right-hand man of such things? No one would believe me, and even still, I'd be a complete outcast — if not killed for such an offense."

"The *king*?"

Ava paused, a cold chill going down her spine.

Oops…Did I say that aloud?

"Umm…" she toyed nervously with her hair that fell over her shoulder. *Well, hell, Ava. You already let the cat out of the bag. No sense lying about it now.*

She heaved a long-suffering sigh and turned to meet his bewildered gaze. "Um, yeah. My father is the king of the vampires."

He looked as if she'd just punched him in the gut. "The king. Like, *king*-king?"

Ava gave a sharp tug on her hair. "Yes."

He scrubbed his hands over his face. "Jesus fucking Christ."

Ava shifted her weight to one leg. *Good gods.* If she could crawl under a massive rock and hide away for the rest of her life, she'd be perfectly content. "Sorry," was all she could mutter.

He let out a bark of laughter, though there was no humor in it whatsoever. "My life is getting crazier day by day. That's a bit of information you could have mentioned back at the motel."

She tilted her head to the side. "Would it have made a difference?"

He gave an impatient shrug. "Yes... No... Hell, I don't know." He sat down on the bed, his expression a mix of frustration and unease. "You're a real princess. Not just a Royal, but the actual daughter of a demon king. Shit, no wonder you're being sought after by bounty hunters."

She grunted uncomfortably. "Yes."

"And that's why you said it's too complicated for you to join a clan for protection?"

"Yes," she said again. "There are only eight Royals left alive, and everyone knows we are all the children of the king. I couldn't risk letting anyone find out about that. My family would have been notified immediately."

He closed his eyes tightly and didn't speak for several minutes.

A feeling of apprehension washed over her. She'd been so afraid of telling him the full truth of her heritage because she was the only daughter of Cyrus, the powerful king of the vampires, who no doubt was feared by many. It was why all the bounty hunters she'd come across had done their best to keep their identities hidden from her, for fear of the king's retribution. With Marc only being a human, it would be no surprise to her if he decided he wanted nothing more to do with her for the same reason.

It wouldn't be a surprise, but it would still be quite painful. She really did care for him. A lot. She had all those months she'd been working at the diner and those feelings had only grown more profound over the last week. With all they'd been through, she didn't want him to have a change of thought about her because of this new information she'd told him.

Marc slowly stood to his feet and made his way to the connecting bathroom. She frowned as she watched him. She could hear him rustling around before turning on the water to the bathtub.

Not wanting to disturb him, she walked back over to the armoire to fix another cup of blood. All this talk, being in this mysterious house, meeting her brothers and father after a century of being absent... She needed a distraction to calm her nerves before she went crazy.

She'd just finished her third cup of blood, downing it like a shot of whiskey, when the water turned off and Marc exited the bathroom.

She turned and gaped as he walked toward her.

Completely naked.

Her mouth went dry and her cheeks warmed, heat pooling low in her belly. All those hard, chiseled muscles rippled under his skin with each step. *Yummy.* The gods had surely been generous when they'd made him.

Marc reached for her hand and led her to the bathroom. She didn't protest.

The scent of lavender filled her nose, and she swallowed thickly when she saw the large clawfoot tub filled with bubbles and water. She watched Marc enter the tub and immerse his body under the bubbles. He sighed and held out a hand, beckoning her to join him.

"Come relax with me while you finish your story," he demanded.

Her gaze wandered to the clean gauze at his shoulders, widening as it dipped beneath the water. "Your wound. Be careful."

He peered down at the gauze and peeled it off, letting it drop to the floor. Ava's eyes widened further at the clean, smooth skin that didn't have a single mark on it—no blood, no scar, not even a faint redness. "It's...healed," she breathed, moving close to rub her fingers across his shoulder. She turned to him. "Did they give you some kind of special ointment or cream?"

He shook his head. "Nope. Just cleaned me up and slapped a bandage on the old-fashioned way."

"Impossible," she breathed. He'd been bitten by a hellhound. That much she knew. She'd seen it happen, had smelled his blood pouring from the wound. It had just been the previous night, but there was no way a human could heal that fast. Hell, even a week from now no human would have healed that fast without even a scar. The hellhound had bitten deep enough into his shoulder to have ripped through muscle.

"Look, we'll discuss it later," he said, seeming far less concerned than she was. He reached out a hand to grip her fingers. "I want to focus on you. You're wound too tight, and we both need to be level-headed, so we can face this...whatever it is, together."

Ava's heart gave a lurch. He was so...caring—and gentle. *Gosh, why can't he be a selfish, loathsome toad who has more brawn than brain?* It'd be so much simpler to get over him if he was a complete asshole.

He should fear and hate her very existence, should want nothing to do with her. All she'd managed to do was bring danger to his doorstep and put his life in peril.

Yet he continued to treat her as if *she* were the fragile one. He pushed aside his own feelings and worries and made her feel like she was important.

He was unlike anything she could have ever imagined. And she wasn't sure if it was a good thing or a bad thing.

Slowly, Ava began to undress. She admired the way his eyes darkened as he watched her.

She knew full well she possessed the unearthly beauty all vampires had, but a measure of insecurity always plagued her. She was only a half-breed, neither full vampire nor fey. She could never fit in with either side.

Marc was beyond handsome, and no doubt he'd had more than his fair share of gorgeous women. Hell, how many times had she seen women at the diner fuss and fawn over him and Duncan? A freaking a lot, that was how many. Of course, she'd acted like she didn't care, but Edith had noticed her petulant attitude or the way she would scrub the counter a bit too much force.

However, in this moment alone with him, with his gaze roaming her body, he somehow made her feel as if she were the most beautiful woman in the world. He seemed to place her on a pedestal, worshipping her as if she were the goddess of beauty.

She joined him in the tub, relaxing between his thighs as the hot water began to melt away her stress.

He wrapped his arms around her, pulling her more securely into his chest.

"Now, love, about your powers... You are able to see anyone's thoughts and memories by touching them?"

Relaxing under the heat of the water, she nodded slowly. "Except you."

"How is that?"

Ava leaned her head back against him. "Honestly, I don't know. You are the first person I've come across that I couldn't read."

"Is that a good or bad?"

"I have no idea." She sighed deeply. It was just another one of the many thoughts plaguing her mind. "But I have to admit it pleases me how much I'm able to relax around you. I've never... It's impossible to feel this kind of intimacy with someone whose every thought and memory pops into your head. It makes you surprised to realize there are a lot of creeps in the world."

"I don't need to see someone's thoughts to know that. Well, we'll figure it out eventually. So your father's second-in-command is the one who told you that you were a burden to your family?"

She nodded.

"And one day when you bumped into him, you happened to see something he did in his past, something that could ruin his reputation?"

"It could more than ruin his reputation," she said softly. "If I were to tell anyone what I saw and it turned out to be true, he would be considered a traitor and killed. But since it was a mere glimpse, there's no way I could possibly prove that what I saw was real. And if I told my family, no one would believe me. I would truly be considered a burden then—one who was thought to spread false rumors about the higher-ranked vampires."

Marc was silent for a long time as he ran a soaped-up washcloth over her body. He was thinking, she knew.

In the meantime, she basked in the tender caress of the fabric on her skin, the gentle way he ran it up and down her body, washing away the events of the day before. With just his touch, he was able to make her greatest worries fade away, providing her with an inner peace only he could.

It was remarkable.

It was also terrifying with the way she was falling for him — not just for his sake, but for hers. She'd have to leave him soon, go back to her life on the run. Even if he decided he wanted to drop everything and join her, there was no way in hell she'd ever allow it.

She cared way too much. He loved his job. Besides, it was too dangerous. She'd never be the same if something fatal happened to him because of her.

When he spoke, she could feel the timbre of his voice vibrating all the way from his chest through her back. "Love, I know I'm just an outsider in all of this, but I have a rather keen sense when it comes to reading people. Last night when your brothers came to your aid, even long after you passed out, all I could see was love in their actions. It has been so long since you all last saw each other, but from the outside looking in, it appears that your brothers really missed you. Hell, I had to jump through hoops and deliver futile death threats just to get them to let me stay by your side all day and night. They care about you so much. I can guarantee that if you tell them the truth of everything, they will believe you. They will not look at you any differently. They all just want to see you safe and sound."

His words touched her. Truly, they did. She'd been so afraid to face her brothers and father after all these years, but somehow, having Marc at her side gave her courage. She felt she could do anything as long as he was with her.

Which was rather frightening.

She didn't know what to make of the feelings she had for him. She cared about him, that much she knew. But in the last several days what she felt had...intensified. She more than just cared for him. She couldn't explain it and she certainly didn't understand it.

She was just stumped.

But she would have to dwell on them later. Much, much later. Right now, she just wanted to enjoy his pleasant touch on her skin.

Chapter Ten

Dressed in casual clothes that must have been bought for them while they had been unconscious, she and Marc followed a female vampire down the winding halls of her father's mansion. The luxurious black marble flooring and the high-class paintings lining the walls gave the place a majestic presence fit for a king.

From what Marc had told her he'd learned while she'd been unconscious, this was just one of her father's many estates, though he primarily preferred living here. It was located in St. Charles, an hour away from Chicago. Ava had been shocked to learn he'd been so close to her and she'd never known.

Then again, she'd done her best to avoid most of the demon world, so it wasn't like she went out and socialized with anyone. All she'd known was that Chicago was home to a rather powerful and influential vampire clan, similar to many other big cities. While it still had a large number of demons roaming the streets, they did well to avoid causing trouble, especially among humans. It was either behave or have the Imperials barreling down on them.

And the Imperials were the demons no one wanted knocking on their door, under any circumstance. If the demons in the human world refused to behave and their own rulers couldn't control them, the next step was to call on the Imperials. Being in the presence of those old bastards was about as lovely as standing in the middle of a swamp full of hungry gators.

As she walked through the halls, Ava was well aware of the large number of other vampires posted about, though they remained out of sight.

Her father was powerful, but he wasn't a fool. He was well-guarded at all times. While several demons respected his leadership, there was always someone who opposed it and wanted him dead.

It was the same with all great rulers, she supposed — human or otherwise.

The servant led them to exquisitely carved double doors, where she gave a deep bow. "The king and his sons await you," she said simply. With that, she wandered off.

The massive doors were guarded by two imposing hooded vampires, who each gave a small dip of his head in greeting. They didn't say anything, just opened the doors and allowed Ava and Marc to pass.

Ava stood openmouthed. At the same time, Marc mumbled, "No fucking way."

The sight took her breath away. Tall bookshelves lined every inch of the room, both on that floor and the one above them. They were filled completely with books, scrolls and every so often a little trinket, novelty item or priceless artifact, each row separated by colossal fluted white columns. On the far side was an extravagant mahogany desk taking up a great deal of the corner it sat in. In the center of the room was an elegant living room set in ornate gold-and-white. A massive crystal chandelier hung from the domed ceiling, splashing the vast room with a brilliant glow, and far above their heads were the most stunning paintings she'd ever seen. Angels, cherubs, sprites, fairies, elves... They were all so breathtaking. A little slice of heaven on earth, for sure.

Yes, her father possessed a great deal of wealth, and he'd never minded showing it off. *And why should he?* Not only was he a king, but he'd also lived more lifetimes than anyone should be allowed. He'd earned his wealth, so there was no point in not rolling in the dough, so to speak.

Sitting on the various couches and armchairs were all six of her brothers and her father. They all stood, but it was Cyrus who stepped toward her.

Like all vampires, he was an exceptionally beautiful man with pale blue eyes and black hair in a ponytail that fell to his knees. He was still as tall as ever, with muscles bulging beneath the elegant purple toga wrapped around his body, giving him the appearance of a powerful Roman emperor. Though to humans he'd only look to be in his early thirties, only a fool would be able to ignore the ancient aura surrounding him, the keen intelligence of an aged scholar dancing in his eyes or the dangerous power swirling beneath his tan skin from the many millennia he'd spent honing his skills.

His eyes shimmered as if holding back tears as he gave in to a watery smile. Ava's own eyes began to sting, the back of her throat burning as she futilely tried to restrain her emotions. *Damn, I'm such a crybaby lately.*

When he was just a few feet away from her, he held his shaking arms out wide. "*Filia mea*," he whispered in an ancient language that still accented his and his three oldest sons' words. His voice was full of emotion. "At last, you're home."

Ava's previous reluctance to join with her family melted away in an instant. She stepped into her father's arms, no longer able to hold in her sobs.

Home.

Such a small word, but the impact behind it was far more intense that anything she could have imagined. That was exactly what this felt like. It was the same as when she had been younger, crying on her father's shoulder while he comforted her. He planted a long kiss on top of her head, and Ava got a flash of him sitting alone in his private study back in Tuscany, crying over losing her after she'd run away.

Ava's heart clenched painfully, making her cry harder.

She'd missed him so much. He'd been so loving and accepting of her from the very beginning, regardless of his not being in her life as a child.

At last, he pulled away, smiling down at her with red-rimmed eyes. "Come, Ava. We have much to discuss."

She gave a single nod, using her fingers to wipe her eyes.

A warm hand was placed on her back, and she looked up to see Marc giving her a reassuring smile. She returned the gesture, leading the way to one of the empty loveseats. Marc sat next to her and she relaxed. She'd told Marc repeatedly that he didn't need to accompany her, that he'd probably just feel out of place, but he insisted on staying by her side.

He was exasperating and stubborn, but she couldn't help but be pleased that he was with her. He was an ever-present comfort, a fortress giving her a strength she hadn't known she'd needed.

All six of her brothers were watching her, their emotions mirroring her father's.

Lucian, Cassander and Andreas sat on one couch, Julius in an armchair and Salvator and Darius on another couch, while her father took a seat in a large wingchair, facing them all in a semicircle.

Of all of them, Lucian looked the most like their father, with his black hair and tan skin. His eyes were pale silver and had always reminded her of the moon. He was the eldest and was well known to be cold as ice to anyone not in the family, though he was a great leader. He was a man who was as feared as he was adored. And, to be honest, he was usually a grumpy sourpuss more often than not — like a true old man.

Next up was Cass. He had their father's pale blue eyes with his mother's fair hair. Just like he had when she'd first met him, he wore his platinum hair pulled away from his face in a series of half-braids that made him look like a Viking warrior. He had always been more reserved, and she understood he'd been tormented on the inside due to an incident in his past. He was all warrior and fiercely devoted to his family. Once upon a time, he could always be found working out or honing his fighting skills.

Sal was third, also born from their father's first mate, with long silvery hair and the same pale blue eyes. He was... Well, he'd always had more exquisite taste than the rest of them. Though he was as deadly as they come, he was a man who enjoyed the finer things in life —

women, fashion and all. Like Cass, he shared his mother's Norse features.

From their father's second mate had come the twins, Darius and Julius. Darius had short brown hair and pale eyes, along with a couple of piercings decorating one eyebrow. He'd always had a special talent for cooking. Julius was the artist in the family. No doubt he was the one who'd painted the magnificent artwork on the ceiling above them. His eyes were pale blue as well, and his brown hair was shaved into a mohawk, the longer hair pulled into a neat manbun. He had a black hoop pierced through one nostril. Both had been troublemakers and dumb as rocks when she'd met them, but they were still fine fighters, back when vampires hadn't been as peaceful as they were now.

Then there was Andreas, who was just a few years younger than the twins. When she'd first met him, she'd known he wasn't their biological brother, as they all knew, but no one ever talked about it. It might not be by blood, but he was still their brother regardless. Like the others, he was a pureblood Royal vampire, but the twins' mother had taken him in as a baby, and Cyrus had been more than happy to raise him as his own. Andreas had black hair to his chin and bright amber eyes.

And that was her Gordano family — a name widely known, both respected and feared.

As Ava looked around at each of them, she had to hold back another wave of tears. Her brothers were as familiar to her as the back of her hand, yet strangers at the same time.

But there wasn't the slightest bit of awkwardness in the air.

She felt at home.

For several long moments, it was dead-silent, as if no one knew what to say. Or rather, it was more likely that they had a lot to say but didn't know how to break the ice.

So she was rather thankful when Julius spoke at last. He threw a leg over one arm of the chair. "So...what's with the human? Is he your pet?"

Ava's cheeks rose to scorching temperatures, and someone made a choked noise. *Wow. First time speaking to him in ninety-six years, and that's the first thing out of his mouth.*

Okay, *now* things were pretty awkward.

Cass glared at him. "Idiot, that's not the way to start a conversation."

Julius raised his hands in exasperation. "What? No one was talking, so I stepped up," — he studied his nails in a casual fashion — "natural leader that I am."

"Yes," Sal drawled, "but you stepped in the wrong direction there, brother."

He merely shrugged, humor twinkling in his eyes. "Well, no sense jumping down my throat. I'm just trying to make her feel at ease." He paused then muttered, "Although, it really was a genuine question."

Cyrus shook his head. "Ava, you'll have to forgive him. I'm afraid he hasn't changed much since you last saw him. He still has a rather disturbing knack for saying inappropriate things at the wrong time." He sent a warning glare toward Darius, who'd opened his mouth. "His twin is no different." Darius' mouth snapped shut, as if he, too, had been about to say something out of line.

Cyrus' gaze warmed as it met hers. "I know this must be terribly uncomfortable for you. We have missed you dearly over these decades. So much so that we've spent a great amount of time looking for you, but it all seemed so futile. You simply...disappeared."

Ava lowered her head, guilt hammering through her. It was Marc's warm arm brushing against her that gave her the courage to even face them. "I'm...sorry. I'm so sorry for any trouble I've caused."

"Trouble is a very nice way of putting it," Darius grumbled, taking a sip of the beverage inside the cup he was holding.

Next to him, Sal smacked him in the back of the head, making the twin spill the brown alcohol on himself. "Bastard," he growled. "What the hell did you do that for?"

Sal sat back, crossing one long leg over the other. He was the very definition of grace. "Because *you* are an idiot."

Darius was about to protest, but Ava spoke up. "No, he's right. I should have never taken off without a word. It was really inconsiderate of me. I only thought my being there was troubling to everyone, so I figured it was best if I left."

Seven pairs of wide eyes looked to her. Lucian sucked in a sharp breath. "Why on earth would you think that?"

"Yeah," Andreas chimed in, "there wasn't a day that went by when we weren't happy to have you with us."

Her cheeks heated more, her heart beating so loudly it was thrumming in her ears. "Someone put it in my head that I didn't belong, since I was only a half-blood, and I believed them. I didn't want to burden anyone any further, so I left." She paused, thinking it was best if she started from the beginning. But before that, she just had to know. "How did you all manage to find me? I thought you would have still been in Italy."

"We still travel home from time to time," Cass stated. "But, primarily, we prefer Chicago. After all, it's home to Lucian's clan and we like to stay together, for obvious reasons — not to mention we all have prospering businesses within the city."

Ava paused for several moments. It was her turn to be shocked. "*Lucian's* clan?" Her gaze met his. "*You're* the Chicago clan chief?"

A hint of pride touched his proud Roman features as he nodded. "I am."

Her frown deepened. "So you've known that I was living there for the last several months?"

There was another hushed silence as they all looked at one another. Cyrus cleared his throat. "Actually, *cara*, none of us knew until a few days ago. As I said, we lost your trail but never stopped looking. I've had many of my informants keeping close eyes on all black markets, slave trades and whatever whispers among the demons they could use to help find you. For decades we came up short. It seemed hopeless, but I couldn't accept the worst. However, just a week ago, one of them sent a report about a group of ghouls suddenly rushing toward the city. It was just a hunch, but I made sure he followed them, just in case they led him to you. And sure enough, it was a hit. From there, your brothers managed to track down your place of employment, apartment and finally, where you ended up last night with" — his gaze slid over to Marc — "your friend."

Ava's frown didn't lighten in the least. While her father'd had people looking for her for years, ever since she'd moved to Chicago, she'd been so close to all of them and not once had she known. It was so ironic.

Fate could be a cruel bitch that way.

"Ava," Lucian spoke to her. His expression held its normal unreadable mask. "I know it's sudden, and though we are all genuinely happy to have you home, there's a rather pressing issue we must address." He leaned forward, his elbows resting on his leather-clad knees. "Your life is in danger. That much is evident from last night. Do you know who it is who's been hunting you down? Or why they want you?"

Ava shifted in her seat, her spine stiffening. "Yes."

His eyes narrowed. "Who." It was more of a demand than a question. Such had always been common with him.

She gave her loose hair a sharp tug. She gulped. This was it, the moment she'd feared for years.

Marc placed his large palm on her back, providing her with the warmth and encouragement she needed. In fact, it was a great amount of warmth. He might as well have been placing a torch to her back. She didn't miss the way her father's eyes narrowed in on their closeness, but she ignored it. "Mikhail Nilsen."

Someone sucked in a sharp breath and the room went quiet again. She met her father's gaze, but it was unreadable. She hunched a shoulder, feeling ridiculous. She'd known they wouldn't believe her. Mikhail was not only a powerful clan chief, he had been her father's right-hand man, his most favored soldier and the only person he'd entrusted his life to a thousand percent.

And she...

Well, she was just the king's bastard daughter, who'd gone into hiding for a hundred years. It was her measly words against a well-respected man.

For what seemed like an eternity, everyone was silent. Deathly silent. She might as well have been in a room full of mannequins. It seemed as if her pounding heartbeat was the only thing to be heard.

When her father at last spoke, his tone was flat, giving nothing away. "Explain."

She gave another sharp tug on her hair. As ancient as he was, Cyrus was a very intelligent man. There wasn't much those sharp eyes of his missed. Even the slightest of movements could tell him how someone was feeling or what was going through their head.

"He is the one who told me I was a burden to you, that my being a half-breed was a mockery to our bloodline. The king siring a bastard child from a late-night hookup with a wood sprite was a disgrace. That's why I ran away. His words sounded true enough. I just didn't want to be a shame to you all." Her gaze dropped down to the glass coffee table in the middle of them. There was a priceless vase holding a beautiful arrangement of flowers in the center, along with a large bottle of brandy and several glasses. She didn't drink, but with the anxious feeling in her heart, she contemplated starting today.

"A few years later I ran into Mikhail and a few of his clansmen in London. We were both in an alley, and when I bumped into him, I got a glimpse inside his mind." She shuddered as the images raced through her head. "He allowed me to go free, which I thought was a relief at first. But then I became aware of him and his men following me. I have been on the run ever since, decades later. It was as if after encountering him, the number of hunters after me have more than doubled. I can always tell which ones are sent by him and which ones are the rare ones who happen to be looking to make some money off a clanless vampire."

Again, the room was silent for several beats. It was impossible to tell what any of them were thinking, not without touching them.

It was incredibly nerve-racking.

"What is it that you saw when you touched him?" Sal asked in silky tones. He casually poured himself a glass of brandy.

Ava lifted her head a fraction, shaking her head slightly at the images that arose. "He had plans to create a new race of vampires."

Andreas' eyebrows drew together. "A new race? What the devil does *that* mean?"

She heaved a sigh. "As I said, it was only a glimpse. But...there were...bodies, a lot of them. There were both humans and vampires, and they had been very recent at the time. I didn't know what it meant. I still don't, but I've always had a feeling that whatever I saw is the reason why he wants me dead. It can't be anything good."

"Well, gang," Julius said on an expel of breath. He rose to his feet, stretching his arms high above his head. When he spoke, he lightened his voice to mimic Fred from *Scooby-Doo*. "It looks like we have a mystery on our hands." His lips twitched in amusement, and he looked around with raised eyebrows at everyone, as if expecting them to share his humor.

He merely received a handful of glares and aggravated groans.

Sal shook his head, sipping at his drink. "Idiot," he muttered.

Marc moved his leg a bit to brush hers. If not for him being there, she would not have had the strength to face her family, to tell them the truth of why she'd lived her life the way she had. All that was left was determining whether or not they believed her.

Cyrus sat back in his chair, drumming his fingers on the armrest. His eyes were searching. For what, she had no idea, but she prayed that whatever he found was good. To Ava's surprise, he didn't look nearly as angry with her as she'd thought he'd be. "I understand your fear of seeking help from us, but honestly, *cara*. I wish with every fiber in my being that we would have found you far sooner, so we could have protected you."

Ava frowned, tilting her head to the side. "You..." She licked her suddenly dry lips, confused. "You believe me?"

His lips twitched into a small smile. "You are my daughter. I will never doubt your word. Also, I sense no lies coming from you."

"Besides," Sal added, "Mikhail was exiled decades ago. There's no reason to not believe you."

That shocked the hell out of her. "He was?"

He nodded, his silver hair tumbling over his shoulder. "Shortly after you left, there was a...an incident, if you will. It came to light that a handful of Mikhail's clan members were responsible for several humans going missing, and he chose to look the other way. His flunkies were tried and executed, while he was stripped of his title as chief and forbidden from joining any clan."

Her mouth parted and her eyes widened. *Well...shit.* That was news to her.

All this time he'd been sending goons to hunt her down and capture her, when he was already exiled. If preventing her from ruining his reputation wasn't the reason he wanted her...then why? He'd already lost his position as chief on his own. Granted, it was a great dishonor to lose such a worthy title, but that had nothing to do with her. She hadn't even been there to witness it at the time.

Or maybe it was his way of seeking revenge against Cyrus. She had gone unprotected for so long that she was an easy target. Maybe he wanted to punish her father for exiling him by using her.

She flashed back to the two Rogues she'd fought the previous night. She'd faced plenty of Rogues in her life, but those two... Something about them had just seemed off. Rogues lost their humanity. All they knew was to feed and kill. But the ones last night had said they had a master who wanted her.

Rogues were loyal to no one. They were just a fraction below rabid animals. They didn't have masters, and they didn't carry out orders.

She didn't understand it.

"Well," Cyrus said, pouring himself a cup of the alcohol, "for the time being, it would be best if you stayed here — for your own protection. You can claim a spot in Lucian's clan, as the rest of your brothers have. You are safe with us."

Her head perked up at that. "What about Marc? He isn't safe out there alone."

Her father's eyebrows lifted as if he hadn't even considered the possibility. "Ahh, yes. Your human." He took a sip of his drink, his eyes calculating them over the rim.

"You should not have gotten him involved in our world," Lucian remarked.

"Yeah," Darius uttered, "you should to erase his memory and send him home. Now that you're under our care, I doubt anyone will come looking for him."

Marc stiffened beside her.

"I can't," she said calmly. "None of my powers work on him. I've already tried a couple of times. But even if I could, I refuse. Marc has been a big help to me these last few days, even risked his own life to save mine — more than once, mind you. He deserves to know as much as I do."

"Be reasonable," Lucian said. "He's only a human. For him to know this much about us, and still — "

Ava growled, rising to her feet. "If your protection will not extend to him, then I will not stay here, plain and simple."

Lucian rose to his feet as well. He was as stubborn as any vampire, refusing to back down. "You are willing to continue facing danger over a mere human? Has being alone all these years made you completely stupid?"

She winced, clutching her fists at her sides. Marc rose next to her, wrapping his hand around her wrist. "Ah...excuse us, please," he said to Cyrus. "Before this gets out of hand, I'd like to speak with Ava alone."

Cyrus gave a curt nod. "We've been here for a few hours now, so I'm quite sure you're famished. I will have a servant bring sustenance to your room shortly." He looked at Ava. "Take your time and join us when you're ready, *cara*."

Marc nodded and tugged Ava out of the study. She sent one last glare at Lucian over her shoulder before allowing Marc to lead her back to their room.

Chapter Eleven

Watching Ava and her human leave the study, Lucian stalked across the room, pacing with his frustration.

By the gods, how can she be so...thickheaded?

Her life was already in danger as it was, and yet rather than staying under their protection, she was more than willing to go back out — *alone* — over a damn human? Was she really that daft? What point was she trying to prove by being so ignorant?

It was damn annoying. He'd missed his little sister so much it hurt. He was overjoyed at having her back home, but he still had to worry over her making foolish decisions.

"Luc, take a seat," Cyrus said smoothly, tapping away at his phone.

He paused, turning harsh eyes on his father. *How can he possibly be so calm over this?* "You know I am right," he growled, moving to flop back down on the cushioned couch. "Humans are vulnerable to any number of vampire charms. He could spill our secrets or bring danger to our kind."

His father didn't even look up. After several more taps, he cut the screen off and slid the device inside a hidden pocket in his robes. It was strange how the man preferred his ancient attire yet still used something as modern as a cell phone—and a smart phone, at that. "Have you taken a good look at that male?"

Lucian frowned. *What kind of senseless question is that?* As the clan chief to one of the most powerful vampire clans around, it was his job to study everyone he came across. He was damn good at what he did. "Of course I have."

Cyrus' gaze turned thoughtful. "Then I believe you are losing your touch, son." He looked around at Cass, who was leaning back on the couch with cool indifference. "Did you see it?"

Cassander nodded. "Yep."

"As did I," Sal murmured.

Luc growled, growing impatient. He was already wound up as it was with the Rogues let loose in his city. Add to that spending the last several days searching for his sister and he'd had very little to no sleep. He was a time bomb just waiting to explode and his family could test even the most patient of saints. "Enough of these subtleties. What are you talking about? What the hell did you see?"

Humor gleamed in his father's pale eyes. "That Marc fellow isn't entirely human."

Lucian blinked in surprise. "How is that possible? Even when Andreas tracked his scent, he said the man was human."

Cyrus nodded. "Yes, that's true. Even now he smells human. However" — he took a deep sip of his drink — "I can sense him going through the 'Change'."

To say Lucian was stumped was an understatement. "Come again?"

"Is that the reason she claimed her powers doesn't work on him? Because he's part shifter?" Darius asked.

Cyrus drummed the fingers of his spare hand on the armrest. "In part."

"Well, what's the other part?" Andreas demanded. "Only a handful of demons are able to block out the powers of a Royal. Even if she's a half-blood, no human can resist a Royal telepath."

Cyrus' lips twitched in suppressed amusement. There was a mischievous twinkle in the ancient man's eyes, one that Lucian wasn't sure was good or bad.

"I'm afraid that is something the two of them will have to figure out on their own."

Lucian shook his head in exasperation. He hated the way his father spoke in riddles. It was so damn annoying. He glanced over to see Cass grinning. At once, Lucian put the pieces together. "Don't tell me he's her truemate." When both of them remained silent, just smirking with humor, Lucian's mouth parted in surprise. Then he began muttering a series of Latin curses. "Terrific." He gave a sharp shake of his head. "So, what are we going to do with him?"

Cyrus shrugged. "It's entirely up to him. If he would like our protection, he has it. I usually don't care to take mortals under my wing, but for Ava's sake I will. We only just got her back. I do not wish for her to feel put off by us because we cannot protect her…friend, nor do I want her back in the world living on the run. But if he decides he wants to return home and continue with his life, I am powerless to stop him. In the meantime, I've reached out to an associate of mine who is also a shifter. I've invited him here to have a talk with Marc and to see about training him." He stood to his feet, moving over to his desk to retrieve a bottle of expensive Scotch.

"Moving on to other things," Sal said, "what are we going to do about Mikhail? He's been hunting down Ava but I don't think it's simply to get revenge on you for banishing him."

Cyrus opened the expensive bottle, inhaling its aroma. "No, I believe there is something more at play here. I've had eyes on him ever since his exile, but he's been...undetectable recently."

Lucian stiffened. "Father, why are you just now telling us this?"

Casually, Cyrus poured himself a glass and strolled back to his seat. "It was best not to alarm any of you before I knew more information. As it is, I'm waiting on another status report from my Guard." He turned serious, his eyes narrowing as he peered at each of his sons. "I believe Ava saw more than what she told us, but she's unconsciously blocking the memory. Whatever she saw when she touched Mikhail, no doubt he thinks she knows what he's truly planning. Have you all noticed the sudden increase in activity of Rogues?"

His brothers nodded, and Lucian leaned forward on his elbows. "They've been terrorizing the city, leaving a trail of bodies in their wake. And the ones who attacked Ava last night... It's like they were being controlled, which is something I've never seen or heard of before."

"Same. We need to get to the bottom of this, and soon," Cyrus said. "If Ava is correct in what she saw, then creating Rogues to control must be Mikhail's plan for creating a new race of vampires. We just need to find out how he's doing it, where he's located and put an end to him before he causes any more damage."

* * * *

Ava let out a string of Italian curses as she paced the bedroom floor. Marc was leaning casually against the bed post, watching her with his arms folded.

That jerk Lucian. She'd kick his ass for talking to her like that, as if she was a clueless child. *How dare he.* How dare any of them expect her to casually throw Marc aside. She'd understand if he were a weak and terrified human, but he had put his very life on the line, more than once, to protect her. He'd proven that he was more than worthy to keep their secrets. She owed him for that.

With a deep sigh, she turned to face him and abruptly narrowed her eyes. Perhaps in her scrambled mind she hadn't noticed it, but somehow…he seemed different.

In the soft glow of the overhead bedroom light, those golden eyes of his watched her with that same observant gleam, but it was more prominent. The very air around him was peculiar. If she didn't know any better, she would have thought he was a demon because of the way his eyes glowed — which was absurd, since she'd known him for several months now. She'd even tasted his blood. And while it had tasted more diverse than any other human she'd fed from, she could still differentiate demon from human.

She was a vampire, after all. Blood was her life.

She shook her head, hopping to sit on of the elegant wooden dresser. Her feet dangled off the ground and she leaned back against the mirror attached to the piece of furniture.

"What do you make of all of this?" she asked him. These last few days she'd been more focused on her own problems. She hadn't even stopped to see what was going through Marc's mind. Not that she could even if she wanted to. His mind was completely blocked to her.

He lifted a thick eyebrow. She found it frustrating how calm he was. The only time he'd freaked out after everything he'd been through had been back in the cell. Afterwards he'd accepted everything much too casually. In all honesty, it worried her. No human should be so unruffled after facing vicious demons and coming close to death a time or two.

"I think your family is happy to have you home," he said simply, his deep voice rolling over her, making her insides quiver. "They only want to ensure your safety, as do I. However, since I'm an outsider, I understand their reluctance to think twice about me. Besides, I can't hide away here forever. I have a life to get back to. No doubt I'm already causing my coworkers concern over my absence."

Ava stiffened. *Wow.* She'd momentarily forgotten all about his being a cop. Unlike her, he had a life, and she was ruining it.

She hung her head. "I'm sorry, Marc. Dragging you into this is all my fault."

"How so? I volunteered to go check on you that first night, and though I've had plenty of opportunities to run away, I chose to do otherwise—because I wanted to."

She peered up at him suspiciously. "I thought Edith asked you to check up on me that day."

His dimples flashed when those full lips cocked into a half grin. "That wasn't completely true. She asked both Duncan and me, but I insisted on going alone after my shift." He shrugged. "Truth be told, I was planning on going regardless of whether she asked or not."

Ava opened her mouth but no words would come out. She found herself smiling as she shook her head. *This guy.* She couldn't even find it in her to be mad at him for it.

He began to stalk slowly toward her. A lick of desire shot through her at his sexy prowl, making her lower abdomen clench. That walk was much like a feline about to pounce on a canary. And Ava knew with absolute certainty that even as a vampire, she was the canary in the scenario.

"There's no need to be so worried over me," he stated, still gliding toward her. "I can handle myself, love. So long as you're safe, I can return to my life peacefully."

She tilted her head to the side, a ping of sadness running through her. "Aren't you going to miss me a bit?"

"A bit?" With a blinding speed that shocked her, Marc was standing before her, making himself comfortable between her legs. He splayed his hands across her lower back and, with a quick jerk, pulled her against him. She gasped aloud at feeling his erection pressing into her. He buried his face in her neck. "I'm going to miss you a hell of a lot." He brushed his lips across her neck. "It's going to be agonizing going to bed every night without you in my arms." He gave the tender skin a little nip, making her gasp. "Without the taste of you on my tongue."

She tilted her head back as he kissed her neck. "Marc," she breathed, clutching at his shoulders. *Good gods.* Vampires were known to be at the top of the list of the most seductive demons in the world, just under succubae and incubi, but Marc was putting them all to shame. "Now is hardly the time to— Mmmm." Ava let out a soft moan when he began sucking on the sensitive area just below her ear. "I can't think when you're doing that," she breathed.

He nipped at her skin, making her jump in delicious surprise. "Then don't think," he murmured.

She slid her hands beneath the collar of the T-shirt he wore, but she gasped when her palms touched his skin. It was hot to the touch, far warmer than was normal. "Marc, you're burning up. Are you feverish?"

"Yes, but only in the best of ways," he growled, licking a path up to her ear. He began toying with her earlobe with his tongue and teeth, sending wonderful shivers across her skin.

"This isn't normal," she said, breathless. With one hand cupping her ass, he used the other to slip beneath her blouse. "I'm serious." She was concerned for him. His skin felt like a furnace against her palm. She was worried that one of his wounds from the hellhounds had become infected, even if it had somehow healed overnight. After all, their bites and scratches were often lethal for humans if left untreated.

"So am I." Kissing his way back up her cheek, he caught her lips in a scorching kiss that was deep enough to make her toes curl. For just a moment, she tossed sanity out of the window as she melted into him. She hadn't been lying. With just a light touch, he set her body aflame, making her thoughts a jumbled mess.

"Gods," she whispered, rubbing her fingers through his scalp.

There was a low, primal rumbling in his chest and he gripped her thighs in a near bruising grip. "I need you, Ava," he rasped. His temperature was continuing to rise, and it was that concern for him that brought her back to reality.

"Stop," she breathed. Before she lost her nerve to resist him, she pushed him back, gasping in shock as she peered into his eyes. His eyes were burning bright, his pupils narrowed to thin slits.

Taking in her worried expression, Marc pulled back and glanced over her shoulder in the mirror, his eyes widening when he got a good look at himself. "What the fuck?" he murmured, leaning to take a closer look.

There was a sharp knock, and before either of them could utter a word, the heavy wooden door was being pushed open and a very tall male they both recognized stepped inside.

Ava gaped and Marc spun around, his shock evident. "Duncan? What the hell are you doing here?"

Dressed casually in worn jeans, a crisp white T-shirt and a black windbreaker, Duncan grinned, taking in the sight of them. "Am I interrupting something?" There was a great deal of amusement in the deep Scottish drawl.

Ava hopped off the dresser and made her way over to him, frowning. "You know my father?"

He gave a dip of his head. "I am a trusted confidante of his. I didn't know you were the missing princess, so forgive me."

"Wait a damn moment," Marc growled, crossing the floor to stand beside her. "You know about her being a vampire? How?"

Duncan continued to smirk. She'd learned it was his trademark. Just like Marc, the man hardly ever had a straight face. "I've known since the day I met her. Demons can always sense the presence of another demon."

Dumbfounded, Marc looked between both of them with accusing eyes. "Duncan, you're a demon too? Wha— How? Just what the fuck is going on here?"

Okay, so much for his keeping calm, Ava thought wryly. Sensing his building frustration, she placed a gentle hand on his shoulder. "Calm down a moment, Marc." She turned to Duncan. "Just what *exactly* are you doing here? How did you know where we were?"

His dark green gaze met hers, his expression becoming more serious. Just a bit. "For the first time in five years, my partner didn't show up for work, nor did he call in, so naturally I grew worried. I went searching, but I didn't have to look for long. Your father sent me a text. He said your friend is going through the Change, so he wanted to see what I could do to help. It's purely coincidental that you two so happened to be the ones I was looking for."

Ava stiffened. *No way... Can that mean...?*

"Wait! What change?" Marc demanded, frowning.

"You've taken a good look at yourself, haven't you, my friend?" Duncan asked, moving to lean against the door behind him. "If not, surely you can feel the difference in your body."

Marc frowned, rubbing his hand through his hair. *Of course I feel different.* Though he was only in his early thirties, he'd started to feel his age catching up to his body. Not much, but little aches and pains had plagued him in the mornings after a long work day. He was still physically fit, but the pain had sometimes made him realize he wasn't getting any younger.

Now, an incredible buzzing energy was flowing through him, and though his body seemed on fire, he experienced an unbelievable surge of strength. He'd never felt so good in his life, truth be told.

As if reading his thoughts, Duncan nodded. "What you're experiencing is what we wereshifters call the 'Change'."

Marc's frown deepened. "Wereshifters? You mean like werewolves?"

Duncan crinkled his nose in disgust. "They're only one of many different shifters. There are wolves, lions, tigers, bears...oh my." His lips twitched at his own piss-poor humor then continued. "And before you ask, I'm a tiger."

Marc held up his hand, stopping him. He peered at Ava, feeling a headache coming on.

"I don't suppose there's a spare bottle of Scotch in here, is there?" Marc demanded.

Ava gave an uneasy smile, shaking her head. No doubt she was just as confused as he was. He felt a bit betrayed that she hadn't mentioned that Duncan was a demon too, but he couldn't really hold it against her. She had a lot on her plate as it was. Besides, he wouldn't have believed her in the first place. Granted, Duncan had some odd tendencies, like he'd always order his steaks super rare, pretty much not even cooked at all, when they went out to eat. Then again, there were others who had tastes like that, he supposed.

With a deep, exaggerated sigh, he walked over to a large armchair and sat down. Ava and Duncan followed. Duncan sat in the matching chair, while Ava went back to sit atop the dresser. He swallowed a groan. He'd like nothing more than to kick Duncan out of the room and continue where he'd left off with her, but this was more important.

Barely.

"As I was saying," Duncan drawled when he had everyone's attention, "I'm a weretiger. In our world, when a human is bitten or scratched by one of us in our demon form, they are infected with our bacteria and begin to go through the process called the 'Change'. This is the development where a human becomes a were."

Marc gave a slow blink. "I wasn't attacked by either." He gave a lift of his brows. "Unless those hellhounds from last night have the same...bacteria?"

Duncan scoffed. "No, they don't. They're not shifters."

"So how am I going through this Change you speak of?"

Duncan leaned his elbows on his knees. "Normally in our community, only shifters can mate with other shifters. It's nearly impossible to produce children outside of their race. However, in very, very, *very* rare circumstances, it can happen—like, one in every thousand. A shifter is able to mate with a human and give birth to a half-breed child, but the child's demon side remains dormant throughout its entire life unless it is bitten by any other full-blooded demon. When this happens, the mixblood goes through the Change and gains its full demon potential, meaning the ability to shift, faster speed, strength, heightened senses, and"— he leaned back in the chair—"an extended life. You know, the usual perks. The only downside is if the mixblood, like other changelings, cannot control its instincts, it will go crazy"—his gaze slid over to Ava—

"much like the way vampires turn Rogue. They are dangerous and must be put down immediately."

Marc rubbed his temples, not liking where this conversation was going. "What has any of that to do with me?"

His partner peered into his eyes. "Obviously, my friend, it is because you are one of these rare mixbloods."

Marc sighed. Call it his intuition, but somehow, he'd known that was what his partner would say. "Of course I am," he muttered. *Why am I not surprised?* Everything else in his life these last few days should have been impossible, so why not add him being half demon to that list?

Duncan eyed him with interest. "You don't seem particularly shocked."

"Oh, quite the contrary," Marc dragged out, his tone dripping with sarcasm. "I am utterly *gobsmacked.*"

Duncan's lips twitched in clearly suppressed amusement. "Don't you even want to know how long I've known? Or how I figured it out?"

Marc just shrugged, spreading his hands in mock curiosity. "Sure."

"Do you remember that day we were answering a domestic call and the lady's boyfriend caught you in the side with a knife?"

Marc grimaced, touching the old scar just under his rib cage. He'd needed stitches to close the wound, and it had hurt like a bitch. The blade had been a mere inch from slicing through one of his organs.

Duncan continued, "It was faint, but I knew from the scent of your blood that you were half shifter — feline at that."

Wonderful. Just what I wanted to hear. Well, it certainly answered one question he'd wondered growing up. He's always been a bit stronger and faster than everyone else. Also, while he'd met his birth mother, he'd never had any clues to his father's whereabouts. If he was a demon, it didn't surprise him that his father wasn't able to be found. He doubted the demon world kept a database of their own kind, complete with Social Security cards and birth certificates.

Finding out he was part demon was… Well, he didn't know how to feel. Despite his sarcastic words, he really was shocked. He just didn't know how to react.

Am I supposed to freak out? Faint on cue? Deny all of it, hyperventilate and spend the next several days locked in this room thinking about how much I'm a monster?

He gave a humorless snort. He supposed his reaction would have been different had he been told this information days ago, *before* he'd found out demons were real, *before* he'd let one drink his blood and *before* he'd developed a strong attraction to one. He was baffled, but all he could do was accept it.

"So, where do I go from here?" he asked Duncan, leaning back in his chair. "When do these…instincts start to kick in? And how am I supposed to keep them in check?"

Duncan studied him for several moments, his expression unreadable. He was as good at hiding his thoughts as Marc was. It was what made them both great at their job. "You're taking this remarkably well."

Marc only shrugged. "Freaking out will do nothing but make matters worse, right? Not to mention make me look like a fool."

"I suppose so." Duncan was quiet for another few minutes then said, "The first few times you shift into your demon form, you must be under close watch. You will feel a near-uncontrollable hunger, but you must not go overboard. If you fully give in to that bloodlust, you will not be able to return to your human form, and you would be considered feral."

Marc nodded, thinking everything over. He had so many thoughts, so many questions. And yet the only one that would form was—

"How old are you?" Marc demanded.

Duncan's eyebrows lifted on a scoff. "Really? Of all things, that's what you want to know?"

Marc shrugged, tapping his index finger on his jean-clad thigh. "Unfortunately I can't think of anything to really ask other than that." Duncan only continued to look at him in disbelief. Marc wondered if maybe it was considered rude to ask demons how old they were. A rather strange insecurity for them to have, but who was he to judge?

"I have a question," Ava said from her perch on the dresser. She hopped down and made her way over to them.

Just watching her, Marc felt his body hardening. The gentle sway of her hips, the sweet lavender scent of the soap he'd used on her in their bath, mixed in with her own natural essence, filled his mind, making him ache to be buried inside her. He was again struck with the need to kick Duncan out of the room and have her spread naked on the silken sheets on the bed.

And in the tub. And the shower. And on the dresser.

A slow smile curved Duncan's lips as he glanced between the two, no doubt sensing Marc's reaction to her. Every time they'd gone into the diner, his partner had been aware of his attraction to Ava, often encouraging him to make a move before someone else did.

Hell, it wasn't like I didn't try. Breaking through Ava's aloof defenses had been about as easy as strolling into Fort Knox with an AK-47 strapped to his chest. Now he knew why she'd worked so hard to keep him at a distance.

Ava asked, "Most humans who go through the Change don't survive the transition. Sometimes their blood isn't compatible with the disease. Will Marc face that same problem, or does it not affect him since he was born and not turned?"

Duncan gave a helpless lift of his hands. "Mixbloods are still pretty much a mystery to us. As I mentioned, it's an incredibly rare occurrence, and since the majority of mixbloods we do know go through their human lives without being bitten or scratched by a full-fledged demon, they simply continue to age as humans until their life runs out." He shifted his gaze back to Marc. "So, my friend, whatever amount of time you have left, welcome to our world."

Marc became aware of Ava chewing on her nail as she nervously paced the floor. He didn't even have to guess what she was thinking. She was more than likely blaming herself for biting him, for turning him into a demon. Before he could hop up to reassure her anxious mind, there was another sharp knock on the door. A cold prickling washed over Marc's arms, and somehow, he knew it was her brother Lucian. That arrogant bastard's cold power followed him everywhere he went, as if announcing his presence to everyone within thirty yards.

She walked over to the door, and to Marc's surprise, he could hear everything as if he were standing next to her. *This must be one of those perks Duncan mentioned.*

"Do you have a moment?" Lucian asked, his deep voice seeming to echo throughout the room, despite the quiet tones he used. "I'd like to apologize for my actions earlier."

Ava looked over her shoulder and excused herself from Marc and Duncan before stepping out of the room, closing the door behind her. He could feel the two of them walking away, and he felt a near uncontrollable urge to follow. Even just having a mere door separating them felt like they were a thousand miles apart.

Damn it all, he had to get his bearings. He was a lot of things, but clingy was not one of them.

He forced himself to lean back in his seat and meet Duncan's amused look. "What?" he growled.

Duncan's ever-present smirk was in place. "Your attachment to her seems to have increased greatly."

"She saved my life."

"Is that all?"

"Yes."

"No other feelings involved?"

"No."

Duncan's smile turned smug. He made a show of rising to his feet. "Well, I suppose you won't mind if I go ask her to accompany me to dinner. You aren't the only one to notice her beauty, after all."

For a beat, Marc just sat there, dumbfounded, unable to accept that his friend was truly in such a rush to be buried ten feet under. But it was only for a moment. In a flash, Marc pinned his partner of many years to the chair, holding him by the front of his shirt. He glared daggers at the man, baring his teeth. "Stay the fuck away from her."

Smirking as if he'd just proved some point, Duncan held his hands up in surrender. "You got it."

With another frustrated growl, Marc shoved away from him, turning to pace across the vast room. "Damn, I'm sorry," he grumbled, shoving his fingers through his hair. That rage…that possessive, near blinding rage had come out of nowhere, and what was worse, he hadn't been able to contain it in the least bit.

Out the corner of his eye, he noticed Duncan rising to his feet again, casually rolling his big shoulders. *Shit.* Duncan had been his partner and friend for going on five years. He couldn't believe he'd attacked him like that.

"That," Duncan said calmly, "is what I mean by controlling your instincts. You need to learn to or else you will end up attacking the wrong person." He gave him a lazy glare. "You are fortunate I consider you a friend. If not, you would have been dead for putting your hands on me."

Marc winced—not at the subtle threat in his partner's tone, but because he still couldn't believe he'd just assaulted him over a mere taunting. "What do I need to do?"

Duncan folded his arms again. "First things first, you need to leave this place." He paused, hesitating briefly over his next words. "You especially need to get far away from Ava."

Marc stiffened, feeling that rage well up inside him again. His body shook with the effort it took to keep from launching across the room. "What?" he demanded, his fist clenching.

Leave Ava? Yeah, he'd known he couldn't stay here. He hadn't been lying when he'd said he wanted to get back to his regular life. He still loved being a cop, after all. But he hadn't expected the overwhelming pain that created a hole in his chest at the mere thought of leaving her.

Duncan's smug look disappeared, his eyes softening. "The first few weeks during the Change are the most critical. You will experience extremely high levels of hunger, fatigue and" — cue a dramatic pause — "lust, both for blood and sex. However, sating your sexual lust is very dangerous during this time, because if you aren't careful, you'll end up screwing around with someone you have feelings for and you will want to claim them as your mate. And before you deny it, it is abundantly clear you have strong feelings for Ava." He shifted his weight to lean against the heavy armoire at his back. "But claiming someone who may not be ready to return your feelings — or who does not wish to claim you back — will only result in you getting hurt in the long run."

Marc clutched at his chest, feeling like the gaping hole had just widened into a deep cavern. "What does it mean, 'to claim someone'? When she and I...you know...I felt the urge to do so, but I didn't understand it."

"Ahh, then it is good you did not give in," Duncan murmured. "When a shifter wishes to claim a mate, he or she engages in lovemaking with their desired lover. While in this intimate setting, the shifter opens himself completely and imprints on the partner. In other words, bites into them hard enough to draw blood. This bite mark will eventually transform into ancient runes binding you to that person, but if their partner doesn't return the gesture, the mating is incomplete. You will forever be bound to them, unable to take another lover or mate, but they will be free to do so — or vice versa, if it was the other way around." Duncan paused, placing his hand on his forehead in an exasperated way. "Holy mother, I feel like a father giving his son the talk about the birds and the bees."

Marc ignored him and took a seat on the edge of the bed.

He couldn't ignore the fact that he cared for Ava as much more than friends. In all honesty, when he'd first seen her, he'd only been interested in her body. She was beautiful, and he wanted to see that aloof air around her melting underneath his touch. However, as the months passed, he'd begun to realize it was much more than something purely physical. Somewhere down the line he'd become selfish. He wanted her to smile only at him, to laugh at his jokes, to fix those bright, warm eyes on him and him alone. He'd stopped taking lovers. He'd lost all interest in any other female, only wanting her time and attention.

And these last few days he'd spent with her, getting a taste of that exquisite sweetness, being wrapped in her heat while she moaned for him and having her take his very essence into her body, he didn't want to just throw it all away. He wanted Ava all to himself, to become one with her in the most primal of ways, to protect her and show her what it meant to be loved by a man.

Christ, I'm desperate. He could have women far less dangerous than Ava, women who wouldn't have demons running him off the road and trying to eat him. And yet he couldn't allow another to take her place. Just the mere thought was revolting.

Pathetic, pathetic, pathetic.

"I was once in your shoes," Duncan murmured.

Shaking the painful thoughts from his head, Marc peered at his friend.

Duncan nodded.

There was something...distant in those dark green eyes, an old pain Marc had never seen before.

"It gets better over time."

Marc shook his head again. Somehow, he doubted that. Whatever Duncan had gone through obviously still pained him to this day. He just did one hell of a job hiding it. He didn't think something like this would ever get better. Maybe he'd become accustomed to it, but that would be the best he could hope for.

He'd always preferred lovers to girlfriends. With the hours of his job, he hadn't had time to seek romantic relationships. He enjoyed being able to come home to a peaceful house and call up someone for a quick bout of hot, sweaty sex before sending them on their way — no complicated feelings, no petty arguing over nonsense, no worrying over a painful breakup. It was simple, and he loved it.

But without him even realizing it, Ava had become a thorn that had lodged herself deep within his side. They had only made love twice and truly gotten to know each other in a few short days, and yet he found himself wanting her in every possible way. His pain at the thought of leaving her behind was raw, and he didn't like it one bit.

He found these feelings for her were far more frightening than facing any number of hellhounds.

Duncan's heavy hand landed on his shoulder, bringing him out of his musings. His partner's eyes were somber.

"There are many other lovers you can take," he said, as if to make Marc feel better.

It didn't.

"After you have successfully gone through the Change, you will find these feelings fading. They're only this strong because you are still in the beginning stages. The longer you stay away from Ava, the less the pain will become. But you need to fight it, for both of your sakes."

He stiffened. "For both of our sakes?" he demanded, his chest aching.

"Simply put, it could never work out," Duncan said. "I hate to say this to you, but there is no sugarcoating it. Ava is a vampire who happens to be the only daughter of one of the most powerful demons in the world — a king, at that. Her mother is also from a highly conservative fey tribe who has a great number of fey rivals looking to kill them off. The joining of her parents created a child with blood so rare that, without proper protection, she is an easy target to any number of demons. Her very existence is a danger for anyone to be around. It's only under the close supervision of her family here that she can be safe. You, however, are the only thing she is willing to toss that protection aside for. If she does that, then she will only continue to live her life on the run. And believe you me, as strong as I'm sure she is, she is not invincible. Sooner or later her luck will run out, someone will have the upper hand on her and it could prove to be fatal. So if you want to protect her, the best thing you can do is keep your distance. *This* is where she belongs."

Marc clenched his teeth and closed his eyes, inhaling deeply. Duncan was right. As much as he wanted to argue and come up with a different solution, he had to refrain. Ava had already told her brothers and father that she refused to stay if they didn't allow Marc to. And though Marc wanted her all to himself, his desire to protect her was greater than his needs.

He had a lot of work to do. This 'Change' would be just the distraction he needed. Ava was now securely under her family's defense. His mission was complete. He had to focus on himself and work on preventing himself from turning feral, as Duncan had mentioned. After all, he was a demon now — or turning into one, whatever the case was. He should be far more worried over what was going to happen to him from now on.

When he opened his eyes, he made sure his expression was guarded. He gave his friend a stiff nod. "I am in your care."

With a sad, sympathetic look, Duncan nodded in return. "I will go speak with the king before we leave. As I mentioned, your training will take some time. We can both take some vacation from work, and using some of the vamps' charm on our coworkers will help to keep any suspicions away. Three weeks should be sufficient, I hope."

Marc just nodded numbly. In less than a week his normally peaceful, albeit lonely, life had turned completely upside down. He could only imagine how much worse it'd become over the next few weeks.

Chapter Twelve

Sitting on the cold, wooden bench in the private garden on her father's vast grounds, Ava breathed in the crisp fall air. Several yards away was a large lake shimmering under the moonlight, small ripples forming each time a fish breached the surface. Lucian was looking up at the midnight sky, his long lashes nearly brushing his eyebrows.

Thick shadows surrounded them, and Ava could feel the vampire guards hiding in the depths, blending in so much so that if she weren't a vampire herself, she would not have noticed. She had a feeling that with Lucian's power and strength, the protection wasn't needed, but he was a clan chief and the heir to the throne. It was always better to be safe than sorry.

"It's beautiful out here," Ava murmured. It had been many years since she'd been able to enjoy gazing up at the night sky without having to glance around and creep in the shadows. She could never be out in the open for very long, and if she ever let her guard down for just a moment, it would give her enemies enough time to attack.

"Yes, it is," Lucian responded. "You can never see the stars like this in the city."

He'd apologized to her for being an asshole earlier, and she couldn't very well stay mad at him. Vampires had their rules. They only looked out for their own. She knew that, and she shouldn't have been surprised at their reluctance to accept Marc.

Besides, she had the type of heart that couldn't stay mad at anyone she cared about for long.

"Do you remember back in Italy at father's estate, you used to lie under the stars for hours and no one could find you?"

A nostalgic smile curved Ava's lips. "Everyone used to scold me all the time for that."

Lucian smiled as well, something he didn't do very often. "It scared the hell out of me. We were always afraid you'd wandered off in the nearby mountains and gotten lost or worse. The mountains have tunnels running through them, and as curious as you were, no doubt you would have stumbled into them and *really* gotten lost."

"Well, truthfully, I did get lost more often than not," she admitted, chuckling at the glare he sent her out of the corners of his eyes. "But I was never worried because I knew eventually one of you would find me."

A companionable silence descended, and Ava found her stress melting away bit by bit. She was still pretty damn nervous being around her family, but they'd done their best to make her as comfortable as possible, treating her as if she was still one of them. For this moment in time, she was happy.

Her mind wandered back to Marc. He was a mixblood, Duncan had said. There was very little knowledge on them among shifters and even less for her. All she had was her own experience to go by and the memories of the people she touched.

No doubt Marc was confused, worried and stressed, but she was relieved Duncan was there for him. Marc had the best teacher in the world to train him on his newfound powers.

She just hoped she hadn't ruined his life by being the demon to bite him and bring forth those powers. It was bad enough she'd opened his eyes to the demon world. Now he was a part of it due to his blood — all because of her.

"Ava," Lucian said, pulling her from her thoughts, "tell me again about the vision you had when you ran into Mikhail."

She stiffened at his words. *Does he really doubt me after all?* "Why?" she demanded.

He continued looking up at the stars. "I believe there is more to it than you might remember. And since Mikhail has been after you for this long, we will need to know every possible detail to find out where he's hiding so we can bring an end to...whatever he's plotting."

Ava turned back to stare at the lake. "I told you what I remember, and I certainly don't know anything about where he's hiding. He's only ever sent people after me rather than fetch me himself. Not a lot to go on there."

He paused for a moment, as if considering his next words. "Those two Rogues you fought last night... Did they not seem different to you?"

It was her turn to pause. She turned to meet his silvery gaze. "You sensed it too?" she breathed.

He nodded. "In the last few months, there has been an increase of the number of Rogues in Chicago. It isn't rare for them to be in a large city like that, but in the last several decades, Rogues have become less and less common. I do not tolerate them leaving a mess in my city. However, all of a sudden it is like they are crawling from nowhere. Only, these newer Rogues have been very much like the two from last night. They're smart. They actually seem to have a working brain that isn't solely focused on killing. I have a suspicion that all of this can't be a coincidence."

Ava frowned in realization. "You believe they might be the new race Mikhail wanted to create?"

"It's just a feeling, but yes. My hunters have been investigating the matter for a while now, but we have no leads." His gaze slid to hers. "Until now."

Ava's heart lurched, worry clenching her chest. "What do you need me to do?"

He sat up straight, turning to face her on the bench. "Close your eyes. I want you to see that night you ran into Mikhail, the sights, the scents, the sounds— everything. Even the smallest detail could reveal a clue."

She hesitated a moment, crossing her arms over her stomach. "What if I don't see anything? I won't be of any help," she whispered.

He gave her a small smile. To anyone else it may have looked cold, but she knew he meant it as a reassurance. He was a man who didn't often show expressions. He gave a playful tug on a loose strand of her hair. "It's okay if you don't, *piccolina*. Either way, we will find him and stop him. Just having you here with us is more than enough help, not to mention we're all just glad to have you back home. I promise that no matter if you do or don't see something, it won't change the way we feel for you a single bit."

She worried her lip for a few minutes before at last giving a nod. "I'll try my best." Knowing full well she'd been manipulated, she smiled then straightened on the bench and closed her eyes. *Deep inhales, slow exhales.* She did everything she could to clear her mind, to summon the memory of that night so many years ago. It had been so long it that took minutes before fuzzy details began to form.

She pulled off the thin leather glove she'd put on after returning to her bedroom with Marc. Though touching others allowed her to see their memories, if she concentrated enough, she was able to send her own to someone the same way. Her father had taught her how to do it decades ago when he'd helped her control her powers, and though she hadn't practiced much at it since then, she still remembered the steps. She held Lucian's big, cold hand in her bare one and unlocked her powers, focusing enough to send one particular memory to him.

It was a few hours after midnight, and the streets of that area of London were dark and silent. Ava had just finished feeding and sent a human on her way, charming her to ensure she went straight home to rest. Now it was time for Ava to retire to her own hideout. Dark storm clouds blocked out the night sky, and she could smell the oncoming rain. The bright flashes of lightning told her that it would be a bad storm. She wanted to hurry up and return before getting caught in the nasty weather.

She raced down the alleys, using her speed to blend in with the shadows and stay out of sight lest more bounty hunters came looking for her. She was moving so fast that she didn't even see the side door of what looked like an old building being opened, and three men walked out. Before she could halt in time, she rammed into the one in the middle and they both tumbled to the ground. His smell was familiar, and she knew right away he was a vampire. The sudden chill in the air was always a sign.

In the entanglement, Ava caught a flash of his memories.

There was a large room filled with the scent of death and blood. She nearly gagged on the smell alone, but when she saw the sight, all she could do was watch in horror. There was a small mountain of bodies being burned — some human, some vampire. They were all dead. She could hear a familiar male voice saying, "It's time for a change. The dawn of a new race is approaching." *The image disappeared, and another flashed before her. But...it was so fast she couldn't catch it. She jumped up and backed away from the man, crying. He rose to his feet and turned to her, and she could see his face clearly. It was Mikhail Nilsen.*

Ava backed away, apologizing over and over. He only smiled at her, but it did nothing to hide the stark coldness in his eyes. She was terrified. He was going to kill her. But then he bowed and let her to move past him. Without hesitation, she took off running, trying to get very far away from him. However, it wasn't long before she realized the three of them were chasing her. It was only thanks to the rain washing away her trail that she was able to elude them.

"That's good, Ava," Lucian said softly. "I know this is hard, but let's go back to the scenario you saw. The first one disappeared, and a new one appeared. Pause the image in your mind and try to focus on it."

Ava's brows furrowed, a shiver racing down her spine. "I-I can't. It was too fast."

"You can," he encouraged. "When that second scene flashed, you saw something, but you were so afraid of touching him that you forgot what the memory was. Whatever it was, it is a vital piece to this puzzle."

As Lucian continued his gentle coaxing, she replayed the scenario in her mind. She'd spent years blocking it from her brain, trying to banish the image of burning bodies, the revolting scent of death choking the air. It was a sight that had given her nightmares long after she ran away.

She thought about all the innocent people who had been killed and would continue to die because of Mikhail, and she sucked in a deep breath.

She called on the image in her mind, willing it to come into focus. It was like trying to look out of a window smeared with Vaseline. All she could make out were blobs of colors. She focused harder, willing the image to become clear. For a while, all she could see was the same blurriness, followed by muffled voices in the distance.

After what seemed like an eternity of straining, the image rippled, similar to the effect of a rock being thrown in water. The blurriness slowly began to fade, and she was soon looking through Mikhail's eyes.

The smell of fear was so thick it was near tangible. A woman's sobs filled the air. She was screaming in pain, begging Mikhail to stop. She let out another ear-shattering shriek, and the vision cleared.

A once-beautiful fey woman, a siren, was chained to a bed with iron shackles. There were several IVs attached to different parts of her body, all drawing blood from her. Her skin was a sickly gray from the blood loss. Tears ran from her dull violet eyes as she sobbed, straining against her bonds. "Damn you, Mikhail!" she cried, her voice hoarse from hours and hours of screaming.

There was a small chuckle and Mikhail moved closer toward the woman. He stroked a loving finger along her hollowed cheekbone. She shrank away, but it did not help. She was trapped.

"Don't be like that, darling," Mikhail purred. "It won't be too much longer. You should be happy knowing your blood birthed a new breed of vampires. Well, your daughter's will, actually. Yours will merely be a jumpstart." His hand shifted to cup her chin in a painful grip. "Now tell me, Lila, where is she?"

The woman bared her teeth, her eyes filling with hatred. "I'll never tell you, bastard. If you lay one finger on her, not even death can save you from my wrath."

"We'll just see about that, dear," he chuckled, turning away from her.

The image returned to colorful blobs, and a split second before the memory vanished, Ava could hear Mikhail murmur, "Just you wait, Cyrus. It's time for a change."

Ava opened her eyes slowly, feeling them sting with tears. That woman... She'd never seen her before, but it was as if Ava could feel her pain like it was her very own. Her heart was pounding in her chest and she gulped in deep breaths of the chilly night air to erase the scent of death and fear.

Lucian murmured something in Latin, pulling his hand away from hers. He shook his head and turned to her with a small smile. "Thank you, Ava. You were very strong for that. I'll go relay this to father, while you describe the image of Lila to Julius for him to draw. Do you think you can do that?"

She nodded, still thinking of that poor woman trapped on the bed. She didn't know how long the woman had been imprisoned, but Mikhail had been using her blood to create a new race of vampires. She wondered if he'd somehow been using it to make all of the Rogues, but if that were the case, then how? And what was special about the woman's blood that made him choose *her*? Or her daughter, for that matter? Had he ever found the daughter in question, and if so, was that why the Rogues seemed so...controlled?

She shook her head and stood to follow Lucian. There were far too many questions that didn't have any answers, but she was determined to find out. Mikhail had hurt a lot of people and was going to continue doing so unless they stopped him.

* * * *

Cyrus eyed the image of the woman in the picture, rubbing his chin.

Ava watched in silence, her brothers once again sitting around the private library. They'd been given copies of the drawing and they were all studying it.

"Lila..." Cyrus murmured to himself. "She looks familiar." He peered up at Ava, who sat in between Lucian and Andreas on one of the couches. "Do you recognize her?"

Ava shook her head in denial, and he frowned even more, turning his attention back to the picture.

Darius held a crystal goblet of blood in one hand, the picture in the other. "So, if her blood is the key to creating these...Rogues, how is it possible? Fey are magical demons, not gods."

"Not all fey," Cassander murmured. "Sirens are rumored to have life- and death-defying abilities."

Salvator gave him a dry look. "Really, Cass? I would have expected such foolishness from one of the twins—"

"Hey!" said twins cried in outrage.

"But not from you. You're usually the sensible one," Salvator continued.

Cass shrugged, rolling his big shoulders and threatening to rip apart the tight black shirt he wore. "It was a serious statement."

"Sirens died out centuries ago."

"It's possible Mikhail managed to obtain one."

"Possible, but not likely." Sal took a deep sip of his goblet of blood.

"Actually," Cyrus cut in, "Cassander might be right."

Cass raised an eyebrow. "I am?"

At the same time Sal said, "He is?"

Cyrus put the photo down on the coffee table and leaned back in his seat. "A long time ago, when Lucian was just a child..." he paused, turning a glare on one of the twins when he made a choked laugh. "What the hell is so funny?"

Julius grinned. "When Lucian was a child, they'd just learned to make a wheel out of stone." Darius and Andreas snickered at that, eliciting a middle finger from Lucian. If Ava wasn't so wound up, she would have been giggling along with them. It wasn't so much that they were funny, but something about their asinine jokes and getting under Lucian's skin was rather amusing.

"As I was saying," Cyrus said, a hint of annoyance in his tone, "my first mate Camilla was friends with several different fey, a few of whom were sirens. They indeed possessed many shocking abilities that regular fey do not have. However, when the demand for their power came to a high peak, they were hunted down and slaughtered until they disappeared completely. Nevertheless, Camilla was still in contact with a few of them, but for their sake, she never spoke of it. Before I promoted Mikhail as my second, rumors began of sirens being seen, and it piqued his interest. He spent many years tracking down the sources of these rumors, but it was never confirmed or denied if they were true. So it is entirely possible he managed to find one. This Lila, however... I don't so much remember her, per se, but she looks eerily similar to one of Camille's friends at one time. Aurelia, I believe, was her name—or something like that. She could be a descendant."

It would be simple to confirm whether or not she truly looked like whoever her father mentioned by peeking into his memories, but she preferred to avoid skin contact with Cyrus at all costs. In his vast number of years, he'd experienced so much sorrow, had seen so much death and destruction and had even caused it on several occasions. He'd killed thousands of his enemies and had come close to death a handful of times. Though he was a master at hiding his emotions, Ava knew from experience that there was a world of darkness and pain in her father's mind. He was a great king and loving father, but he'd endured more hardships than anyone else she'd ever encountered.

And while he was one of the few demons who were able to block her empath powers, she had still caught glimpses of his past every now and then when she'd lived with him. 'Purging' was what her brothers had called the results that followed. She'd lock herself away for several weeks until she was able to clear the darkness that had entered her mind, learning to cope with it.

While her powers were handy, for the most part, they were a double-edged sword. She could see into someone else's mind, but she ended up feeling their every emotion as if it were her own. And for her to touch someone like Cyrus, who was constantly filled with dark energy, the repercussions would send her into a deep depression that remained until her powers could filter it out of her body.

So yeah, she loved her father dearly, but he was one person whose memories she'd rather continue avoiding if she could help it. Her brothers were no better.

"Well," Sal huffed, "I stand corrected. So if—and this is a big if—Mikhail managed to capture one of these magical sirens and has been using her blood to create a new form of Rogues, why now? Ava ran into him and saw his memories almost a century ago. It's been a significant amount of time since he captured that woman and used her blood. So why has he only waited until now to begin unleashing Rogues? And how has her blood lasted so long?"

There was a pause among the group before Andreas spoke softly. "Well, for one, he said her blood was only going to jumpstart his plans and that he was looking for her daughter. Maybe the daughter is who he really needed. And he must have found her if he's only now letting the Rogues out."

Julius shook his head. "Or gotten Lila pregnant." When people started to glare at him for making yet another ridiculous statement, he raised his hands defensively. "No, seriously. Think about it. What better way to continue using siren blood, without worrying over one dying, when you can continue to make more? I mean, it's sick as hell, but who am I to understand the inner workings of a psychopath?"

Ava felt a chill down her spine at the mere thought. Mikhail forcing himself on the poor woman to impregnate her? *Gods...* She hoped that wasn't the case. It was enough to make her tremble in revulsion.

There was a knock at the door and Marc and Duncan entered. Ava felt a flare of heat race through her body at the sight of Marc. He was wearing faded jeans and a hoodie, but he was still sexy enough to make her tingle with desire.

Instead of returning her hungry gaze, he stared at the ground, his expression unreadable. His body language was stiff, and immediately she knew he was...upset. Even if she couldn't see his face, she could feel his sadness pulling at her.

The two men strolled in the room and Duncan bowed his head to all of them, his accent thick when he spoke. "Thank you for having us. I've come to inform you we'll be taking our leave now."

Ava frowned, rising to her feet. "You're leaving? Both of you?"

Duncan turned an easy smile on her, one that didn't quite reach his eyes. "Yes. We have a lot of training to do since Marc is changing."

She fiddled with her hands. "But, what if someone tries —?"

"Don't worry, lass. I will be with him in case any danger comes his way."

"Yes, Duncan is a rather skilled warrior," Cyrus reassured her. "Your friend is in good hands."

Ava swallowed hard. "But...will you return after the Change is complete?"

Duncan's eyes softened. "There is no need. He has brought you home. After his transformation, he will be free to return to his life before...this."

Marc refused to meet her eyes, making her heart throb. He was leaving, just like that. No goodbye, no hug...

She gave a bitter laugh inside. *Well, why should he?* Because of her, he'd been knocked unconscious, held chained in a cell, beaten by ghouls, run off the road, ruined his car and to top it all off, her drinking from him had awakened his demon blood and now he was turning into a shifter.

So yeah, why on earth should he want me anywhere near him? Sure, they'd made bone-melting, delectable love twice and shared an intimacy she was sure no other man would ever be able to compete with, but that had been before he'd found out the truth of his heritage. It wouldn't surprise her if he wanted nothing more to do with her. She had ruined his human life.

Knowing that, it still hurt, like a poison-tipped dagger stabbed into her chest. It was a slow pain that spread all throughout her chest.

Accepting that there was nothing she could say or do to change a thing, she gave a stiff nod, lowering her gaze to the floor. "Best of luck to you, Marc," she murmured. She sat back down between her brothers, the ache in her chest growing bigger with every moment.

"Thanks," was all he said, his tone matching hers. She looked up to see him turning away.

Duncan's own gaze was rueful, but he faced her father. "If you wish, I will send updates on his progress."

"Yes, do that," her father murmured. "Also, if you happen across any Rogues, please notify me at once."

Duncan placed his fist over his heart and gave a deep bow before exiting the room. The door pulling shut behind him echoed in her mind, so loud he may as well have slammed it with all his strength. Her heart gave another painful lurch.

That was it. Marc was gone.

It was for the best, she supposed. That was her usual lie, and she was still sticking to it.

Jeez, why am I sad anyway? Sure, she'd been attracted to him since the first day, and yes, she'd come to care for him on a deep level, but it wasn't like there had been anything more than that. They weren't dating, and they weren't committed in any way. They were just two people who'd made the best of a shitty situation, and now they had to go their separate ways.

Besides, with him going through the Change, he'd be susceptible to his sexual lusts, sating his needs with whatever female was willing. She would be no more than a passing memory in his life.

It's for the best.

It is.

Even as she thought it, however, she had a feeling that it would be years before her heart decided to move on.

Careful not to touch her skin, even though she was wearing a light jacket and gloves, Andreas pulled her in for a hug, patting her on the back. "It's okay, sis. Forget that guy. There are plenty of fish in the sea."

"Or plenty of shifters in the pack," Darius drawled.

Lucian growled at him in warning, but despite the pain she was in, Ava found herself laughing. She pulled away from Andreas, chuckling as she wiped at her burning eyes. "You really are an idiot," she said to Darius. Then she gave him a small smile. "Thank you. I'll be fine. We have more important things to worry about, right?"

Darius nodded, a pleased smile forming on his handsome face. She had a feeling he and Julius said nonsensical things in an attempt to ease the delicate air surrounding them.

When Ava relaxed in her seat, she sent her father a nod. He was watching her with worried eyes. He nodded in return.

"In order to get to the bottom of this, I want you all to use your connections to do some digging, starting tomorrow morning. Lucian, your hunters are already investigating the Rogue attacks in the city. Make sure to update them on what exactly to be looking for. Sal and Cass, your clubs have a large number of demons who attend every night. Use your words cautiously and see if you can discover any whispers on the whereabouts of Mikhail, sirens, Rogue nests or anything relating to this case. Andreas, take a hunter and return to the area where you all found Ava last night. Search for any clues and trace the scent to where the Rogues and hellhounds came from. Darius and Julius?" The twins perked their heads up, eager to receive their special mission. "Just…stay the hell out of trouble."

Their mouths dropped open, as if they'd just received the gravest of insults.

Cyrus continued, ignoring their sputtering protests. "I will send out word to my own informants to do some investigating. Whatever any of you find, make sure to keep the rest of us updated. And please be safe."

Having received their orders, everyone nodded. Ava leaned forward. "What about me?"

There was a brief pause, and everyone looked around, clearly puzzled.

"Is that a genuine question?" Cassander demanded. "It's too dangerous for you to be out and about during this time."

Ava twitched in annoyance. "That doesn't mean I can't be helpful. Hello? The power to see the memories of anyone I touch? If we come across some Rogues—"

"Out of the question," Lucian said, his tone cold. "Cass is right. We only *just* got you back. None of us are in a rush to risk losing you again."

"Well, I don't want to sit around twiddling my thumbs all the damn day," she said, rising to her feet. She knew she probably looked ridiculous, but since she was surrounded by men who were all over six feet tall and well-muscled, standing over them made her feel a little empowered. She placed her hands on her hips, glaring at them all. "I know you're only looking out for me, but I can fight my own battles. I've been doing it for a century, for the gods' sake."

"Yes, and whose fault was that to begin with?" Andreas demanded. "We only want to ensure your protection, Ava."

Ava winced, guilt slicing through her. She was silent for several moments. "Look," she said at last, sitting back on the couch. If she continued acting like a child, they would continue treating her like one. Even being absent for nine decades hadn't changed their fierce protectiveness over her. That, and they were all stubborn as hell. They were vampires, after all. Gordano vampires, at that.

But then again, so was she. She forced her tone to remain calm. "All of you in this room are mighty warriors, feared by thousands of demons and have been for centuries. Do you mean to tell me that you are incapable of protecting me outside these walls? Yes, it was my own decision, but I *have* managed to stay alive for this long. I'm not nearly as inadequate as you seem to think. I'm as much a part of this as the rest of you."

She let out another breath, her tone shrinking to a plea. "I can't just sit around doing nothing." She'd just spend all day thinking about Marc. She didn't say it aloud, but they all knew the hidden words. "So please..."

Call her conniving, but there was nothing like a soft whine and well-executed puppy-dog eyes to move her oh-so-hardened brothers. A few of them repositioned themselves in their seats. Even the all-powerful king of vampires glanced away, closing his eyes in a clear attempt not to give in. All through her teens up until she'd left, she'd always used 'the look' on her brothers to guilt them into doing what she'd wanted. She hadn't thought it would work after all this time, but it was.

Just for an even more dramatic effect, she forced tears to her eyes. She looked at the man who had always been the most vulnerable to her pleading look. "Dad, please," she whispered, forcing her voice to break.

Cyrus brought his fist to his mouth, clenching his teeth around his knuckles. He was resisting her expression, she knew. Still, she could tell it wouldn't last long.

Five. Four. Three. Two.

His gaze met hers, and whatever resolve he had left crumbled. He heaved an exacerbated sigh, shaking his head ruefully. "Very well, *cara*, you win. You can join the twins in their search. That way, I'm sure you can keep them out of trouble. However, if you get a lead or if you are attacked, do not wander off on your own."

Hiding her triumphant grin, Ava gave an eager nod, ignoring Lucian's groan of frustration. Even Sal and Cass looked displeased. As the three eldest brothers, they all had a relentless desire to protect their younger siblings. Even if most times they didn't show it on the outside, it was evident.

As she glanced around at each of them, her heart gave another painful clench. She forced the ache to the back of her mind. No, she wouldn't have to keep looking over her shoulder, and yes, she'd be able to get a good night's sleep without waking up every hour for fear of an intruder, but having something, *anything*, to keep her mind off of Marc was welcomed.

Now, if only she could make the hole in her heart disappear.

Chapter Thirteen

"Mommy, why are you crying?"

The woman kneeling on the floor jerked her head up, her limp blonde hair falling in her face. Her eyes were red and swollen, and makeup streaked down her face from her tears. When she glanced up at the child, her eyes grew wide with horror. She pointed a shaking finger at him. "Stay away from me, demon!" she yelled. "I hate you! I hate you!"

When the child took a hesitant step forward, the woman's eyes grew wider.

She threw her head back and yelled at the top of her lungs. She reached for a knife lying beside her on the floor and began frantically slicing at her wrists and forearms. The child covered his ears, his own tears forming. He ran back into his own room, hiding his small body under his bed. He squeezed his eyes shut, but nothing he could do would block out the sounds of his mother's wailing.

With a deep, desperate gasp of air, Marc shot out of the twin-sized bed beneath him, clutching his dry throat. He was forever tormented by that same dream, a small fragment of memory from his damaged childhood ages ago. He couldn't recall who his father was, but he remembered his mother. He'd always thought she'd been in a panic due to her addiction to drugs, always calling him a demon. Now he knew better. She'd been terrified of him, even though he'd been a human at the time.

Marc shook his head, sucking in gulps of air to cool down his body.

He was on fire. Everything burned. His very skin felt like it was sweltering from the inside out. He squeezed his eyes shut for fear they would pop out under the intense heat. It was as if he'd drunk an entire gallon of gasoline and swallowed a lit match while standing under a shower of acid.

It had been a little over two weeks since he'd begun his transformation, and with each day, the pain became increasingly worse. His body ached. His head was pounding. Every twitch of his muscles sent a searing hot pain through his veins. His very blood felt like lava flowing through him.

Good…God! This was only the beginning. He howled in pain, feeling another burst of heat streak through him.

At the sound of approaching footsteps, he looked up at his friend, who was watching him with somber eyes.

"Wa…Water," Marc rasped, reaching out a hand to Duncan.

Duncan moved forward, holding a bottle of water, having already known what he needed. Marc downed half of it in one swallow, then poured the rest of it over his head. To his chagrin, the icy water did nothing to ease the burning ache, and Marc threw the empty plastic bottle across the room in frustration.

"Shit, how...much longer...before...this is over?" Marc demanded, panting between words.

Duncan leaned against the wall. The dark chamber was just a step above a jail cell, with thick stone walls and floors, a small barred window letting in the rays of the setting sun, a plain twin-sized bed bolted to the floor and a connecting bathroom with a shower and toilet. Even the door separating him from the rest of the house was made of thick steel, making it impossible for him to escape.

Not that he was a prisoner, but Marc was being kept in this room for his own sake. They were far across the state in spacious private land, the nearest town miles away. If Marc happened to get free during this time and ran off unsupervised, he'd feel the urge to attack anyone crossing his path. And killing humans without just cause was an even bigger no-no in the demon world than it was in the human world.

Damn Ava for awakening my powers. Not that she'd known or that he regretted her biting him, but still... He needed something to pin the blame on.

At the mere thought of Ava, his body hardened, his muscles bunching beneath his skin as a fierce need to seek her out shook him to his core. He wanted — no, *needed* — her to be lying beneath him while he punished her for causing him this pain — punish and punish and punish her over and over again with his mouth and cock. He was desperate to be inside her, to feel her heat surrounding him, to be wrapped in her sweet scent as she took his blood while he pounded away at her.

"Fuck!" he groaned, pacing the length of the room. He ached everywhere as it was. He didn't need a straining erection plaguing him as well.

He didn't even care that Duncan was standing just a few feet away, well aware of what was happening to him. And the bastard was taking great amusement in watching him suffer, judging by the smirk curving his mouth.

"I would tell you to relax, but that wouldn't help you, would it?" Duncan remarked.

Marc glared at him. "If I kick your teeth down your throat and tell you to smile, would you?"

Duncan's cocky grin only widened. "Fair enough. I believe that's your inner demon talking. How do you feel?"

What the hell kind of stupid question is that? His very blood was on fire, he was starving, his head felt like it was about to split open and, worst of all, he wanted to be buried balls-deep inside a woman who was more than three hundred miles away. "Fucking fantastic," he growled.

"I can sense your demon forming beneath the surface. It's nearly complete, and once it is, you will be able to shift. Afterward, I will allow you to leave these rooms and show you how to hunt. Is there anything you need?"

Marc continued his pacing, his tone just a pitch above a growl. "Food and Ava."

Duncan shifted to move toward the door. "Food will be brought to you shortly. As far as handling your...other needs, I can have women brought here. They are succubae, so you will not harm them no matter how...rough things get."

Marc stopped and pointed a shaking finger at his friend. "Do not bring any female other than Ava anywhere near me. No matter how much worse this shit gets, I refuse to touch another until this is over."

Duncan's jaw clenched as he regarded his friend with narrowed eyes. "Do not be so stubborn. You will only cause yourself more pain."

"So be it." Marc refused to back down. He didn't want another woman, damn it. Though he was annoyingly erect like a horny teen with a constant stiffy, he wanted one woman and one woman only. It didn't even matter if his body thought otherwise. Until he was done with this Change and he could confirm where his feelings were when it came to Ava, he would not give in.

He thought about the way she'd looked at him when he'd last seen her. She had been hurt, he knew. He could almost feel her pain. Or had that been his own? It was hard to tell. He hadn't even had the balls to speak to her. If he had, he wouldn't have been able to walk away.

Besides, she was back home with her family where she belonged. She was safe. If he never got to see her again, at least he could move on knowing she was well protected from her enemies. He could go back to living his peaceful life before he'd gotten entangled in her mess, albeit with demon powers. They would both be happy and move on with their separate lives, forgetting each other soon enough.

He gave a sharp bark of laughter. *Yeah right.* There was no way in freaking hell he'd ever forget her. She was... She was a precious part of him he didn't want to live without.

With another growl of frustration, he entered the bathroom and turned the shower on as cold as it could go. In one tug he had his clothes ripped off and stood under the icy spray of the water.

Too bad it did nothing at all to chase away the scorching heat still flooding his veins.

* * * *

Sitting in the back seat of the stylish black SUV belonging to one of the twins, Ava clutched her ears, failing to block out Darius' and Julius' god-awful duet of a forever-popular Journey song.

Blessed gods above, what has she ever done in her life to deserve such excruciating misery? No amount of burns, whips or beatings could come close to this amount of torment. For hours and hours on end as the twins drove her around, they belted out songs at the tops of their lungs. It didn't matter how much she begged, they just wouldn't shut the hell up. It was a wonder her ears weren't bleeding.

They hit a note in unison, sounding similar to alley cats screeching in the night.

Ava threw herself onto the seats, praying to every god she'd ever heard of to just end her life now.

Let lightning strike her down. Let a meteor slam into her. Or let a cosmic laser beam from thousands of light years away disintegrate her to mere ashes. She could take it.

Her father was a very, very cruel man for sticking her with these two morons for the past weeks. If she had to hear one more minute of their horrible bellowing, or ill-conceived jokes, or who could belch the longest… Well, they were going to end up on the demon world's version of *The First 48*.

Much to her relief, the car *finally* rolled to a stop. The second she heard the switch of the locks, she threw the door open and fell onto the pavement in her haste to get out.

Thank the gods, thank the gods.

Every day with them had been torture. One day they had belted out songs that hadn't even been playing on the radio! They had been singing a capella. The next day they'd played ridiculous road trip games that had no rules and made no sense. The next they'd quoted entire movie scripts, then they'd begun singing again.

It was excruciating. They were two peas in one underdeveloped pod.

"Wow, Ava, you should be more careful," Julius chided, stretching his limbs. "You almost busted your ass on the concrete."

"Yeah, what's your rush?" Darius asked, coming around the truck to stand with them. "The building isn't going anywhere."

She glared daggers at the two of them and brushed herself off as she straightened. She growled an Italian curse.

They shared a look of exaggerated horror. "That is anatomically impossible, sis," Julius rasped, "not to mention very inappropriate language for a young lady."

Ava just rolled her eyes.

She took back what she'd said weeks ago. She'd much, much rather have stayed home with her father doing nothing. That would be far more preferable than sitting another moment trapped in a vehicle with those two howling banshees. She shivered in distaste.

As the days had passed, Ava had grown closer to her family, though she was still a bit wary. It wasn't that they didn't make her feel welcome. Everyone did their best to make sure she was comfortable. They chatted and caught up on the years, laughed and joked around a few times. Even Cassander, who usually spent all his time locked away in his lair, had spent several hours each day at their father's mansion. But after she'd spent so many years alone, it was hard to suddenly accept having people to lean on. At this point, it was just natural for her to be cautious, not to mention that everywhere she went, she could feel someone watching her as if they were afraid she'd run off in the middle of the night again.

They'd made very little progress in their search for answers, too. There had been no whispers of sirens among the demons who frequented everyone's businesses, and though plenty had noticed a rise in the number of Rogues, no one knew where they were coming from. Andreas had spent the last several days tracking down the scents of the Rogues who'd attacked her and Marc, but they had led him in circles all over the city and far into the countryside. He had been on the move ever since, only sending updates every few hours.

She, Julius and Darius had ventured all through Chicago, scouting every abandoned warehouse, home and building for a clue. Though Rogues could be Royal, Aristocratic or Turnblood, one thing they had in common was their inability to travel in daylight. They slept during the day and only came out to hunt at night. So if there were any hiding about in the city, they would choose somewhere permanently dark to remain until the sun set. It was why she and her two brothers did their searching during the day. On the off chance they stumbled upon a nest of them, they had the sun as their greatest weapon and means of escape.

It was a good thing they were thoroughly prepared to beat the heat with several bags of blood in a hidden cooler in the truck. They were Royals, but they were still drained by the rays of the sun if they remained out too long without sustenance.

With her favorite silver dagger tucked at her hip and another one strapped around her ankle, she followed behind her brothers as they made their way into the latest warehouse on the outskirts of the city. The parking lot was old, with several areas of the pavement cracked and damaged. The surrounding ten-foot-high chain fence was rusted, with 'no trespassing' signs adorning it. That was never a good sign.

Pun intended.

Ava gave a wry snort at her wit. She was obviously spending too much time with the twins if their ridiculous jokes were rubbing off on her.

The three of them approached the bolted gate.

"Oh, well, the sign says 'do not enter'," Darius murmured sarcastically. "I suppose all we can do is heed the warning and go home."

Ava let out a long-suffering sigh. "Must you do this at every stop we make?" Honestly. It was like they were in a constant competition to see who could be the most annoying.

"Blame Father," Darius remarked, grinning. The twin always had a freaking smile on his face. When he spoke, she'd occasionally catch the glint of metal from a tongue piercing. "He dropped us on our heads a few times as babes."

Julius nodded in agreement, pointing to a non-existent scar on the side of his shaved head. "Indeed. It's why I have this scar here."

Ava rolled her eyes, reminding herself to give her father a tongue lashing when she saw him again. He'd told her to keep them out of trouble, but if not for her everlasting amount of patience, she would have throttled them both by now.

She bent her knees and used her strength to jump over the fence, careful not to touch the barbed wire. She landed in a crouch on the other side then straightened to face the building.

It was evident that the warehouse on the outskirts of town had been unoccupied for a significant amount of time. A large, two-story crumbling mass of bricks, it was a wonder it hadn't collapsed yet. The broken windows were all boarded shut, the old red bricks faded nearly white with graffiti tagged on them. Vines and weeds crawled up the walls, and with a shudder, Ava tried her best not to think about how many rodents and other creepy crawlies were in there.

In her opinion, Rogues were like cute hamsters compared to big, hairy spiders. Even vampires were allowed to be afraid of the eight-legged monstrosities. She couldn't be the only one.

Darius and Julius landed on either side of her. The sun was shining bright, giving a minimum amount of warmth in the chilly fall air. She breathed in a deep breath, unable to sense any surrounding dangers. Even still, one couldn't be too careful when dealing with Rogues. They were demented, but they weren't stupid. They were lethal predators who used the darkness to their advantage.

Ava's hands were encased in thick leather gloves. After years and years of practice, she was able to control her telepathic abilities, but she wasn't perfect. When her emotions happened to get out of control, so did her powers. She was still very young by vampire standards, after all. She was a long way away from mastering her powers like Lucian, Cass and Sal. Hell, even the twins and Andreas were able to wield theirs perfectly, and they were closer to her in age—not to mention she was only a half-breed, so her power had its limitations.

"Okay, you know what to do," Ava said to them. "Let's split up and meet inside. If you see something, yell."

She and Darius began moving forward but stopped at Julius' halting hand. For once, his expression was serious.

"What is it?" Darius demanded, raising his nose to test the air. Ava did likewise, but again, she couldn't sense anything out of the ordinary—just stale old air and rotted wood.

"There are no animals," Julius said.

Darius stiffened and Ava paused in confusion. Then she froze when realization hit her.

Julius' special power was his ability to command animals of all sizes. The last dozen warehouses and abandoned buildings they'd ventured to had all had some kind of animal inside. Whether they were rats, bats or birds, Julius had been able to sense them all. But for this one to not have any of the sort, that meant there was something in there the animals were afraid to be around.

Ava had a feeling in her gut that she knew what it was.

Wrapping her fingers around the hilt of the dagger at her hip, she faced the building. "What do we do?"

Darius pulled out his phone and began tapping away at the screen. "I'm going to send the others a text to let them know we may have found something."

"Great. Then what?"

A second later, his phone vibrated with an incoming text message. "Well, we have two options. One, we can follow Lucian's orders to stay outside and wait on our dear brothers to get here, however long that would take."

"Or?" she asked.

There was a smile in Darius' tone. "Or we can get a head start and do a bit of investigating before they come."

Ava weighed her options. She'd told herself repeatedly not to do anything stupid, to not put herself or anyone else in danger. If there were Rogues inside the warehouse, they would awaken and attack without question. There could be dozens of them in there — or just a handful.

Or there could be something inside other than vampires. Other demons also chose to bunker down in abandoned places like this until the sun set. They wouldn't know unless they saw for themselves.

Besides, what if her other brothers came all the way out here and it was nothing to worry over? That would be a waste of time and resources.

"Let's go with option B," she at last said. If they got in trouble, so be it. She could take the blame. It wasn't like she would be grounded or anything. She was a grown woman.

* * * *

Andreas and his father's hunter named Seth tracked the scent of the Rogues all the way to Freeport. He was hours away from Chicago, and the farther away he traveled, the higher his temper mounted.

He'd been sent all around Chicago twice before catching the faint scent and following it all the way out to freaking nowhere. It was damned annoying, but he refused to give up. That bastard Mikhail had caused his sister to run away from home. And if that wasn't enough, the man possessed the balls to hunt her down long afterwards, like she was some kind of animal.

Though they were happy to have her back, Andreas would never forget the way everyone had been torn up over her loss. The twins had gone out of their way to pick fights with other demons. More than once they'd come home with cuts and bruises and telling the most outrageous tales. Darius had given up his love for cooking for a while, and Julius' paintings had gone from beautiful, exotic colors to dark and brooding ones.

The ever-calm-and-collected Sal had done well to hold his composure when around his family, but outside, Andreas had known he was drowning himself in debauchery, taking multiple lovers and drinking blood rich in alcohol to make himself forget the pain he was in. Cass had already lost his mother and his human mate. After Ava's disappearance, he'd become even more withdrawn. He'd stayed in his private manor day and night, never contacting anyone. It had taken years for him to come out, but he'd still been reserved. To this day, if the man wasn't overseeing his business, he was cooped up in his private lair, playing around with his computers and other techie stuff.

His father had remained the strong, powerful king he was known to be, but every night behind closed doors Andreas knew his father was weeping over the loss of his only daughter. He'd lost two mates before, a number of comrades and loved ones in his life, but never a child. Andreas could only imagine the pain he had been feeling.

And Lucian...

Lucian had taken the loss far harder than anyone else. Though there was a thousand-plus-year age gap between them, Ava had formed a close attachment to him. Given her sad background, Lucian had felt a strong need to protect her. He had always been strict and overprotective of his family, and he was generally a sourpuss, but he'd also smiled far more during Ava's time with them. He'd come to their events and had a good time.

After Ava left, however, Lucian had turned cold. He'd spent a decade searching for her, and when that turned up unsuccessful, he'd withdrawn even more. His temper had grown shorter. He'd busied himself with his clan responsibilities, taking on more tasks than he could handle, as if burying himself under a mountain of work would keep his mind off Ava.

Of course, with her being back, there was no forgetting the pain they had endured over the years. And while Andreas wished she would have thought to tell them her worries over their opinions of her, he did understand her reasoning for leaving. He didn't agree with it in the least bit, but he understood. She had been new to the family, after all. She'd spent all her life under her mother's care, unable to trust anyone else. When she'd died, a young Ava had suddenly been thrown into a house full of relatives she'd never met prior to that point. Who wouldn't be uneasy over that?

Andreas shook his head and glanced around the open field of untrimmed grass. They were miles from the nearest town, but the trail ended here. He inhaled deeply, calling on his powers to tell him what had happened in this spot, but there was nothing. The two Rogues had just...disappeared.

He kicked at the grass, growling to himself. *Cazzo*, all of that work just to come to a dead end. It was a massive waste of time. One thing he hated more than anything was wasting time. "This is where the trail ends," he said to the other vampire.

Seth's own annoyance stirred in the air. "That's not possible. Even if they took to a vehicle, we should still be able to follow their trail."

Obviously. Every vampire was blessed with incredible senses, the hunters especially. Andreas' were even more sensitive than that. All he had to do was sniff the air and he could see what someone had been doing in the spot he was standing in. Hell, even if they crossed the Mississippi River, he'd still be able to track them.

The only explanation for their scent to disappear like this was if they'd used magic to hide them — or if there was a portal.

Which was absurd, because Rogues couldn't think to do such things. All they knew was how to hunt and kill.

He frowned to himself, remembering having seen the two the other night. Then again, they had been following orders. It was entirely possible Mikhail or someone had altered their blood somehow to change the very way they defined Rogues. It was unnerving as hell.

A cold breeze blew across his face, bringing with it the stench of death. He and Seth stiffened, both drawing their weapons. Something was coming toward them, and it wasn't friendly. Standing back to back with Seth, Andreas scanned his surroundings.

Beyond the field, he could see the woods far off in the distance, so there was no way anything could sneak up on them. Yet the scent of death and decay grew closer and closer. Andreas sniffed the air again, his body going cold as he recognized the stench.

"Bloody hell," he murmured, alarm racing down his spine.

"Abaddon," Seth muttered.

Abaddon were vile, nasty demons from the lowest ranks of hell. They weren't the most skilled at fighting, but with a small scratch they could inflict a deadly disease on their victims, one that would make the Black Plague look like the sniffles. And the only way to be cured before an ugly death was to have that same abaddon break the spell.

Andreas shivered in revulsion, sweat beading across his forehead. He wasn't afraid of death, but to die a slow, agonizing one from an incurable disease? *Yeah, I'll pass on that.*

In a puff of black smoke, the demon appeared several feet away from them, its repugnant odor nearly choking him. The creature itself looked no better. Though its body was mostly humanoid, that was where the similarities ended. Its flesh was hanging in tattered shreds, revealing inky black muscles on the inside. Its hands were gnarled, with black-tipped claws dripping with some kind of slimy gunk. The face was elongated like a seahorse, with sunken holes for eyes and a gaping mouth oozing more slime. It was truly a creature of nightmares. It was because of their horrifying looks and deadly skin that they had been banished to the lowest pits of hell, unable to rise and spread their diseases.

Andreas gulped. Behind him, Seth was still as a statue. Andreas held his sword even tighter in his hands as realization dawned on him.

This was a trap.

The Rogues' wandering scents had lured him all over the city and finally away from the safety of Luc's clan. Andreas didn't know how Mikhail could have possibly summoned an abaddon, but for him to do so against demon laws, he was either unafraid of the wrath of the Imperials or unconcerned that he'd be caught. Either way, it wasn't a good sign for them. This went far above a simple act of revenge.

There were very few demons whose blood was strong enough to be unaffected by an abaddon's touch, and unfortunately vampires, even Royals, were not one of them.

The creature opened its mouth wider, and though there were no lips moving, it was speaking in a raspy tone. "Vampire, I have a message for you."

Andreas kept his tone steady, though his heart was pounding in his ribcage. *Merda*, he'd faced some pretty badass demons in his life without a shred of fear, but this creature was understandably far more terrifying than anything else. Or rather, his powers were more so.

"Who sent you?" he demanded. It was a question he already had the answer to, but he still needed the confirmation.

The creature gave him its own version of a smile. "Master goes by many names."

Andreas rolled his eyes. *Always with the cryptic bullshit.* If this demon was going to give him the runaround and vague answers to his questions, he'd pass on all of it. His patience was thin as it was. "What's the message?"

"The great kings of the past will fall, giving way to the birth of a new era."

Andreas' tilted his head, frowning. "What the hell does that mean?"

The abaddon just gave a low, sinister laugh before crouching, as if to attack. "It means change is on the horizon, vampire, and your kind will be no more." With a hiss, the demon slinked forward, its claws outstretched.

It was slow but crafty. Also, the buggers were damn hard to kill, because getting close to them could be lethal. Escaping was easy, but an abbadon would follow a trail until its contract with its summoner ended, which could be years. And Andreas in no way wanted to have the demon leaving a trail of death and disease in its wake.

Andreas gulped deeply. "Don't let it touch you, Seth," he demanded.

The other vampire nodded once. Andreas sent a silent prayer to the gods for a quick, easy kill. But somehow he had a feeling deep within his heart they would not hear his plea this night.

Chapter Fourteen

There were two regular-sized doors leading inside the warehouse. The rest were large slabs of steel, rusted shut. Ava and the twins didn't even attempt to open them. Hell, even if they'd wanted to, they couldn't. With them having been closed for decades, the metal was so old that it was permanently sealed. Not even their superior strength would enable them to yank the steel free.

Not to mention, any attempt would be far too loud and alert whatever creature — or creatures — could be lurking inside.

Darius went around the back to another door, while Ava and Julius approached the one in the front. The paint on the metal door was faded and chipped, revealing the dark copper-colored rust beneath. It took a bit of force, but with a few tugs, Julius managed to wrench it open enough for the two of them to slip inside. The air was stuffy with a musty odor, making Ava crinkle her nose in disgust. The other abandoned buildings they'd entered had all had similar smells, but that didn't make this one any less foul.

Ava's vision pierced the pitch darkness. At the entrance, there was a small lobby with an open doorway leading to the warehouse beyond. On the right side of the lobby was a plain wooden door, the large window next to it showing them an empty office space.

She and Julius both wore combat boots, but they were light on their feet, their footsteps silent as they made their way to the open warehouse.

The darkness stretched into the wide expanse of the manufacturing area. There were several storage bins and crates lined against one wall and a few wayward ones littering the concrete floor before them. The other side contained the heavy machinery that had once run this place. A metal staircase led upstairs to the second-floor landing with a balcony overlooking the perimeter of the room.

Ava tested the air, sifting through the stagnant odors. That familiar prickling danced down her spine and she readied both her daggers. Julius, feeling the danger too, pulled out a sleek gun with a silencer attached to it. Regular bullets couldn't kill vampires and most demons, but silver ones sure as hell could if one pierced the heart or brain and was left untreated.

Entering from the back door, Darius joined them, a long razor-sharp silver sword held in one hand. Though the two of them were troublesome and downright asinine, they were both just as deadly and skilled as any vampire, even more so considering who their father was. Only a fool would underestimate their capabilities.

"There's someone else here," she whispered.

There was a faint rustling sound from above them, followed by shuffling—a lot of shuffling. Ava tensed when over two dozen pale faces with gleaming red eyes peered down at them from all around the balcony.

Rogues. And a hell of a lot more than she'd anticipated.

Slow, heavy footfalls sounded, and the air suddenly dropped several degrees. That prickling on her spine intensified, sending needles of fire throughout her body.

While Lucian was the only vampire who could command ice and could always 'wear' his cold power around him, any number of other vampires were able to raise or drop the surrounding temperatures if they procured enough strength.

A figure approached the balcony railing, a lean man sporting a thick black cloak. With a dramatic flair of his hands, he threw his hood back, revealing the Slavic features she knew all too well.

"Mikhail," she growled.

Like all vampires, the man was especially beautiful, with his pale yellow hair brushed back, a tall, slender build and chiseled features. However, it was the sinister curve of his lips and the soulless depths of his dark eyes that made him far more malicious than handsome.

"Hello, Ava," he purred.

A chill crept over Ava's skin at the nefarious tone. Since she'd first met the man over a hundred years ago in her father's home, she'd always been uncomfortable around him—and now more so than ever. Being hunted down and chased all around the country tended to do that to someone. *Go figure.*

He gazed over to Darius and Julius, his smug smile widening. "And the Gordano twins. What a delectable twist of fate meeting you all here."

A sliver of dread began to form in her stomach. Something about Mikhail being here didn't sit right with her. It seemed...too convenient.

"Why don't you come down here and join us for a grand reunion," Julius commented with a shrug.

"Oh, trust me. I intend for a reunion to take place very soon," Mikhail promised. "Unfortunately, I have other matters to attend before such a woeful event."

"What matters?" Ava demanded.

He zoned in on her. "Wouldn't you like to know, darling?"

"Yes, I would."

He held out his hand to her. "Then come to me and I'll show you."

Ava felt cold sweat slide down her temple. Her grip on her dagger became so stiff her fingers started to cramp. "The next time I come anywhere near you it will be to bury a stake in your heart."

He chuckled as if her words were a joke. They weren't. "So bloodthirsty," he murmured humorously.

"Yeah, well, being chased around the country and nearly killed by your goons put me on edge."

Ava didn't like the secretive gleam in his eyes. Not one bit. "A necessary ruse that worked in my favor."

Darius took a small step forward, pointing the tip of his sword at Mikhail. "What the hell is that supposed to mean? You've been trying to kill her all this time and have failed miserably. How is that 'working in your favor'?"

"Foolish boy, if I truly wanted the princess dead, she would have been so a long time ago."

Ava stiffened, her temper flaring. She'd faced countless bounty hunters, ghouls, hellhounds and other demons he'd sent to capture her, and each time she'd either managed to escape or kill them. Her entire life had been a fight for survival. She'd grown strong enough to defend herself. She was an easy target, but in no way was she an easy kill, not for anyone.

"So you don't want her dead?" Julius demanded.

"Of course I do," Mikhail smoothly countered. "I just have need of her first."

Ava's fangs lengthened, and she flashed them at him. "Stop speaking in circles, Mikhail. Your secret is already out, and you were banished long before I got to mention it to anyone. So what is your endgame?"

He leaned forward on the rusted railing, smiling down at her. Another cool blast of power washed over them. The Rogues surrounding Mikhail began to shift uneasily, anxious to pounce. The fact that so many of them were just standing there, as if waiting for a command, only confirmed their previous assumptions. Somehow Mikhail had managed to gain control over Rogues.

"My goal is simple, my dear. Our kind are natural predators. We are at the top of the food chain in this world, yet it is because of your father's inadequate rulings that we have been forced to slink about in the shadows while the mortals run amok, all high and mighty. A change is long overdue, and I will personally free my brethren from the shackles Cyrus forced us into. Vampires will once again rule the night without fear of banishment or death."

Ava's spine stiffened. "The laws are in place to protect all humans *and* vampires. The times have changed. Humans and demons coexist. There is no longer a need for wars or killing humans for their blood. Your cause is unjust and your reasoning is just a pathetic excuse to steal the lives of innocents to help you seek revenge."

The temperature dropped even more. With every exhale, a small white cloud formed past her lips.

"Innocents?" He gave a sharp bark of laughter. "You are even more of a fool than your father if you think humans to be innocent. They are just as cruel and vicious as any demon, killing their own and destroying families without a second thought. They have far too much arrogance for them to be so weak. We are and have always been superior, therefore a mortal's life should never, ever hold more value than a vampire's." He straightened, smoothing his cloak down. "I will give you one more chance, my sweet. Join me willingly, and I will spare your life for now. I'll even allow your brothers to leave this place alive."

Both Julius and Darius stepped in front of her protectively. "You are too quick to belittle us, Nilsen," Darius said. "Ava is not going anywhere with you."

His smile returned and he backed away, disappearing into the shadows. "Very well. It's your loss. *Attack.*" A tingling sensation slid across her skin and she caught the smell of some kind of sweet dessert before it vanished.

Then she pushed it to the back of her mind. Before either of them could chase after Mikhail, the dozens of Rogues above them began leaping over the balcony, fangs extended, their eyes red with bloodlust. The three of them took battle stances, preparing to fight their way through the horde.

Ava and her brothers spread out, giving each other some space to fight. Ava was always more of a close-up fighter than a long distance one, so she held both daggers in her hands. The first Rogue who ran at her did so without thinking. She stepped to the side, avoiding the claws that swiped at her. Standing behind it, she used the blade to slice it across the neck, cold blood spraying out. It hadn't even dropped to the ground when she turned on the other one, ducking low under its arms and stabbing both blades into its gut. She gave a sharp jerk, wincing at the Rogue's high-pitched shriek of pain.

Without looking, she could hear the sounds of Darius' sword slicing through the Rogues and Julius' shooting bullets with his silenced gun and refilling in the blink of an eye when the clips ran out. Even if he used up all of his ammunition, he had a number of other hidden weapons on his body.

They were too far into the warehouse and surrounded by too many Rogues to try to escape into the sunlight. *So much for that plan.* With the large number of Rogues they were facing, it was only a matter of remaining standing until the cavalry arrived.

Never taking her eyes off her opponents, she gave a dry snort. Though these weren't the average Rogues, Ava was in no way afraid of them.

What did worry her was how the hell she was supposed to explain this mess to Lucian when he arrived. Though he was her brother, he was more like an annoying mother goose who would no doubt be furious to learn they'd ignored his commands and entered the warehouse without him. Not only that, but they'd also let Mikhail get away.

Yeah, these Rogues were a piece of cake. If they didn't kill her first, Lucian in his cold rage certainly would.

She fought on — and on.

With a growl, Ava rammed her blade into the skull of yet another Rogue, the sickening crunch of bone making her stomach churn. But she didn't give up, not when there were still another dozen Rogues left. She didn't know how much time had passed, but it had to have been over an hour. The first wave of Rogues had been simple kills. They had only charged forward with no tactics. The second wave, however, were smarter. It was clear they were older.

They were able to dodge blows, which made them more of a nuisance. What was worse, they were faster and stronger than they should have been. Whatever Mikhail had done to create them, it was one hell of a concoction. It was like fighting any sane vampire, which even for a Royal could be challenge if the other vamp was skilled enough.

With her back against a wall, she held both blades steady, her breath coming out in pants. She was holding up pretty well on her end, but not without a few repercussions. She had some cuts along her arms, one on her cheek and a pretty deep bite on the back of one of her calves. It just went to show how hungry Rogues could be that one of the bastards had bitten straight through her jeans and taken a pretty good chunk of flesh. It would heal after she fed, but for the time being, it was impossible to put pressure on it without collapsing.

There were three Rogues facing her. Beyond them she could see Darius and Julius with a handful of them as well. Julius had resorted to using blades after having run out of ammo. Both of them were bleeding from minor wounds but nothing that seemed serious. They certainly didn't have a gaping hole in the back of their leg that she could see.

Cripes. How was she supposed to prove her independence when she was the only one with a serious injury? Granted they had a couple of centuries on her, but still...

Another Rogue pounced and she dodged, balancing on one leg. She brought one blade up, slicing it across the arm. It screamed in pain but didn't slow as it swung at her again. She dodged once more, but another one raked their claws across her back, making her hiss. *Damn, that one actually hurt.* Her light jacket hadn't done a damn thing to prevent the Rogue's nails from slicing through her skin.

She staggered forward, almost losing her balance as her weight fell on her injured leg. She dropped one of the daggers, reaching out a hand to brace herself against the wall. She spun around, avoiding another blow. There was very little time for her to catch her breath.

This time when a Rogue came at her, she caught it by the throat, holding it away from her. Its rancid breath washed over her face, smelling like the very ass of hell. *Freaking gross.* Its yellowed fangs snapped at her, making her squeeze her fingers harder. Her nails bit into its neck, and with an awful squelching sound, she crushed the Rogue's throat. Cold blood poured onto her fingers, and she flung the dying creature at the other two. They leaped out of the way then ran at her at once.

With only one weapon in hand and favoring an injured leg, Ava bared her fangs at the two.

Fortunately, she didn't have to worry about fighting the creatures anymore. Appearing out of the blue, Lucian loomed before her. With one strong swing of his sword, he lopped off both creatures' heads, killing them on the spot.

Well...hell. He made it look so easy. With a faint shake of her head, Ava straightened. She'd taken down more than her share, she acknowledged with a pout. He was late to the party, after all. She'd spent the last hour or so fighting off the rabid creatures while he was looking all pristine and immaculate, like a perfect ice prince. The deceased bodies of the Rogues were turning to ash, any evidence of their existence fading to dust.

She looked up to see Cass helping Julius and Darius take out the remaining Rogues. "Wait!. Leave one alive," Ava shouted. Cass gave an annoyed grunt before slamming the butt of his dagger on the last Rogue's head. She growled before slumping to the ground with a thump.

Cold air pinpricked Ava's skin, making her aware of the death glare Lucian was giving her. She grimaced before giving him a sweet, innocent smile. "Heyyyy — "

"How could you have disobeyed the simplest of orders?" he demanded, his voice a low growl. "It's not rocket science, nor is it hard to comprehend the meaning of staying put until we arrived."

Ava's brows lifted at his tone. She'd known that he'd be mad, but it had been many a year since she'd seen him *this* mad. The cement floor was beginning to turn to ice around his shitkickers, a sure sign of his fury. Even the leather hilt of his sword began to coat with frost.

"Bro, do you need a Snickers?" Darius drawled, sheathing his sword.

As always, his inopportune humor only added fuel to the fire. And despite Lucian's ice abilities, his rage was definitely turned on high.

"Because you're not you when you're hungry."

Lucian's silver eyes flashed with anger. He pointed a finger at the twins. "I'm in no mood for any of your ill-conceived jokes. You had direct commands, and instead of listening, you deliberately put yourselves and Ava in danger. You could have been killed. We only just got her back and you two fools went out of your way to try to lose her again. What the hell is wrong with you?"

The fact that neither of the twins had a smart remark to say to Lucian showed just how guilty they felt. The miserable looks on their faces made Ava's heart clench regretfully. She always hated how sensitive she could be. She placed a gloved hand on Lucian's arm, forcing him to meet her glare. He opened his mouth to bark something at her, but she spoke first.

"Listen to me, Mr. Hissy-Fit," she said with a poke to his chest.

His silver eyes widened, as if offended by the gesture—or the name.

Oh well.

"First of all, it was *my* decision to investigate this place, not theirs. They were only following me to make sure I was safe. So if you have anything to fuss about, direct it at *me*." Another hard poke. "Second, you and *Brock Samson* over there were sure taking your precious time getting here. Mikhail could have left undetected and we wouldn't have any new information had we waited outside." Another poke, this one hard enough to make him wince in pain. "Lastly, I am neither your servant nor one of your clansmen. You will *not* bark orders at me and expect me to obey like some faithful mutt. You might be used to having everyone else scrambling around to do your bidding, but I am Ava

Gordano. You will treat me with the same respect you want to be given. So I suggest you tone it down ten notches before you join these Rogues in a pile of ash."

Darius', Julius' and Cassander's mouths all dropped open in unison, and Lucian's eyes were so wide they nearly bugged from his head. She ignored them, though, and gave a toss of her hair before limping over to the unconscious Rogue. Going by their reactions, she was sure no one had ever talked to Lucian in such a way for fear of his temper. Even her brothers knew what buttons not to press.

Ava, however, couldn't give a rat's puckered ass. She was tired, she was in pain, she was hungry and she was pissed to *still* be treated like a child. Yes, she was young by demon standards, but she was in no way in need of someone telling her what to do and what not to do, especially someone who was definitely *not* her father.

She snatched one of the torn gloves off her hand and bent to touch the Rogue female on her forehead. When no memories came to her, she called forth her powers to search deeper within the Rogue's mind.

She'd seen the memories of the Rogues that had attacked her and Marc when they had been in the car accident. Their thoughts and memories were jumbled messes, but all she could see was their anger and desire for blood. It was disturbing, to say the least.

In the background, she could hear Lucian grumbling to himself in outrage. "Mr. Hissy-Fit? I have never in my life thrown a hissy fit."

"Actually —" one of the twins began.

"Shut it," he growled, effectively cutting off all three brothers from whatever any of them were about to say.

Ava ignored them and focused on the task at hand. With this Rogue being unconscious, she hoped it could give her an idea on how she'd gotten here, where she'd come from and if there were any clues leading to Mikhail's whereabouts.

The wall blocking the Rogue's mind cleared, and Ava shifted through the memories. Oddly, there weren't very many, as if being Rogue wiped away all recollections of their past lives. There were glimpses of grassy fields, riding in the back of a commercial truck for hours, coming across humans and draining them of their blood...but nothing particularly helpful.

Wait...

One image came through, and with a frown, she could see Mikhail smiling directly into the Rogue's eyes. *"Hello, lovely. I knew sooner or later you'd see this."*

Stiffening in shock, Ava realized belatedly he was talking to her. He must have known she would use her powers on a Rogue to try to locate him. But there was no way he could have known she'd use it on *this* particular Rogue. With a horrified shudder, she concluded he must have imprinted the memory on all these Rogues.

Mikhail was peering directly into the Rogue, which in turn made Ava feel like he was looking directly at her.

"I'm going to keep this short and sweet. If you want the cure, I'll be waiting in the place where it all began."

With that, he raised an orange lily to his nose, inhaling deeply. Then, the image disappeared.

With a confused frown, Ava rose to her feet. Her brothers gathered around her.

"What did you see," Lucian demanded. When she cut her eyes at him, he cleared his throat. "Ah, what did you see?" His voice still held its commanding tone, but this time he actually *asked* her. It was a start.

Ava shook her head. "Something that didn't make any sense. Let's report back to father and get everyone caught up."

She could tell he wanted to press her, but he gave a simple nod. "I'm going to check upstairs to make sure nothing else is lingering." He didn't even wait for anyone to respond, just silently took off in a blur, leaving her behind with the twins and Cassander.

When he was out of sight, Cass turned to look at her, raising an eyebrow. "*Brock Samson?*"

With a smile, Ava turned and began limping out of the door. The animated character she'd called Cass wasn't too far off the mark. Body wise, their builds were pretty similar. She lifted her hands. "If the shoes fit, *fratello*, wear them proudly."

Cass grunted in disapproval. Behind her, she could hear the twins muttering between each other. "I still say Luc needs a Snickers."

Off in the distance, though it was very faint, Ava could hear Luc's voice quietly drifting down to them.

"I heard that."

* * * *

To her utter relief, Ava rode back to her father's mansion with Cassander instead of the two howling monkeys, while Lucian drove alone in his Jag. It was so like Cass to ride in his decked-out pickup truck in complete silence. No music from the radio, just the smooth purr of the engine as he drove through the city and out into the countryside. The quiet would have been unnerving had it not been for Ava spending most of her time gulping down bottles of blood to heal herself.

She was slowly becoming used to the taste of bagged or bottled blood, though she still would much rather drink it from a live host. It was just...fresher that way.

She thought briefly about her feeding from Marc, feeling the familiar pain in her chest. She'd kept her mind busy for the past few weeks, but she'd see him standing there smiling, those sexy dimples present in each grin. She missed him. Just the thought was enough to send heat rushing through her body before she quickly banished his image.

From what her father had told her, Duncan had sent an update a few days before. Marc hadn't been able to shift yet, but his progress seemed to be going smoothly. She didn't know exactly what the procedure included, but from the stories she'd heard over the years, the first two weeks seemed awfully painful. She didn't envy him in the least bit.

Still, she couldn't help the twinge of guilt sliding through her. Had she known he possessed demon blood, she would have never bitten him to awaken that side of him — not without his permission, anyway. Now he was stuck being a demon for however long he lived.

"You're thinking of your human?" Cassander asked, his deep voice startling her. Before she could lie, he gave a small smile, the harsh lines around his handsome face smoothing. "You can be honest with me. Unlike the rest, I can keep my mouth shut when need be."

Ava didn't doubt it for a moment. Cass was silent and brooding. He spoke only when he felt like he could contribute to the conversation. Other than that, he preferred to sit back and carefully watch his surroundings, like a hawk.

It was one of many things that made him a great warrior. That, and his powers to blend in and manipulate even the faintest of shadows. It was a skill that was as effective as it was terrifying.

With a small sigh, Ava leaned back in her seat. "He's not *my* human."

He looked at her out the corner of his eyes. When he spoke, his deep voice was filled with humor. "From the time we began following your trail up until the day after he left, his scent has been all over you. Even now I can still smell him on you."

Ava blushed, resisting the urge to sniff at her own skin. As far as hygiene went, she made sure hers was immaculate. She was far from a germaphobe, but she enjoyed a good long shower or bath. She was so used to being around humans that she'd nearly forgotten how strong demon noses could be. *Drat it all.*

"That doesn't make him mine," she muttered. "Besides, he's a shifter now, not a human." *Great.* Now she'd be self-conscious about her odor around the rest of her brothers, especially Darius and Julius. Those two had a knack for putting people on the spot.

Cass only chuckled. "There's nothing to be ashamed of. Sometimes we can't help who we fall for." His tone and expression remained calm, but Ava saw the slight tightening of his hands on the steering wheel. She could also feel his sadness.

A pang of sorrow struck her heart. *That's right.* Cassander had lost his human mate a long time ago. It had come before Ava was living with them, but she knew her brother was still hurting over it.

Her name was Maria, and she had been born with an illness in her lungs. It was like an old Shakespearian tale, a beautiful love story ending in tragic heartbreak.

Because her body was so weak, Cass hadn't been able to turn her, so he'd been forced to stay by her side until her very last breath. He'd watched her suffer through her disease, unable to do anything but watch her fade away at far too young an age.

Ava reached out her gloved hand and lightly placed it on Cass' arm. "When you put it that way, I can't deny it. How did you decide you wanted Maria as your mate?"

He looked at her again before focusing on the road. His Adam's Apple bobbed when he swallowed. Underneath that cool exterior was a man who'd been deeply hurt. Just like her father, he was good at hiding it. However, her empathy allowed her to see deep within his heart.

And his words had struck true. She couldn't deny the strong pull she felt toward Marc. Somewhere along the way, whether it had been during her time at the diner or in the few days they'd been together, she'd developed a deep attachment to the sexy cop. As much as she tried to fight it or push him away, it was clear to see. She had feelings for him, feelings far deeper than those of a friend — even more than a mere lover.

Unfortunately, there was nothing she could do about it. It was for the best that they remained separated. He had an entire new life to live, without her.

"I never decided."

Ava's brows lifted, confusion swirling around her. "*She* decided?"

His lips twisted wryly. "*Fate* decided."

Ava's lips parted in disbelief. "You don't strike me as the type to believe in all that destiny crap."

This time he chuckled sincerely. "What I mean is, all vampires have a destined truemate. It doesn't take years to get to know someone for us to decide, as is the case with humans these days. With just one look — or a scent, or a small touch — once we come across that one person fate created just for us, there can be no other until one of us leaves the world."

Well...hell. This was news to her. "All vampires have a...truemate?"

"*Si.*"

"So no one chooses who they get to mate?"

He thought about it for a while before shaking his head. "For us, mating is a life-long commitment. You do not want to be attached to someone for an eternity if they aren't your truemate. Ofttimes we take lovers or find someone we trust enough to develop a friendship with, but it can never be more than that. Well, I suppose it *can* be, but somewhere down the line one will grow tired of the other, and the only way to end a mating is death." He looked over to her again. "Finding a truemate is the greatest feeling in the world. It's like the missing half of our soul is found, even if you didn't realize it was missing. We have a reason to live. There are times, however, when it can be downright painful. Our truemate can be anyone — a shifter, another vampire, another species...or a human."

Ava's heart gave a painful lurch as she thought about Marc. Was that why she'd felt so drawn to him since meeting him? *Is he my truemate?*

"How can you tell?" She swallowed the lump in her throat. "How do you know if someone is really your truemate?"

He sighed softly. "You will feel it in your heart. You may try to fight it or reason that it's just lust or temporary infatuation or any other excuse, but no matter how long you resist or how far you travel, you will always feel a connection with that person. And once you become...physical, that connection becomes stronger."

Ava stiffened, absently rubbing a hand over her aching heart. *Marc...* He wasn't her truemate...Fate couldn't possibly be that cruel.

She hoped.

"I know you've been doing your best to stay busy so you do not have to think about him," Cass continued.

Ava clasped her hands together in her lap and pressed her lips tightly together.

"I'm not going to give you some big lecture, but I want you to know we are all here for you. None of your battles, mentally or physically, have to be fought alone, *piccolina*. You don't have to feel you need to show off how strong you are. You have us to lean on, and we'll never think any less of you."

Ava turned to face the window, staring out at the vast landscape passing by as they traveled farther and farther away from the city. She didn't want him to see how much his words had touched her. "Thank you," was all she said. However, she curved her lips into a small smile.

"Another thing..."

Oh dear. She didn't like that tone. Hadn't he just said he wasn't going to lecture her? It was bad enough he'd already dropped a bomb on her that one day some stranger would come into her life and wreak havoc on her soul. That is, if hadn't happened already. "Yes?"

He paused for a moment, seeming to choose his words carefully. When he spoke, his voice softened. "While every vampire has a truemate, sometimes it can take up to centuries before we meet them. And very,

very few are fortunate enough to have more than one per lifetime."

Ava opened her mouth to respond but closed it. She thought about her father and his two mates. He had met them centuries apart, and yet he'd lost them both. Cass had lost his own mate as well. It must be terribly lonely, finding that one person to spend an eternity with, only to have it all snatched away just like that. She'd never even had a boyfriend, let alone a mate. She couldn't begin to fathom how they dealt with the pain.

With a small shake of her head, she turned back to gaze out of the window. She didn't want to think about that. It was far too raw for her sensitive nerves.

The landscape nearing her father's estate became more familiar. Though each of her brothers had their own homes and personal living areas, they'd been staying at their father's mansion most of the time to be close to her. Cass rolled to a stop at the outer gate that was securely locked. As ancient as Cyrus was, he was up-to-date on all the latest technologies, including high-tech security systems. Not even a field mouse could cross his lands without him or his security knowing.

The winding driveway seemed to go on for another mile, and there were two more checkpoints along the way before Cass parked his car in the garage large enough to house a small jet. Ava got out, eyeing the multitude of expensive cars.

King or not, who the hell needed *that* many vehicles? It was ridiculous.

With a shake of her head, she followed Cass through the sprawling mansion in search of their wayward father. As they passed, Ava continued to admire the priceless paintings and vases, the body armor and life-sized statues, the polished marble flooring, the high ceilings and the intricate designs along the paneling. Not for the first time, she wondered just how much money her father had put into this place.

Then again, she didn't want to know and didn't care. Cyrus had enough wealth to fund a small country, and this estate was just one of many.

They were just about to approach Cyrus' study when an alarmed shout called from the distance. Startled, Ava and Cass bolted toward the back on the mansion, turning what seemed to be an endless number of corners before coming to an abrupt halt before the back door. A feeling of trepidation crept up Ava's spine when she saw Seth and Andreas tumbled onto the floor. There was no blood that she could scent, but Andreas was unconscious and foaming at the mouth, the front of his black shirt torn from what looked like a claw mark.

Cyrus knelt beside him, holding his son's head steady as seizures racked his body. "What happened?" he demanded of Seth, his tone booming throughout the halls.

Seth's eyes were wide, but something about him was...off. Ava couldn't say what it was. It was just a feeling in her gut. There was an odd mix of fear and regret, which was understandable, given whatever had happened. He likely blamed himself for not protecting Andreas enough. But it was...more, like an almost-corrupt feeling cloaking the air around him.

There was a choked noise, drawing her attention. Andreas' entire body shook, his clothes were drenched in sweat and his pallor was a sickening gray. Footsteps thundered through the hall, and Ava knew without turning that her other brothers had joined them.

"Abaddon," Seth hissed. "It was a trap. The scents of the Rogues disappeared and an abaddon sent by Mikhail attacked us."

Cyrus lashed out in fury, knocking the priceless portraits off the wall. "*No*," he growled.

Ava covered her mouth, her heart sinking to her toes. Abaddon were literally walking plagues. Just the tiniest of scratches had the potential to create deadly viruses that could wipe an entire nation off the face of the earth.

"Where is it?" Lucian demanded, his face set in hard lines. There was a hint of desperation in his voice. If anyone contracted an illness from an abaddon, the only way to recover from it was to seek out the exact demon who'd caused it. Otherwise, one would experience a painful, horrifying death. It could either be instant or drawn out to make the victim suffer.

Seth swallowed. Cyrus' power in the hall was spreading to a painful pressure, his grief palpable. "It escaped," Seth rasped. Though he appeared terrified, Ava was once again struck with the feeling that there was more to it. The uneasy feeling she had only grew stronger. She was an empath, after all. She was never wrong about these things.

She took a step toward Seth, but Cass held her back, probably thinking she was about to launch herself at him. She paused. Then again, her father had trusted him enough to send him out with Andreas, so she could be mistaken.

"Its message was '*The great kings of the past will fall, giving way to the birth of a new era*'," Seth said.

There was a quiet sense of despair permeating the room. Cyrus clenched his teeth so hard that his jaw popped. When Andreas' seizing slowed, their father scooped him up into his arms as if he weighed nothing. "Meeting in my study ASAP," he snapped.

With that, Cyrus took off at a blinding speed, disappearing through the house, carrying Andreas. Seth followed behind them. Ava's knees went weak and she slumped to the ground, placing a hand over her heart. "Andreas," she whispered, her voice cracking. Her heart was breaking into a million pieces. She'd only just been reunited with her family and now there was a risk they were going to lose one of them.

Dropping her head into her hands, Ava tasted hot tears sliding down her face. She'd never really prayed to any of the gods, not seriously. She wasn't a religious person. In fact, she'd always been bitter toward them for cursing her blood, making her a desired target for countless demons.

On this day, however, she prayed to any entity listening to not take her brother away from her.

Chapter Fifteen

Though Cyrus had called for a meeting ASAP, he didn't show up in the grand study until two hours later. His expression was a cold, dark mask. His eyes, however, were filled with fury. He was a father first and a king second. His children were his greatest treasures, and the fact that someone out there was hunting one of them down and had cursed another one with a deadly disease made for a very, very pissed-off vampire.

And when Cyrus the Conqueror was angry, only the absolute bottom-of-the-barrel stupid would dare cross his path.

With each passing minute, Ava's own mood had grown darker. No one spoke a word, only sat in a melancholy silence.

Cyrus sat in his preferred chair, though she knew by his clenched fists he was anxious to hop up and tear someone's throat out. "I have several doctors currently looking over Andreas, but for now, all we can do is keep him comfortable until we find the abaddon who did this."

"How the hell did an abaddon make it through the Gates in the first place?" Julius growled, referring to the guarded entrances separating Hell from the human world. There were no ill-mannered jokes, no goofy voices, no sarcastic remarks. One of their own lay dying. In this room, they all wanted one thing and one thing only — blood.

Specifically, the blood of a traitorous Slavic vampire.

"He isn't afraid of the wrath of the king or the punishment of the Imperials for summoning a forbidden creature," Sal murmured. "We need to reevaluate exactly what we're dealing with."

"Someone with a death wish," Darius stated, his fangs flashing.

"It's deeper than that," Lucian said. His tone was smooth, his face impassive. However, the cold power swirling dangerously in the air was the only sign that he was as furious and concerned as the rest of them. He focused narrowed eyes on their father. "This is more than a simple act of revenge for banishing him. His hatred of you is far more than that, isn't it?" As per usual when it came to Luc, it wasn't really a question. It was a demand.

Cyrus' eyes flashed with guilt. He rose to his feet, his own barely contained power spreading through the room, threatening to tear down the very foundation of the library he'd obviously spent a large fortune creating. He walked over to his desk and withdrew an expensive bottle of Scotch. He didn't bother pouring it into a glass. He took a long, deep swig.

Ava frowned. Lucian had touched a nerve, one that was enough to make Cyrus uneasy.

"What happened between the two of you all those years ago?" Lucian demanded again.

Cyrus set the bottle down roughly on his desk, hanging his head as if it pained him to dredge up those old memories. With a drawn-out sigh, he made his way back to them with deep regret in his eyes. He sat down, his jaw clenched.

"It was a long time ago," he started. Ava leaned forward in her seat, zoning in on her father. His features were tight with an ancient pain. "I've known Mikhail since he was an adolescent. His father, Vladimir, was a great friend of mine who fought alongside me through many battles. He was one of the rare few people I trusted with my life. Before I took the title as king, there were others before me who were in power."

"The Ancients?" Ava asked, trying to recall the old tales. It was all so long ago, and there were so many different stories spread over the millennia that it was hard to pinpoint what was true and what wasn't.

Cyrus gave a single nod. "Yes, the Ancients. They were even older than I. During their reign, there was no order. Only complete and total chaos. They were unjust and just wanted to torture and kill their victims — humans, demons and even our own people. There was no prejudice. They killed them all without mercy, and it was time to put an end to the anarchy. Alongside Vladimir, we formed a clan of our own and fought our way through hell before facing the Ancients. A great battle broke out and we won, but it didn't come easily. We lost many comrades, and even in the final battle, I was unable to protect Vladimir in time. He took a blast of power meant for me, allowing me to land the killing blow.

"With the Ancients dead, the title of king descended to me. It was a position I did not want, but it was my old companion's last wish that I bring balance to our people and watch over his family." Cyrus' eyes lowered, and even from a distance, Ava could feel his pain. "I took his wife and Mikhail under my wing as I worked to restore order among our kind. Under my training, Mikhail proved to be a capable warrior, and he quickly rose to the highest ranks. At this time I met my first mate and we had Lucian. Several years later Mikhail had his own family, and I didn't see either of them for a while. They moved across the seas to a safer, quieter land. Our kind continued to prosper and become civilized, and things were finally becoming more peaceful."

He sighed deeply, shifting in his chair as if restless. When he couldn't find a comfortable position, he rose to his feet again and stared at the nearest bookshelf. His agitation only further showed how disturbed he was by everything. He had thousands of years' worth of patience.

"Hunters began to cleanse our people of Rogues and those who opposed these new laws. No one was forced to join a clan, but it was widely known that if a vampire, regardless of status, chose to not join a clan, he was a target to other demons. There was no protection for him. Anyhow, just after Luc's twentieth birthday, news reached my ears of a Rogue running free in a city off the coast of what is now Croatia. I went personally, because I knew it was where Mikhail had retreated to. It had been many years since I'd last seen him, so a reunion was in order. However" —his eyes darkened, and his ancient accent grew thicker— "when I arrived,

I learned that the Rogue in question was Mikhail's own daughter. She was no more than fifteen."

Ava gasped. The crackling power in the air intensified, but she paid it no mind as she imagined being in her father's position. "He could not bring himself to kill her, even knowing our laws, and so he was allowing her to continue rampaging, killing any human or demon she came across. As deeply as it pained me to do so, I had to do the right thing. I couldn't show favoritism by overlooking this travesty."

His shoulders sagged beneath the elegant robes he wore. "Mikhail was devastated, of course. *Merda*, the look on his face was one I'll never forget." He shook his head, rubbing the heels of his palms across his eyes. "I knew he despised me after that. Who wouldn't after my killing their child? Their *only* child, at that. Rogue or not, a parent's love is...immeasurable. There was no making up for it. However, I left a spot open in my Guard for him, should he ever decide to take up the offer. It was nearly a decade later, but he finally accepted. In truth, I allowed it partly so I could keep an eye on him. The other part, I'd hope to rid myself of the guilt I felt."

He let out a deep sigh and strolled over to his desk, taking another long swig of the alcohol.

"I knew he was still hurt, but he accepted his role and eventually became my second-in-command. I always sensed the darkness within him, but so long as I kept a close eye on him, I was reassured. From then on, everything was... Well, you all know the rest."

The room remained silent after Cyrus finished his story.

Ava's gaze was lowered toward the floor. She hated how sympathetic she could be to creatures who didn't even deserve it.

Mikhail was like any other person. He'd lost someone very dear to him, and the desire for revenge had become too great for him to ignore. He was a terribly cruel man with a darkness in him that couldn't be redeemed, yet at the center of it all was a father hurting over the loss of his child.

However, though his vengeance was understandable and she felt a small measure of pain on his behalf, she couldn't overlook the way he'd hunted her down for all these years, forcing her to cower in moldy rooms, dusty barns and damp cellars just to hide from people *he'd* sent after her. Nor could she ever forgive him for siccing an abaddon on one of her brothers, causing him to suffer whatever god-awful disease was now plaguing his body.

Not to mention all those people he'd killed in his attempts to create Rogues he could control...

By the gods, the man needed to be sent to the very depths of hell, and she'd make sure to do it, even if it killed her.

"I still don't understand why he spent all this time hunting me down," Ava whispered, "or why he wants me alive."

Cyrus grimaced. "What?"

Darius leaned forward, squinting in irritation. "He was just trying to get inside your head, Ava."

Cyrus stepped toward them, his large frame seeming even more imposing from her seat on the couch. "You encountered him? Today?"

Ava frowned, only then realizing they hadn't yet discussed the events in the warehouse. "Darius, Julius and I came across an old warehouse, and Julius couldn't sense any animals inside." She nodded to Cyrus, knowing his cell phone was in a hidden pocket within his toga. "Instead of waiting, we went inside to investigate, and on the second floor were about two dozen Rogues — and Mikhail."

Cyrus stiffened, as did Sal, who sat beside her. "What happened?" Her father's tone was now bitter, and she could sense the rage continuing to bubble inside him.

Ava licked her lips, hesitating for a moment. It wasn't as though she was afraid of her father. He'd never lash out at her or any of them, not unless he absolutely had to.

However, with his pale blue gaze burning into her, she had to choose her words with care lest he lose his temper and blow the roof off the place.

It was Julius who spoke up, beating her to the punch as he relayed the details of their encounter with Mikhail. Cyrus' expression grew colder with each word.

"So we fought the Rogues until Lucian and Cass arrived, but by then, Mikhail was already gone," he finished.

With obvious effort, Cyrus returned to his seat in his preferred wingchair. He leaned one arm on the armrest, placing his chin in the palm of one hand as he thought. Ava wondered what he was thinking, but with the thunderous look on his face, she could guess.

If not that, she could feel the dangerous crackling of power in the air as he struggled to keep his temper in check.

She expected an angry outburst or a scolding. Hell, he might even sentence her to a timeout. But all he did was sit there, his expression guarded as he watched them.

She remembered the tingling sensation she'd felt across her skin back in the warehouse, followed by a faint sweet smell. "I think he used a portal to escape," she murmured. "I could sense magic being used before the Rogues attacked us." Her brothers looked surprised before sending nods her way. They all knew she was the only one of them who could sense magic, thanks to her mother's blood. Besides, there was no other way Mikhail could have escaped the warehouse. He was only an Aristocrat, so he didn't possess any of a Royal's special powers that could have helped him. That sweet smell had to have come from an imp. All fey tended to smell either sweet or woodsy, and imps were able to create portals. "He could be anywhere by now."

"What did you see when you touched the Rogue?" Cyrus asked. His tone was detached, which was far more intimidating than if he'd yelled at her. She shivered. *Cripes, talk about scary.*

She thought back over the image she saw in the unconscious Rogue's head. She froze, her spine stiffening in remembrance. "No," she murmured to herself.

"No?" Cyrus demanded, thinking she was declining to answer him.

Thankfully, Sal understood her reaction. He turned to her. "What is it?" he asked. "What did you see?"

She repeated Mikhail's words back to them.

'If you want the cure, I'll be waiting in the place where it all began.'

She looked up at them with wide eyes. "I didn't know what it meant at the time, but" — she clutched at her stomach, feeling a wave of nausea rolling through her — "I think he means the cure for Andreas."

Lucian growled. "That bastard. He had to have imprinted that memory on the Rogues a while ago."

Ava nodded, having already come to that conclusion. "How could he have possibly known Andreas would be there that day?"

"Furthermore, *'I'll be waiting in the place where it all began'*?" This from Julius. "What the devil does that mean?"

Ava shook her head. "Seth did say the scents of the Rogues who attacked them suddenly disappeared, then the abaddon came out of nowhere. It was likely the creature was hiding away, waiting for Andreas to show up."

Then again, she didn't even believe that. Abaddon were forbidden to be summoned into the human world. Andreas had begun his search nearly two weeks before. There was no way the creature could have been lying in wait for so long without raising some suspicion. The Imperials would have sensed it or other passing demons would have reported it.

There were far too many questions with no answers and it was pissing her off. She recalled that uneasy feeling she'd had when she'd first seen Andreas lying on the floor. She rose to her feet, looking at her father, alarmed. "Where is Seth?" she demanded.

Her father's eyebrows raised at her question. "In one of the private rooms recovering from the shock. I have yet to fully question him." Seeing her tight features, he rose as well. "What is it?"

Ava bit her lip. The reason she'd run away in the first place was because she'd trusted the words of another, and instead of being honest and open with her family, she'd decided to hide it for ninety-six years, when in the end, they'd accepted her regardless. She wouldn't make the same mistake again.

Squaring her shoulders, she said, "I can't say for sure, but it's a feeling I had when I saw him earlier. The vibes I got from him were...off." She shook her head. "I don't know exactly what it is, but it's almost the same feeling I had when I first met Mikhail." She made a fluttering movement with her hands around her heart. "I can feel these things."

Cyrus' pale eyes widened a fraction before he nodded. He rushed over to the door, his long ponytail swaying with each hard stride. He poked his head out and murmured something in low tones. The two vampires standing guard outside disappeared through the halls in search of Seth. Cyrus closed the door and turned back to Ava.

"You're absolutely sure?" he asked.

"Positive," she retorted, with not a moment's hesitation. Something had not sat right with her when she'd looked at Seth. She'd have to touch him to figure out what that feeling was, but he was without a doubt a shifty fellow.

Ava's hands were twitching fifteen minutes later when another knock sounded on the door. Cyrus opened it, and there was hushed murmuring, too low for even Ava to hear. However, she could tell by the tightening of her father's shoulders that whatever news he'd received wasn't good.

He slammed the door closed. "Don't tell me he escaped," Darius said, agitated.

"Worse," Cyrus growled. He turned around, the shirt Seth had been wearing clutched in his hands. It was covered in blood. "He's dead."

Alarmed, her brothers all rose to their feet. "How the hell did that happen? Didn't you have guards posted outside his door and windows?"

Cyrus' fangs lengthened, his anger struggling to be released. "Of course I did. He took his own life. He slit his throat before Lynx could stop him," he growled, referring to the leading warrior in his Guard.

A grim silence descended on the room, and Ava was the first to sit back down. It frustrated her to no end that she hadn't the slightest clue what was going on. The only reason Seth would kill himself was if he were truly guilty of something. And if he'd somehow been working with Mikhail, it meant the bastard had eyes and ears on the inside to keep track of their every move.

Worse was that a wave of guilt flooded her. If she'd spoken a bit sooner, they could have had him in time to question his motives.

'If you want the cure, I'll be waiting in the place where it all began.'

Ava frowned. That still didn't make any sense. *Mikhail has the cure for Andreas, but it's in the place where it all began?* How in the hell was she supposed to know where that was? Even knowing it was an obvious trap to get them where he wanted them, she knew her family would risk it all for one of their own.

Cyrus closed in on them, speaking in low tones, as if afraid someone other than them was lurking about, spying. "Listen to me very closely. We need to work fast, but efficiently. I will call every one of my workers here and, one by one, I want you, Ava, to get a reading on them. See if anyone else is working against us."

Ava stiffened. *Every vampire here?* She'd have to touch them and sort through their memories, no matter how painful, scary, or…repulsive they could be. Another wave of nausea rolled through her at the mere thought. *I don't want to do that.* It was what she wanted to say. It was right there on the tip of her tongue, but she refrained. She swallowed her own fear and tilted her chin.

She would do it for Andreas.

But she would not like it. Not one bit.

With an almost inaudible sigh, she gave a slow nod.

"Lucian and Julius will be with you, doing their own interrogations. Start with the members of my Guard. I want to make sure they're clear first." To her relief, he added, "You don't need to go through each individual's head unless you want to. You can sense the way they're feeling, as you did with Seth. If anyone seems suspicious, read them." Ava gave another nod, this one a bit more relieved. "Sal, Darius and I will patrol the grounds and keep an eye on security. I don't want anything or anyone slipping in or out undetected. Cass" — his eyes hardened with pain — "stay with Andreas. I need eyes on him at all times in case…anything happens."

Cass gave a solemn nod and left the room. He didn't walk out of the door. He vanished, his large body molding into the shadows until she sensed him traveling away. Ava didn't miss the hint in her father's words. In case Andreas didn't survive through the night or if someone tried to further the process, he wanted to be notified immediately.

Ava felt a painful throb in her chest. She would not let Andreas die. She didn't have the slightest clue how she could prevent it, but she would force a mountain to move if she had to.

She only hoped she could do so before her dear brother's time ran out.

* * * *

With a howl of pain, Marc crouched low to the ground, the cool dewy grass beneath his fingers doing nothing to soothe the scorching fire in his veins.

Food. Hunger. Food. Fuck.

The savage thoughts exploded in his mind with a ferocity that would have scared him had he been in his right mind. But he wasn't. And it didn't. He was angry. He was hungry. He was horny.

He needed to eat something, fuck something and kill something — not so much in that order.

With another howl, he arched his back in pain. His bones shifted and popped until they became dislocated, rearranging themselves as he began to shift.

"That's it," a male voice murmured. "Allow the shift to overcome you."

Marc growled, the noise low and animalistic, even to his own ears. His teeth were clenched together so tight that he couldn't even speak. His face rippled as the muscles shifted. Thick brown fur sprouted from his skin, transforming him from human to animal. When the change was complete, he let out a loud yowl.

The world around him clarified, his vision zoning in on every small movement, his ears twitching with every sound. When he heard footsteps, he spun around, crouching low and baring his sharp teeth at the approaching male.

Duncan watched him warily, holding his hands out in a non-threatening manner, but his stance indicated that he was prepared for an attack. "Easy, Marc," he soothed. He didn't blink. Not once. "I'm your friend, Duncan."

Duncan. Food. Duncan. Food. Kill.

Marc gave a low growl, his front legs bending as he prepared to attack.

Duncan's eyes narrowed. "Listen here, you big bastard. Don't you even think about eating me," he said, pointing his thumbs into his chest. "This meal bites back." His eyes flashed, letting Marc know he was a dangerous enemy.

Kill.

With another low growl, he leaped at the man. His meal rolled out of the way then jumped quickly to his feet again. "Watch it, Marc!"

Marc jumped again, swiping at him with his massive paw. *Food.*

Duncan dodged. "Damn it, you're lucky I'm your friend." With that, he took off toward the woods. In a flash, Marc gave chase.

Food. Hunt. Kill. Eat.

Marc's prey was fast, but so was he. His heart raced as he ran, enjoying the cold night air flowing through his fur. He hopped over fallen logs, dodged low-hanging branches and ducked smoothly around every tree. He was agile as he ran.

Free. Free.

The chase forgotten, he continued to run for a while, excited to no longer be trapped in that cell. At last, he paused in the middle of a clearing, his keen eyes alert as he scanned the area. He jumped high into one of the thick trees, climbing his way up to a branch where he could get a better vantage point. His ears twitched back and forth as he listened closely to the approaching steps.

A large buck came into view, its chest puffed out. Its antlers were high and proud, a sure sign of its virility. Marc crouched low on the branch he was on. *Food.* Instinctively, he crept forward until he was close enough to the animal without alarming it. He licked his lips in hungry anticipation.

Instinct took over. With one strong surge, he jumped down toward the buck with his claws outstretched. The unsuspecting animal realized too late its life was about to end. Marc dug his claws into the creature and sank his massive teeth into its neck. It vaulted around wildly, kicking its hind legs out to dislodge Marc, but he wouldn't budge.

He sank his teeth even harder into the animal. The copper taste of blood touched his tongue, but all it did was increase his hunger. The buck gradually slowed before letting out a low, pained sound as it took its last breaths. With a jerk, Marc released the dead animal. He gave a small, pleased growl and went to work polishing off his meal.

He'd just taken his last bite when he heard the crunch of leaves. He jerked his head up, growling in warning at the approaching man. Duncan only smirked at him, crossing his arms. "I hope you feel better now that you've eaten."

Marc licked his lips and raised to his feet. Now that at least one of his hungers was sated, his bones and muscles begin to shift, morphing back into a man. To his surprise, it didn't take nearly as long to transform as it had earlier, nor was there any of the expected pain. It took all of five seconds before he was standing on two legs again.

The fire burning inside him had died down, though he was still pretty hot. He shook out his arms and legs and tilted his head to both sides, popping his neck. "That was incredible," he said, smiling. He was so energized. The entire world around him seemed far clearer than he'd ever seen it. He looked down at the dead carcass and grimaced. "Mostly incredible," he murmured.

"Don't worry. The desire to hunt eventually goes away," Duncan said, still smirking. "Welcome to shifterhood, brother."

Marc waved that away. "Don't ever say that again. That sounds far too close to *sisterhood*."

Duncan paused, thinking it over. He gave a small grunt. "Yeah, you're right. How do you feel?"

How do I feel? After spending the last three weeks with a lingering fever, constant hunger, stiff muscles and an annoyingly consistent state of arousal, he felt pretty damn great.

"Come. I have a gift for you," Duncan said.

"What is it?"

"You'll see."

Marc followed his friend through the tangled forest. He was naked, but with the heat flowing through his body, the cold air didn't affect him at all. After several minutes, they left the woods and Marc could see the secluded cabin Duncan owned, a large two-story wood-and-stone structure with modern utilities. It was a beautiful piece of work. More than once Duncan had spoken about his 'private getaway' with an unmistakable amount of pride. Marc could see why. He'd never seen the secluded cabin in person, but he admired the handiwork done on the place.

He walked up the steps behind Duncan. Though his hunger had subsided, he couldn't deny the other lusts still plaguing him. The unnerving desire to fight something and screw something was strong.

A musky scent filled his nose long before Duncan opened the door to one of the spare bedrooms, and somehow Marc knew it belonged to a woman. He almost choked on his own tongue when he saw her.

Sprawled out on the fur blankets was a naked woman too beautiful to be human. She smiled up at him and her plump red lips were pouted sensually. The very scent in the air around her had him hard and aching, even more so than before.

"What —?"

"This is Mariel," Duncan said smoothly. "She's a succubus — and more than willing to sate your needs."

"It's true," she purred. She rose to her feet and walked over to him in a way that most men would drool over. When she was standing before Marc, she trailed her fingers down his bare chest. Her scent intensified, as if throwing off some kind of pheromone he couldn't resist. "I am eager to please." She roamed her fingers down to his dick, where she gripped it in a way that nearly made his knees buckle.

He closed his eyes at the feeling of her stroking him. He was acutely aware of Duncan leaving the room and closing the door behind him. He let out a soft noise. The feeling of her soft fingers wrapped around him made him squeeze his eyes shut even tighter.

Shit.

Her touch felt wonderful. Why had he been fighting it for the last few weeks? If he'd known it would feel this damn good, he would have given in the first day Duncan mentioned it.

A sharp, gaping hole abruptly opened in his chest, causing his heart to clench. Frowning, he opened his eyes. The heady, aphrodisiac scent of the succubus cleared from his mind, and he could see her better. She was a tempting woman, but she couldn't even hold a candle to the one he wanted the most.

The pain in his heart tightened, and he felt deep in his bones that something was wrong. *Ava is hurting.* He couldn't put into words how he knew, but some way, somehow, he did. It was like her heart was calling out to him, and he needed to answer.

With a low growl, he pushed the woman away from him and threw the door open, dashing out of the room. Duncan's alarmed shout rang in his ears, but he ignored it. He exited the back door and leaped down the five steps, feeling his bones and muscles shifting again. Before he even touched the ground, he was back in his animal form, racing through the vast fields and tangles of forests.

Duncan was following behind him, trying to stop him. However, none of that mattered.

He didn't want that succubus in the room. He didn't want a single damn woman unless it was *his* woman. He wanted Ava, and not even the fierce tiger chasing him could keep him from her.

Chapter Sixteen

Ava spent the next several days studying her father's workers, hours and hours on end, reading each one separately and sifting through the memories of those who were suspicious. She was trying to see if anyone else was plotting against them. To her annoyance, more than a handful had given off guilty vibes, forcing her to dip inside their minds. She felt like she was invading their privacy, and more than a few times she'd seen some disturbing, gruesome images from their pasts. When she was finished, a sense of relief washed through her that everyone had ended up clean.

But she was devastated all the same. Seth had been their only lead to finding Mikhail, which in turn was their only lead to saving Andreas. Her brother was still hanging in there. It was both fortunate and unfortunate. The good news was that whatever illness the abaddon had cursed him with was slow in moving through him. That meant they had more time to find the cure. The bad news, however, was that Andreas was suffering a slow, agonizing death. She could look into his eyes and see the anguish he was in. It only made her want to find Mikhail even more and rip him apart. She couldn't stand to see sweet Andreas wrought with so much misery. The demon doctors were doing all they could to ease his pain, but it didn't seem to be enough.

The rest of her siblings and her father had been no better. Each of them had had very little sleep as they worked to put an end to this. When she'd finished searching everyone, she'd stepped outside into the midnight air.

She covered her face with her hands, shaking as she tried to scrub the images of what she'd seen out of her mind. So many of her father's workers, though they were happy to have a place to call home and many of them had their own families and lives when they were off duty, had seen so much bloodshed. They'd lost so many loved ones. They'd done unspeakable things once upon a time just to get by.

It was too much. Ava wasn't old enough to have lived through the uncivilized times centuries ago, but she felt as if she had been there after watching so many of the same visions. She was thankful that in her desperation to heal Andreas, she had fought her need to go into one of her Purging episodes. It had been sheer determination that had kept her from locking herself away.

While not a single one of the vampires had been pleased with her having to intrude into their most private memories, no one had fought against it — either out of fear of their king or loyalty to him, no doubt.

Ava clutched a hand to her stomach. The stress of the last few days had put a strain on her body, and she was constantly vomiting. *Gods.* It was too much for one person to handle. The ability to see someone's memories and absorb their feelings was truly a curse. It was a burden to carry so many flashes of death, carnage and destruction. There were memories that weren't even hers, and yet she now had to carry them with her until she could cope with the darkness they brought. She could feel everyone's pain and sorrow as if it were her own. To say it was disturbing was an understatement.

She wasn't strong enough to endure this much. No one was.

She heaved the contents of her stomach onto the ground, wave after wave of nausea rolling through her, threatening to make her drop to her knees.

When the feeling began to dissipate, she wiped at her mouth, grimacing. She pulled out a pack of gum from her pocket, and popped two sticks into her mouth. Back when she had been working at the diner, she'd picked up the habit from Edith. The older woman said chewing gum had helped her quit smoking over the years.

Ava didn't smoke cigarettes, but she did have a rather annoying habit of chewing her nails. Chewing gum helped to control that, as well as aiding her to keep composed.

With a deep sigh and refreshed breath, she strolled over to sit on a bench. She propped her elbows on her thighs and dropped her head into her hands.

Bloody hell, she was devastated. She'd been so happy to finally reunite with her family, but at what cost? It seemed as though her very presence among them had only caused more pain and misery. Andreas lay dying, and there wasn't a thing any of them could do to make it any better, not without any leads to where Mikhail was holing up.

And if only she'd been swifter in seeking out Seth, she could have gotten *some* answers from him. She clutched her chest above her heart. Everything was falling apart just as it should have been falling into place.

With a deep, forlorn sigh, she replayed the Rogue's memory in her mind. There had to be something more to it.

'I'm just going to keep this short and sweet. If you want the cure, I'll be waiting in the place where it all began.' With that, he'd raised an orange lily to his nose, inhaling deeply.

Ava felt frustrated tears sting her eyes. *Porca miseria,* what did that freaking mean? He'd known she would be the one to see the memory, and clearly it was a clue for her to find him. But it was the vaguest, most unhelpful clue in the universe. She was tearing her mind apart thinking about it but couldn't come up with an answer.

The place where it all began. Was it a reference to a place her father knew? Maybe the place where Cyrus had killed Mikhail's daughter? Or where Cyrus and Vladimir had fought the Ancients?

Ava was in the middle of yanking her hair from her scalp when she froze. *Hold on a second.*

"I'll be waiting in the place where it all began," she murmured softly to herself. Her brows furrowed as she concentrated. "Orange lily. He raised a fully blossomed orange lily to his nose. *The place where it all began.*"

With a sharp, humorless laugh, she dropped her hands and rose to her feet. She started making her way back to the house.

Of course! It was all so simple now. She knew exactly where to find that bastard, and she kicked herself for not realizing it sooner. In the heat of the last several days, she had overlooked that not-so-subtle clue of the orange flower. *I am so freaking stupid!*

She was halfway across the grand landscape when a familiar prickling touched the back of her neck. She reached for the dagger she always kept at her hip, grunting in annoyance to find it wasn't there. Damn her carelessness. She'd taken it off when she'd gone to the bathroom before coming outside. Having a distracted mind could lead to certain death in the demon world.

Something she'd be wise to remember in the future.

Always assuming she survived the present, of course.

She cursed her stupidity yet again as she scanned the darkness for the threat. From high up in an oak tree near the lake, her narrowed gaze met two bright golden eyes. Her body went cold and she stood defensively, glaring at the creature. She knew instinctually that it wasn't a normal cougar.

Its body was much larger than a regular animal's, and the heat radiating from it was far too hot, not to mention that the astonishing amount of intelligence in the creature's eyes as it watched her told her there was no way it was stray animal.

It was a damn were-cougar.

She wasn't afraid of the shifters. They were large and powerful in their animal forms, but there were few creatures that could actually stand a chance against a skilled vampire.

She grunted again. Not that she was a particularly skilled one herself, but she did know enough to get by.

However, the stark, possessive hunger gleaming in this cat's eyes made her wary. She could call for help, but the creature was close enough that it could pounce on her before she even opened her mouth. All she had was her hands and fangs to defend herself.

And as strong as vampires were, those massive teeth looked sturdy enough to bite through steel, not to mention she wasn't a full vampire, so she didn't possess the strength and powers of pureblood vamps. *Curse it all.* She was strong enough to lift a man twice her size off his feet, but that was nothing compared to what she'd seen full vampires do.

The shifter hopped down from the tree, landing gracefully a mere few feet away from her. He smelled of rain and blood and...oddly familiar. She studied the cougar even more. The desperate, greedy sparkle of his eyes made her take a cautious step backward.

Bad move. Never, ever do anything to provoke a hungry animal. And this massive cougar before her was starving.

She just wasn't sure if it was for food or something darker.

In a single bound, he leaped forward, and Ava fell on her back with an 'umph'. The cougar stood over her, baring its teeth a mere few inches from her face. She held her breath and kept her head to the side, trying to keep as still as possible. It couldn't see really well if she as prey remained immobile, right?

Then, with a humorless snort in her mind, she chided herself. *Idiot, he's not a damn T-Rex.*

Ava's heart was pounding in her ears. The shifter's heavy paws were on either side of her shoulders, his heavy body hovering over her in such a way that it was impossible for her to even twitch without him feeling it.

He lowered his head and Ava squeezed her eyes shut, expecting to feel pain at having her throat torn open.

It never happened. Instead, the cougar laid its bulky head on her chest and purred. *Purred!*

Opening her eyes, she stared down in shock at the animal nuzzling her like a huge, overgrown housecat. *What...the...shit.*

"Ava!" someone shouted, alarmed. At the same time, there was a loud roar.

The cougar backed off her, allowing her to rise to her feet, but it stood in front of her, growling at the newcomers. Cyrus and Salvator approached her with drawn weapons while another shifter, a large, bulky tiger, sprang from the same tree the cougar had come from.

What...the...shit?

"Ava, are you all right?" Sal demanded, his wary eyes on the cougar and tiger.

"Um...I think so."

The cougar growled again, his muscles tensed and poised, as if he were about to attack. Cyrus glared at the tiger. "Duncan, what is the meaning of this?"

Duncan? Ava glanced over at the tiger, only then noticing the familiar jade-colored eyes with yellow flecks she knew to be Duncan. So that meant...

Her gaze slowly slid down to the cougar guarding her. Easily as tall as her breastbone, he was a beautiful wildcat that had a pelt of silky brown fur. She recalled the eyes of the beast and the scent. She was just full of dumb moments tonight.

She put her open palm on the cougar's head, right between his ears. He tensed, but she stroked him with loving pats. "Marc," she whispered. The painful dull feeling in her chest over his absence disappeared and was replaced by warm heat.

He let out a low hiss in warning at the other males before turning under her hand and rubbing his head against her, letting out that soft purr. With a smile, Ava threw her arms around Marc's furry neck and hugged him. She'd missed him, but she hadn't realized she'd missed him so much. *Gods.* It felt like a bit of the darkness plaguing her mind melted just by being near him.

When she felt his bones begin to shift, she took a small step back, watching in awe as he reverted back to his human form. Duncan did the same, and with flaming cheeks, she looked away from their naked bodies.

She wasn't a prude, but it was all she could do to avoid gawking at such masculine perfection — both Duncan and Marc.

Marc wrapped his strong arms around her shoulders, pushing her behind him so as to shield her from the other men, as if *she* were the naked one.

And going by the disbelieving looks on their faces, they were just as startled as she was. His irrational behavior was territorial. She knew it was due to his awakened animal instincts, but... *Good Lord.*

Cyrus cleared his throat, looking at Duncan. There was absolutely no shame as he stood tall and nude, placing his hands on his muscular hips, his broad chest rising and falling with heavy breaths. "I've been chasing this bastard since last night," he growled, huffing. In his exhaustion, his accent came out thicker than usual. "He's a fast bugger."

"Has he hurt anyone along the way?" Cyrus demanded.

"Only my lungs."

Cyrus clucked his tongue, turning away from them. He growled something in an old language. "Well, come along. It seems he is in enough control and obviously not going anywhere anytime soon. You two can assist us."

Ava stiffened, peeking from behind Marc's large frame. "You're just going to leave me here with him?"

Without looking back, Cyrus threw his hand up in a dismissive gesture. "Where you are is the safest place you could possibly be. Get him a change of clothes, *cara*, and meet us in the library to catch them up. Time is ticking."

* * * *

Marc probably looked like an idiot, but he couldn't get rid of the wide grin splitting his face.

He watched Ava dig through the wardrobe in her bedroom for some clothes for him to wear. Standing butt-ass naked a mere few feet away from her, he allowed his gaze to trail down her luscious body, now bent over at the waist.

Unable to help himself, he strolled forward and wrapped his arms around her from behind, pulling her soft body against his hard one. She let out a startled noise and struggled against him, making him groan when she rubbed herself against his aching erection.

"Marc," she breathed, "let me go."

"I can't," he murmured, burying his face in the curve of her neck. He inhaled, hardening even more at the sweet scent of lavender. "I've missed you."

He sensed her own lust spiking in the air, but instead of allowing him to put them both out of their misery, she pulled his arms apart with a rough tug and pushed him away, tossing a handful of man-sized clothes at him. "Put these on so we can go," she murmured, heading toward the door.

Oh, no. She would not be getting away from him, not when he'd only just gotten her back.

With his newfound speed, he was standing in front of her in the blink of an eye, blocking the exit. Those beautiful emerald eyes widened and she took a step backward. "Well," she huffed, giving an uneasy smile that didn't quite reach her eyes, "I see you're putting your new skills to use."

His grin returned and he waggled his eyebrows. "I have other skills I can put to use, love. Wanna see?"

He didn't miss the darkening of her eyes or the way her desire became more prominent. His heightened hearing could even pick up on the fluttering of her heartbeat. To his frustration, however, she gave a sharp shake of her head and took another step back.

"Why are you running from me?" he demanded, taking a step forward.

She licked her lips, and he had to swallow a groan. He remembered all too well having her kissing down his chest, wrapping those lips around his cock as she took him in her mouth. *Good Lord, I need her.*

"You're the one who ran away from me," she whispered.

Halted dead in his tracks, he gave her a bewildered, stunned look. "I didn't…"

She shook her head again, hugging herself. She lowered her lashes. "I'm sorry for turning you."

He sucked in a sharp breath then reached his hands out to cup her chin. "Ava…do you think I'm upset over being a demon?"

She looked guiltily to the side but didn't say anything.

"Look at me, love." He waited until she did. "I was born a mixblood, from a human and a shifter. Yes, it was your bite that awoke my demon side, but I now have super strength, speed and I won't grow old anytime soon. Tell me, where is the downside in that?"

She gnawed her lower lip and his eyes dropped to focus on the innocent movement.

"Eventually you'll have to quit your job and move away from everyone you know to avoid raising suspicion that you aren't aging. You will now have to follow demon laws, which aren't all peaches and cream. One day you might…make love to a woman you care about and accidentally get too rough and hurt her. It's a long list of downsides. I've ruined your life as a human."

He took another step toward her, closing the small distance between them. He allowed his hands to gently trail down her arms to cup her hips, pulling her against him. "The only thing that's happened to me this past month that I regret is not being by your side every second of the day."

He heard the fluttering of her pulse. "Then why did you leave?" she asked.

He used his fingertips to trace the curve of her cheek, down to those sweet lips. "For your protection."

Her forehead furrowed in confusion. "*My* protection?"

He nodded, using the pad of his thumb to outline her lips. "Yes. You were willing to leave the safety of your family if they didn't allow me to stay. I couldn't let you make such a foolish decision."

She narrowed her eyes, clearly outraged. "You don't get to make my decisions for me. I'm perfectly capable of —"

"Hush," he commanded.

"Hush? Did you just tell me to *hush*?"

He pressed his lips to hers, sliding his hands through the thick waves of her hair, cupping her head and he pulled back slightly. "Yes," he murmured, feeling pleased at the lovely blush rising to her cheeks.

Her lust perfumed the air, and he could see her battling the urge to pull him in or push him away. "Why did you come back?" she asked.

He studied her face, remembering every perfect inch of the bronzed skin covering her beautifully carved features. "That's a good question."

She frowned with a hint of impatience. "Good questions deserve a respectable answer."

He kissed her again, smoothing a hand down her backside. He trailed his lips across her cheek, down to the hollow just below her ear where he knew she was most sensitive.

She gripped his shoulders as if she'd crumble to the ground if she let go.

"I feel connected to you in a way I don't understand," he murmured. "I felt your pain. I knew you needed me, so I came running to you. Literally."

Ava stiffened in his arms. He could sense the conflicting emotions swirling through her.

Who could blame her? The feelings between them were…strange.

It wasn't just a matter of lust. Lust didn't make him want to be at her side every second of the day. It didn't make him run over three hundred miles across Illinois just to be with her. It didn't make him want to face any demon who posed a threat to her and rip them apart.

What he felt was...

Hell, he knew precisely what it was. He just couldn't bring himself to admit it aloud.

Not now, anyway. The timing had to be perfect.

"You...*felt* my pain?" she asked, her voice shaky.

He pulled back to gaze deep into her eyes. "Yes, as if it were my own. But somehow I knew it was you." Realization crossed her features, as if she knew full well what he was talking about. He shook his head. "I'm glad you bit me. Honestly, I've always known I was different from everyone else. Even my mother—" He broke off, an old pain choking him.

She framed his face, peering up at him with a tenderness he felt deep in his heart. "What is it?" she questioned.

"I have a recurring dream of her from when I was about four or five. It's always the same. She was yelling at someone, crying because she didn't want to raise me. When she saw me, she became terrified, calling me a demon, a monster and other horrible names. Then"— he sighed and turned his face into her hands, kissing her palm—"she tried to kill herself right in front of me."

Ava gasped in horror. "She *what?*"

He nodded. She pressed her lips together, her eyes shining as if she felt his pain through whatever bond connected them. She studied him for several quiet moments. "It's not just a dream, is it?" she questioned.

He shook his head again. "I read the police report when I started looking for her when joining the academy. That night, I'd locked myself in the room, but she'd kept screaming, so one of the neighbors called nine-one-one. They took her to the hospital and determined she was suicidal, so they placed her in a psych ward until she was released a few years later. She lost custody of me, and I was placed in foster care."

When a single tear fell from her eye, he used the pad of his thumb to swipe it away.

"That's horrible. I'm so sorry, Marc."

He sighed again. "All this time I thought it was the drugs that made her that way, but now I know it's because she knew what my father was. In turn, she knew I wasn't full human." He smiled gently, kissing her forehead. "I'm not upset over this Change, Ava, not one bit. This is who I was meant to be. I should be thanking you, actually. So please stop letting guilt eat you up. I'm...content."

She closed her eyes and relaxed her expression, her relief washing over him. He leaned forward and kissed her on the lips, loving the way she opened to him. He gave her lower lip a teasing bite before drawing it into his mouth. "Now, love," he murmured against her lips, "what was it that had you in so much pain?"

"Andreas," she breathed. "He's dying. It's a long story, but father will explain it to you and Duncan in the library."

He froze, seeing her deep sadness. He pulled away with wide eyes. "Holy hell, woman, why would you try to seduce me at a time like this?" He jerked on the clothes she'd handed him then headed toward the door, looking back to see her mouth dropped open in disbelief.

"I didn't seduce—"

He waved that away and motioned for her to hurry along. "Come on, love. They're waiting for us."

She murmured something under her breath in Italian, and he didn't need a translator to tell him what it was.

He hid a smile and took her fingers in his hand. He gave her a brief kiss before tugging her down the corridor toward the private library.

* * * *

"I know where Mikhail is hiding," she said

In the library, Marc refused to let Ava move more than a foot away from him. While it filled her with an immense burst of happiness, she still felt the dark dread looming in her heart. Andreas' life lay on the line, and they would be able to find the abaddon and heal him if they moved fast.

Marc and Duncan had been updated as to what was going on, and both were eager to help them track down Mikhail.

Eight pairs of shocked eyes turned to Ava at her statement. She nodded, her face solemn. "He's in Tuscany."

Those same eyes widened, half with curiosity, half in disbelief.

"How do you figure?" Lucian demanded, clearly on team disbelief. He looked between her and Marc with blatant disapproval. No doubt it was in his elder-brother instincts to dislike any guy who looked her way. It was the same as it had been many years ago, when other vampires had shown interest in her.

Thankfully, however, he didn't say anything.

"He said he'll be waiting in the place where it all began," she elaborated. "At first I thought it was a reference only father would understand. However, he was holding an orange lily. I assumed it was random, but it isn't. Do you all remember the first time I got lost after I came to stay with you? I went exploring the lands around the villa but ended up losing my way. Turns out I'd wandered farther away from home than I expected and wound up near the mountains in a field of lilies. Mikhail was the first to find me, and I remember he picked an orange lily and put it in my hair. He said it was his daughter's favorite color. It was the very first time I ever met him."

She peered around at each of them. "I know it sounds crazy, but I'm sure he's back home in Tuscany, probably hiding in the mountains." She fiddled with her hands in her lap, her voice beginning to lose some of its confidence at their incredulous stares. "It's our only clue to finding him."

Cyrus leaned forward on his elbows. "You're right, *cara*. Those mountains have any number of secret tunnels leading deep into caverns. There was even an old myth that the first natives built secret passageways to escape the intruders taking over the land."

"Old myth?" Duncan demanded with obvious skepticism. "Weren't *you* there?"

Ava twisted her mouth, trying not to laugh, despite the circumstances. Someone else let out a tiny snicker before covering it with a fake cough. Duncan hadn't said it to be funny, but the insulted look on Cyrus' face threatened to make her lose her composure.

"For your information," Cyrus said with indignance, "I'm old, but not *that* old. *Merda*. Jupiter, strike me down. The myths go back long before the Etruscans lived in the lands. The tunnels are still there, of course, but their origins are unclear to this day."

"Ah, my mistake," Duncan said, shrugging. Like Marc, someone had given him spare clothes, though his legs were just a bit too long for the jeans he wore.

"Soooo…a trip to Italy?" Darius asked, a flash of excitement in his glacier-like eyes.

Cyrus nodded. "*Ita.* I'll warn my lieutenant there about what is going on so he can keep an eye out for anything peculiar and scope out the land ahead of us. That, and I need to make sure our travels are covert and not alarm anyone else who may be working with Mikhail."

"Just one question," Ava said, her tone dry. "How the hell are a group of vampires, a tiger and a newly turned, inexperienced cougar supposed to travel thousands of miles across the world without drawing unwanted attention?"

Her brothers gave her bland looks, as if she were daft. She shrugged. "And I'm quite sure not even Sal can carry us all."

Sal bristled at her statement, offended. "I beg your pardon, *piccolina*, but I can teleport an entire army if I so desire."

Ava rolled her eyes. Sal's Royal power was the ability to teleport from place to place. As far as she knew, he could only flash a few people at a time. Any more than that and their molecules might become so jumbled that when they reappeared, they could be muddled up as one. It was a risk she so did not want to take.

"Nonsense. We will take the private jet," Lucian said, waving his hands as if it should have been obvious. "It's faster, it's secluded and when we land, we can quickly begin our hunt."

Ava placed a hand over her stomach as another wave of nausea slid through her at the mere thought. *Flying? Yeah, that's the easiest 'hell no' in the world.* "Polite pass," she said, a small tremor in her tone.

Lucian's frown deepened. "I suppose you have a faster choice?"

No, she didn't. *Smart ass.*

"Don't tell me you're afraid of heights?" Darius asked in disbelief.

Ava worried her bottom lip, refusing to meet their gaze. When she'd traveled from England to America all those years ago, it had been by boat. At least if there had been an accident, she could have swum or drifted until she reached land. Planes, however, were another story. Flying any number of miles in the air with no sturdy ground beneath them and the possibility of freefalling until she became soup for the ground...

Afraid of heights? Me? Nahhh.

"Come now, darling. It's not that bad," Cyrus soothed. "The jet is spacious and designed to provide you with the utmost comfort."

"Exactly," Julius chimed in. "It won't even feel like ten hours once you —"

"*Ten* hours!" she exclaimed.

Julius' mouth dropped open in surprise at his accidental words and Cass smacked him in the back of the head. The blond then turned to look at her, his eyes softening. "If it makes you so nervous, the doctors infused sleeping aid into Andreas' bagged blood. You can drink one of them and sleep the majority of the way there. By the time you awaken, we will have landed or be close to doing so."

Ava shook her head, not at all liking the thought of being drugged just to board a plane. *How embarrassing. Besides...freefalling thousands of feet in the air while unconscious? Like hell.*

"That's not necessary," she said on a sigh. "Let's just go and get this flight over with."

Ten hours on a damn plane. Gods help me.

"It's okay to be afraid of flying," Julius said to her in a chipper tone, as if he could possibly ease his earlier words to her. "Lucian is terrified of boats."

Lucian's eyes went wide with horror at his secret being revealed, and he growled threateningly at Julius, who in turn gave an innocent smile.

Ava shook her head again, a tiny grin splitting her lips. If it was Julius' attempt to make her feel better, she had to admit it had worked.

A little.

Chapter Seventeen

As promised, Cyrus' private jet was nothing short of luxurious. With the cabin lined in white leather furnishings and custom wood veneer, it was just another ridiculous illustration of her father's immense wealth. There was even a small built-in theater, complete with high-speed Internet and a mounted TV where the twins were playing some video game, no doubt to have a distraction from the impending battle.

The back half of the plane contained a private bedroom where Andreas slept. They hadn't wanted to leave him behind in case they were able to get the cure and could heal him in a timely fashion.

That, and they wanted to keep a close eye on him at all times. Even after determining that the remaining vampires were all innocent and loyal to the king, there was no guarantee one of them couldn't be manipulated just as Seth seemed to have been.

Cyrus sat with his ankle crossed over his knee while he tapped at his phone as he communicated with his men — or played Candy Crush. The man had a rather odd fascination with the childish game. More than once, Ava had caught him muttering and cursing to himself after losing a level.

Lucian was sitting still as a statue, looking out of the tinted window, his mind no doubt in a different place. Cass sat polishing his already-clean blades and Sal was reading a magazine on the latest fashion trends in the modern world.

Duncan was sprawled out in one of the recliners, his mouth hanging open as he snored. He'd been in that very position in a deep slumber since they'd boarded. Ava rolled her eyes. If there had been a question in her mind about what type of demon he was, she could just look at him at that moment and tell he was a big, lazy cat.

Mingled with the rest of them was a handful of other vampires, including her father's Guard. A team of seven vamps, they were essentially a modified, far more lethal version of the Secret Service. They were employed by the king, each trained by him, making them seven of the most deadly vampires walking the earth.

To anyone outside looking in, they would all have looked utterly outlandish, dressed in a variety of black jeans and leather, riding casually in a lush private jet — like *The Expendables* in first class. Ava would have laughed at the ludicrous getups if she wasn't doing her best to hide just how sick she was. She made her way to the bathroom and clutched at the smooth stone countertop, using every bit of willpower she had to keep from darting over to the toilet to empty her stomach.

Marc was standing just outside the door. She refused to let him come in. She didn't want anyone seeing her in this weakened state. It was so freaking humiliating. She could spend hours fighting and killing her enemies without a second thought over the blood and gore spilling out.

Yet flying in the safety of a jet piloted by vampires with many years of experience was enough to make her queasy.

Pathetic.

There was a knock on the door and the knob turned. She opened her mouth to tell Marc not to enter, but it was Cassander who appeared instead. She straightened.

"Cass, what are you — ?"

He gave a tiny smile. It might as well have been nonexistent. Such was the norm with him. Where Lucian always wore an ice-cold, oftentimes grumpy mask, Cassander's expression was always just...blank. Unless one truly knew him, he was impossible to read. Hell, even for Ava and the rest, it was *still* hard to get a feel for what he was thinking. The man may as well have been a walking statue.

"I'm just checking on you."

She eyed him quizzically. "I'm surprised Marc let you in here without him."

He rolled his shoulders. "His protective manner over you is admirable. Annoying as hell, but admirable. It took a fair amount of bribing, since threats from Luc didn't work."

"What's the bribe?"

His smile turned secretive. "That's between men, *piccolina*. However, I only have five minutes."

She shook her head, resisting the urge to scoff. "I'm fine. Just air sickness."

He nodded but obviously didn't believe her. His look turned somber. He reached under his leather jacket and handed her a small box. Ava took it, her eyes growing wide in disbelief when she studied the pink cardboard. Her mouth parted. She looked up at him, but he held out a hand, cutting her off.

"Take it," he said, his tone soft but stern. "You can lie to the rest of our family but not to me. Remember, I was mated once before. I know the signs."

Ava's heart clenched as she felt his pain. "Maria was pregnant?" she whispered.

A wounded expression crossed his face, but he gave a small nod to the box in her hands. "I will not tell anyone, but I want your promise that you will take care of yourself. We're heading into a dangerous battle, one that could be fatal for some of us. I know asking you to stay behind will be futile, but I don't want you to take any unnecessary risks."

Ava swallowed before nodding. He gave another small smile before exiting the bathroom, closing the door behind him. Ava strolled over to lock it, leaning against the wall and sliding to the floor.

She clutched the pregnancy test in her shaking hands, that sense of dread filling her even more. The throwing up, the fatigue, the rise and fall of her emotions... It all made sense.

She placed a hand over her mouth, her eyes stinging with tears. She couldn't be pregnant. Not now. Not with all the dangers and drama surrounding them, not with them so close to facing off against Mikhail. Most of all, not now because she and Marc weren't even an item.

Oh, no, what will he think? They hadn't even had the chance to explore what was going on between them. And though he was protective of her and refused to leave her side, that didn't mean he wanted to mate with her. For vampires and most other demons, mating was a sacred ceremony between two lovers who wanted to become one with each other. It was deeper than marriage. Once two became mates, they were bound to one another for the rest of eternity.

Mating gave a literal meaning to 'till death do us part'. As Cassander had told her, it didn't take years of courting to decide whether or not a vampire wanted someone as a mate. It was an instant connection of the heart. Their mind might fight it, but once the heart found its truemate, there was no getting rid of the feelings.

She covered her face. She'd always felt drawn to Marc. Ever since the first day, she'd wanted him. It was far more than simple lust, though she'd tried to convince herself otherwise. In reality, Marc was her truemate. She knew it. She'd known it the day Cass had explained it to her, but she'd been forcing herself to not think about it. It had hurt too much.

However, that didn't mean he would agree to hop all willy-nilly into a lifelong commitment to her. He was only a newly awakened demon. He wasn't accustomed to their ways, so no doubt if she revealed the meaning of their mutual feelings, he'd freak out—or deny it, like she had.

She looked down at the pink box and gulped. She already knew what the answer to the test would be. The signs were all there. She'd been a fool to think otherwise. Still, she wanted to be one hundred percent sure. No, she *needed* to be. She needed to see proof with her own eyes. And if it was positive…

Well, if it's positive, I'm just magnificently screwed, aren't I.

* * * *

Marc had never left the country before. Hell, he'd only left Illinois a handful of times, and it had always been for business. He just hadn't felt a need to go anywhere. He'd always been content.

Well, not completely content, he thought ruefully. He'd always felt an odd ache in his heart, but it wasn't like he'd ever tried to examine it. Hell, he hadn't *wanted* to examine it. He merely spent his years pushing it aside and focusing on what was ahead of him.

Now, however, he had a feeling that vast emptiness had had everything to do with Ava. When he was around her, he was always filled with warmth. Her scent, her smile, her very presence filled that void in the best of ways. He wanted her in every sense of the word, to have her rely on him and him alone. He had such an unfathomable desire to make her his, to hell with Duncan's warning. He would protect her with his very last breath. Come hell or high water, he would die before he let anything happen to her.

Admitting his feelings to her would have to wait, however. Seeing the pale, stricken look on her face as she sat next to him in the blacked-out SUV worried him.

After being briefed on what they were dealing with and knowing that one of her brothers lay sick and dying, Marc had felt pure rage. He didn't know her family on a personal level, but they were important to her, which meant they were important to him, no matter how much the oldest continued to glare and threaten him. He would kill for them if it meant making Ava happy.

A notion that should have disgusted him. He was a cop, after all. He'd spent the last decade serving and protecting his community, upholding the laws and setting an example for young eyes. However, demon laws were different. So long as humans weren't involved, Marc would kill who or what needed to be destroyed in order to save Ava. *Call me prejudiced, but hey...*

At least, that was how his inner demon felt. The more mundane side of him wondered if he'd actually be able to take another's life, demon or not. He'd killed those hellhounds to protect her, but what about demons who really looked like people? Or even Rogues. They had once been human, right? *Can I do it?*

He glanced down at Ava. She was stiff, her body ramrod straight as she sat on the other side of the seats. Sweet Jesus, just the foot between them was far too great a distance, but he refrained from crossing over. He sensed her desire to be alone. She was worried over her brother and nervous about the upcoming battle, but he had a feeling there was something else bothering her.

Maybe some lingering guilt that she'd caused him to turn into a demon? He turned to look out of the window, though they were far too tinted to see anything. He hadn't lied to her earlier. While her world was indeed new, strange and quite startling, he didn't regret being a demon, not one bit.

Perhaps it was further proof of his fading sanity, but it was true. He was learning that being a shifter was pretty damn awesome. He had more strength and energy than ever, he was faster, his senses were sharper and, best of all, he wouldn't age. No doubt most people would find the entire experience starkly terrifying, and he had too, at first, but the pros greatly outweighed the cons.

Besides, it wasn't like he had any family to worry over. His adopted parents had both passed, *may their souls rest in peace*. His birth mother was also dead, and he'd never met his father. There were no other siblings, no distant relatives that he knew of. He was entirely alone in the world. Now he could live a long life without the fear of watching his family fade to nothing while he continued living.

He even had more time to do what he really wanted, which was open up his home as a safe haven for kids who'd grown up like him. Ever since being saved by his foster parents, he'd always known he wanted to follow in their footsteps. He wanted to get kids off the street, clean them up and provide them with the type of love and warmth that would inspire them to become something greater. Of course he wanted kids of his own as well, but it had always been his desire to help those in need of a parent's love.

After another hour or so of driving, the vehicle rolled to a stop and they exited. Marc darted around to Ava's side and opened her door, holding out his hand to help her exit. She took it with a small hesitation, sending a jolt of heat through him.

To his dismay, however, she refused to meet his eyes. He didn't miss the way her fingers gave a slight tremble.

Frowning, he tilted her chin to look up at him. "Ava, are you okay?"

She darted her tongue out to lick her lips and he swallowed a groan. Though his Change was complete, he still was on edge. Both of his hungers were haunting him, but he pushed back his lust. Now was not the time.

Now, his desire to fight? Oh, he was so looking forward to kicking some ass.

She let go of his hand and took a step back, turning to her brothers. Her reaction was odd and jerky, but before he could question her further, Cassander stepped between them. A frustrated growl bubbled inside him. He knew the male was her brother, but he couldn't help the flare of jealousy rolling through him at another man being so close to her.

He blamed it on the predatory instincts that were still new to him.

He forced himself to focus on their surroundings. He couldn't help but gawk at the sprawling property stretched out over the broad landscape. Like his mansion back in Chicago, Cyrus' villa was a wonderous, massive structure filled with beautiful gardens and trimmed grass. *Jesus, how much money does this man even have?*

It was also secure enough to make the Pentagon look like a local flea market. The land was set in a valley of small, rolling hills with an astonishing close-up view of a portion of the Apennine Mountains in the background. With the sun dipping behind the picturesque ridges, it left a miraculous halo shining over the villa.

The breathtaking scenery was something he burned into his memory, making him wish he had a camera. It was unlike anything he'd ever seen before, and there was no guarantee he'd ever be granted a chance to see such a mesmerizing image again—not in person, at least.

His gaze slid over to where Ava stood with the rest of her brothers and her father's workers, who'd all joined together after exiting the line of SUVs. Her back was turned to him, but he couldn't find it in him to be angry. She was dressed neck-to-toe in a fitted leather suit and he couldn't help but admire her long, slender limbs and the gentle curve of her back down to her perfectly round ass. Her thick black hair was pulled into a neat bun, the graceful curve of her neck tempting him. His body hardened.

How one person could look so gentle and fragile yet be such a badass at the same time was beyond him. He didn't complain, though. He loved every bit of it.

Her brothers and father—even the other vamps who'd traveled with them—were all dressed in similar attire, their faces set with grim determination. Among the leather, shitkickers and dark battle attire, Marc and Duncan looked as out of place as...well, two cats in a lair of vampires. They were dressed far more casual in loose jeans and hoodies, so if the need to shift came, it'd be easy to undress to transform.

The rest looked every bit the deadly warriors Marc knew them to be. He felt a teensy flare of fear on Mikhail's behalf. The man had harmed one of their own, and they were coming for him with a vengeance. This group before him would stop at nothing to ensure justice on Andreas' and Ava's behalf, as well as the multitude of their fallen brethren who he'd either killed or turned Rogue.

With a hidden smile, Marc joined them, Duncan beside him. Somehow...he felt as if he was right where he needed to be. He loved being a cop, but he'd always had a minute gut feeling that there was something else out there that was his calling. He had yet to figure out what it was, but this was a large step in that direction.

Inside the villa, Cyrus began barking out orders to the vampires who'd been waiting for him. The men and women hastened to carry out their duties. Marc admired the loyalty they had for the king. There was no hesitation, no question, just swift obedience.

With everyone prepared for war, they stood around a large conference table with several maps spread across the glass. Cyrus and Lucian broke everyone down into teams, pointing out all the known entrances into the mountain. They knew there was danger lying in wait. They knew there would even be several traps. Each team had at least one vampire from the Guard, who had a telepathic line to each of the other Guards and Cyrus.

The orders were given. The very second the sun disappeared behind the crest of the mountains, each of the teams exited the villa and went to their designated tunnels, fanning out in search of any enemies who lurked around.

There was no need for vehicles. They were far too noisy, and with everyone being a demon, their speed and stamina exceeded those of a human, for which Marc was grateful. It took about an hour to check through the surrounding woods and another before they reached the entrance of their designated tunnel.

The rest of their team made their way inside. However, Ava paused before entering, raising her nose to the air. He did the same, though what he was sniffing for eluded him. Even with his heightened senses, he was still learning to differentiate the diverse smells.

"What do you sense?" he asked her.

Her eyebrows were pulled together in frustration. "Nothing."

"Isn't that a good thing?"

"It's never a good thing." At his questioning look, she elaborated, "Do you hear anything?"

Marc frowned in return, pausing to strain his hearing for anything surrounding them. "No."

"Exactly. We're surrounded by miles and miles of forestry, but there isn't a single animal scurrying about."

His frown only deepened at the realization that she was right. There was a possibility the colder fall weather had the animals tucked away in their homes, but even the nighttime creatures that were immune to the weather should have been heard — or the drumming of cicadas and other small insects. But there wasn't a single sound. He understood her unease.

When she started to go into the tunnel, he grabbed her wrist, turning her to face him. She still wouldn't meet his gaze. In a swift movement, he leaned to press his lips to hers in a brief kiss. Her eyes were wide when he pulled back.

He gave her a small smile. "I will protect you no matter what, love. I promise."

Her cheeks turned a lovely shade of pink. She narrowed those pretty eyes. "How many times must I say I can defend myself?"

This time Marc was wise enough to hide his amusement. He and her family had spent a great deal of time trying to get her to stay behind in the safety of the villa with Andreas. Unfortunately, the woman had insisted on joining them. Compared to Marc and her towering, over-muscled family, she was like a cute little rabbit standing up to a group of bears, but it in no way kept her from backing down. She was so stubborn.

They'd at last given in to her demands, because they knew if they had forced her to stay, she would have found a way to sneak off and head into danger without backup.

With another swift, bone-melting kiss, he turned toward the tunnel. "I know, love. You're a big bad vampire. *Rawr.*"

She opened her mouth, no doubt to call him all sorts of sordid names. However, there was an abrupt shift in the air, making both of them tense. He sniffed the air, nearly gagging at the sudden stench of death and rotting flesh.

"Good lord, what the hell is that?" he demanded in disgust, his stomach churning as his hairs stood on end.

Ava's eyes were wide. "Abaddon," she breathed. Then, without another word, she took off, heading away from the tunnel.

"Ava, wait!" He shouted, chasing after her.

He caught up to her, but she was fast, maintaining several feet between them as she dashed along a narrow path up the mountain.

The rising slope turned into flat ground, revealing the wide mouth of an opening hidden by thick overgrowth. Not once did she slow her pace. The horrid scent became stronger and, without a pause, she dashed inside the cave.

"Stop, Ava!"

He started to follow her but slammed into something with enough force to crush his nose. He shouted out a curse then tried to enter again and again, to no avail. "Ava!" He yelled, pounding on the invisible barrier she'd disappeared through.

His panic rose, his frustration exploding inside of him as fear gripped his heart. He was utterly powerless to chase after her.

"Fuck!"

Ava dashed inside the cave, following the scent of the abaddon. She realized that Marc was no longer following her. He was trapped outside at the entrance of the cave. She'd felt the shimmer of magic as she'd entered through the invisible barrier, but she'd been too focused on finding the forbidden demon to pay it much attention.

Vampires were vulnerable to magic. Only a very rare few had the ability to sense it, but it was practically an invisible weapon to the rest. Ava was half fey. She couldn't wield magic or create portals or…hell, anything really, but she could see it and, in some instances, repel it.

The barrier she'd stepped through, however, had obviously been put up to prevent anyone else from entering. Only her fey blood working against the magic had allowed her to push through it.

She stopped in the middle of the dark tunnels, debating whether or not to turn back.

She was so close, not that she knew what she'd do when she got to the abaddon. She couldn't touch the demon or she'd contract a disease as well. And she didn't have anything on her to capture the beast and drag it out.

But she could lure it away, somehow. She could get the demon to follow her out into the open where one of the other vampires could capture the disgusting thing.

That was, *if* she could even get it to follow her. Pulling two wicked silver daggers out of her boots, she continued along the trail, keeping her eyes and ears peeled for any sudden movements.

She turned several corners, keeping a steady jog before coming to a halt in a small, empty cavern that led nowhere at all.

She peered around the small room. The walls were far too thick to hold a hidden door, and there wasn't an illusion spell hiding anything. She would have sensed it. There was only one way in and one way out.

But that was where the abaddon's scent led…

With a scowl of frustration, she gripped the hilts of her blades, cursing herself for her stupidity.

By the gods, I've been fooled. She'd walked straight into a trap.

As if confirming her theory, there was a low, sinister hiss, followed by a painful prickling dancing down her spine. She kept her back to the cavern wall on the far side of the entrance, getting into a defensive position, even as she tried not to gag.

The stench of rotting flesh filled the room, wrapping around her and clinging to her skin, making her desperate for a hot shower. She watched as the abaddon crept into the room, followed by a handful of Rogues and, lastly, Mikhail.

She kept her blades up, baring her extended fangs at the entourage. It was a show of bravery she didn't feel. Not that she feared a mere few Rogues or Mikhail… It was the abaddon she did her best to keep from peeking at. The horrid creature wasn't just feared for its deadly skin and blood. Its visual presence alone instilled nightmares among even the most hardened of soldiers.

With a small shudder, she glared at a grinning Mikhail, who stepped forward.

He was dressed in a dark cloak with a hood covering his head, his soulless eyes drinking in the sight of her. *Cripes.* Between his sick perusal of her and the abaddon's gods-awful stench, she wanted to flay her own skin and soak in a hot tub in an attempt to clean the dirty feeling that seemed to cling to her. "Not bad, darling," he murmured. "You always were quite the beauty."

She curled her lips in distaste, but she didn't say anything, not when the smell of decay was threatening to make her puke.

He lifted a pale eyebrow. "No witty banter? No sarcastic remarks? No curses of how despicable I am? You disappoint me."

"Give me Andreas' cure," she demanded simply.

He tilted his head curiously and took on a stance as if pretending to be confused about what she was saying. "The cure? Hmm. I can't say I know what you're referring to, milady."

Ava growled, not for the first time wishing she had the powers of a full vampire. Unlike everyone else, she didn't have blasts of powers radiating from her body. Some could send nearby objects flying, shatter glass or create fissures. Any of those would damn sure come in handy right now.

Half vampire and half fey, unable to use magic and unable to wield the full powers of a true vampire. *What a freaking nuisance.*

With her embarrassing lack of abilities, no doubt she just looked like a snarling shih tzu. *Yeah, very ferocious. What a joke.*

"Don't screw with me, Mikhail. Your pet abaddon is the only thing that can take the illness away from Andreas."

He pondered her words for several more moments before snapping his fingers, as if suddenly recalling his own devious plot. "Oh, yes. *That* cure. My mistake."

The Rogues around him grew agitated, shuffling and twitching with the suppressed need to jump forward to drain her dry. It was proof that while he was able to control them, they were still bloodthirsty beasts beneath the surface.

"Where is it?" she asked again.

He waved a slender hand toward the drooling demon. "You're more than welcome to approach the abaddon and retrieve it yourself."

Ava gave another shudder of disgust. Black gunk was dripping from its mouth…*if that's even a mouth.* Its grayed skin lay in shreds, hanging from its gnarled body like ripped clothing.

Oh gods, oh gods, oh gods. Gross.

Swallowing the bile that rose in her throat, she looked back to Mikhail when he chuckled. "Something funny?" she demanded coldly.

"For someone who has managed to outsmart and escape me for so many years, you so readily fell for such a simple trap. It's so deliciously ironic."

"It'll be deliciously ironic when I rip out your throat with my fangs."

"Ahh, there's the witty banter." Mikhail pulled back his lips, revealing fangs even longer and thicker than her own. He stroked his tongue up the length of one. "I suppose if you don't want to get the cure for yourself then…"

He made an odd gesture to the abaddon, and before she could prepare herself for an attack, she screamed, watching in wide-eyed horror as the abaddon used a sharp talon on one hand to slice open its own throat.

Shocked, she saw black blood spill from the creature and begin to bubble away before turning into a puddle of black dust.

Ava let out a loud, furious shout before lunging across the room at Mikhail. "You bastard!"

He didn't even move. The Rogues around him charged forward, far too fast for her to counter. She only managed to land a few slices and stabs before she was forced to the ground. One of the creatures had a handful of her hair and slammed her face-first into the solid rocks. Stars danced before her eyes and she struggled against the Rogues, but with another painful blow, she fell unconscious.

Chapter Eighteen

The need to get to Ava had Marc shaking with fury.

Idiot, idiot, idiot. The words continued pounding away inside his head.

If only he'd been faster in catching up to her. He punched the nearest tree so hard that the bark cracked beneath the force of the blow. Pain rippled through his hand, but it did nothing to stop him from beating his fist into the tree again and again.

It was either that or give into the urge to shift. His skin was rippling, his bones vibrating as he barely suppressed the need. Learning to recognize the signals was one of the mini lessons Duncan had given him during his self-imprisonment. If he knew the signs, then he'd be better at controlling the urge to shift around humans.

However, if he couldn't get to Ava in the next couple of minutes, the thin, fragile thread that was holding him together was going to break.

It was the firm hand on his shoulder and cool blast of power pulling him away from the battered trunk that stopped him. He glared into the hard silver eyes watching him with a combination of sympathy and frustration.

"You need to calm yourself, brother," Lucian commanded, his voice calm. "Going around destroying the wildlife isn't helping a thing."

Marc shrugged his hand off, running his hands through his hair in annoyance. "I can't just sit here and do nothing," he growled, turning to pace back and forth. He was beginning to feel like a caged animal. *A rather fitting description*, he acknowledged. "God knows what's happening to her in there. She needs me. I just know it."

Lucian took a step back, his eyes narrowing. "You think my sister is helpless?"

Marc let out a sharp laugh. "I've seen firsthand how well she's capable of defending herself. She's a natural survivor."

"Then you need to trust that she will do whatever is needed to escape or live until we can get to her. She was taught by the best, after all." With that, his shoulders straightened and he tilted his chin in a proud manner, letting Marc know *he* was the one who had trained her.

Marc gave a dry snort. "Yeah, let me thank you for that. I fell in love with a woman who can literally rip my throat out."

A silence fell upon them and Marc belatedly realized his own words.

Love.

It was true. He was in love with Ava. It was an emotion that had always eluded him when it came to past girlfriends, but he'd found it in a half-blood vampire—a vampire who was beautiful yet deadly, and strong, with a vulnerability that tugged at his core.

He'd always had feelings for her, even when he'd thought she was just a regular waitress.

He grimaced. *Well, not regular.* Nothing about Ava had ever been regular.

But it had never once deterred him from developing feelings. He'd come to care for her. He'd spent every other day coming to see her at the diner. She hadn't said much, but he hadn't missed the way her eyes would heat when she looked at him. He'd wanted to breach those defenses and see her without that aloofness around her.

He only wished he'd been bold enough to tell her his feelings earlier. He'd wanted to wait until the time was right, but at what cost? He knew better than anyone that the future wasn't guaranteed. There was no such thing as perfect timing.

He loved Ava with every fiber of his being, and he kicked himself for not having the balls to say it sooner. Now, by the time they got to her, she could be—

He shook his head. *No.* She'd be okay. She'd be safe and alive, and he would tell her how he felt and make her his. The need to claim her was powerful, and he didn't want to wait anymore. He *wouldn't* wait anymore.

He was brought from his musings when he sensed the other man still watching him with a strange expression. "What?" he demanded.

Lucian's lips twisted into a faint smile. "I've seen this before. You really are her truemate."

Marc frowned, unfamiliar with the term. "What is that?"

"I—" he cut himself off, tensing as he scented the air. "*Cazzo*. I'll tell you later." He turned to his father and brothers, who were attempting to break through the barrier around the cave. "We'll take care of it," he told them, and the other men nodded. "Come on," he directed at Marc before taking off.

Marc was still confused as he followed Luc. What was the 'it' they were taking care of? His speed made him able to keep up with the vamp, but just barely. He'd known vampires were fast, but...*holy shit*. The man moved like lightning, ducking and dodging trees and branches as if the forest were his home. And he was silent, too. Not even the fallen leaves and twigs on the forest floor made a sound beneath his heavy bulk.

'Unnerving' was a good word for it.

Meanwhile, Marc was far less graceful. It was annoying as hell because *he* was the cat. He should be the one with a fluid, agile gait, not sounding like a toddler stomping around in a tantrum.

They came to an abrupt halt in the middle of a clearing. Lucian pulled out the big-ass sword strapped to his back, scanning the eerily still forest around them. His dangerous power swirling in the air sent cold needle pricks over Marc's skin.

"Why did you bring me here?" Marc demanded, his nostrils flaring at the strange shift in air. There was something...big lurking nearby.

"You sense them," Lucian said. "There's at least a dozen Rogues. And you, my friend, are in dire need of a distraction."

No argument there. Marc was itching to sink his teeth into something—a lot of somethings.

Really, really hard.

With a feral grin, he heard the steps of the Rogues approaching, could hear their furious hissing as they crept forward. "You're right about that," he said, undressing before giving in to the impulse to shift.

His bones shifted and stretched as he transformed into the large cougar that had been clawing to be free. Just as the change was complete, the first few Rogues stepped out of the trees. They were ragged, dirty and no longer possessed the unearthly beauty all vampires had.

"I always am," Lucian said with pride, anticipation lilting his tone.

* * * *

Thirteen-year old Ava watched the men around her with bleak eyes. All she could think about was that her mother was gone. Dead. She'd said she would come find her, but she never had. She'd lied.

A man approached her wearing an ancient Roman toga brushing the top of his sandaled feet. He was tall, with the palest blue eyes she'd ever seen. He was scary-looking, with an imposing presence, but she wasn't afraid. Why should she be? She had nothing left to live for. Her mother was dead. She had no family.

The man knelt before her, bringing him just a touch below her eye level. She just watched him, uncaring what he'd decide to do. Even still, he smiled. There was kindness in that smile, but pain shone in his eyes. He was hurting on the inside, just like she was.

Yeah, right. *He was a king. He had a vast amount of wealth and the strongest security team to protect him day in and day out. What on earth did he have to be sad about?*

"I am your father," he murmured in Italian. Ava had learned the language after she'd turned five, when she and

her mother had moved to the country. "My name is Cyrus, and all six of these boys behind me are your brothers."

Ava blinked, unimpressed. Her tone was flat with a hint of accusation. "If you are my father, why have we never met? Why were you unable to protect my mother?"

His eyes widened, that deep pain intensifying. "That... I am deeply sorry, piccolina. *If I had known her...circumstances, I would have offered her protection right away."*

Ava didn't say anything, only continued staring into the man's eyes with disinterest. Something about that pain tugged at her curiosity. Why was he so hurt? What had happened to him? She wanted to know. It couldn't possibly match her own sadness. She had lost her mother, after all. You only get one.

She took a glove off one hand and raised it. Cyrus watched her with hesitation, but he didn't back away. She placed her palm on his warm cheek.

Her eyes flew wide at the images she saw. There were so many bodies. So much blood. So much carnage. Cyrus' pain flooded through her, choking her with its intensity. She saw a beautiful woman with fair hair twisted into a series of braids and kind blue eyes smiling at him. The vision of her made Cyrus happy. There were three sons — an adult, an adolescent and a child. Cyrus was proud of them. He loved his family. The image changed. Now he was holding the woman's dying body in his arms, screaming in pain. Sobs filled Ava's mind. There was more death. More carnage. Cyrus felt sadness and rage. Soon there was another woman. She was also beautiful, with light brown hair and forest-green eyes. She was holding the hands of twin boys, with another baby cradled in her arms. Cyrus was happy again. Then, there was a fire. His second mate was trapped inside the house. He couldn't save her in time. More screams of pain filled Ava's mind.

She snatched her hand away from Cyrus' face and placed it over her mouth, hot tears running down her cheeks. Her coldness was gone, replaced by fear and sorrow — for her loss and this man's loss. He was in deep, despairing pain. He'd wanted to end his life, but he couldn't, for the sake of his children.

Ava shoved her glove back on and wiped her eyes. "I'm sorry," she whispered.

He gave her another one of those sad smiles. "As am I, darling." He tore off a piece of fabric from his sleeve and wiped at her eyes. "You are one of us now, Ava. We are your family. And as long as we are all one, there is no pain we can't overcome together." He smiled, and this time it was much warmer. "You are a Gordano now."

Ava opened her eyes with agonizing slowness. It took several blinks for her fogged memory to clear. She sat up, wincing at the pain in her head.

Crap, that hurt. She reached up a hand to wipe away the blood sliding down her temple. She scowled, however, when she heard the familiar rattling of chains. She glared down to see her wrists were now encased in silver shackles, as were her ankles. Much to her annoyance, the leather sleeves of her bodysuit had been cut off to reveal her bare skin, allowing the silver to burn into her.

Why, why, why *does it always have to be silver?* She yanked against the chains, testing their strength. *Gods, what a nuisance.* Why couldn't her enemies ever use rope, or iron shackles, or, hell, even a shock collar. If the material was thick enough, it was as effective at binding as silver, just without the severe burns.

But nooo. They didn't care about her tender skin. Sure, she could use her strength to break through anything else, and okay, she supposed silver was the only surefire way to capture a vampire, but still. They could've at least left the leather covering her wrists and ankles.

This shit hurts.

Freaking jerkoffs.

Heaving an annoyed sigh, she peered through the metal bars, her temper flaring more when she sensed they were silver as well. Full silver, at that. They were smart jerkoffs.

With another deep sigh, she leaned back against the cold stone wall, peering into the darkness beyond. Not even her heightened vision could pierce through the inky blackness. Her nose worked just fine, though.

"Come on out, Mikhail," she said, forcing her tone to sound bored.

There was a dark chuckle that made her skin crawl before the vampire stepped into view. He was grinning, a triumphant look in his black eyes. "Such strength is admirable, my dear," Mikhail said.

He was slimmer than most men, but the dangerous power swirling in the air around him was a warning that he wasn't a foe to dismiss. She frowned at his immaculate figure. Even in movies it seemed the villain always had to be handsome. It was a pain in the ass, for sure. Plus, it gave all other good-looking men a bad rap.

She thought about when she'd seen the abaddon slicing its own throat open at Mikhail's command. Of course, he'd never planned on keeping the creature alive. It took a tremendous amount of strength to keep from launching herself at the silver bars.

"That's hardly a compliment coming from you."

He grinned, moving to stand close to the bars but not touching them. "The energy around you seems rather dark. Tell me. Has tragedy struck the mighty Gordano family?"

She kept her expression impassive. "It's about to strike the Nilsen family — or what's left of it," she taunted.

His eyes flashed with anger before smoothing over. "*Touché*. I supposed Cyrus has finally admitted his sins to you, then?"

"I'm afraid I'm not sure what sins you're referring to." She brought her hand up to study her nails, pretending the silver shackles didn't hurt like a bitch. "My father happens to be a righteous man."

It was an obvious lie. In his long, long, *long* life, Cyrus had made decisions that would have horrified even the most brutal of psychopaths. He was far from an innocent, but one thing was certain. He was a fair and just king whose decisions were for the good of vampire-kind.

Mikhail sneered in derision. "Defending a murderer, I see."

Ava narrowed her eyes. The memory of the mountain of dead bodies caused by Mikhail flashed in her mind. "As if you have any room to talk. Unlike you, he carried out his duty and did what was necessary to uphold our laws."

He didn't bother to hold back his anger. A blast of power slammed into her, crushing her against the wall she leaned on. That was the exact type of power that she lacked, but would have come in handy at least fifty times in her life. He let out a dark growl. "He killed my child in cold blood."

She gritted her teeth against the pain, continuing to glare into his eyes. "She was a Rogue. She was killing anyone who crossed her path. For her own sanity, she needed to be put down. It's the only thing we *can* do for them."

"She was a *vampire!*" he barked. "Humans are nothing more than livestock for us, yet for some reason we are supposed to treat them as our *equals*? She was my only child and that arrogant bastard took her from me. Of course you wouldn't know what that's like. Even as an empath, you can't possibly understand my pain." He raised his hand as if to send another blast of power at her.

Before she could stop herself, she clenched a hand over her belly. She held her breath as he watched the movement, his nostrils flaring. The moment realization hit him, his face smoothed over and he reined in his power. A delighted expression crossed his features, one that caused a cold chill to inch down her spine.

"Well, well," he purred. "The king is soon to be a grandfather. What a lovely turn of events."

She paled, her blood turning to ice. "What events?" she demanded, her voice coming out shaky.

He grinned, his white teeth gleaming in the darkness. "Cyrus doesn't know what it's like to lose a child." He placed a hand to his forehead, chuckling. "But he will. Blessed gods above, he will."

Ava swallowed the cold lump of dread in her throat. "You already sentenced Andreas to death."

His eyes gleamed with joy, but there was nothing warm in those soulless pits, only malice. "That was just insurance. However, a father losing his daughter, his *only* daughter, is a far greater pain than losing a son, especially when there are five others to replace him."

A growl tore itself from Ava's throat. "He's lost more friends and family than you could ever imagine. All he knows is suffering, and you—"

Her words were cut short when the rocky walls began to tremble, bringing down a shower of dust and pebbles. She gave a small smile and forced her tense shoulders to relax when a familiar power rippled through the air. "And you just ran out of time."

Instead of appearing fearful, he kept that smug grin of his. "Afraid not, my dear." He unlocked the door to her cell and strolled over to her. She cringed away, doing her best to mold her body into the cold wall. He only reached out a gloved hand and wrapped it around her throat, cutting off her air supply. She struggled against him, but with the silver shackles holding her in place, she was powerless. "It's your time that has run out."

* * * *

Marc was in a full-blown rage as he bit, swiped and tore his way through the horde of Rogues. They were strong, but nothing could stop his determination to get to Ava.

Icy needles washed over him, but it was the sheer heat of his adrenaline that left him unaffected. The trees surrounding them shielded the beasts, making it impossible to tell how many there were exactly.

He had a faint awareness of Lucian fighting around him, which was no doubt the source of the drop in temperature. He was swinging his sword through the air as he slayed his share of Rogues.

The coppery taste of cold blood fueled Marc's bloodlust. His vision narrowed and everything turned red. His moves became swifter, his bites harder, his growls deeper. His only thought was to kill everything in sight. With each passing second that Ava wasn't near him, his rage only grew. He soon began shredding through his enemies as if they were paperweights.

Kill. Find mate.

The words continued to echo around in his head. With a furious growl, he sank his massive teeth into the throat of the last Rogue. It let out a gurgling scream of pain. Marc shoved away from the creature, turning to face Lucian. He didn't see the tall male as a comrade. In his red rage, all he saw was another enemy. He crouched low, growling at the vampire.

Lucian's silver eyes went wide before he returned the growl, flashing his fangs. "Don't even think about it, Whiskers," he snarled. When he noticed Marc slowly inching forward, poised to spring, he hid his sword behind his back and held out a passive hand. "Do not give into your rage, Marc. We have more enemies to face." He paused then said, "We need to save Ava...together."

Marc straightened, the red fading from his eyes as he blinked. Lucian nodded. "That's right, brother. Let's go get her."

Marc let out a low hiss before turning and darting into the forest, Luc running beside him. He continued following Ava's scent through the narrow path up the mountain, back toward the mouth of the cave she'd run in to. Cyrus and the others were still there, waiting.

Cyrus' hands were on the invisible barrier, his eyes closed. Marc watched as the vampire called forth his ancient powers. Electricity buzzed through the air, causing Marc's fur to stand on end. He paced, anxious to seek out his love. The electric heat grew and he fought to keep from snarling at the looming threat.

There was a pulsating blast of power, and the ground beneath Marc's feet trembled. He growled, taking a step back. One more strong blast of power and there was a loud crackle, like thunder in the sky. In a strong gust of wind, the barrier was destroyed, and without waiting for any orders, Marc flew past everyone and dashed inside.

He ignored the men calling his name, instead focused on Ava's faint scent through the tunnels. Any Rogue unfortunate enough to cross his path was slaughtered in a blink.

His mate needed him, and nothing was going to stop him from getting to her. *Nothing.*

His demon vision pierced through the darkness as he turned this way and that. He was acutely aware of some of the men following him. The rest had fanned out through the other winding tunnels.

After what seemed like an eternity, Marc came to an abrupt halt in a wide cavern. Torches lined the walls and towering stalagmites stretched high up into the ceiling that was more than fifty feet high, with beautiful yet sinister-looking stalactites of all sizes hanging down. Shadows danced along the rocky walls, and Marc could sense dozens upon dozens of Rogues hiding about. There was a small body of water separating them from the dark tunnel on the other side of the cavern, the clearness of it showing its depth.

Lucian and Darius appeared on one side of him, while Cyrus and Salvator appeared on the other. His additional two brothers and the vampires who'd come along had left them to hunt throughout the vast tunnels.

"So kind of you to finally join us, old friend," a sinister voice called out.

On the far side of the cavern, a slender man stepped out of the shadows. He was dressed in a dark cloak, with everything but his head covered. He had pale

Slavic features with pitch-black eyes twinkling with mischief. His smile was full of smug satisfaction.

Cyrus' power crackled in the air. "Mikhail," he said, his powerful tone bouncing off the rocky walls. "Where is Ava?"

"Close, but you should be far more worried about your own predicament, Cyrus."

Cyrus took a threatening step forward. "Kidnapping my daughter and cursing my youngest son *is* my predicament."

Mikhail looked bored as he regarded them. "Ahh. A daughter you did not meet until she was a teenager, and a son who is not yours."

"Blood or not, they are my children and they carry my name."

"Now you are beginning to feel my pain."

Cyrus hissed, his dangerous power whipping in the air. Even Lucian's snapped forward, clashing with his father's. Lightning and ice. Not the best combination. "You cannot begin to know what true pain is."

Mikhail's own power surged forward, bringing a gust of wind through the cave, causing the water to stir. Marc stiffened in fury. He smelled blood. Ava's blood.

He growled.

"Easy, Marc," Lucian warned in hushed tones. "I smell it too."

Marc could hardly restrain himself as he shuffled back and forth. He scraped his claws on the ground, like a bull getting ready to charge.

Or a cougar about to pounce. *Whichever.*

"True pain is watching your father's so-called friend let him die in battle," Mikhail growled. "It's also watching that same man ruthlessly kill your own child."

Cyrus pointed a thick finger at the man, his muscles tensed. "Your father was a great warrior who gave his life for the greater good. And your daughter was too far gone to be saved. There isn't a day that goes by that I don't suffer from the choices I made, but one thing I will never do is betray my own kind."

Mikhail scoffed. "No? You leashed an entire race of demons, confining them to clans and preventing them from hunting the way nature intended."

"He saved our people from eternal damnation," Lucian shouted. "If not for his rulings, vampires would still be at the mercy of other demons. There is now order, peace and no need to lurk about in the shadows."

"Yeah! Plus, there's Wi-Fi!"

Sal, Luc, Cyrus and Marc all turned to glare at Darius. He looked taken aback, shrugging. "Just trying to contribute."

"*Idiot*," Sal growled before turning his attention back to Mikhail. "Return Ava to us, Mikhail, and bring forth the abaddon."

"I'm afraid that's something I cannot do. You see, the abaddon no longer with us."

Lucian hissed, his icy power swirling in rage. "You *killed* it?"

The other man shrugged, his smile widening into a deliberate taunt. "It had fulfilled its purpose."

"Bastard," Sal snarled. Fury radiated from his body. "Andreas will die because of you."

"Well, that was the purpose, after all."

Lightning crackled in the air, making Marc's fur stand on end. "No matter how unjust your need for revenge is, this feud is between you and me. Why bring my children into the mix? You plotted to separate Ava from us all those years ago and spent the entire time tracking her down. What is the true purpose of it all, if you just want me dead?"

"Oh, no, Cyrus. I don't want you dead." Mikhail sneered, curling his lip in disgust. "Though nothing would please me more than to rip your heart out, death is simply too kind a punishment for you. I want you to feel what I feel. I want you watch everything you worked so hard to build crumble at your feet as a new nation takes over."

Marc watched as the man turned to the side, waving behind himself. There were some grunts, following by shuffling then a rattling of chains. Ava was pulled into view by three Rogues. Her wrists and ankles were bound in silver shackles, making it impossible for her to move more than a few inches at a time. One of her eyes was swollen shut, blood trickled from her temple and even from this distance Marc could see the bruising around her neck, as if someone had choked her.

Red rage leaked into his vision again and he snarled. He'd only taken a step when Lucian stepped in front of him. His own body was stiff, his fury evident in the freezing temperatures. The clear pool of water a few yards away began to ice over. "Not yet," Lucian growled.

Marc growled in return, one second away from flinging the man aside with his teeth. All he could see was Ava and that someone had dared to hurt her. Every fiber in his soul was screaming to get to her, and it only further pissed him off that Lucian was interfering.

Mikhail wrapped his arm around Ava's neck, hauling her against his body. He produced a silver blade and he stroked it down her cheek. Even from the distance, Marc could hear the sizzling as the blade burned her soft flesh. She struggled against him, but his forearm tightened around her throat, making her good eye squeeze shut in pain.

"Let her go," Cyrus commanded, a hint of desperation in his furious tone. "This is between *us*!"

"Yes, it is," Mikhail purred. His trailed the blade down her collarbone, over the curve of her breast to where her heart pounded in her chest. Marc shook with rage, bouncing on his paws with the need to tear the other man apart.

"Sal," Lucian whispered, so low that if Marc wasn't a demon he wouldn't have heard it.

"I got it," the silver-haired vamp responded.

"Darius."

"Right," the twin said in the same soft tone. Marc didn't know what the hell they were planning, and at the moment, he didn't care. He just wanted to get to his woman.

"I have waited for this day for centuries," Mikhail hissed, his fangs flashing. "The one and only daughter of Cyrus the Conqueror." He trailed the blade down her flat stomach, pausing with the tip poking just under her navel. "And his first grandchild."

Someone made a choked sound of shock and Marc stiffened, his heart stopping for several frightening seconds. *Ava...is pregnant? With* my *child?* And this man dared to harm them.

Oh no. Hell. No.

Possessive, white-hot rage flooded through him, causing him to dig his claws into the ground. He didn't wait for whatever the brothers were planning. All he saw was Mikhail raising the blade and ramming it into Ava's gut. At the same time, a loud gunshot rang through the caves, entering from the back of Mikhail's skull and lodging itself somewhere in the man's brain.

Ava let out a piercing cry of pain and Marc was charging forward with a speed only certain demons could match. Several Rogues detached themselves from the shadows and came at him with fangs bared.

Marc didn't let a single one of them stop him as he charged around the pool. He used his heavy bulk to slam into several of them, knocking them into the ground before biting and clawing through them. More than once he felt nails scratching him and fangs biting into his skin, but with the fierce way his blood was pumping, there was no pain — only anger and a brutal need to get to Ava.

Her brothers and father charged after him. Marc noticed the walls and ceiling shaking from the combined force of their powers.

From his peripheral vision, Marc could see Mikhail's body falling forward, sending him and Ava tumbling into the water. Fear clutched Marc's heart when he saw Ava sinking into the pool, her and Mikhail's combined blood turning the clear waters red. He let out a loud snarl of fury, fighting against the damned Rogues. Everything was a red blur as he made his way through the horde, no doubt looking nothing short of a rabid beast.

Chapter Nineteen

The freezing water Ava was drowning in did nothing to ease the silver burning into her wrists and ankles, nor did it do anything at all to soothe the scalding pain of her latest wound, the silver dagger still buried deep in her belly.

What was worse, the heavy chains binding her made it impossible for her to swim to the surface. So she just hung there, unable to do a damn thing as she sank to the bottom of the pool of water.

And isn't this just a bitch? She'd faced mages, Rogues, ghouls, hellhounds and all sorts of other demons out to get her. She'd always come out victorious. Always. Maybe a little beat up, battered and worse for wear, but victorious, nonetheless.

Yet it seemed the one thing that would take her down was freaking drowning.

Damn the gods.

Her lungs were on fire and blackness was creeping into the corners of her vision. In a matter of seconds she'd be forced to take a breath, and it would all be over. There wasn't a damned thing she could do about it.

For once in her shitty life, however, it seemed luck was on her side. There was quick flash of silver hair. Then her body began to tingle, feeling as if her bones were melting away to nothing.

Just as quickly, she found herself sitting on the rocky interior floor of the cavern. She sucked in huge gulps of air, all the while coughing up the bit of water she'd swallowed before being saved.

Her shaking arms supported her while a big warm hand patted her on the back, another under her torso to help keep her from falling forward. When she felt she could breathe again, she turned and fell onto her back, putting her weak hand on the hilt of the blade protruding from her belly. She groaned in pain when she tried to pull it out, but it was too deep. And she'd lost far too much of her energy.

"Don't move, Ava," Sal commanded, kneeling over her.

Yeah, no problem there, she thought with a wry twist of her lips. Every drop of energy she had was depleted. She couldn't even lift her limbs anymore. They were just too heavy. Her whole body screamed in pain. Even her vision and hearing were fading away, the sounds of battle around her growing more and more faint. It took everything within her to keep from blacking out.

Marc... She had to see him. She had to make sure he was okay. There were so many Rogues charging him at once. Her entire world had frozen in horror.

With effort, she tried to muster whatever remaining strength she had, but she was no match against Sal's slender, yet firm, hand holding her down.

"Don't push yourself, *piccolina*," he commanded again, his accent thick. "You're safe now."

Ava wanted to protest and force him to help her up despite the pain she was in, but no words would come out. All she could do was lie there and fight against blacking out. In the end, unconsciousness won.

When their battle ended, Lucian pulled Mikhail's limp body from the cold water of the pool, tossing him like a ragdoll onto the rocky ground. The bastard wasn't dead yet, but he would be within the next few minutes. Cass had shot him in the head with a silver bullet, and so long as it remained lodged in there, the man would stay unconscious until they either removed the bullet or waited for his body to turn to ash.

He glared down at the despicable traitor, wishing with everything within him that he could remove the bullet and make the bastard suffer a slow, painful death.

A very *slow, very painful death.*

Too bad he had his orders. There was no redemption for Mikhail, nor would there be any trial. Far too many had been killed and had suffered at his hands. There was no undoing what he'd done.

He wanted to hang Mikhail by silver chains and leave him out for the sun to burn him alive. He was an Aristocrat, so he wouldn't turn to ashes right away. However, he would suffer massive third-degree burns if left out for a few days with no blood to feed on.

Or he could skin him alive, leave him for the rats to feast on his flesh, give him blood to replenish what was lost then start the process all over again.

Or Lucian's personal favorite nightmare — strip the bastard butt-naked and drop him into a pit of hellhounds in heat.

He shook his head. Okay, maybe that was a bit too far. Despite what people claimed, he was no longer an uncivilized beast like his brethren had once been before establishing clans and peace. Those days were long behind him.

Nor was he the type to enjoy watching someone being tortured, no matter if they deserved it or not. He would do it if it were required, and he had before, but it had not been entertainment for him, only duty.

He glanced over at his unconscious sister, his belly becoming a twisted ball of fury. Hell, maybe he would enjoy a few punishments for the bastard at his feet.

With a frustrated growl, he signaled to one of the vampires hovering nearby to watch over Mikhail then strolled over to where Marc was kneeling over Ava. The shifter was ass-naked, but he didn't seem to care in the least bit as he held a shaking hand out to her, stroking her bruised face with a gentle caress.

Lucian had to admit that he had a newfound appreciation for Marc. Despite being thrown into a world of dangerous demons, finding out he was a half-breed, turning into a full shifter and charging head first into danger, he'd showed a remarkable amount of courage and strength.

Lucian hadn't cared for him at first.

However, he had to admit Marc had shown he was a worthy mate to stand at his sister's side. He had put his very life on the line for her. It was that type of devotion that made Lucian want to call the guy 'brother', no matter how annoying and arrogant he was.

Lucian joined his father and brothers as they gathered around Ava, ignoring Marc's warning growls.

Damned truemates. It was bad enough he was a shifter. Add to that he was a newfound truemate, his territorial instincts were off the freaking charts. Lucian had seen it with his own father and Cass. New mates were a pain in the ass. He wanted nothing to do with it.

Cyrus' eyes were full of rage and pain when he looked at Marc. He pointed to another handful of vampires who'd returned from scouting out the caves. "Follow them back to the villa. The healers working on Andreas will help her, but you need to back off. For her sake. And her child's." His voice cracked on the last word, and Lucian didn't blame him. They'd all been shocked to learn Ava was pregnant, and after seeing Mikhail stab her in a vital organ to kill her and her unborn baby had enraged them.

Marc hissed but gave a curt nod. Despite the heat and fury radiating off him, he lifted Ava in his arms with loving gentleness, as if she'd break if he used too much pressure. Then, in a blur, he and the chosen vampires exited the cavern.

Lucian rose to his feet, shaking his head in frustration. "There are still far too many questions left unresolved."

"It pisses me off," Darius grumbled.

They were all covered in blood from their recent battle, but no serious wounds had been inflicted. *Thank the gods.* Lucian was a powerful man, but he didn't think he could take it if another one of his siblings were on the verge of being taken away from him.

Cyrus barked out a series of orders to the remaining vampires. Some of them were to return to the villa, while some were to head out in search of the surrounding woods and nearby towns to make sure none of the Rogues had escaped.

The only ones who remained were the five brothers, Cyrus, Duncan and a couple of Cyrus' Guard warriors. He looked at the them and Julius. "Did you find anything?"

Julius answered, "No one else inhabited these caves. However, I did find an iron cell. It's been abandoned for quite some time, but there was some kind of fey there not too long ago."

"If it's been abandoned for a while, how do you know a fey was there?" Duncan demanded, crossing his arms. Unlike Marc, he was still dressed. It was clear his entourage hadn't come across any of Mikhail's minions to fight.

Julius opened his mouth to no doubt say something ignorant, as per usual, but he paused, considering his words. Lucian's idiot brothers had their intelligent moments, as brief and fleeting as they might be. "Because, Puss, the iron was recently damaged, as if whoever was there had escaped, but they left behind blood. And while it's dry now, I can sense it's only a few weeks old."

Duncan glared at the name-calling. They knew Mikhail had kept the fey Lila trapped, but that had been over eighty years ago. It was possible the poor woman had died decades before, but if Mikhail had held another fey here, who was it? And why? And how had he managed to create so many Rogues that he was able to command?

"Did you catch onto a trail?" Lucian demanded, but Julius was already shaking his head in denial, the braid of his mohawk swishing back and forth.

"The trail vanishes just outside the caves."

"*Cazzo*," Lucian murmured, shaking his head. The fey must have used a portal to escape. And with Andreas too sick to leave his bed, he couldn't use his skills to see the past of whatever had happened here. They were essentially back at square one.

"Was this really the best Mikhail could do?" Darius grumbled, kicking at a stray pebble. "I get the idea of trying to make Pops suffer, but there's no way he spent all those years hunting Ava down and making Rogues just for...this."

Sal hissed, narrowing his pale eyes. "What are you saying?"

"Think about it," the twin elaborated. Lucian wondered if the twins had their strokes of genius at the same time. It wasn't the first time when they said something intelligent, it was back-to-back. "Mikhail said he's been waiting on this day for centuries, as in plural. Ava only came to us a hundred and eight years ago, meaning Mikhail had been trying to make a new race long before he met her. That tells me that killing her was just a bonus in this whole revenge strategy, but unleashing Rogues had been his true plan all along."

"Yes, is there a point to this?" Duncan demanded, eliciting an eye roll from Darius.

"My point, *Garfield*, is that for him to truly want his plan to take effect, he has to have more Rogues out there hiding, waiting to be let loose. Every smart villain has a backup plan, after all."

"And as much as I hate to say it, Mikhail isn't a stupid man," Sal murmured. "Insane, but not stupid."

Lucian rubbed his temples. Again, far too many questions with no answers.

Cyrus spoke next, his tone weary from the events of the days. "We'll do another search of the tunnels for any clues and check all the places Mikhail once lived. We can probably get Ava to..." he glanced over at Mikhail's body turning into ashes. His power crackled in the air in annoyance. "*Cazzo*, never mind. We now have no leads, and our one clue to explaining what's going on or how this mess started lies in a wayward fey we know nothing about and have no possible way of tracking. Terrific."

Lucian shook his head, sharing his father's frustration. "What's more, with the abaddon dead, we can't do a damn thing for Andreas."

A distressed silence fell among the men in the room, each mourning the inevitable loss of their brother. No doubt they were all feeling guilty for their inability to catch the abaddon in time. Even as Lucian tried to tell himself it wasn't his fault, that it wasn't anyone's fault except for Mikhail's, he couldn't help but assume the blame, just like he took the blame for everything that had happened to Ava — her running away, her being hunted down all these years, her nearly dying at the hands of Mikhail...

Jesus Christ. Fate had tormented his family enough over the centuries. When would it end? Did they not deserve the peace they strove so hard to establish among their people?

"We'll find some way to cure him," Cyrus said with a confidence Lucian didn't feel. "On my life, I will not allow him to die such a horrible death. There has to be another way to fight the illness in his blood. For now, we just have to lend him our strength and do what we can to make him comfortable. Until then, let's do another sweep of these tunnels and caves, then meet back at my villa for some much-needed rest. We've all had a long-ass day."

Lucian had no argument there. He was ready for this mystery to be solved already so he could get back to his clan duties in Chicago. It was just the distraction he needed from this chaos.

* * * *

When Ava first awoke, her initial thought was that she was alone. The bed beneath her was made of the softest material, making her feel as if she were floating on a cloud. There was complete darkness in the room, and the only sound she could hear was her own steady heartbeat.

She sat up, frowning at the odd sense of déjà vu.

It was pitch black, but her eyes pierced the darkness. The bedroom was smaller than the one in St. Charles, but no less elegant, with its polished wooden floorboards and crimson-and-gold interior decorating. There were two tall windows on either side of her bed, both deeply tinted and covered with thick drapes to block out the setting sun.

A slew of memories flashed in her mind, making her heart skip a beat.

This was her old room in Cyrus' palace in Tuscany, the one she'd been given when she'd first come to live with her father and brothers. At first, Cyrus had spent several weeks trying to get her to tell him exactly how she wanted the room decorated — what colors she wanted painted on the walls, whether to add more of a 'girly' touch to it or not. But Ava had insisted that the room was perfect as it was. Growing up with her mother, they had always been on the move, so Ava had never had a place to call home, let alone her own room. She'd been pleased with whatever she was given.

A small, wistful smile curved her lips.

Then, remembering the reason she was in Italy in the first place, a small gasp escaped her lips. She peered down at herself, spotting her bare wrists that were now healed. There wasn't even a faint redness to reveal the burns she'd endured. She pulled back the thick red covers to discover that the skin around her ankles was restored as well.

Swallowing the big lump of dread in her throat, she lifted up the hem of her satin nightgown — wondering how she'd gotten into it in the first place — and smoothed her fingers over the thin white scar below her navel. A flare of panic raced through her as she spread her hands flat against her belly, as if it was possible to feel a tiny heartbeat in there.

The doorknob to the connecting bathroom twisted open and Marc stepped out, a thick red towel wrapped low around his hips.

Holy…shit.

Ava's panic was forgotten for a moment as her mouth went dry. It wasn't her first time seeing him without clothes — or even her second time. But hot damn, he never failed to make her heart leap with excitement. He was always a gorgeous man. However, it seemed as if the Change had made every inch of him more defined.

His smooth skin stretched taut over powerful muscles. His hair was trimmed, the longer strands lying damp across his forehead. The angles of his face were sharper, his eyes almost glowing across the dark room.

When he saw her sitting up, his golden eyes widened. With a speed that revealed he wasn't human, he was kneeling on the bed beside her in the blink of an eye.

He reached out to cup her face with a gentleness that warmed her heart.

"You're awake, love," he whispered. His breath was warm, with a faint scent of mint. "How are you feeling?"

She had to clear her throat several times before speaking. It felt like she'd swallowed a pound of gravel. Marc reached across her to grab the glass of water on the nightstand beside her.

Ava swallowed a groan at the delicious scent of him—warm blood mixed with sandalwood. It was an erotic combination that sent heat racing straight to her pelvis.

Ava took the glass from him, taking deep sips while peering at him over the rim. His nose flared, sensing her blatant arousal. His own eyes darkened in response, making Ava hide a smile behind the glass.

When she was finished, she placed the glass back on the table. "Thank you," she murmured. She cleared her throat one more time. Satisfied that it wouldn't give another embarrassing croak, she said, "What happened in the caves? The last thing I remember is Sal teleporting me out of the water and...nothing."

His look flashed with pain and anger, as if the memory of seeing her hurt made him want to rip someone's throat out. "We won," he said tightly, his voice thick.

She thought back to when Mikhail had stabbed her. There had been a loud gunshot, but she'd barely heard it in her moment of fear. Everything had happened so fast, and before she'd known it, she was falling into the water with Mikhail on top of her. "Mikhail is dead?"

He nodded with grim satisfaction. "When we separated from the others, their orders were to circle around the rest of the tunnels to make it so Mikhail couldn't escape in the midst of the battle. It was Cassander who took the killing shot from behind him. His Rogues attacked us after that. There was a helluva lot of them, but in the end, we killed them all."

Ava frowned. *Just like that? It seemed...too easy.* "Something doesn't seem right."

Marc nodded, coming to the same conclusion. "We figured that, too. While we killed the Rogues in the tunnels, a great number of them escaped. Not to mention Mikhail no doubt had several more of them hiding in other cities." He shrugged. "Mikhail is dead now, so as the leader of...whatever it was he was plotting, the main threat has been terminated. All that is left is hunting down the remaining Rogues — wherever they're hiding — and things will be back to normal." He paused, thinking over his words before giving a dry snort. "Well, whatever normal means to demons."

She frowned as she tried to understand everything going on. She still felt foggy from waking up. "Exactly how long was I out?"

"Three days," he muttered, shaking his head. "It's a combo of all the silver draining you and stress. You were...*dead* to the world." His lips twitched, and she narrowed her eyes at him. If it was his attempt at a joke, it was a piss-poor endeavor.

With a small shake of her head, a feeling of dread twisted in her gut. "Andreas," she breathed. "Mikhail killed the abaddon."

Marc gave her a sad smile. "He's stable for now. Your father has some powerful witch and demon friends who crafted a special amulet. That's all still freaky to me, by the way."

"A what?" Witches and mages were universally disliked among vampires. It shocked her that her father was willing to allow a witch into his home, let alone to perform whatever hoodoo on Andreas, even if they were *friends*.

"Whatever it was, as long as he keeps the amulet, the illness is held back. It's only a temporary solution until we can find another way to cure him. But for now, he's okay."

While fear for her brother still gripped her heart, she couldn't help the sense of relief she felt that they had more time to find a cure.

Then, she froze when his words registered. "We?" she asked, unsure.

His hard look softened, and he reached out a hand to cup her cheek. "Yes, love. *We*. Whatever your worries, your burdens or feelings, I want you to share them with me." He used his free hand to hold her own, bringing it to his mouth. Heat surged through her at the electric sensation of his lips touching her knuckles. Gods, even the smallest of his touches were enough to have her desperate for more. *Much more.*

"I know you feel this chemistry between us," he murmured between kisses. "It's more than lust, or a fling, or a passing crush. I...I feel complete with you."

Ava's heart filled with a sudden, inexplicable warmth at his honest words. "It's because you are my truemate," she whispered.

She expected him to frown, question it or even call her crazy. Instead, he nodded. "Your brothers told me what that means. We are destined for each other. I've never believed in anything like that, but I can't deny that from the day I first saw you, I just knew you were important to me."

Ava smiled as stupid tears stung the edges of her eyes. Heat pooled in the pit of her stomach at the feel of him nibbling on the tender skin of her inner wrist. "Marc," she murmured. Then, her earlier panic returned. She placed her hand on her flat stomach, feeling the cool, silk material of her gown.

Reading her train of thought, he smiled, genuine delight shining in the golden pools of his eyes. He covered her hand with his larger one. "While you were unconscious, your father's doctors looked over everything. Our child is just fine."

Her heart skipped a beat. "Our child," she breathed. "Are you sure you want this? Us?"

Instead of a direct answer, Ava found herself flat on her back with Marc hovering above her, his towel discarded. She pressed her hands against his chest, unable to help herself from stroking the satin skin.

"I want all of it," he whispered, his breath fanning across her face. Then, his lips met hers in a way that was both possessive and demanding.

Ava let out a soft moan and melted against him, deepening the kiss. If there was ever a doubt in her mind that either one of them was uncertain about the other, it disappeared under the tender warmth.

He traced the shape of her full lips with his tongue before dipping into her mouth. She roamed her hands up his pecs and over his broad shoulders. He was shuddering, as if fighting to hold back his need. Ava was right there with him. At the same time, he was sliding the silk gown over her upper thighs, her stomach, her aching breasts and over her head.

He sat back on his heels, smiling down at her with a sense of pride. There was such male appreciation in his dark gaze, as if he were looking down at a trunk full of priceless gems.

"I'll never get tired of looking at you," he murmured, leaning down to kiss a hot trail over her throat and the soft curve of her breast. He flicked out his tongue to lick at her straining nipple before pulling the tight bud into his mouth.

Ava let out a soft moan, arching her back in silent invitation. "Marc," she breathed when he spread her legs apart, revealing the slick wetness of her arousal.

He responded by dipping a finger into her heat, followed by another.

Lust perfumed the air, a heady combination of both hers and Marc's. Every kiss sent a shockwave of electricity through her blood, from the top of her head to the tips of her toes.

Marc dragged his tongue down the length of her body, pausing long enough to kiss the small scar under her navel before continuing his downward path of torment. "You're so beautiful, my love," he whispered against her skin.

"So are you," she breathed in response, squirming beneath him. "So damn beautiful."

"Mmm." He settled between her legs, his eyes glittering with desire. "You're mine, Ava." Never taking his eyes off her, he gave her damp flesh a loving lick. "You're *mine*." Another lick.

Ava moaned, her hands latching onto his head to hold him in place. However, he paused his torment to stare into her eyes. "What is it?" she questioned.

"I'll never let you go, Ava," he murmured. "Do you know that?"

"Yes," she whispered in response. There was no hesitation.

"Good."

He dipped his tongue inside her, stroking her in a way that had her toes curling. She tangled her fingers in his hair, her hips arching off the bed as his tongue went deeper, sending jolts of electricity throughout her body. When the pressure became too much, she pulled away from him, her legs shaking as her release hovered one stroke away from the edge.

She pulled him up her body for a passionate kiss. "I need you, Marc," she groaned, spreading her legs to let him settle his cock between her legs.

Marc hissed when his straining erection rubbed against the wetness awaiting him. "You have me, Ava. Forever."

His erection was hard as a rock when she took it in her hand, guiding it to her entrance. He slid inside with one smooth stroke and they both hissed. By the gods, nothing had ever felt so right, so perfect.

He tilted his head to the side, baring his neck to her. "Do it," he commanded. When he spoke, he sported his own set of fangs. They were shorter than a vampire's, but they were sharp enough to break skin. She didn't know much about shifters, but she was aware that such a thing happened when they were ready to claim a mate.

"There's no going back from this," she warned. Her own fangs were lengthened, throbbing with the need to sink into Marc's warm flesh.

Beneath the stark desire heating his eyes, she could see his absolute certainty. Her heart melted beneath his look, an emotion that only he could bring filling her. When he kissed her, it was nothing but tender love.

He pulled back to be nose-to-nose with her. "I don't want to go back, love. Never."

It was all she needed to hear. With him stroking in and out of her, she kissed the soft spot above the vein pulsing in his neck. He shuddered. Ava sank her fangs into him.

Hot blood washed over her tongue, a potent aphrodisiac that only increased her lust. Unlike the other times when she'd taken it, this was different. It was far more intense. She didn't know whether it was the newfound demon blood coursing through him or just the fact that their mating was taking place, but she didn't complain. It was delicious.

Each pull sent a cool tingling through her. His pace quickened, and she retracted her fangs, licking the holes closed. She turned her head as well, gasping with each thrust.

Marc leaned forward, placing tender kisses to her neck. Ava shivered. She'd heard stories of the explicit, pleasurable effect a vampire's bite had on people, but she'd never experienced it for herself. She didn't know if a shifter's bite would be the same, but she licked her lips in hungry anticipation.

"Bite me, Marc," she panted, baring her neck to him in total submission. "Take my blood."

He gave a low, pleasurable growl. With a precise skill as if he'd been doing it for years, Marc's canines broke the tender skin at her throat. There was a small prick of pain followed by immense pleasure.

Good…gods.

Marc let out a small groan and sucked her blood, all the while quickening his thrusts.

All Ava could do was moan and gasp at the sheer excitement raging through her. She wrapped her legs around his waist, her nails scoring down his back as he dragged her to the very edge of pleasure yet again.

With a sharp cry, she tumbled over with a crashing force, black spots dotting her vision. Even still, Marc continued pumping his hips, biting down even harder before pulling back.

Through their completed mating, Ava could sense his every feeling—love, joy, lust...uncontrollable, insatiable lust. It slammed into her with enough force to have her nearing that sweet edge yet again.

With a surge of strength, he used his hands to reach her inner thighs, pulling apart the death grip she had on him. Before she could guess his intentions, he had her legs stretched over his shoulders, her knees almost touching the pillows around her head.

The new position angled him even deeper inside her, every pump of his hips hitting a delicious spot within her that had her gasping for air.

"Marc," she moaned, her breath coming out in short pants as those black dots danced in her vision again.

He let out a feral growl and gave another hard, deep thrust, sinking as far as he could into her before shouting his own release.

They were both still shaking minutes after they'd come down from their high. Through their mating bond, she felt his satisfaction, though he was far, far from sated. To her shock, she could say the same.

With a loving smile, she rolled over to rest her head on his chest, his pounding heart against her ear the sweetest music she'd ever heard. He brought his arms around her, pulling her close in an intimate embrace.

Marc had awakened hungers within her she didn't think would ever dissipate.

And now they had an eternity to tend to each other's needs.

There would no longer be any running. No hiding. No looking over her shoulder and fearing the shadows she was forced to remain in.

She had a family now. A mate. A child growing in her womb. A new life with a bright future ahead of her.

She was complete at last.

Chapter Twenty

Weeks later...

Perched on the edge of the desk in his father's private study in St. Charles, Illinois, Lucian ignored the expensive wood groaning under his considerable weight. Instead, he focused on the written report he held in his hand. With a feeling of utter disbelief, he read and reread the paper at least fifty times.

He was far from illiterate.

He could speak a hundred different languages. The simple words written in perfect English on the paper were straight to the point, no cryptic messages hidden between the text.

Yet he was...dumbfounded.

He glared over the top of the paper at his father, who sat in his wingchair, sipping at a glass of warm blood as he played some colorful game on his phone. A muscle twitched under Lucian's eye in annoyance as the game continued shouting out, "Delicious! Sweet! Yummy!"

"I don't understand," he admitted. He tossed the paper aside, having already memorized everything word for word. "A siren? A *real* siren?"

Cyrus, the only other person in the room, gave a solemn nod without looking up from his phone. "From what Lynx gathered, there's a woman rumored to have siren blood."

Lucian frowned. Lynx was his father's second-in-command, and the powerful leader of Cyrus' Guard. It was the most honorable position any vampire could hope to have — well, any vampire who wasn't one of the king's seven children. "You believe the woman to be the daughter of Lila?" he demanded, referring to the female fey in Ava's vision.

His father shrugged, shutting off the screen of his phone and sliding it into a hidden pocket under his traditional toga. He looked as clueless as Lucian felt. "We don't know much about the woman, except that she's employed at a demon pub located in St. Louis, owned by an imp named Keegan. However, he is..." Cyrus trailed off, a look of frustration crossing his Etruscan features. "Well, let's just say he's managed to slip the radar."

Lucian raised an eyebrow. "And?"

"The woman has as well."

"What has that got to do with me?"

Cyrus stabbed him with a hard look. "I want you to track them down."

"Excuse me?" He was a powerful clan chief, not a damn hound dog. He had far more important duties to tend to than chasing down a stray imp and a woman who might or might not be a siren.

Cyrus took a casual sip of his beverage. "I don't give a damn about the imp, but I want you to track down the woman and bring her here."

"And your beloved Guard can't do this because...?"

His expression turned frustrated. "They did. However, she is... Well, there was interference."

Yawn. "What kind of interference?" Luc demanded, in truth not giving a single care.

His father hesitated, as if conflicted by the whole situation. "Another woman. She's fey, but—"

"But?"

"Her scent is similar to the one from the caves."

Well, that was...interesting. "Similar? Or the same?"

Cyrus shook his head. "It's too difficult for either of them to be sure. The scent from the caves was faded and old. She smells of fey, but...more. She may be a siren as well."

"So, while Lynx and Caesar were searching out a rumored siren from a demon pub, this new woman—another siren—comes along and causes an interference?"

The ancient vampire gave a dip of his head. "Precisely."

Lucian rolled his eyes at the simple answer. That told him exactly nothing. "Care to elaborate a little further, father? Why not bring both women in for questioning?"

His father's expression was back to one of frustrated puzzlement. "The first woman's trail disappeared, and Lynx lost her scent. Before he could continue searching, he came across the other woman, but he lost her as well. What has my attention, though, is two sirens in the same city just after defeating Mikhail, who we hypothesized to have been using siren blood, is far too much to be a coincidence. It's...intriguing."

Lucian glared at his father. "You called me all the way over here just to send me on a tedious quest to search out two women who may or may not be sirens?"

A hint of impatience touched the dark features. "No, I want you to find the first woman and bring her in."

"Shouldn't Geoffrey know anything about her or the missing imp? They are in his territory, after all," Lucian said, referring to the St. Louis clan chief.

"I've already had a word with him. He claims that if a siren lived within his city, he'd know about it." The look in Cyrus' eyes told Lucian just what he thought about the man. Geoffrey had the power and skills worthy of the title clan chief, but the man was oftentimes more concerned with riches rather than anything else, not to mention that he was far too arrogant for his own good.

Then again, so was Lucian...and his father...and all his brothers. Hell, all vampires were.

"Siren or not, what is so special about this woman?" he demanded, folding his arms over his chest. "Why bring *her* here and not the one who may have been in the caves working with Mikhail?"

"I want you to bring her in because of her gift."

Lucian shifted with impatience. His father could never just outright say what he wanted to say. "What kind of gift is that?"

"As the rumors go, the woman at the pub is a siren whose singing voice could heal any illness or wound. It was very rare that she was put on display, so whenever she was, patrons had to pay a fortune just to be in attendance and listen to her."

Lucian leveled his father with a flat, disbelieving stare. "A woman on the run whose voice is so magical it can heal anything. Really, father? Do you truly believe that bullshit?"

Cyrus shook his head and gulped down the remainder of his drink. He set the glass on the coffee table and leaned back, crossing one long leg over the other. Though Lucian looked the most like his father out of all Cyrus' children, in this instance Cyrus looked eerily similar to Sal, who often sat in such an elegant pose — minus the fancy toga, of course.

"Son, in my many, many years of living, you would think I've seen it all — and I have. However, there are still rare times when even I become surprised. I will not say I truly believe such a wonderful gift resides just a few miles south of here, but if there is any chance that she is able to heal Andreas, I will go to the edges of the world to determine if it is true or not. It may merely be a pipe dream, but I will not take any chances of letting the opportunity get away."

Lucian clenched his teeth at the mention of his youngest brother. It had been several weeks since the battle with Mikhail, but Andreas was still plagued by the illness of the deceased abaddon. It was only thanks to a series of magic from powerful witches and demons that the disease had been stalled. He was well enough to leave his bed and walk around, and some of his strength had returned, but it wasn't permanent. Sooner or later the spells of the amulet would wear off and he would be back to suffering a slow death.

He couldn't very well blame his father. They all wanted to find a cure for Andreas.

"Very well, I'll accept that," Lucian said on a huff of air. "However, do you realize I am the clan chief of Chicago? Once again, why can't your Guard continue their search for the woman? It's their job, after all."

The older man's lips twisted in obvious displeasure at the question. "As I mentioned, the other woman interfered, so the trail was lost to Lynx."

"And? He and the rest are the best trackers our kind has. Even if the trail is lost, he would be able to pick it up if no one else can."

"Indeed. However, he's convinced the other woman is searching for the same siren. Twice now she has interfered in their search, making it far more difficult to find the siren than it has to be."

Again, he couldn't just outright say what he wanted. "What kind of interference are we talking about? Magic? Portals?"

Cyrus shook his head, frowning. "She possesses a rather startling amount of courage and strength that has managed to leave my men outwitted and incapacitated."

Lucian frowned again, a rather common expression of his. He had to take a few moments to consider his words with care. In the end, however, he just said what the hell he wanted to say. "You mean to tell me that the baddest of badasses hand-selected by the king were beaten up by a mere fey woman?"

Cyrus shrugged, a confused mix of both amusement and frustration swirling in his pale blue eyes. "I find it rather hard to believe myself, but they would not lie to me."

Lucian clenched his fists. "Was anyone killed?"

Cyrus gave a helpless lift of his hands. "Only their pride."

Lucian rolled his eyes, pushing away from the desk. A fey—siren or not—couldn't even come close to causing injury to a vampire, least of all a group of hunters who happened to be trained by the king himself. No doubt the woman had used magic. It was the only way to truly have the upper hand on a vampire. Only a rare few vampires were able to sense magic, let alone defend themselves from it.

"Okay, so before I waste my precious time on this senseless mission, what do you want me to do with the interfering woman, should I come across her?" Lucian didn't care for harming women, but he wouldn't hesitate to kill them if he needed to, especially if they dared to attack first.

Cyrus gave another helpless lift of his hands. "If she is a siren, it would be rather nice to get some answers from her, especially if she's the one from the caves or related to whoever it was. I'd also like to know what her purpose is in seeking out the other siren, why she attacked my men and whether or not she truly was an ally to Mikhail. If so, she is to be brought before the Imperials for judgement for her participation." He linked his fingers together at his knee. "However, if you fear she poses a threat to you in any way, you know what to do."

So...put an end to her.

With a grudging sigh, Lucian straightened. "Is Geoffrey aware that I'm stepping into his territory?"

"*Ita*, but it's wise to stop by formally, just in case."

Lucian nodded and headed out of the door. "I'll be on my way then." He'd just placed his hand on the doorknob when his father stopped him.

"One more thing, son."

Lucian looked over his shoulder and raised an eyebrow.

"If the woman's singing abilities are real, it's best not to piss her off before receiving her help. I don't want her making Andreas' curse any worse. You will have to be nice."

Lucian scowled. "I beg your pardon?" *What the hell is that supposed to mean?* He was nothing if not diplomatic.

Okay, maybe he had the personality of a viper, and maybe he was more of a 'kill first, ask questions later' type of man, but he wasn't impervious to swaying people to do his bidding, least of all a woman. Whether it was charm, manipulation or brute force, he never failed. His presence alone was enough to instill fear among other demons and lust among most women he came across.

"Just remember she is a woman," Cyrus said, as if that made any difference.

Lucian's scowl became a glare. "She will come along, even if I have to toss her over my shoulder and throw her into the dungeons until she agrees to help."

"That's exactly my fear." Cyrus gave a rueful shake of his head. "Very well, son. Be careful."

Lucian gave a wry snort before leaving the room. He had a few calls to make and a few ends to tie up before starting his journey.

A rather tedious journey at that.

Lynx was a six-foot-five vampire warrior with muscles on top of muscles. He was a man who was widely known and feared all throughout the demon world, both for his lethal powers and his title as second-in-command to the almighty king of vampires.

Yet the proud, vigorous fighter had been bested by a mere fey. A woman at that.

Pathetic.

Want to see more from this author?
Here's a taster for you to enjoy!

The Royal Gordanos:
A Royal's Pursuit
Makayla Roberts

Excerpt

St. Louis, Missouri

Contrary to its elaborate name, The Golden Crown was nothing special in appearance. It was decent enough, with its green wooden exterior and tin roof catching the soft glow of the moon, which was partially hidden behind snow clouds. The two-story building had the sort of welcoming air meant to attract the local demons.

However, the Irish-inspired pub was at the bottom of the barrel compared to its competitors in the nearby city. The beverages were cheap and ofttimes flat, the food was bland and the layout was rather simple — a rustic bar with a handful of worn stools, metal tables clean yet unadorned and a small stage where amateurs belted out karaoke songs.

The pub catered to those who didn't care for the over-the-top glim and glam that most demon establishments had. It had been created for those who just wanted to get out of their lairs, caves or nests for a casual night out.

Whether it was fancy or modest, Siovon would much rather spend her nights curled in front of a fireplace to exercise her art skills or brew new potions to add to her collection of medicines. She wasn't an introvert, but as a rare demon whose ancestors had been wiped off the face of the earth centuries ago, making friends and enjoying a night out were next to impossible if she wasn't careful.

Tonight, however, she was on a mission, and until she completed it, her hobbies would have to wait.

It'd been ten years since she'd been separated from her beloved younger sister. Ever since she'd escaped Mikhail's clutches a few months before, she had been searching high and low for Calysta, a task that was proving to be far more difficult than she'd hoped.

Out of habit, she touched the golden hoop at the top of her right ear. One of five enchanted earrings, the cold metal didn't do a damn thing to improve the worry twisting in her gut.

At one point in time, she'd been able to touch the hoop to locate her sister—and vice versa. It connected them, so even if they were on opposite ends of the world, they'd always be able to find one another. Of course, like all magic, it needed to be refilled every few months to keep its effect. But since they hadn't seen each other in a decade, the magic was long gone, rendering the earring a useless piece of jewelry. So, she'd had to bust out her rusty tracking skills and search for Calysta the old-fashioned way.

After spending weeks with no results, Siovon had caught a break when an old friend had informed her of a rumor about a siren with a healing voice working at The Golden Crown. It was a long shot, but it had been her only lead, so she'd traveled from the coast of South

Carolina all the way to the outskirts of St. Louis to investigate.

To add to her mounting annoyance, the rumor had turned out to be true, but Caly was long gone, right along with Keegan, who'd likely held her against her will. Siovon didn't believe for one second that Calysta would use her singing voice for something as simple as entertaining a crowd of greedy demons.

What was worse, Siovon had learned that some vampire leeches were trying to find her as well. Whether it was for her blood or to use her unique gift for their own heinous plots, as Mikhail had done to Siovon, the sooner she found Calysta, the quicker they could go back to living their lives under the radar from the wretched demon world.

Siovon had first ventured to the pub a few weeks prior, but she'd had to leave after being harassed by two huge vampires. She'd eluded them, but several days later she'd run into them again, and when she'd learned they were looking for Caly, she hadn't hesitated to kick their asses and send them on their way with a clear message—'*Back off.*' It wasn't until after they'd left the pub unguarded that she'd returned.

After a quick look around the imp Keegan's office to find any clues to their disappearances, she crept past the bouncer, who was dead-asleep in a rocking chair next to the door.

Siovon rolled her eyes. *Some guard.* She didn't even have to tiptoe. A parade of elephants could come tromping through and the schmuck would snore right through it. *Lazy-ass trolls. Always more brawn than brain.*

She returned to the bar downstairs, drawing her hood over her head. Then, sticking close to the shadows, she made a swift exit. She took out an ink pen and a folded piece of paper from her pants pocket and scratched *The*

Golden Crown from the list. There was nothing in the imp's office to indicate where he or Calysta had vanished to, but she had a few addresses to places he frequented.

With any luck, she'd find the jackass, catch him off guard and do what was necessary to get some answers. If he didn't have Caly, he had to know something.

Shaking her head, she jogged across the snow-covered fields back toward the city. She willed her adrenaline to kick into gear to keep her warm against the cold December air. Not for the first time, she was thankful for her disciplined — some might say cruel — mercenary training growing up. She'd learned to tolerate hours and hours on end of strenuous exercise, including running long distances without losing breath. Her drills had been good for something, at least.

Siovon grimaced at the dark memories threatening to rise and she shook her head again. Now was not the time to reminisce about her less-than-cheery childhood. Besides, those days were behind her. She was a new person. She was a healer, dedicated to the sick and dying.

A pacifist.

She snorted at the absurd statement. Well, she was an *aspiring* pacifist. She'd been trying to channel her inner peace and not be so hasty in resorting to violence to resolve every issue. *I let those two vamps live, after all.*

Sure, she'd roughed them up a teensy-tiny bit, but she could have killed them if she'd wanted to. Hell, in another day and age, she *would* have killed them.

She was learning to focus on blue skies and sunshine. That kind of progress had to count for something.

When Siovon made it to the city a little while later, she kept to the alleys as she zigzagged her way to her hotel. Even in large cities filled with varying scents to wash away her own, she was wise enough to cover her tracks. It was second nature to be cautious. As much as her newly birthed pacifist soul wanted to be trusting and look for the best in people, like Calysta could, she wasn't stupid.

Still, having a vehicle to get around in would have made everything a hundred times simpler — and faster. *And warmer.* She made a mental note to find a local car rental service before nightfall.

Her hotel was an old building, but it was up-to-date with an air of cleanliness. That was a must for Siovon. She liked to keep a low profile, but that didn't mean she had to slum about in rinky-dink motels to keep her privacy. *A lady has needs, after all.*

She took the stairs two at a time until she got to the fourth floor. It was her preferred method. When it came to choosing between a cement stairwell with a sturdy structure or a metal cage waiting to get stuck in a shaft, it was a no-brainer.

Polite pass on elevators, thank you very much.

Exiting the stairwell, she pulled out a keycard when a sudden chill filled the air, making her hair stand on end. The humans inhabiting the hotel would assume the dramatic drop in temperature was a result of the snowy weather outside and resort to cranking up their individual heating units.

Siovon, however, knew the source was something far more alarming than the threat of catching a cold.

There was a damned vampire approaching — and a powerful one, at that.

Cursing under her breath, she unlocked the door to her room and ducked inside, bolting the locks. *Yeah, as if that will keep out a bloodsucker,* she thought. They had the uncanny ability to get past any obstacle that wasn't made of pure silver.

Of course, there was no guarantee that the particular vamp was after her. It was possible he had his own room, was meeting someone or was up to any number of things.

Possible, but not freaking likely.

After her run-in with the other leeches, it wouldn't surprise her if they'd sent someone to avenge them. Or perhaps it was Mikhail looking to continue where he'd left off.

Either way, the vamp was far too close for comfort. She'd already escaped one maniac.

It was a good thing she was quick on her feet. If one plan failed, it would take only moments for her to develop another.

As the ice prickles from the vamp's power danced along her skin, she grabbed her prepacked bag and darted for the window. She'd just pushed the glass open when the leech worked his powers to unlock her door.

A handy skill, no doubt, but Siovon had no interest in staying to admire his efforts.

She stood on the window's ledge, gritting her teeth against the cold. *Christ…* She didn't know which was worse—Missouri's winter air whipping at her face or Frosty the Vampire's powers creeping over her skin.

Her window faced an apartment building with a fire escape seven feet away, and below her was a dark alley with a solid forty-foot drop. A human would have been screwed.

Fortunately, she was a siren, which meant the demon blood in her veins provided a substantial amount of strength and speed.

She bent her knees and, with a strong spring of muscles, leaped across the distance and grabbed hold of the rickety fire escape, her light weight giving it only the slightest of creaks in protest. She pulled herself over the railing and planted her feet on the rusty landing.

Siovon shivered as she pulled off the jacket that had kept her warm for the past few days. With nothing more than a tank top covering her torso, she fought to keep her teeth from chattering. Hell, she'd endured worse. She'd once had to survive stark naked for a week outside in the snowy mountains in Siberia as part of her training. She'd endured great levels of frostbite and hypothermia before her natural demon healing could kick in gear, but she'd made it.

This Missouri weather? Easy-peasy.

Stiffening her spine, she tucked her bag inside the jacket and dropped it to the ground. Assuming her plan worked, the stalker would follow her scent.

She dashed up the crisscrossing stairs to the roof. Once there, she ducked behind the brick ledge and peeked over just in time to see a large figure peering outside her room window.

She twisted her lips in grim amusement as the schmuck looked around in confusion, trying to determine which way she'd disappeared to.

* * * *

As Lucian entered the hotel room, he had to swallow a groan as the overwhelming scent of sweet cherry blossoms hit him. He'd been tracking the fairy ever since coming to St. Louis a week before, and with every passing day, her scent was growing on him more.

His sole mission was to locate a mythical siren whose singing voice could heal anything. It was the most ridiculous, insulting use of his skills.

The job was a tedious matter better suited for the Guard, the uber-elite group of vampires who acted as the Secret Service for Cyrus, the king of all vampires, except they were bigger, meaner and far more intimidating. There was nothing in the world or the depths of hell that would halt them from protecting Cyrus or carrying out whatever obscure missions he sent them on.

So why was he—the first in line to the throne and a powerful clan chief of Chicago—the one performing the menial task of searching for a woman who may or may not exist instead of the almighty Guard?

The answer was simple. Annoying, but simple.

The fey woman had gotten the upper hand on Lynx and Caesar. Not only had she been able to disarm and rough up a couple of the most lethal vampires around, she'd done so *and* eluded them. Twice.

It was pathetic.

Thus, instead of sending others with nothing better to do with themselves—that is, any one of his five brothers—*he* was the lucky one. *Yay.*

His objective had been to track down the source of the rumor and determine if it was true. If it were false, he'd return to his territory and continue with his life. If it were true, he'd been ordered to find the woman and somehow convince her to travel with him to Chicago to heal his youngest brother from a lethal disease.

It was so simple that it should have taken a few days…tops.

Unfortunately, things could never be that easy. All he'd gathered were the same few rumors of the siren who'd disappeared, along with the owner of the establishment. To his dismay, so long as he had no solid proof the woman wasn't real, he'd have to stay.

Lucian then turned to tracking down the missing imp, charming lesser demons to spill what they knew about the man. He'd just finished his interrogation when he'd run across the most tantalizing scent he'd ever smelled. He'd latched onto it and followed the creature all throughout the city until he'd caught up to her at the hotel.

When Lynx, the leader of the Guard, had described the woman who'd attacked him, all he'd remembered was a specific scent and her height. The woman had concealed her identity, but both men stated she'd been short. Lucian knew it was embarrassing as hell for them to admit they'd been bested by a little fairy, but if either of them had been distracted by the woman's sweet scent like Lucian, he couldn't very well say he blamed them.

However, he wouldn't allow some woman to get the upper hand if it came down to a fight. He'd faced women who were as beautiful as they were deadly, and none of them had ever sidetracked him from his purpose. Tonight would be no different.

Except, in a way, it already was. He had strict orders not to approach the woman without provocation, but Lucian had convinced himself that it was necessary. After all, she *could* be a siren, just not the one he was looking for.

Not to mention she could very well have been Mikhail's ally. Her scent was similar to the blood they'd found in the Apennine Mountains after their fight with him several weeks before. They'd hypothesized that Mikhail had used siren blood to create a band of Rogues to control, though they had no solid proof, just a bunch of 'maybes' and 'what-ifs'. If the woman he was following was a siren who was tied to Mikhail, she would need to be brought in to be held accountable for her actions.

Cyrus wanted to admonish anyone who'd been a part of Mikhail's schemes.

As Lucian strolled down the narrow corridor, common sense told him to turn his ass around and not waste any more time. Another part of him argued that the woman reappearing couldn't be a coincidence. She had to have some information, and the sooner he figured out her role in everything, the sooner he could be done with this ludicrous ordeal and return to his lair.

In truth, it was the curious part of him that sought out the fairy. Her scent was intoxicating. He was damn near two thousand years old, so he'd come across more than his fair share of demons of all shapes and sizes. He could differentiate the blood of a wood sprite and a dew fairy from a mile away, and the two were almost impossible to tell apart.

All fey tended to have a sweet fragrance with a hint of something outdoorsy. But hers was far more potent than a normal fairy's. There was an underlying sense of power in her scent that tugged at his more primal instincts.

Plus, he wanted to see what kind of woman could defeat a couple of vampires well over six feet tall. She had to be some sort of Amazon warrior with god-like strength. Sure, Lynx and Caesar had said the woman was tiny, but they'd also said she moved fast, so they could be mistaken.

Yes, that's it, Lucian thought with confidence. *They only thought she was small, but in truth, she's built like a Roman gladiator.*

When Lucian heard a soft *thump*, he rushed to the window.

He frowned in disbelief at the darkness below. Not even his night vision could pierce the thick shadows, but he smelled the woman down there. If she was a swift healer like most demons, the fall wouldn't have killed her, but it would likely have broken a bone.

Amazon, he thought again. *She's an Amazon.*

He was convinced, and a lick of excitement flared within him — not just at the woman's delicious scent but also at the idea that she would prove to be a challenge to him.

And, by the gods, it'd been so long since he'd had a good rumble.

His title was boring, more often than not. He no longer felt the need to expand his territory. He'd created an air of peace and wealth in his domain, a place where his vampire brethren could escape the small clan wars that still broke out from time to time.

So he looked forward to seeing what the fairy was capable of.

Not that he truly believed she was a fairy, but until he discovered the truth, the name would stick.

In a smooth manner that not many creatures could match, he leaped and landed in a crouch. The snow crunched under his shitkickers as he ambled to where the woman's scent was strongest.

Far too late, however, he realized he'd been outwitted. He glared at the backpack wrapped inside a jacket. There was no other scent telling him she'd taken off down the alley, nor were there any footsteps in the snow, which meant she'd never jumped in the first place. He took a step back, unable to believe her cunning.

Lucian glanced up in time to see a pale limb push from the rooftop high above him. Curling his lip in annoyance, he caught the fire escape and hauled ass up the old railing.

With his blinding speed, it took all of ten seconds to reach the top. He cursed his ignorance, but he couldn't help the tiny smile playing at his lips. He'd already known the woman was intelligent from the clever way she'd backtracked throughout the city to cover her tracks, but to pull off such a move — on him, no less — was rather impressive.

Too bad for her it only made him more eager to face her. And once a vampire was on the hunt, there wasn't a force in hell that could stop him.

Once at the top, Lucian scanned the surrounding buildings and concentrated on her sweet scent. He dashed through the snow, leaping over two more rooftops before coming to a stop.

Blood tainted the air — not enough to cause alarm, but enough to make him wary — especially when the very scent made his fangs lengthen and his gut clench with hunger.

He followed the trail of small footsteps. He narrowed his eyes as he neared a large vent, spotting a corner of the cold metal stained with fresh blood. He drew a dagger from his boot and rounded the corner, pausing when he saw a woman lying face down in the blanket of snow.

For just a moment, he eyed the curve of her lower back expanding into a rounded ass defined by tight black jeans. He shook his head and used the toe of his boot to roll the woman over onto her back.

For all that is holy...

Lucian went hard as a rock. Her barely-there shirt outlined a tight, flat stomach and full breasts that could fill his hands. Judging by the straps on her shoulders, she was wearing a black sports bra, yet even through the fabric, the cold temperature had her nipples in tight peaks.

His fangs throbbed as he trailed his gaze up the slim column of her throat to a serene face. Smooth, ivory skin stretched over high cheekbones, a dainty little nose and the delicate line of her jaw. Her bow-shaped lips were pink and damp, and her lashes lay motionless over blushed cheeks. Short dark hair peeked from under the black beanie she wore, and swooping bangs lay across her eyebrows. There was a small stain of blood from a gash on her temple.

He snorted. The daft fairy must have tripped and hit her head in her haste to escape him. Such clumsiness made it far too easy for him.

Then again, nothing about her thus far had indicated she was anything short of intelligent.

He eyed the tattoos covering her arms. On one inner forearm was a short sword crossed over a jagged dagger, both with worn hilts.

The shimmering tattoo on the other arm was far more elaborate. It was a black serpentine dragon with iridescent golden scales, two bat-like wings tucked close to its body, four short legs baring sharp talons and sea-green reptilian eyes that seemed to be glaring at Lucian. Its tail curled around her index finger while the rest of its body wrapped around her arm from wrist to elbow. Its head was nestled on her inner biceps.

For several moments, Lucian was stunned. He'd never seen a tattoo so…lifelike. It was as if he could stroke the creature and feel its scales rising from her skin.

As for the rest of the woman, she was exquisite — tiny and delicate with soft curves made to be kissed and caressed. She didn't seem capable of taking down a man twice her size.

With a frown, Lucian scanned the rooftops again. It had to be a trick, some kind of sorcery to fool him into lowering his guard. The Amazon he'd chased was no doubt lurking in the shadows, and somehow she'd used magic to create an illusion of the woman lying on the ground.

It was that thought that had him bringing his dagger up, coiling his body in preparation for an attack. He'd fallen for the wench's trap once. He wouldn't do it again.

On the verge of sending his power out to freeze anything in the shadows, he didn't notice the sudden shift in the air, not until a kick strong enough to crack his ribs caught him in the middle of his back. He sucked in a sharp breath and whipped around in time for the pint-sized female to deck him in the jaw.

For such a tiny thing, the blow hurt like a bitch. He tasted his own blood. Surprised and annoyed, he caught one flying fist in his hand, then her leg in his other when she attempted a kick. It took more strength than he would have liked to admit to detain her. She was strong as hell. And fast.

Just as Lynx and Caesar had described.

With her balanced on one leg, he smirked down at her face hidden in his shadow.

She sneered in return. Before he could guess her intention, she jumped and wrapped her free leg around his waist, using her weight to bring him down on top of her. Stunned, he allowed her to roll him onto his back. She straddled his chest with her knees pressing into his forearms to hold him in place.

Lucian stared with a mix of surprise, frustration and…lust—a hot, unexpected wave of lust.

Hard violet eyes with a small upward slant flashed down at him in triumph. It was the cold tip of a dagger at his throat that had him snapping out of his stupor.

"Why are you following me?" she growled, sounding sexy rather than frightening.

"The answer is pretty obvious," he drawled.

She narrowed her beautiful eyes. "I've done nothing to warrant the attention of leeches."

A bitter scent filled his nose. For her to outwit him twice, she was far too intelligent not to know vampires had the greatest senses in the demon world. They were masters at studying the body language of their prey. Most of them, including Lucian, could even *smell* when they were lying.

He lifted an eyebrow. "You attacked two of my men."

Her eyes widened in disbelief. "Are you kidding me? Those two brutes attacked me first. Am I not allowed the right to defend myself?"

She was telling the truth. Well, not that they'd attacked her. From what Lynx had reported, he and Caesar had tried to speak with her, but she'd grown defensive. Even Lucian knew the men had such imposing presences that they appeared threatening, even if they weren't.

"Maybe so, but those two happen to be members of the Guard. For you to lay harm to them is to challenge the king's authority."

As predicted, she went still above him. Non-vampires weren't under Cyrus' command, but that didn't mean he was any less terrifying. Vampires were at the top of the demon hierarchy chain, and Cyrus sat on a golden throne at the very tip. Lesser creatures scurried away in fear, while greater ones bowed at his feet.

And though he chose to live his life instilling peace among his people, he was still every bit the powerful Etruscan warrior he'd been millennia ago.

The woman above him swallowed hard, and Lucian found his eyes glued to her throat. His fangs throbbed with the desire to see if her blood tasted as sweet as she smelled.

She made a sound of disgust. "I barely even touched them. There's no way they were harmed."

Lucian fixed her with a disbelieving stare. By the time he'd met up with Lynx, the great warrior had already healed, but he'd been nursing a broken nose, a bruised jaw and a few broken ribs. Meanwhile, Caesar was recovering from a dislocated shoulder and a dagger protruding from his foot. After several bags of blood, they were healed within the hour, but there was no repairing their wounded pride.

He could see now why they had been so embarrassed to admit what had happened. The woman was half their size, but she packed one hell of a punch. Gods, his own cracked ribs and jaw repairing themselves from her assault still ached.

He should be furious that she'd dared to attack him. He had a reputation for being a cold-hearted bastard, a lethal foe only those with a death wish were foolish enough to take on. He was a man who preferred action to diplomacy, and he'd kill anyone who ever tried to disrupt the peace of his clan or family.

Point. Blank. Period.

However, as he lay on a bed of ice with an angry waif of a woman perched on his chest, he was far from pissed.

His body heated as his lust stirred, and, above all, he felt a great amount of amusement.

And it had been many, many years since he'd felt anything other than pure boredom or disdain.

How peculiar.

Home of Erotic Romance

Sign up for our newsletter and find out about all our romance book releases, eBook sales and promotions, sneak peeks and FREE romance books!

About the Author

Makayla's love for reading began at the age of twelve when her mother introduced her to the world of mystical creatures. From then on, she discovered a talent for turning her own imagination into words. From fanfictions to short stories to full-length novels and novellas, if she wasn't focused on school activities, she was either reading or writing.

Raised on the coast of Mississippi, Makayla juggles her everyday life between work and being a mom. In her free time, she enjoys binge watching criminal suspense shows, shopping, painting, wood burning, and of course, working on her books.

Makayla enjoys writing stories with strong elements of romance, adventure, and paranormal. Vampires, shifters, fairies, dragons — she loves them all!

Makayla loves to hear from readers. You can find her contact information, website details and author profile page at https://www.totallybound.com